THE PURSUIT OF JUSTICE

"Remember that button?" Tommy asked.

"The black button? Yes," Laura answered. "Did you hear from the FBI?"

"I did."

"What were they able to find out?"

"A button like this costs a lot more than plastic. In fact, it's most likely European. It came off a nice piece of clothing."

"So it's more likely to be Belew's than Jervis's?"

"Could be. You need to check his entire wardrobe either to show it was his or eliminate it. I was thinking along the lines of you finding a guy you thought was good for the murder—then, if he had a cuff button missing from one of his jackets, you'd be able to link him in."

"So all I need to do is find this guy."

"Yes."

"Then let me ask you the million-dollar question: Do you believe there is a guy to find?"

"I'm not a detective, and I don't know anything about your case, except what I've seen in the lab here and read in the newspaper. But based on that, I have to say yes. I think there's at least one other person besides Roland Jervis involved here."

"You know something?" Laura asked. "I think you'd be a pretty good detective."

When Laura hung up, she was sure of two things: there had been a second person involved in the murder of Lawrence Belew, and she was going to find him.

Books by Lelia Kelly

PRESUMPTION OF GUILT
FALSE WITNESS
OFFICER OF THE COURT

Published by Pinnacle Books

OFFICER
OF THE
COURT

Lelia Kelly

PINNACLE BOOKS
Kensington Publishing Corp.

http://www.pinnaclebooks.com

PINNACLE BOOKS are published by

Kensington Publishing Corp.
850 Third Avenue
New York, NY 10022

All Kensington Titles, Imprints and Distributed Lines are available at special quantity discounts for bulk purchases for sales promotions, premiums, fund-raising, and educational or institutional use. Special book excerpts or customized printings can also be created to fit specific needs. For details, write or phone the office of the Kensington special sales manager: Kensington Publishing Corp., 850 Third Avenue, New York, NY 10022. attn: Special Sales Department, Phone: 1-800-221-2647.

Pinnacle and the P logo Reg. U.S. Pat. & TM Off.

First Printing: November 2001
10 9 8 7 6 5 4 3 2 1

Printed in the United States of America

This book is dedicated to the friends who shared
Bay Head: The Norbert Years
Carmel, Elaine, Jill, Dave, Kae, Charles,
and especially Kathy Jones Rapetski

ACKNOWLEDGMENTS

I owe thanks to Kay Kidde and John Scognamiglio for advice and support, and to Laura Langlie, who has been a pleasure to work with for the past four years. I was also fortunate to have technical advisors who contributed materially to this story: Steve Skoumal, M.D., of the Pocatello Regional Medical Center; Ian Smith, a fine pathologist and a darn good brother-in-law; and Tom Patton, my armaments expert; all of whom provided much information and inspiration. Inspiration of more than one kind came from the Reverend Frederick Pope.

I am grateful, too, to have an opportunity to thank the real Tommy Wood; without his help, none of my books would have been published. Thanks, Tommy, for your fearless willingness to hook up computers and DSL lines, as well as your unflagging friendship for many years.

Thanks are due to all my friends, especially my book club, the patient and understanding folks at Wachovia, and my wonderful family, especially the "Jefferson branch": Harry, Jayne, Bill, Jane, John, and Karen Bryan, and the "Mobile branch": Kathy and Mike Conwell. My mother contributed her considerable editorial and secretarial skills, and my sister-in-law Karen and my Aunt Lillian continue to act as my most effective marketers.

Finally, I'd like to thank the little people: Cameron and Grantland Smith and Elizabeth Kelly and her new sister, Lelia Ann Kelly.

AUTHOR'S NOTE

This story could not take place in Fulton County. In the first place, as Laura is careful to point out, death penalty trials are relatively rare in that jurisdiction. In the second place, there are many good resources, both public and private, for defendants faced with a capital charge in the Atlanta metropolitan region. There has not been, to my knowledge, any recent case where a defendant went on trial for his life with inadequate or incompetent representation in Fulton County Superior Court, thanks to dedicated and talented lawyers like those from the Georgia Indigent Defense Council and its Multi-County Public Defender (Death Penalty) Division. An author has to have some latitude, however, in creating dramatic situations, and I have taken advantage of that allowance.

Monday Morning

The minivan barely tapped the rear bumper of the Jaguar. Neither car should have been in the intersection in the first place, but there was a MARTA bus stalled in the right-hand lane of Piedmont Road, forcing all the cars trying to turn right onto Peachtree Road to merge into the center lane with all the traffic that was trying to cross Peachtree. So, instead of stopping behind the white line as they should have, both the minivan and the Jaguar had crept into the intersection of Piedmont and East Paces Ferry Road.

The selfish optimism of Atlanta motorists never ceased to amaze Laura Chastain. Not only did they insist upon running stop signs and red lights, and entering intersections when they clearly would not be able to pass through them, but they never really committed to stopping. Instead, they rolled, claiming every inch of pavement they could.

That was precisely what the lady in the minivan was

doing, rolling, one micrometer at a time, as she blocked the intersection. Maybe she was feeling conspicuous, and not without reason. She could have bought herself a hefty ticket if there had been a cop on the scene—which, as it happened, there was, although she couldn't know that the man at the wheel of the Jeep Wagoneer that was waiting to turn left from East Paces Ferry onto Piedmont was, in fact, a cop. But neither could she have known that the driver and his passenger were not particularly anxious to get through the intersection in a hurry.

Laura Chastain and Amos Kowalski were oblivious to the traffic jam, sharing a perfect moment, listening to an Ella Fitzgerald and Louis Armstrong duet. Amos had just taken his hand off the gearshift and placed it on Laura's knee. As she turned to smile at him, she saw the accident—which was hardly worthy of the name, as it was, by any definition, just a tap.

The minivan could not have been going more than five miles an hour, probably less. The guy in the Jag could hardly have been aware of the impact. The van lady didn't seem to be—at least, she didn't throw her vehicle into reverse, or leap from the driver's seat to apologize. It's possible that she didn't even realize that she had hit the Jaguar. Maybe she wondered why its driver came out of the car, storming toward her with a golf club in his hands.

Laura certainly wondered what he was doing, right up to the moment he swung the club—it was an iron—and smashed the van's windshield. Laura gasped in shock. His actions were extreme to the point of being bizarre, and he looked so . . . normal, just an average guy, maybe in his forties, attired in a "business casual" ensemble of gray trousers and a slate-gray shirt, open at the collar. Laura noted, as he teed off on the van's headlights, that he was balding, and that he had allowed his hair to compensate by growing over his collar in the back. It was funny, she thought later, how much detail she had taken in. He wore little wire-framed glasses, which he pushed up onto the bridge of his nose as he proceeded around to the passenger side of the van, which positioned him directly in front of Amos's Jeep.

Laura started to say something to Amos, but by that time he had already vaulted out of the Jeep and sprinted into the intersection. "Call 911!" he shouted over his departing shoulder. Laura fumbled with her cell phone, not willing to take her eyes off him as he ran straight at the man with the club, holding his ID and shield above his head and shouting "Police!"

The club-wielding man turned as Amos neared, pausing only a moment before swinging again and shattering the front passenger window. Laura could hear the shrieks of the woman and children inside the car; they almost drowned the voice of the 911 operator. She tried to concentrate on the questions the 911 operator was asking—where was she? What was the closest address? Was the attacker armed?

Now Amos was trying to talk to the man, holding his hands out, showing that he was unarmed, trying to reason. Laura would have preferred him to draw his gun and stand the man down without all the discussion, which she felt was unnecessary under the circumstances. The golf-club man apparently agreed; he hefted the club over his head and warned Amos away. Laura jumped from the car, ready to do something if the man swung at Amos. He didn't. He took another step toward the van, raised the club again, and brought it across one of the rear windows. Laura could see the children inside, scrambling for safety, screaming and howling in terror. This time the window didn't break. The man prepared to swing again.

Amos took advantage of the fractional second when the assailant's backswing had him off balance. He lunged at him, and hit him low, like a cornerback bringing down a wide receiver. They both crashed to the pavement. She saw the attacker's head hit the street, and bounce. Laura expected that he would remain there, prone and unconscious, but he didn't. He fought Amos furiously, trying to reach the gun Amos wore in a holster on the back of his belt, and when that didn't work, flailing at Amos with his club, landing ineffective foreshortened blows on his shoulders.

When she saw that, Laura abandoned the cell phone and the 911 operator, and ran, murder in her heart. "I will kill you!" she heard herself screaming. "I will kill you!" She wanted to bounce his head off the pavement again—that would be lovely. She wanted to land a kick in his ribs with the toe of her sling-back pump; she imagined the satisfying crunch of the pointed toe connecting with the man's ribs.

In her anger and fear, Laura didn't notice the house painter who had gotten out of his truck. She was almost there when the painter reached down, with an economical gesture, and jerked the attacker to his feet, Amos still grasping his knees. The painter held the man, one brawny arm across his neck, the other behind his back, wrenching the golf club away in the process.

Amos stood, and unhooked handcuffs from his belt—the handcuffs that always embarrassed Laura so much when he took his jacket off in public. The man saw the cuffs, gave up, sagged against the painter with a strange moaning cry. Amos snapped the handcuffs on him, and then they heard the sirens. It was over.

Laura stood, shaking with frustrated rage. Her fists were still clenched, still hopeful of landing a punch on the Jaguar driver, who was now sobbing pathetically in the custody of the house painter. Amos was inside the van, checking the children for injuries. A patrol car pulled up, followed by another, and blue-uniformed cops poured out of them. Laura stumbled to the curb and sat down, disregarding the potential damage to her skirt and panty hose, heedless of the stares of the drivers who were by now pulling around the Jeep and passing through the cleared intersection, off to work a little late, but with a great story to tell at the water cooler.

Laura waited while the van was moved to the parking lot of the restaurant on the corner, and the Jaguar hooked up to one of the omnipresent tow trucks that homed in on accidents like bats on moths. No one took any notice of her, not even Amos. He was talking to one of the uniformed cops, describing what had happened, and laughing. *Laughing*, when just a few minutes before he could have been killed. Laura's fists tightened, and her nails dug into her palms.

Finally, after what seemed like an age, Amos approached her. "You okay?" he said. Laura didn't answer, but landed a glare on him that could peel paint. "I know," he said. "You're mad at me. You wanted me to wait for the *real* cops. You don't like to have your boyfriend jumping on maniacs in public. But, sweetheart, it's my job."

She hunched her shoulders and looked away; she was furious with him, all the more so because he was right. She wanted to hit him, almost as badly as she had wanted to hit the golfing man a few minutes earlier. Amos, shrewdly, guessed what was running through her mind. "I bet you want to hit me, just smack the crap out of me, don't you? It's just the adrenaline—you'll come down in a minute. C'mon. Let me help you up."

He was right; the anger and the fear were both ebbing away. She reached up and took his hands, and allowed him to pull her to her feet and into his embrace. He snorted. "Buckhead," he said. "Some damn neighborhood you live in, Chastain. If this is what they do here on a Monday morning, I don't wanna know what goes on on a Saturday night."

She laughed. Then she punched him.

Chapter 1

"I don't give a fat damn what you *think*, young man. I want to know what you *know!* Don't come into my courtroom unprepared because you're too damn disorganized to talk to your client."

Laura Chastain winced. Even when it wasn't directed at her, Judge Root's wrath was a terrible thing. The hapless defense lawyer straightened his tie, playing for time, and tried to recover his poise. "Your Honor, I haven't had an opportunity to discuss a strategy with my client...."

"Strategy? Who the hell needs a strategy? This is an arraignment, son—head 'em up and move 'em out. Is he guilty or not?"

"Well, that's the thing—you see, we haven't had a chance to discuss the case, not really, Your Honor, and I just thought if I could have a little more time ..."

"Why haven't you had time? And what the hell is there

to discuss? It's an arraignment. He's accused of robbing a liquor store. He's supposed to enter a plea, and then we'll talk about bail. You don't need to take a meeting to do any of that, do you?''

"Yes ... I mean, we *did* meet, Your Honor, but we disagreed on what course we should take at this juncture.''

"*Juncture?* What the hell are you talking about? You're a public defender, son, and this ain't the Supreme Court. I don't allow *junctures* in my courtroom. Get on with it.''

"Yes, uh, but ... you see, there's some question as to whether I should be representing him at this hearing ... he doesn't like me, Your Honor,'' the unfortunate tyro concluded lamely.

"Then he's got more sense than I'd have given him credit for. You! Defendant!''

"Yes, sir,'' the accused answered, grinning at his attorney's discomfiture.

"I bet you've spent a helluva lot more time in court than your lawyer here. Am I right?''

"I reckon you are, Your Honor,'' came the beaming reply.

"Then you know the drill—are you pleading guilty or not?''

"Not guilty, Your Honor, and I'd like to say that this peckerwood wanted me to plead guilty. At my *arraignment*,'' with a contemptuous glance at his counsel. "I done told him I ain't pleading guilty—I got a sheet, Your Honor, and you gonna have to send me down a long time if I plead guilty. No, sir, I want a trial with a jury,'' he said with the authority of a man who had been there and done that.

"Do you wish him to continue to represent you, son?''

"I wish to fire his ass, Your Honor.'' Titters rose from the courtroom; even the bailiff was having a hard time keeping a straight face.

"Your Honor, my client—" The perspiring defender tried to get back in the game, but the judge pulled him up short.

"It seems to me that your client has decided to represent himself, Counselor. And I might add that it seems like a good call to me."

Laura thought it was time to stick her neck out—probably right onto the chopping block, but nobody had ever accused her of being afraid of a little judicial reaming. "Your Honor, in view of the gravity of the charges, I think the defendant should be encouraged to reconsider his decision to fire his lawyer."

"What the hell difference does it make to you?" Judge Root snorted. "If the man wants to appear *pro se*, I say let him."

"I'm not convinced that the defendant is fully aware of the gravity of his situation, Your Honor. He has a previous felony conviction, and if he's found guilty on this charge, he's looking at a minimum sentence of twenty-five to life. That's not a jaywalking ticket, with all due respect to Your Honor. His, ahh, legal experience may be adequate for the purpose of this proceeding, but I question his ability to sustain a defense at trial."

Judge Root threw up his hands. "I fail to see why the prosecution should want to make its job more difficult, but if I've learned anything about you in the past year, Miss Chastain, it is to expect the unexpected. Defendant! Rehire that skinny boy who calls himself a lawyer, and make him shape up."

Fifteen minutes later, with his client arraigned and on his way back to the Fulton County Jail, the thoroughly cowed defender caught up with Laura in the hall of the courthouse. "Hey—thanks for helping out in there. I'm Avery Daniels. You're Laura Chastain, aren't you?"

"I am."

"You went to law school with a buddy of mine—Jim Norris. When he heard I was coming to Atlanta, he told me to look out for you."

"Well, tell him I said hey."

"Listen, I really appreciate what you did. Is he always like that?"

"Norris?" Laura asked, remembering Jim vaguely as a consummate law-school weiner, and thinking it figured this kid would know him.

"No, Judge Root—is he always such a jerk?"

"He's not a jerk. He's a judge on one of the busiest benches in the country, and he doesn't have time to teach law in the courtroom."

Avery pulled himself up. "He didn't have to teach me anything—I know what I'm doing. I wasn't going to plead my client guilty. Shit, what kind of a moron do I look like?" Laura took the question as rhetorical and allowed him to continue. "I simply suggested to my client that he might want to consider a plea and he went nuts on me. We got called up before I could sort things out. I just met him five minutes before his case was called. But I still think he ought to plead to a lesser charge."

Laura shook her head. Although she was a dedicated prosecutor, she always put herself in the shoes of the defense, and in this case she believed that the accused man was right in demanding a trial. He was probably a cagey courthouse veteran who knew that the only plea bargain he'd get from the district attorney would put him on a bus to a state prison within forty-eight hours. But if he held out for a trial, he'd spend months—maybe a year or more—in the far friendlier, if crowded, confines of the Fulton County Jail, close to home and, if he had the right connections inside, maintaining a lifestyle not so different from the one he was leading now. And after a year, who could say what the prosecution's case would look like? The eyewitnesses who had put him in the liquor store might have moved on, or forgotten what they saw—all in all, a risk worth taking. Laura would have counseled him to stick it out. If things looked grim as his trial date approached, he could still strike the same bargain he could today, with credit for the time served before the trial.

Laura, after a year as a prosecutor, knew that the dimmest-seeming inmate was capable of this sort of crude calculus, but she didn't feel inclined to clue Avery Daniels in on the game. He'd managed to rub her the wrong way—by dragging her into his doofus problems in front of a notoriously fierce judge, or by invoking the irritating memory of one of her least-favorite classmates. She didn't know. But as far as Laura was concerned, Avery Daniels could learn the rules of the jungle on his own. Laura shrugged at him and said, "He's the client. You do what he wants to do, Counselor."

"Well, you heard him—he wants to fire my ass. He hates me."

"He'll hate you a whole lot more if he ends up spending his golden years as a guest of the State of Georgia, which with his record is a real possibility."

"I know that. I was gonna ask you if we could plead him on a misdemeanor."

"No."

"Why? He didn't hurt anybody."

"He attempted to rob a liquor store at gunpoint."

"But the gun wasn't loaded."

Laura was becoming exasperated. "How was the poor clerk to know that—or the cops who caught up with him? Your client's lucky he didn't get shot full of holes. And he's going to serve his time if I have anything to say about it.'' What she didn't add—what she shouldn't have needed to add—was that it was an election year, and her boss, District Attorney Marshall Oliver, wouldn't thank Laura for going easy on a career criminal three months before the primary. Laura looked at her watch. ''Look, I have to get going. My only advice to you is this: represent your client. Get to know the facts and see what you can do with them. And listen to him.''

Avery drew himself up. ''You know, I was in the top ten percent of my law-school class. I clerked for a federal judge in Virginia. I just took this job for the courtroom experience. When I've logged some trial time, I'm going to set up my own criminal defense practice. I think these scumbags are lucky to get a lawyer like me for free.''

Laura started to reply, but she was luckily interrupted by someone shouting. ''Laura! Chastain!'' Laura looked around. She smiled when she saw Detective Carlton Hemingway trotting toward her. ''Hey!'' she said, happy to see Carlton for his own sake, but equally glad to be able to get away from Avery. ''Look, Avery, I'll see you around. Don't take it too hard—consider it your initiation. You'll get the hang of it soon.'' Avery strode off huffily. ''Carlton!'' Laura said, turning to a more pleasant companion.

''Hey,'' the detective said with a grin. ''Heard you and your man mixed it up with a yuppie this morning.''

''There's entirely too much gossip in the police department,'' Laura said sternly.

''Naw, I hear Kowalski was a real hero. Took on a bald guy with a five-iron singlehanded.''

''It wasn't funny at the time,'' Laura said, remembering all too vividly her own rage. She changed the subject. ''What brings you to the hallowed halls of justice, anyway? Testifying?''

"Nope," the detective replied. "Research."

"Research? What for?"

"I've got a missing person case, and I need some background on the victim."

Hemingway was a homicide detective, but missing persons cases went to his squad when foul play was suspected. "Not a child, I hope?" Laura said. There was no worse case for a cop than a missing child.

Carlton shook his head. "Adult male. Got a minute? Maybe you can give me some ideas. You did the corporate law drill for a while, didn't you?"

Laura nodded. "About seven years."

"This guy who's turned up missing is a businessman. His coworkers and family are sure that someone's killed him, but I think they've been reading too much Agatha Christie. Guys like this don't get offed, but they do disappear—usually under their own power."

"What makes you think that's what happened?"

Carlton shrugged. "Instinct. His house was clean as a whistle—no sign of anything violent going down there. His car's missing, too—but he's been gone two, maybe three days. We usually find the car pretty quickly in a murder case. I figure he and the car are still together. What I'm thinking is that there may be something dicey about his business, something that might make it advisable for him to disappear for a while. I came over here to check his name through the court records—you know, see if anyone's suing him or something along those lines."

"Good thought," Laura said. "You'll need to search the federal system, too. I can save you a trip to the federal courthouse, if you've got a few minutes. Why don't you come back to the office with me? We've got all the on-line databases—I can just plug in a few coordinates and we'll see what pops up. And I have a friend who can clue us in to what the IRS thinks of this guy. If it's a money problem, they'll most likely be involved.''

"Thanks," Carlton said. "I was kind of hoping I'd run into one of you lawyer types. I don't mind kicking down doors or reading autopsy reports, but financial stuff bores me to death.''

Laura and Carlton had walked to the end of the hall, where she yanked open the door to the stairwell. The elevators were entirely too slow and crowded for her; she preferred to climb the three flights to her office. "I haven't seen you around for a while," Laura said as they began the ascent. "What have you been up to?''

"Little of this, little of that. How 'bout you? Guess Kowalski's still in the picture.''

Laura smiled. "Yep. He's finished renovating his house, so he's taken over mine. He's building a brick wall and planter boxes on my patio this week.''

"Sounds serious. Any plans you want to tell me about?''

"Nope. I like things just the way they are." They arrived on the landing, and Laura pushed through the door to a dim corridor banked with file cabinets and office doors. She led Carlton to her own patch of county real estate. "Take a seat," Laura said. "I'll just check my messages and fire up the computer." There was nothing urgent on her voice mail, so she launched into a records search, explaining to Carlton what she was doing as she went along. "Okay, we'll look under his name first—what is it, by the way?''

"Lawrence Belew.''

"Oh, yeah—I read about this in the paper yesterday. He's some kind of a computer jockey, isn't he?''

"Yeah, he's a 'systems consultant,' whatever that means. He does a lot of government business. He went to the

'House,' of course," he said, his voice tinged with resentment. Morehouse, the "African-American Harvard," was noted for its tightly networked alumni. Most of Atlanta's black power brokers were "Morehouse Men," or were tight with those who were. "Then he got a masters at Georgia Tech for good measure. Covered both sides of the street, you might say." By which, Laura assumed, Carlton meant that he made contacts in the white business world. And what was wrong with that?

"You don't seem too nuts about Lawrence Belew— what's the name of his firm, anyway?"

"Seventh Generation Systems. And it's not that I don't like him; I never met the brother. But I know the type. Buppie. Born with a silver spoon in his mouth."

"Buppie, as in . . . ?"

"Black urban professional. Slick car, cell phone welded to the ear—you know what I mean."

"Hey, baby, I live in Buckhead. Don't get me started on the cell phones. Okay, I'm coming up empty here. He's not a party to any lawsuits, nor is his firm. Let's check some other sources. I'll switch over to a news database." Laura waited as the search engine did its job. "Lots of pieces on him, mostly about his business. He's not just tied in with city hall—looks like he's got contracts with everyone, from the big corporations to the county and state governments, too. But there's nothing here that makes me see trouble. What do you know about his personal life?"

"Very little. He's a real loner, they say. No girlfriend, few intimate buddies. Even his firm is funny—he's only got a couple of permanent employees, a secretary, and a payroll clerk. He hires people for specific jobs."

"That's par for the course in his line of business. They

get a contract, and hire independent programmers to do the work."

"Yeah, and he hires a lot of kids—college and even high school students who're smart about computers. Very few of them seem to know anything about his personal life, other than the fact that he is a *Star Trek* buff."

"Surprise, surprise," Laura said with a chuckle.

Carlton wrinkled his nose. "Yeah, and I don't recall seeing a lot of brothers on the Starship freakin' Enterprise."

Laura laughed again. "Don't be such a hard case, Carlton."

Carlton shrugged. "I just like to keep it a little more real, myself."

Laura hooted. "Oh, give it up, Carlton. If you could, you'd be driving a Lexus and getting Mr. Sulu's autograph in a heartbeat. You're just jealous."

Carlton grinned. "Oh, sure. Jealous of a herb. That'll be the day." He stood up. "Thanks for the help, anyway."

"No problem. I'll call my IRS contact right away and get back to you as soon as I hear anything. Good luck."

"Yeah, good luck wasting my time. This guy's gonna turn up in a day or two, and I will have missed some real cases."

"Grumpy! Call me when you're in a better mood and we'll have lunch."

Carlton snorted and left Laura laughing.

Chapter 2

The Jeep was there when she pulled into her driveway. She had been all but certain that it would be, but she was relieved just the same. She pulled out the bag of expensive groceries she had picked up on the way home. She had invested in apology food: jumbo shrimp, with beady little eyes still attached, asparagus, and wine that cost more than ten dollars a bottle—which violated one of her principles, but it was a wine Amos especially liked. And ice cream, which was more for her than for him, but he wasn't the only one who'd had a bad day.

She shut the door of the car softly, and crept into the kitchen through the back door. She didn't want him to see her yet, not until she could get a reading on his mood. She put the bag on the counter and craned her neck to look out the window that overlooked the patio.

The signs were good: he had Sinatra on the boom box,

which meant that he was in a good mood. A blue-collar, salt-of-the-earth, none-of-your-fancy-pants-music mood, but that was okay, a good sign, in fact. She would have worried if he had chosen Billie Holiday; Laura didn't care for the Billie mood, which was melancholy and silent. But Frank meant that things were okay. She watched him for a few minutes as he slathered mortar on bricks and tapped them into place with a satisfying *chink*.

Looking at him like this, with him unaware of her gaze, made her knees a little rubbery. They were still in that stage where their mutual physical attraction was a novelty. Sure, Laura had always known that Amos Kowalski was an attractive man. But now he was *her* attractive man, and that made a difference. At one time, not so long ago, their relationship had been professional, and she could remember being embarrassed when she found herself contemplating that six-foot-two frame, the square jaw, and those green eyes. Her knees were getting a little wobblier just thinking about him. She couldn't believe that she had punched him. She prepared herself to explain to him what had happened this morning. Taking a steadying breath, she stepped to the French doors that opened to the patio and stepped outside.

"Looks good," she said, hoping that she sounded cheerful.

He turned and smiled at her. He certainly didn't seem angry. She returned the smile, relieved but still worried.

"You're running late," he said, unconcerned. "Like it?" He stood up and wiped his hands on his cement-encrusted pants.

"Yes. Amos, I'm so sorry. I am *so sorry*. I've just been sick all day. . . ."

A puzzled frown skewed his forehead. "Why? About what?"

"About this morning. I don't know why I did it. It was inexcusable."

"What are you talking about?"

"Amos, I *hit* you this morning."

He laughed. "Yeah, you did. Sucker punched me, to be accurate. Good thing I've been working out; the abs of iron hardly felt it."

"Don't laugh at me! I'm trying to discuss this seriously."

"What's to discuss? You were scared half to death, and something had to give. It just happened to be my gut. Better me than some poor jerk down at the courthouse, I figure."

"Yeah, well, there was one of those, too, but that's beside the point. There is no room in this relationship for violence. . . ."

He threw back his head and howled with laughter. "You call that violence? Oh, sweetie, don't get your knickers in a twist—it is funny. What chick magazine did you get that from?"

Laura bridled. "Listen here, mister, just because you're listening to Frank Sinatra and laying bricks doesn't mean you can start *chick*ing and *broad*ing me. I'll ring-a-ding-ding your bell again if you don't watch it."

"That's more like it. Look, Laura, you have nothing to apologize for. Zero. You're a civilian, and you don't know how to handle the adrenaline rush. I'm a cop; I'm used to it."

"Like the cops handle themselves *so-o-o* well all the time," she said with a sarcastic fling of her hands.

"Well, maybe not all of 'em, but *I* do. Anyway, I know exactly what happened to you. The guy was attacking me, and you wanted to kill him. I thought it was sweet. And I had the punch coming to me. I should have checked on you right away, but instead I let you sit there and stew while I helped clear the mess up. I should have let the real cops handle it."

"Maybe," Laura said, placated. "Or maybe if you had come straight to me, I would have knocked you down. I just wish you wouldn't charge into situations like that. He was trying to get your gun, Amos, and he was hitting you with what amounted to a deadly weapon. Don't they tell you not to go into a situation without backup?"

"I sized it up, and I made the decision. He wasn't going to hurt me. And, by the way, there's no way he could have gotten the gun. I've had a little experience in taking guys down safely. And he was just a big blob of frustration, anyway. I knew he'd fold in a minute."

"What happened to him?"

"He's down at Grady for psychiatric evaluation. Just a stress case, in my opinion—he lost his job, things weren't going so well at home, so when that poor lady tapped his bumper he was ready to flare up. But that was all it was—a flare. You saw how quickly he came down. I knew he would. And by the way, he was *compos mentis* enough by the time they got him downtown to call for a lawyer. In fact, he called your old pal Craig Fannin. So don't cry for him."

"I certainly will not. And I hope Fannin charges him a ton of money. Maybe he'll have to sell the damn Jaguar and buy a Hyundai to pay the bill," Laura said spitefully.

"If he owned the Jaguar—if he's like ninety percent of these guys, he had it on lease; Jaguar style on a Honda budget."

Laura laughed. "You're undoubtedly right, as always. I stopped and picked up something for dinner. Shrimp. And asparagus, for risotto."

"Oh, now I *know* you're sorry. I should let you beat me up more often."

"Shut up, or I will. Are you ready to stop working?"

"Just about. I need to take a shower before dinner."

"That's okay. It'll take a while to get things ready. I've got to change before I start, anyway."

"I'll finish out here and take a shower." Laura started back to the kitchen, but he caught her hand. "You can apologize a little more, if you want." She slipped her arms around him and laughed as he kissed her. She pulled away after a minute. "We better stop, or we won't make it to dinner."

"And?"

"I'm hungry," she said. "Let me go before I faint."

"Bullshit," he grumbled, but he released her.

Thirty minutes later Laura was chopping asparagus and tending a pot on the stove when a cleaned-up Amos joined her in the kitchen. "Want a glass of wine while you cook?" he asked.

"Sure. I bought your Australian stuff; it's in the refrigerator. How was the rest of your day, anyway?"

"About average," he said as he searched for the corkscrew. "Yours?"

"The usual pageant of human folly. I ran into Carlton Hemingway at the courthouse."

"Oh? What's he up to?"

"That missing person case—you know, the computer guy. It's been on the news. Carlton's very sure that he's hiding out somewhere, chortling over his ill-gotten gains. I offered to do a records search for him, to see if there were problems with the business."

"Find anything?" Amos asked as he handed her a glass of wine.

"Nope. Clean as a whistle. I even checked with a pal in enforcement at the IRS. The man is a stand-up, taxpaying citizen. If you want to know the truth, Carlton has a little chip on his shoulder about guys like this Lawrence Belew."

"What about Belew would get Carlton in a twist?"

"Oh, nothing—it's just that Belew's a buppie. You know, a black entrepreneur who knows all the important people in Atlanta. He went to all the right schools, and had it pretty easy, relative to a guy like Carlton, at least. To tell you the truth, I think Carlton is a bit of a classist. He only respects you if you've had some hard knocks."

Amos laughed. "He'd say he's just keepin' it real."

"Actually, that's what he *did* say. Would you mind setting the table? I have to keep stirring this stuff. Anyway, whatever did happen to Lawrence Belew, it didn't involve his absconding with the corporate funds. Why would he? It's his company, one hundred percent. He'd only be robbing himself."

Amos, retrieving plates and silverware, shook his head. "He's most likely off living out some personal fantasy."

"You mean sexual, I suppose?"

"What other fantasies are there?" he replied with a wry smile. "He's probably got a secret life, and he just forgot to manage expectations back in his everyday world. It happens."

Laura waved her wooden spoon at him. "So typical—Carlton thinks it has to be about money; you think it's gotta be sex. Your frames of reference are so totally shaped by your personalities!"

"Oh?" Amos asked as he filled water glasses from a pitcher. "And what's your theory, great and wonderful Oz?"

Laura thought for a moment. "Well, Carlton does have one point—in a murder, the car usually turns up abandoned somewhere. That hasn't happened, so I think he's on to something when he says that Belew and his car are still together. But I don't think he's off in some tax haven—I think he had an accident, and the car slid off the road into a gully somewhere. Someone will stumble across the car, with Belew in it, as soon as the kudzu dies back in the fall.''

Amos laughed triumphantly. ''I should have known! Carlton and I may think the guy's a thief or a pervert, but we at least are willing to offer up a hope that he's still alive. But you think he's dead—that's what being a lawyer does to you.''

Laura started to argue with him, but she stopped and laughed instead. ''Touché. I guess being a prosecutor does give me sort of a Gothic outlook. Well,'' she said, picking up her wineglass, ''wherever Lawrence Belew is, I just pray that he's safe. I get the feeling he was—is—a pretty decent guy.''

''Amen,'' Amos added.

''Okay, it's done—get ready to be dazzled by my culinary skill.''

Laura ladled out the risotto, tossed the salad, and joined Amos at the table. They talked about more pleasant topics while they ate—plans for the weekend, Laura's new nephew, the upcoming election. As they finished, Amos said, ''That was great. You're getting to be a regular Martha Stewart.''

''Sure, I'll be making a chandelier out of ordinary household paper clips and bottle caps any day now. You really liked it?''

''Very much,'' he said, as he helped clear the table. Then, in a blandly disinterested tone, he asked, ''Anything particular you wanted to do tonight?''

''No,'' Laura replied, as she cleared the table. ''But I'm guessing there's something *you've* got in mind.''

"As a matter of fact, I wouldn't mind catching the hockey game."

"Hockey? Good grief, it's practically summer—they're still playing hockey?"

"Yeah. They play indoors now, you know, so they don't have to worry about the ice melting," he said.

"There's no need to be smart with me, mister. Of course we can watch the game. You can explain it all to me."

"As if you cared. You don't have to humor me anymore; I accepted your apology."

"I'm not humoring you. I have ice cream, and one box of frozen Girl Scout Thin Mints left. Give me thin mints, and I can watch anything. . . ."

"Even *Oprah*?"

"No, for *that* I need booze. Go on and turn on the TV. I'll finish up here."

When Laura arrived in the living room, Amos had tuned the television to the Blackhawks game, and had settled onto one end of the sofa. Laura gave him a dish of ice cream, placed a plate of cookies on the coffee table, and sat on the other end of the sofa. She pulled her feet up onto the sofa and took two cookies. "Don't let me eat too many of these. What's going on?"

"It's just started," he said. "The Blackhawks are up one game in the series."

"So if they win this one they go on to the next round?"

Amos laughed. "No, I hate to break it to you, but these aren't the playoffs. This is still the regular season."

"So what you're saying is that we have *weeks* of fun to look forward to."

"Potentially, yes."

They watched in silence for a while, Laura wincing theatrically when the skaters collided and bashed each other into the walls. Amos laughed at her. "Oh, lay off. I watch the figure skating when you want to. And *that* would be a lot more interesting if they could body-check. It would add a real element of suspense—get two of those gals in the skimpy costumes out there and let 'em go at each other. Then you'd get the male viewing audience."

An hour later Laura was sound asleep, oblivious to whatever high-sticking, icing, or what-have-you was happening on the ice up there in Chicago. Amos nudged her awake shortly after eleven.

"Did I miss anything?" She yawned.

"Just the most exciting hockey game ever played," he said.

"Shucks. Tell me all about it." She extended her hands to Amos, who was standing. He pulled her to her feet, a little too hard; she overbalanced into him. He caught her, and held her. She looked up into his eyes. "Tell me about it later," she said with a smile.

Chapter 3

There was nothing predictable about life in the district attorney's office. Laura never knew when her plans for the day would be bowled over by a new case. And as a member of the major cases division, she could count on being involved in the most highly publicized cases—which made the job exciting, although sometimes it could be exciting in the way a minefield is exciting. Despite a few false steps, and some near blowups in her first year on the job, Laura had just been made deputy to the head of the division. Very little happened that she wasn't in on, so she wasn't surprised when she arrived at the office Tuesday morning to find that her boss, Meredith Gaffney, was looking for her. Laura took her cup of high-test coffee and her notebook into Meredith's office before she even logged on to the computer.

"Oh, there you are," Meredith said, clearly distracted. "What's on your schedule today?"

"Not much. A couple of meetings, a pretrial conference. Nothing I can't move. Why?"

"Carlton Hemingway says he spoke to you about the Lawrence Belew case."

"Yesterday. Yes, I helped him with a background check. He thought Belew had absconded."

"Well, he was wrong. Belew's dead."

"How?"

"Beaten to death. It looks like the perp was after his car. Shit—why don't people just give up the damn keys?" Meredith, a fifteen-year veteran of the district attorney's office, seemed to have a hard shell, but Laura knew that every case ate at her. Meredith had once told Laura that the only reason she stayed in the game was that she imagined it would be worse to read the newspaper, see the stories, and not be able to at least *try* to do something to help the victims.

"Where is the investigation now?" Laura asked, pen poised over paper.

"Closed," Meredith announced, to Laura's surprise. Seeing Laura's arched brows, Meredith explained. "They found the guy driving Belew's car—with the body still in the trunk." She shook her head. "Talk about your criminal masterminds. Anyway, Marshall wants this to go without a hitch—so dump what you've got and come with me to the zone headquarters where the cops are holding this moron."

Laura hurried to do her boss's bidding, reflecting sadly that she, Amos, *and* Carlton had all managed to be wrong—the triumph, she knew, of hope over experience. Of course they all should have known that the man had been murdered; responsible professionals don't simply disappear for no particular reason. But no one wants to believe the worst, not when a decent, productive citizen is involved. *We may have been naive,* she comforted herself, *but that's a whole lot better than being cynical.*

And I'm not cynical, she thought as she strode out of the office at Meredith's side. *It's a miracle, but I'm not.* This was not the first murder—brutal, senseless murder—that she had prosecuted, but it never got any easier. She thought back guiltily to her conversations about Lawrence Belew with Carlton and Amos. *He was probably already dead,* she thought, *and we were talking about him in that abstract way that cops and lawyers have. We owe him more than that,* she thought, grimly determined to deliver a conviction by way of apology to the dead man for her irreverence.

They took Laura's car, a slightly shabby Toyota. "When are you going to get a new car?" Meredith groused.

"When are you going to give me a raise?" Laura retorted. "Where are we going?"

Meredith sighed. "Cherokee Avenue."

"What else do you know? How did they catch the guy?"

"I don't know much more than you do. The police got in a tip early this morning—just after midnight—that they would find the car in Kirkwood, at the house of"—she referred to her notes—"one Roland Jervis. He seems to be pretty much your average loser; he's got a record for petty theft and public intoxication. Looks like this was his first try for major thug status. They picked him up around one A.M. He said he 'found' the car down by Oakland Cemetery, but he had a little trouble explaining what the body was doing in the trunk."

"Any history of violence?"

"Not that I know of."

"Seems like a big leap—drunk and disorderly to violent murder, don't you think?"

Meredith shrugged. "Who knows? He might have been

a ticking bomb, just waiting for the right time to blow. Or maybe this is the first time he's been caught. Anyway, we're not here to psychoanalyze the guy. All we have to do is convict him—and fast. Marshall doesn't want any mistakes on this one.''

"What's that supposed to mean?" Laura asked, stung by the implication. She and Marshall had never fully mended their fences over Laura's last big murder case, which, in all honesty, she had come close to bungling, even though everything had turned out for the best in the end.

"Don't get all huffy. This is politics, that's all. The primary is less than three months away, and Marshall's running scared. It's bad enough to have to face a Republican in November, but now he's spending all his energy—and his money—running against another Democrat. He doesn't need any distractions, and he doesn't want to hand the opposition any ammunition. Plus, the victim's family has quite a bit of pull.''

"Who are they?"

"They're from DC. Dad's an army surgeon—he fixed the president's hernia a couple of years back. And Mom is press secretary for some senator. They've already been in touch with the mayor.''

"Great," Laura said. "Just what we need—more pressure.'' The district attorney's office, usually a calm backwater as far as the electorate was concerned, had become a political lightning rod in recent years. This year, so far, a couple of big cases—none, thankfully, that Laura had had anything to do with—had been mishandled, and the backlog at the Superior Court was becoming worse, not better. A federal judge was threatening to start releasing inmates from the Fulton County Jail if the district attorney didn't do something about the overcrowding. So a big murder case, with ties to the Washington power structure, was not exactly what the doctor ordered.

Meredith sensed Laura's dismay. "Relax. This one's a lay-up. How many times do you find the perp with the body still in his possession?"

They were approaching the police station. "If it's really such a chip shot, why don't we just offer a plea, and get this one off the radar?" Laura asked as she signaled a turn.

Meredith paused before she answered. "No. It's felony murder, and Marshall wants it to go all the way."

That meant death penalty. Laura clamped her lips shut. Meredith knew how she felt about Georgia's death penalty. And Laura knew how Meredith felt: that it was the law of the state, and that they were bound to uphold it. Period. Usually the death penalty issue just went away, and Laura wished it would this time. But she didn't start arguing with Meredith. For one thing, it would be pointless, and for another, they had arrived at their destination.

The zone headquarters was an unlovely building, but functional. Laura and Meredith did some practiced badge-flashing at the front desk and were quickly ushered into a room where several cops—some identifiable by their uniforms, others by their weary demeanors and ugly ties—were sitting drinking bad coffee. Carlton—neither weary-looking nor badly dressed—stood out among them. "Hey," he greeted Laura and Meredith. "Glad y'all could make it." He jerked his head to a door on the far side of the room. "He's lawyered up—a public defender showed up about half an hour ago."

"What did you get out of him before his lawyer got here?" Meredith asked.

"Not much," an older detective, one Laura had not met before, replied. "He's sticking to his story: he found the car with the keys in the ignition, and he was just trying to return it to its rightful owner.''

Meredith snorted with laughter "That's a good one." She thrust out her hand to the detective. "Good to see you again, Alex. Do you know my assistant, Laura Chastain?"

"I haven't had the pleasure," he said, shaking Laura's hand. "I'm Alex Devereaux. I've heard good things about you."

"Thanks," Laura said. "So what else do we know— what did the medical examiner say?"

"Not a lot he *could* say at the scene. He figured the guy had been dead maybe forty-eight hours, give or take. Cause of death was probably severe trauma—he was beat to shit, the poor guy. I've frankly never seen anything like it in thirty years as a cop. Must've used a tire iron," he said, glancing at the closed door with sudden fierce hatred. "The body and the car are on their way to the crime lab. We won't know much more for a day or two."

"Has his family been informed?" Meredith inquired.

"The mayor and the chief are doing that now," Carlton said. "Mayor wants a press conference to announce the arrest later today."

Meredith nodded, and gestured at the closed door. "Who's the attorney?"

"Some guy I've never seen," Devereaux said. "Tall, skinny kid. Must be new."

Laura had a sinking feeling, which was confirmed a moment later when the closed door opened and a satisfied-looking Avery Daniels entered the room. "Everything my client said to you people is inadmissible," he said in a warning tone. "He tells me he asked for counsel right away, and that he was denied an opportunity to speak to a lawyer for several hours."

"We called you folks as soon as he asked for a lawyer. If he was denied anything, it's because it took you three hours to get here," Devereaux replied belligerently. "As for what he said to us before you came, you can tell your 'client' that I don't need a lawyer to tell me what's bullshit—and that's all he gave us."

"My client maintains that he found the car, and that he was attempting to drive it to the nearest police station so that its rightful owner could claim it."

The cops hooted in unison. "Was he going to stop off at church on the way?" one of the uniformed officers jeered. Avery shot him a dark glance. "Make light if you will, gentlemen—and ladies—but if my client tells me that any more of his rights have been violated, you will be hearing from me. Now," he said, as if he had successfully ticked off *that* item of business, "I see the district attorney's representatives are here. I'd like to speak to the two of you in private, if I may."

"Certainly," Meredith said, raising her eyebrows at Laura. Laura was sorry that she wasn't going to have a chance to tell Meredith what she was up against. But the boss wouldn't take long to get the measure of Avery on her own.

The three lawyers were shown into another room, and Avery closed the door and looked at them portentously. He nodded curtly at Laura and looked inquiringly at Meredith, without bothering to introduce himself. "I'm Meredith Gaffney," she said. "Head of the major cases division. And you are . . . ?"

"Avery Daniels. I'm with the public defender's office. Has my client been charged with anything yet?"

"No, but we'll soon see that he is, if that's what's worrying you," Meredith answered cheerfully.

"You can file all the charges you want to, Ms. Gaffney, because I've already found so many procedural irregularities in the arrest that your case will never see the light of day."

"For pity's sake, Avery . . ." Laura began, hoping to get the young Clarence Darrow to climb down a bit. Meredith held up a hand, barely suppressing a smile. "Would you care to tell me what these violations are?" she asked politely.

"Certainly. You've already heard that he was denied access to counsel, despite his request for representation. But even earlier—when he was arrested—there were serious errors made. For one, the police officers failed to properly identify themselves. For another, my client was not informed *why* he was being stopped—"

Meredith interrupted. "He was stopped because he was driving a car that the officers knew for a fact was stolen. You're not trying to argue that there was no probable cause, I hope?"

"No," Avery said with a serpent smile. "I am asserting that my client was stopped on the basis of an anonymous tip received by the police, and that the tip was insufficiently corroborated."

"Hardly," Laura interjected. "Possession of the stolen vehicle is way beyond adequate corroboration, Avery. This is just nonsense, and you know it."

Avery became genuinely angry, and for a moment Laura thought he was going to lose his cool. "It's not nonsense, and I'm warning you that I plan to move for dismissal the minute you charge him with anything."

Meredith stood up. "Thanks for the heads-up, Avery. I'd like to speak to your client now—with you present, of course, so you can let him know when I start trampling his rights."

Avery narrowed his eyes, as if he suspected that he was

being mocked. But he nodded his assent. "So long as it's clear that everything he says is off the record," he said.

"Naturally," Meredith replied.

Avery led them back through the waiting room and into the side chamber where Roland Jervis sat, attended by a lone uniformed officer. Laura guessed that the suspect was in his early thirties, although he looked much older. He had the beaten-down look of a man who had lived hard, and had amazed himself by surviving. He was tallish—it was hard to say how tall, since he was seated—and slightly built. His clothes were a polyglot combination of designer labels and thrift-store rejects.

"Good morning, Mr. Jervis," Meredith said. She introduced herself and Laura. "Are you aware, Mr. Jervis, that you have been arrested on suspicion of being involved in the murder of Lawrence Belew?"

Jervis cut his eyes to Avery, who nodded. "Yeah," Jervis said. "But I didn't kill him."

"Then why were you driving his car?" Laura pressed.

Jervis shrugged. "Found it. The keys was in the ignition. I was just . . ." Avery caught his client's eye and shook his head. "I was just going to return it to the police."

"It didn't occur to you to call the police to the scene?" Meredith asked.

Jervis's eyes brightened with sudden inspiration. "Wasn't no phone anywhere near that place—that's a bad neighborhood, ma'am."

"I see," Meredith said dryly. "Care to tell me what an upright citizen like yourself was doing there?"

"I was on my way somewhere. Passing through."

"Passing through a bad neighborhood. And saw a Lexus. Tell me, Mr. Jervis, was Mr. Belew very hard to kill? Did he fight a lot?"

Jervis's head jerked up, and he protested, tearfully, that he had never seen Belew.

"Of course not. Not after you put his body in the trunk of the car, anyway."

Jervis broke down in sobs. Meredith, so genial most of the time, had the ability to switch on this tough persona at will. She could intimidate confessions out of harder cases than Roland Jervis, and had done so. It was a part of the game Laura knew that she'd never be able to play as well as her boss. And she didn't want to. Avery should stop this now, if he cared about his client.

As if he could read her mind, Avery stepped forward. "That's enough. He's got nothing more to say to you people."

Meredith stood and patted Jervis lightly on his shoulder. "That's okay. We'll talk again, Roland. You call me any time," she said. Glancing at her watch, she snapped back into her professional character. "We'd better be going now—we've got work to do. It's been a pleasure meeting you, Mr. Daniels. Look forward to seeing you again real soon." She walked out of the room, and Laura followed without glancing back at Avery.

"Book him for felony murder," Meredith said to Devereaux and Carlton, who were waiting outside. "And if you can arrest Perry Mason in there for impersonating a lawyer, that would make me real happy, too."

The cops laughed, and Laura smiled. Poor Avery—if he thought blowing his classmates away in moot court meant that he could take on a Meredith Gaffney, he would soon realize his error. But it was one thing to have a laugh at the expense of a jackass like Avery, and quite another to pretend that the kid could mount an adequate defense of his client. Laura said as much to Meredith on the trip back to the office.

"Listen, Laura," her boss replied. "I hired you because you're a damn good lawyer. And I like the fact that you have a conscience. But we're not here to judge the skills of the defense. There are adequate safeguards in the system to protect Roland Jervis. If you don't want to be a part of this let me know, and I can arrange for someone else to take on the case."

Laura was taken aback by the harsh tone Meredith used. "No, that's not what I want. It's just that—I've seen Avery in court, Meredith. Can't you talk to Julia Walton about him?" Julia had recently been made head of the public defender's office, and she and Meredith went way back.

"No. I certainly wouldn't appreciate a call from Julia telling me how to run my office, and I'm not going to start telling her how to run hers. There's a lot at stake here, Laura. This is not the time for us to stick our heads up. We've got a job; we've got to do it. *Capisce?*"

"I understand," Laura replied. But her mind was uneasy. Roland Jervis, murderer or not, was about to become a burnt offering on the altar of Marshall Oliver's ambition. And that just wasn't right.

Chapter 4

The triumphal press conference to announce the arrest was held at City Hall East, where Police Chief Charles Sisson's office was located. The building—a former department store—was located just to the east and north of downtown. It was not a terribly convenient location; that is, not for anyone but the mayor, who could avoid having to appear at press conferences like this one by claiming urgent business at his offices in City Hall proper downtown.

His Honor had reason to avoid the searchlights of the press these days, as he was rumored to be in the crosshairs of the ongoing federal investigation into irregularities in the City's contracting practices. The remote location made it convenient for the busy mayor to skip this press conference. But Laura liked the City Hall East building, and never minded a trip there. It was an interesting example of adaptive reuse of a historic building. And Amos's office was there.

Marshall Oliver, who had arrived early to confer with the chief and his press team, saw Laura and waved her to his side, behind the podium. "Where's Meredith?" he asked.

Laura, accustomed to the district attorney's abrupt style, chose not to be insulted by the implication that her presence was inadequate. "She had to stop at the ladies' room. She'll be along in a minute."

"What's happened? Did you get a chance to question the guy?"

Marshall had been in high-level meetings all morning, out of reach even by the cell phone that never left his side. While Laura filled him in, Marshall's eye wandered across the room where the participants were assembling. His gaze—and Laura's—fell on a group of four people. "Are those the Belews?" Laura asked. She knew that Marshall, a member in good standing of the black power elite, would know the family.

Marshall nodded. "Helen and Martin, his parents, and his sister Diana and her husband. This has crushed them, just crushed them. They're good folks."

Helen Belew stood slightly apart from the rest of her family, surveying the room. Laura recalled that she was a Senate press secretary in Washington, so this must be a familiar setting for her. She was a tall, striking woman, dressed soberly in a navy suit with an asymmetrical neckline, the kind of suit that every powerful woman in Washington— and no one else in the world—wore. Her husband, though retired from the army, carried his six-foot-plus, muscular frame with military dignity. But it was the daughter who wrung Laura's heart. She was leaning heavily on her husband, and trembling so violently that Laura could see it from across the room. "I wonder if she should be here," she remarked.

Marshall shook his head. "I doubt they could have kept her away. She was exceptionally close to Lawrence." He shook his head violently. "What a waste—with all the no-damn-good people in the world, why did that punk have to choose Lawrence?"

"You knew him?"

"Sure. You knew he wrote our case-assignment software?" Laura shook her head, and tried not to raise an eyebrow. A politically well connected contractor won a sealed bid? It was exactly what the FBI was looking at. Marshall was continuing, "I don't think Lawrence was all that interested in politics, but the rest of his family lives for it. Diana was a political consultant before she had a child. She and Julian have two now. Bright girl, very bright. She worked for both of Harrison's campaigns."

"Did she?" Laura asked, noncommittally. Mayor Harrison Broad was not one of Laura's favorites, but no politician had much of a chance of making it onto her Top Ten list, not even Marshall, on the days when he was more politico than lawyer, which were occurring more frequently as the election neared.

"I had better go speak to Helen," Marshall said. "I'll talk to you later."

He crossed the room and positioned himself with the Belew family. Laura was not naive; she knew the value of a grieving relative in a courtroom or a newsroom, but that didn't mean she liked playing that particular card. Marshall wouldn't mind, she reflected. Not that Marshall was a cynic. If he had been a cynic—or maybe a "more able politician" was the polite phrase—he might have regularly manufactured scenes like this out of the flimsy fabric of Atlanta's everyday tragedies. But Laura knew that Marshall was either too principled or too stubborn to take advantage of folks who didn't know the score. The Belews knew the score. They knew there was a closely fought election on the horizon, and if their interest in getting justice for their son happened to align with Marshall's need for a little good press, that was the way things worked.

The conference was about to begin; the doors were opened so that the assembled dignitaries could file into the larger room where the press waited. Laura was always surprised at how many reporters attended these events, given that she never seemed to be able to get local news from any source. But there were five television stations, the morning and evening papers (which were really one and the same), and a handful of radio stations represented. The balance of the crowd consisted of freelancers and representatives of community papers and the out-of-town news sources that considered Atlanta worth the effort of reporting. Laura and Meredith were strictly supernumeraries at this production. All that was required of them—and of Devereaux and Carlton—was that they stand behind the speakers at the podium and look solemn.

Chief Sisson went first, reading a statement about the loss Lawrence Belew represented to the city, followed by the announcement of the arrest. Then Marshall took over to reassure everyone that the perpetrator would be prosecuted to the fullest extent of the law. Was there an extent of the law that was less than full, Laura wondered?

All the time she watched the Belews, especially Lawrence's sister. Although Laura had feared that Diana was close to fainting, she managed to remain standing throughout the ordeal of hearing the details of her brother's death, and the identity of his presumed killer, recited over and over, as the press seemed to require.

Each of the reporters seemed to feel that he or she had

to ask each question, as if it didn't count if he just took notes on some other guy's question. And the questions themselves were numbing in their predictability. Few of them were even answerable at this stage—when would the trial begin? Was the suspect going to plead not guilty? On the whole, Laura thought a printed press release would have accomplished what the press conference did, without traumatizing the family. Unless, of course, you considered the intangible benefits of this public ritual.

Finally, it was over. The chief's press secretary stepped up to thank everyone for coming, and to offer printed handouts listing the names of everyone who had appeared, and reiterating his boss's statement. Meredith tapped Laura on the shoulder. "Marshall wants us to stick around for a meeting with the family."

Laura nodded, not especially glad to receive the invitation. "Why?" she asked. "We're not that far along yet."

"They know that. I think they want us to outline what happens in our system in general, give them a general idea of what they can expect. I told Marshall I want you to handle all the pretrial business, so you should run through that with them. Marshall and I can talk about the actual trial procedures."

"Okay. Where are we meeting?"

"Upstairs in Chief Sisson's conference room. I have to call the office; I'll meet you and Marshall there. Go ahead and start without me."

Laura followed Marshall onto an elevator, and they rode upstairs in silence, Laura wondering if Amos was in the building, and if she'd have time to say hello to him before she had to head back downtown.

The Belew family, the chief, the press secretary, and one or two other aides were already seated around the table in a large conference room when Laura and Marshall arrived. Marshall explained that Meredith would be along in a minute, and they took their places at the table.

"Why don't we get started without Meredith?" the chief suggested.

Marshall frowned. "Meredith had a phone call to make. She might be delayed a while, but she asked me to kick things off. Laura Chastain, Meredith's deputy, will handle the pretrial phase. Meredith and I will actually argue the case at trial," he said emphatically, sensing that the Belews wouldn't want the second string handling things, which was fair enough. He nodded encouragingly at Laura.

"I can go ahead and give you a feel for the pretrial process—if that's okay." She addressed herself to Mrs. Belew, who commanded the room effortlessly.

Mrs. Belew nodded. "Yes. You will understand, I hope, that we don't have any experience in criminal matters. Our attorney in Washington will come down to help us, but he tells me that local practices differ."

"Yes, he's right," Laura said, hoping that Marshall didn't resent the Belews' arranging oversight of the process. "There are a lot of similarities in criminal procedure here and elsewhere, but there are some quirks in our system. Let me just start at the beginning, which may be a little redundant after the press conference."

Mrs. Belew conferred permission by a nod of her head. *Man, she's used to running the show,* Laura thought with some foreboding. But she met Mrs. Belew's gaze evenly and continued. "Roland Jervis, as you know, was arrested early this morning. He's no stranger to the system, and he knows his rights, so—not surprisingly, given the gravity of the charges—he requested counsel. As an indigent accused, he's entitled to representation in Fulton County by a public defender."

"Who are the public defenders?" Diana's husband asked.

Marshall fielded his question. "The public defender's office is a county agency under the supervision of the Fulton County Superior Court."

Dr. Belew frowned. "I thought private attorneys had to take turns defending indigents."

Marshall nodded. "In some jurisdictions, they do. But not here. The bar association does make attorneys available for complex defenses on a pro bono basis, but the legal requirement to provide counsel is met by the public defender."

"So he already has a lawyer?" Mrs. Belew asked.

"Yes. Yes, he does," Laura replied. *And how,* she added silently, thinking of Avery.

"You can't talk to him?" Mrs. Belew pursued.

"I'm sorry—to his lawyer or to the defendant?" Laura asked.

"The defendant."

"Yes, we can talk to him, if he and his counselor agree to it. We can't compel him to talk to us, though."

"Have you talked to him?"

"Yes, as a matter of fact we did, this morning. He told us the same story he gave the police, with some embellishment."

"What will his defense be?" Mrs. Belew asked, leaning forward. Her questions were certainly germane, Laura thought, and belied her professed inexperience of the criminal justice system.

"I can't say with certainty. He says that he found the car, that he never saw your son, and that he didn't know that his . . . body"—she hurried over the word—"was in the trunk. We, of course, have the burden of proof, which means that *we* must prove, beyond a reasonable doubt, that Jervis did, in fact, kill your son.''

"How can you do that?" Dr. Belew asked, coming suddenly to life and slapping his palm on the table for emphasis. "Can you? Or will his lawyer use all the goddamn tricks in the book to get him off—how do you stop that from happening?"

His wife laid her hand on his arm. "Please, Martin. The girl is just trying to explain the process to us."

"Yes," Marshall interjected, while Laura tried on the feeling of being called "girl." "We're getting a little ahead of ourselves, into trial strategy. We'll have ample time to build our case, and we will—I promise you—anticipate any stratagem the defense may have up its sleeve. Go on, Laura, and talk about what's going to happen next."

Laura resumed her explanation. "Jervis has been arrested, and charged with felony murder. That's the equivalent of first-degree murder in other jurisdictions. Our penal code recognizes two murder charges: felony murder and malice murder. Felony murder is murder committed during the deliberate and premeditated commission of a felony. Premeditation of the murder itself is not necessary—only premeditation of the crime that results in the death of a victim. Malice murder is premeditated murder—where the intent of the criminal was to kill."

"Why not charge him with malice murder?" Mrs. Belew asked.

Laura cut her eyes at Marshall, thinking he might want to handle that one, but he nodded, encouraging her to continue.

She cleared her throat. "Let me back up and clarify a point: felony and malice murder both carry the same penalty in Georgia. Death, or life in prison without the possibility of parole. The felony murder concept—well, to keep it short, if you set out to prove malice murder in the case of your son's death, we would have to show that Roland Jervis set out with the *express intent* to kill your son. And that would be hard to do, since as far as we know your son had never laid eyes on him. I think—and I hope Marshall agrees— that it would be nearly impossible for us to prove that he had targeted Lawrence, or anyone, for death. On the other hand, we have a very good case that Jervis was intent upon stealing your son's car, even at the cost of your son's life. *That* we are confident we can prove, on the basis of the evidence."

"Which is?" Mrs. Belew asked. She was taking rapid notes in a leather-bound book.

Marshall fielded the question. "His possession of the car is prima facie evidence that he committed the crime. We also expect that the forensic analysis of the car and Jervis's clothing and effects will provide more physical evidence. And the investigation, you should understand, is continuing. We hope to introduce witnesses who may have seen the crime, or who may have seen Jervis with the car."

Laura nodded. "We can continue to investigate and introduce new evidence and new witnesses throughout the discovery period—which is, as the name implies, the pretrial phase in which we construct our case. And we have to share all our evidence with the defense."

"And they with you," Mrs. Belew stated.

"Yes. We can't keep a surprise witness in the wings, and neither can they. But while all this is going on, there are certain procedures I'll be overseeing. Right now, Jervis is in the Fulton County Jail. He made what we call a 'first appearance' today in front of a municipal court judge— because he was arrested, you see, in the City of Atlanta."

"Which," the mayor added," is not the same as Fulton County."

"Fulton County Superior Court is a division of the Georgia court system—every felony has to be tried at the state court level, in this case the Superior Court. I know that's confusing," Laura said apologetically. "The whole jurisdictional thing is a product of Georgia politics—"

"Which we certainly don't want to waste your time on!" Meredith added as she entered the room. "I'm sorry I'm late," she said, as the mayor made new introductions.

"That's perfectly fine," Mrs. Belew said. "Your able assistant has been giving us a very interesting lesson in Georgia jurisprudence."

"Then I'll let her continue," Meredith said as she took a seat, smiling apologetically at Laura.

"Okay. So let's say that Jervis has been bound over to the Superior Court for trial. From here, a couple of things need to happen: within ninety days, he has to have a bail hearing. He will *not* get bail," she hastened to add. "Then, because it's a capital case, there will most likely be a probable cause hearing, where the evidence that led to the arrest and charge is reviewed."

"That's a chip shot," Marshall interjected. "A formality, really, in a murder case. Sorry to interrupt, Laura."

"No problem. After that hearing, we'll begin preparing Grand Jury testimony. He has to be indicted—formally charged—by the Grand Jury for felony murder."

"Who chooses the Grand Jury?" Dr. Belew asked.

"It's the same pool from which trial jurors are drawn," Meredith explained. "But they serve a fixed term instead of just serving for a trial. There are eighteen of them on the panel, plus five alternates."

"We present the charges and the evidence against Jervis

to the Grand Jury,'' Laura said, ''and they return a 'true bill' of indictment for felony murder.''

''So it's automatic?'' Mrs. Belew asked.

''Well, not really . . .'' Laura floundered.

''It's a virtual certainty, anyway,'' Meredith said. ''I hate to put it bluntly, but the Grand Jury is really a tool for the district attorney. It has an oversight function, to make sure we're not abusing our power, but it's not charged with deciding guilt or innocence, as a trial jury does.''

''So Jervis can't present his case to them as well?''

Laura, Marshall, and Meredith exchanged glances. ''He can testify himself, but he can't call witnesses,'' Marshall said.

''But the Grand Jury can subpoena witnesses,'' Laura added. ''Although they rarely do.''

Mrs. Belew put down her pen. ''But are you saying he could get in there with some sob story, or some fancy technical arguments, and they could set him free?''

''No!'' the three prosecutors said, almost in unison. ''Not at all,'' Meredith elaborated. ''Even if they *didn't* return a true bill on the first pass, we could try again.''

''How many times?'' Mrs. Belew asked.

This woman is fooling with us, Laura thought—*she knows criminal law.* It crossed her mind that Helen Belew might be a nonpracticing lawyer.

Marshall stepped up to handle the air ball. ''We get two chances. But, Helen, I promise you it won't happen that way. We *will* indict Jervis, and we'll do it the first time out. There will be no surprises.''

Mrs. Belew seemed to accept his assurance, at least for the moment. ''So then the trial—when?''

''Well,'' Laura said, ''there are going to be other pretrial events. His lawyer will file motions . . .'' *Boy, will he,* she

added silently, reflecting on Avery's proclivity for compli-
cating things. ". . . and the judge will hold hearings—either
in open court or in his chambers—on those motions. The
trial will take place when we're ready, unless Jervis exercises
his right to a speedy trial, in which case the trial will take
place in the next session of the Superior Court."

"Which is?"

"Each session is six months, so—given that this session
has almost expired—that would mean before year-end. *If*
he so requests, which he probably will not. He needs time
to build his defense."

"It may be to our benefit to wait longer," Meredith
pointed out. "Some types of evidence take time to prepare—
DNA, for one."

Dr. Belew nodded. "I see. So there's not much that we
can count on, really, is there?"

Marshall rapped his knuckles on the polished wood of
the table. "Only this: that we will get justice for your son."

That seemed to satisfy Mrs. Belew, who nodded and rose
to her feet. The rest of the family seemed to recognize a
signal, and they all rose along with her. "Thank you for
taking the time to explain things to us," she said. "I hope
you understand our concerns."

"Of course we do," the chief said soothingly. "And you
know that you have the mayor's, and the district attorney's,
strongest commitment, too. We're going to make sure that
there are no missteps on this one."

Laura, Carlton, and Meredith waited behind as the room
emptied. "You heard the man," Carlton said. "No missteps."

"I hadn't planned on making any," Laura replied dryly.
"I wish that gooberhead Avery would just cut out the civil
rights b.s. and mount a real defense."

"What about your boss's reelection?" Carlton asked in mock surprise. "He should appreciate a weak defense lawyer."

"I didn't know you were such a cynic," Meredith answered. "But it doesn't matter. You need a ride back downtown?" she asked both of them. Laura had taken a cab, but she didn't want to leave without trying to lure Amos out for a late lunch or a cup of coffee. "I'll take a cab," she said.

"I've got some business here," Carlton said.

"I'll see you back at the office, then," Meredith said. "Say hi to Amos for me," she added with a grin.

"Busted," Carlton said as Meredith disappeared down the hall.

Laura smiled. "Am I that obvious? I guess so." She headed for the stairwell that would take her to the floor where Amos sat, with Carlton following. "I have to see somebody, too," he said.

They emerged from the stairwell into an open floor stuffed with desks and loud with telephones. Amos's glass-walled office was visibly empty in the far corner, and she tried to bridle her disappointment. *Maybe he's just gone off for a few minutes,* she thought.

"Hey, Carlton," someone said. Laura knew before she turned who had spoken, and she cringed involuntarily. It was Don Archer, a big blond bohunk of a cop, and one of Amos's intramural basketball teammates. He also happened to be head of the mayor's security detail.

"Hey, man, what's up?" Carlton asked as he shook Archer's beefy hand.

"Same old," he replied. "Looking for Kowalski?" he asked her. Without waiting for an answer, he crushed her hopes. " 'Fraid you're out of luck," he said. "He's been called to a scene. In fact, I hope you don't have plans for dinner, 'cause he may not make those, either. Another attack out on Bolton Road,'' he said in an aside to Carlton. "Bad scene. Guy used a box knife this time.'' He glanced at Laura to gauge her reaction. She offered none.

Amos said that Laura had a bad attitude about Don, a charge she didn't even try to defend. He was everything, in Laura's opinion, that people hated in cops. He was crude and thuggish, and took an unsettling interest in Amos's grislier cases. In fact, Laura believed that Archer liked to hang around Amos for the vicarious thrill of hearing about the latest in sex crimes. He seemed ill-suited, and an odd choice, for the sensitive, high-profile job he held. "You just don't like him,'' Amos argued. "He's in that job because he's extremely well qualified.'' Archer was ex–Secret Service, Laura knew, and she appreciated the elite nature of that force. If only he would go back to it, preferably in another city, where she didn't have to socialize with him.

"I have to get back to the office,'' she said, abrupt in spite of herself. "Keep me posted, Carlton,'' she said. "See you,'' she managed to say to Archer. As she left, she saw Archer bend his head toward Carlton, and take the detective by the arm.

Chapter 5

A week went by, a few days' lull while the legal system began to digest Roland Jervis. The arraignment and bail hearings went with predictable smoothness, and the probable cause hearing was on the court docket. It was time for Laura to familiarize herself with the evidence that the court would need before the case could proceed to the Grand Jury. It was time to visit the crime lab, in other words.

The headquarters of the Georgia Bureau of Investigation's excellent crime lab was in Decatur, a pleasant urban town just east of downtown Atlanta that had so far managed to avoid becoming snarled in Atlanta's traffic and general bad mood. Laura was making a trip to the lab by herself, because Carlton and Alex Devereaux were busy running down some supposed eyewitnesses. She would have preferred to have at least one of them accompanying her, given that they had far more expertise in analyzing physical evidence than she

did. But Marshall made it clear that the case had to be top
priority for everyone involved. So, on Monday afternoon,
precisely one week after Lawrence Belew's body had been
found, Laura drove to Decatur.

Her first appointment at the lab was with Scott Butler, a
technician in the latent evidence area. He had examined the
fingerprint evidence in Belew's car. Then she had a meeting
with Jay Cooper, a forensic pathologist. She was looking
forward to her meeting with Scott a whole lot more than her
meeting with Jay, which would inevitably involve autopsy
photos. She hadn't seen them yet, but Carlton had warned
her that they were hard to look at. She parked and entered
the building, where she signed in and was directed to the
technician's office.

Scott, a slightly built sandy-haired man in his late thirties,
was eager to see her—seething with excitement, in fact, at
the prospect of sharing his findings with her. "Miss Chastain—hi!" he said brightly. "Glad you could come. I'm all
set up in here, got some slides to show you. Got some
interesting stuff!" The fiber guy would join them later,
he said, ushering Laura into a small conference room that
featured a white screen on one wall. A laptop computer was
set up, ready to show Scott's slides.

It was marvelous how quickly the technicians had worked,
given the sheer volume of cases they handled as the central
lab for the entire state. Getting a latent report scarcely a
week after the crime was committed was almost unheard
of. Strings, naturally, had been pulled—not just by powers
in the city, Laura suspected, but in the statehouse as well.
The Belews knew the governor, too.

"Have a seat over there, where you can see the screen,"
Scott said, his excitement barely disguised. "I've got this
all set up." He dimmed the lights and hurried to his compu-

ter. "I gotta tell you, this is strange, real strange. I don't know what you're gonna think. Well, I should just shut up, maybe, and show it to you, huh?"

Laura didn't quite know how to answer that, so she smiled. Scott clicked a button on a controller that extended from the computer, and an image of Belew's goldish tan car appeared on the screen. "This is Belew's car—1998 Lexus LS 400, VIN number 1G8JW82R5YY635834. The car was brought in here after the on-scene techs secured it. Now, normally, there's no way I could get a report to you this quickly, but the weirdest thing . . . anyway, here's a shot of the interior." The camel-colored interior of the car, like the exterior, was covered with the greasy powder the police used to lift fingerprints. Little graphic arrows on the screen pointed to the steering wheel, the gearshift, the window switches, and several other places. "The arrows indicate where fingerprints were found. Now, like I said, normally, we would be still matching the prints through the systems at this time. Do you know how we work?" he hurried on without waiting for an answer. "We first take a set of Mr. Belew's prints from his body. Those would be what we would call 'elimination prints.' Because, you see, we would *expect* to find Mr. Belew's prints in his own car."

"Yes, I see," Laura said. She knew this much, but she didn't mind hearing it again. She liked knowing that Scott was thorough and articulate; he would need to be if he was to testify before the Grand Jury and later at the trial.

"So, we had Mr. Belew's prints before we started our analysis. We took the prints we found in the car and compared them against his. Well, what we found was pretty surprising." He paused for effect, saw that his audience was hooked, and proceeded. *"Mr. Belew's prints were nowhere in the car."*

"What do you mean, nowhere?"

"I mean *nowhere*. And believe me, we know where to look." He clicked again, and a second image of the car's interior appeared, showing the open glove compartment smeared with powder. Another click, and an exterior shot appeared, a close-up of a door handle. "See, Miss Chastain, there are places where we would expect to find the owner's prints—and they are not there. Think for a minute about how you open your car door—do you have flush handles?"

"I can't recall—you mean, the kind that are flat against the car door? Okay, I know what you mean." She visualized curling her fingers under the handle before she lifted it. The door handles on Lawrence Belew's Lexus were similar to her Toyota's. "I would leave my fingerprints on the underside. You're saying there aren't any there?"

"No. Not on the driver's-side or passenger-side doors. And—this is what really baffled me—there were no prints at all inside the glove compartment. Now, if the man had owned the car for over three years, wouldn't you expect that he had opened his glove compartment?"

"Of course."

"And you wouldn't think that the man wore gloves to drive his own car, would you?"

"No, I wouldn't." Laura tried to be patient with Scott's Socratic method, but she wanted to know where this was heading. "Are you saying there were no prints at all in the car?"

"There were prints all right. Just not Mr. Belew's. Let me move on." He clicked again and some reproductions of fingerprints, enlarged to giant proportions, appeared. "These are the prints we *did* find. This is a full set, selected from all that we found. There were a ton of them."

"Were you able to identify them?"

"Yes! That's why I'm able to share all this with you today—all of these prints belong to one individual!"

"And you know who that individual is?"

"It is your suspect, Mr. Jervis."

"Okay, so this proves that Jervis was in the car—but we already knew that, I'm afraid. Still, it's helpful to have the physical evidence—"

"I don't think you understand what this means, Miss Chastain," Scott said, shaking his head. "There are no prints *but* Jervis's in the car!" For emphasis he clicked through a series of photos. "None of Belew's prints on the door lock switch! On the dome light! On the turn signal, or the ashtray! It's as if Belew was never in the car. And as if he never had any passengers, which I doubt. But let's say that Belew actually never did have a passenger in his car, just for argument's sake. How many people do we know with absolute certainty were in that car at one time or another?"

"Two, at least—Belew and Jervis."

"Right! So what does it mean that only Jervis's prints are in it?"

Good Lord, Laura thought, *I'm back in Logic 101. Okay, if that's how he wants to play, I'm game.* Good lawyers usually were; some legal proofs were nothing more than well-constructed syllogisms. This one was a cinch. "It means that someone wiped every surface in the car that could possibly hold a print. Presumably Jervis."

Scott threw up a hand. "Hold on—why would Jervis wipe out traces of Belew, but leave his own fingerprints everywhere?"

Laura shrugged. "Maybe it was an attempt to obscure his guilty knowledge that he had killed the car's rightful owner. There's no saying, really. Someone who kills in order to get a car is not operating on a logical plane, and his actions aren't susceptible to logical explanations. Anyway, we don't need to explain his actions; we just need to prove beyond a reasonable doubt that he committed the crime.''

Scott looked disappointed that Laura wasn't properly baffled and astounded. ''But you've got to believe his defense lawyer is going to ask the question—not to mention why he would carefully clean the interior of the car, but leave the body in the trunk.''

Laura refused to be stumped. ''That's easy—first he cleaned the car, while he figured out how to dispose of the body. He must have had some plan for it. Maybe he was going to the river, or a patch of woods, or out into the country, to get rid of Belew's corpse, when the police caught him.''

''Maybe so, but let me tell you one thing: that car was cleaned by a pro. What do you know about this guy Jervis— was he ever in the military? Was he ever a cop?''

''He was definitely not a cop, but I don't know about his service record. There's at least some probability that he served for a time, given his age. He's about the right age for a Gulf War vet.''

''I'd check carefully on that, because no civilian could do the kind of job this guy did. The military, the spooks, some cops—they all know to wipe the inside of the glove compartment. But not Joe Carjacker. No, sir. Not unless he got taught somewhere along the way. I give seminars right here, twice a year, to cops and military police and intelligence folks, on how to find prints at a crime scene when somebody's tried to hide them. And naturally, the inverse applies—if you know where to look for them, you would know how to scrub a crime scene so no one can find anything. This guy could have taken one of my courses, for all I know.''

"I doubt it. He's a petty criminal."

"Well, whoever cleaned the interior of that car was good—that's all I'll say. And here comes ol' Tommy Wood to tell you the same thing about the fiber evidence."

"Which there ain't none of," a gangly man who had just entered the room said. "At least, none to speak of." He introduced himself to Laura and shook her hand. "Scott here been sharing his conspiracy theory with you?"

"I wouldn't call it a conspiracy theory," Laura answered with a smile. "He gave me a good heads-up on some unusual aspects of the investigation. Doesn't change my mind about what happened, though. Are you going to try?"

"No," he said, taking a seat. "Sorry I don't have any slides. You can turn up the lights, Scott—no need to keep anybody in the dark for what I'm about to say. You've dealt with fiber evidence before, I guess?"

"Sure. It's been a factor in a couple of my cases."

"Then you know it's not an exact science. When I look at any crime scene—including a car—I can only make a positive statement about who was there if I find an unusual fiber, and I can match it to someone who is suspected of having been there. It doesn't do you much good for me to find a unique fiber at a scene if we can't then match it to someone, or someplace. On the other hand, it's not really all that helpful for me to find fibers relating to people we know with certainty were on the scene. All that proves is something you already know."

"So you're saying that you found fibers that you can match to Lawrence Belew and Roland Jervis?"

"Yes and no. I did find fibers matching the victim's hair and clothes, but only in the trunk of the car where his body was found. Not in the interior of the car. And I found evidence that Jervis had been in the interior of the car, but not in the trunk. I found no fibers that were unique to Jervis on or near Belew's body, in fact.''

"But that doesn't mean that Jervis *didn't* put the body in the trunk. It just means that he didn't leave any fibers," Laura interjected.

"Right. I can't prove a negative—that he *didn't* put the body there, just because he didn't leave fibers. But by the same token I can't say positively that he *did* handle the body.''

"Is there any evidence that someone else might have come in contact with the body?''

Wood shrugged. "There were a variety of fibers on the body. Some we haven't matched off yet to Belew's home, office, colleagues, et cetera. Could they belong to a third party involved in the crime? Maybe. But in order to say that with any certainty, I'd have to locate a unique fiber that could be tied to someone who might have been at the scene. And there's no one else you have in your sights for this one, is there?''

"No," Laura admitted. "We're operating on the theory that it was Jervis alone.''

"And I can offer you evidence that Jervis was in the car. I found fibers matching the carpeting in his apartment in the victim's automobile. I can defend that finding to a jury pretty well, I think.''

"I appreciate that, but as I told Scott, since we found Jervis in possession of the car, I don't think I need further proof that he was inside it.''

"And you've got to admit," Tommy said, "that it just makes it all the more likely that Jervis killed Belew and cleaned the car.''

Scott shook his head. "That's where we disagree. I just don't think he could have done that kind of a job.''

"My poor little paranoid buddy here is always looking for a conspiracy," Tommy said confidentially to Laura.

Laura laughed, but she was troubled. If Scott saw holes in the evidence, others—like Avery Daniels—would, too. An idea flashed into her head. "Either of you guys ever have a car detailed? I mean a real hundred-and-fifty-dollar job?"

"I drive a Corolla," Wood said dryly.

"So do I, but I had a boyfriend who drove a Bentley. Twice a year he had that thing detailed—and those guys went everywhere in that car, with brushes, cotton swabs, and an industrial vacuum cleaner. What if Jervis was a detail man—one of those guys who works Saturdays in Buckhead at a luxury car wash? It's a real industry in Atlanta, I'm telling you—there are guys who spend more time and money on their cars than they do on their kids. Maybe Jervis's first instinct on getting a fine set of wheels was to give it a good cleaning. We know that Belew had been dead for a while when we found the car. Who's to say Jervis didn't detail the car in the time he drove it before he got caught?"

Scott looked thoughtful. "You can't say for sure that he didn't. I guess it would be up to you to show that Jervis knew how to detail a car that thoroughly, or that he took it to someone who did. But I still come back to his having the body in the trunk the whole time. It just seems illogical that he would keep the body but clean the car to the nth degree."

"I agree that it's illogical, but as I said, so is beating a guy to death to get his car. And we know Jervis did *that*. So as far as I'm concerned any bizarre behavior on his part fits an established pattern."

"The lady's got a point," Tommy Wood said. "I'm not through with the fiber analysis, of course. When I heard you were coming I told Scott I would give you what I knew after the first pass. I'm still hoping to find something that'll tell us more. There is one other thing I found that I'm a little hesitant to bring up.''

''What's that?'' Laura asked.

''A button. A black button, about five-eighths of an inch in diameter, with some silk threads clinging to it.''

''Does it match any of Belew's clothes?''

''No, and it doesn't match anything Jervis was wearing when he was arrested either.''

''Are you saying it could belong to a third party?''

''No. I mean, it could, but there's no way to prove it. Both Belew and Jervis had buttons missing from their clothes, but this button doesn't match any of the other buttons on their clothing. But that still doesn't mean it belongs to a third party—it could be a mismatched button one of them sewed on to replace a lost one. I've done that before. Anyway, you need to get the cops to go through Belew's and Jervis's wardrobes to see if this button matches anything they owned.''

Laura, who had been listening thoughtfully, spoke carefully. ''Even if you did eliminate all their clothes, you still haven't proved the presence of a third party.''

''But it would be a much stronger possibility,'' Scott retorted.

''Right,'' Tommy Wood said.

''What about the button—can it be traced back to a manufacturer?'' Scott asked.

''Way ahead of you. I've sent it to the FBI.''

''What, they have a button identification unit?'' Laura asked, surprised.

''No,'' he said, laughing, ''but they have the resources to look into a thing like that. They've sent it on to their New York field office. Somebody'll take it down to the garment district and see if they can get a bead on who might have used buttons like it. I've got to say, though, that I don't hold out a lot of hope that they'll come back with anything solid. It's just a plain old black button. Couldn't be more anonymous if it tried.''

Laura chewed the end of her pen thoughtfully. "The silk thread suggests that it came from a more expensive piece of clothing, doesn't it?"

"Maybe. But that just suggests that it was more likely to be Belew's than Jervis's.''

"Where was it?''

"Loose, inside the plastic that wrapped his body. Could have come out of his pocket—I've carried a button in my pants pocket when I've lost it. Sometimes stays there for weeks at a time. See, this is why I didn't bring up the button right away—it's probably meaningless.''

"But if I found a third party who might have been involved, and I found that he was missing such a button . . .''

"You'd have yourself a clue.'' He glanced at his watch. "I'd best get back to work, unless you've got some more questions.''

"I appreciate your sharing what you have so far. You too, Scott—this has been very helpful to me. It's like I've been grilled by a good defense lawyer; now I know where some of the open questions are.''

Both men seemed pleased to hear that. Scott offered to take Laura to the pathology lab, after Tommy ambled back to his lab. He didn't offer to go in with her, however. "I'm not a big one for the real gory stuff,'' he confessed.

"Me neither,'' Laura said, eyeing the door of the lab with misgiving. "All in a day's work, though, I guess. Thanks again for everything, Scott.''

Chapter 6

The pathology lab that Scott directed Laura to was in another part of the building. She found a door marked PATHOLOGY, and she opened the heavy door and peered inside. There appeared to be no one in the lab. "Are you looking for Cooper?" a voice behind her said.

"Yes. I have an appointment."

"He's probably in his office," said a tall man whose clothes and bearing said GBI. "Down that hall, second door on the right."

"Thanks," Laura said, and followed the man's directions. She found a door with Cooper's name on it, and tapped on it tentatively.

"Come in," said a midwestern-accented voice.

Laura entered the pathologist's office, a cluttered and unattractive cell furnished with gray metal desks and file cabinets. Jay Cooper was sitting behind the desk, his face blueish from the reflected light of his computer screen.

"I'm Laura Chastain with the Fulton County District Attorney's office. You spoke on the phone to Detective Hemingway, I believe, about the Belew case."

"Yes. I was expecting him. Where is he?"

"He couldn't make it, but I didn't want to put this off. I have testimony to prepare for the Grand Jury."

"Oh. Well, then," Cooper said without enthusiasm. "I haven't written up my report. It's only been a week," he said accusingly. "I'm not prepared to testify until I've completed my report."

"I don't need you to testify. Carlton Hemingway or his partner can present the forensic evidence to the Grand Jury. I can take notes on your report, but I will need it in final form. How much longer do you anticipate it will take?"

Cooper shrugged. "I don't know. Some of the toxicology won't be back until next week."

"Is the toxicology important?"

"Maybe, maybe not."

Laura was at a loss to explain this man's sullen demeanor, especially after the cheerful crime-fighting bonhomie displayed by Scott and Tommy. She had interviewed defendants who were easier and more pleasant to talk to. Cooper wore an unchangeable bland expression on his face, but he was, Laura suspected, enjoying busting her chops for some private reason.

"Look, Dr. Cooper, I have a job to do and I need your help. I need a few basic facts: how and when did Lawrence Belew die?"

"*How* he died I can tell you. *When* is a matter of opinion. I can give you a range of time, that's all."

"That's fine."

Cooper sighed and opened a file on his desk. "This is a transcription of my autopsy notes. Again, not in final form, but I'll read them to you. 'Subject is black male, thirty-two years old, six feet tall, weighing one hundred and ninety pounds.' Then there are some identifying characteristics— moles, scars, et cetera. They're not important, because we had a positive ID by a family member."

"That's okay. Skip ahead to his injuries and the cause of death."

Cooper ran a finger down the page. He cleared his throat and began to read. " 'External examination reveals multiple contusions and lacerations to chest, head, and extremities. There are abrasions on the palms of the hands, consistent with an effort to break a fall onto a hard surface, and additional scraping evident on the elbows. Multiple facial injuries, including cuts on both lips. One ear is partially detached.' " Laura cringed, but Cooper didn't look up from his report. " 'X-ray examination reveals multiple fractures of the ribs, collarbone, and skull, with intercerebral bleeding.' " He looked up. "You want specific locations of the fractures? I counted forty-six."

"You can skip ahead a bit," she said.

"Okay, internal examination—the right lung was punctured by one of the broken ribs, and there were contusions to the internal organs, particularly the liver and kidneys, with internal bleeding resulting from the injuries."

"Was that the cause of death?"

"No, probably not. He didn't really have time to bleed out from the thoracic and abdominal injuries. I would say he went quickly, from the head injury." He referred to his report. "The skull was fractured, accompanied by intercerebral hemorrhage. I'd say that's your cause of death, right there. Of course, if he hadn't had the head injuries, he might not have survived the abdominal trauma. Hard to say. But what is it you lawyers look for—proximate cause? Well, that's the head injury.''

"Any idea what inflicted the injuries?"

"Hard to say—I'd guess fists and feet."

"You mean someone beat him to death bare-handed?"

"It appears that way. Of course, the injuries were repetitive—there could have been some blunt instrument involved. There were bruises on bruises. Hard to say what caused them. Here," he said, pulling out a sheaf of photos and tossing them toward Laura. "You can see for yourself. He was pretty well beaten into a pulp.''

Laura took a quick glance at the top photo, and immediately looked away. "Who ID'd the body?" she asked.

"His brother-in-law, I think. Yes, Julian Arnold, it says here. Married to Diana Belew, the sister of the deceased."

"You say whoever did this might have used a blunt instrument?''

"Might have, to inflict some of the injuries. He probably didn't need to, he did such a good job with his hands. It was the kicking and the stomping that really took the toll, though. See here?" he said, pulling a photograph from the pile and pointing to a mark on Belew's torso. It was easier to look at than the photo of his face that had turned Laura's stomach, but still horrific. "There's a semicircular impression there, one of the few clean marks I was able to isolate. Could have been the heel of a hard-soled shoe that made it, or something else. I'm inclined to think it was a shoe."

"Can you get any idea of what size the shoe was?"

"From a heel impression? Don't know—you'd have to ask one of the geniuses out there," he said, making a vague gesture that encompassed the entire crime lab. "There's probably one of these guys spending his life on footwear identification."

Laura frowned, and introduced a new topic. "What about time of death—can you pin it down at all?"

"Well, yes and no. There are certain signs, like livor and putrefaction, that can give a general idea. But I can't be too exact. As a matter of fact, there were a couple of aspects in this case that didn't quite tally."

"Like what?" Laura asked.

"Take what we know about the time frame. The guy is last seen leaving his office on a Friday evening, and his body is found in the trunk of his car late Monday night, or in the wee hours of the morning on Tuesday."

"Right."

"That gives you the earliest time of death possible as sometime Friday evening, or approximately eighty hours before the body was found. If I assume that he walked out of his office Friday and ran straight into the guy who killed him, I would expect a couple of things to be present eighty hours later—advanced livor, and signs of decomposition."

"What did you find?"

"That livor was more or less consistent with the victim having been dead for less than forty-eight hours. And I looked at putrefaction. In this weather, we would expect the corpse to begin showing signs of decomposition fairly rapidly. If indeed the body was in the trunk of that car for the entire weekend, there would have been early signs of decay—possibly the presence of insect contamination."

"I take it there was none."

"Not to the extent I would have predicted. Of course, he was wrapped in plastic, which would have minimized insect exposure," he mused. "So you see, there are a couple of contradictory factors at work that make it harder than usual to pin down an approximate time of death. There are some that support a decease early in the time frame. Some were consistent with a decease later in the period."

"Could he have been . . . stored?"

"It might be possible to conclude that the body had spent some time in a place that was presumably cooler than the trunk of that car, yes. And also not exposed to insect contamination. It's a possibility worth considering," Cooper added, speaking blandly and without interest.

"But what would that do to your ability to determine time of death?"

He shrugged. "Not much, really. It broadens out the time frame a little, but dead is dead. You die, your heart stops pumping, the blood pools. Decay sets in, but not on an exact schedule. I sense that you're trying to get me to commit to something here," he said accusingly.

"No, I'm not. I shouldn't need any testimony at all about the time of death, because the defendant—so far—hasn't raised an alibi defense. My concern is that there are some inconsistencies—anomalies, actually—in the other physical evidence. That makes me uncomfortable."

"That's too bad. But it's not my job to make lawyers comfortable. And if you don't mind, I do have other work to do."

Startled by his sudden rudeness, Laura rose hastily to her feet. "Of course," she said. "Forgive me for taking up so much of your time trying to solve a brutal murder. I'll show myself out—don't bother. You've been really helpful."

What an ass, she thought as she strode down the corridor. Okay, so the man didn't write poetry for a living, but a little more professional courtesy wouldn't have killed him. As she turned the key in her car's balky ignition, it occurred to Laura that the whole damn town was in a bad mood. She was glad that she had a date with Amos—whatever they were putting in Atlanta's water system these days didn't seem to affect him.

Chapter 7

There were two cars in Amos's driveway when Laura arrived. One, a sleek Mitsubishi, was unfamiliar to her. The other, a steroidal Ford pickup truck in a livid shade of red, was all too well known. She almost drove on past the house and headed home, forgoing her date with Amos in order to avoid further contact with Don Archer. But a date with Amos was worth a little irritating contact with Don.

She pulled to the curb and parked, quickly running a comb through her hair and dabbing on some lipstick. She left her overnight bag discreetly in the backseat, knowing that the sight of the bag would bring on one of Archer's salacious smirks, and maybe even a clever remark. Slamming the car door a little harder than usual, she started up the walk to Amos's bungalow.

She heard voices in the backyard, so she didn't bother opening the front door with her key—just as well, because she didn't care to have Archer know she carried one, the fatheaded jerk. She schooled her face into a polite smile as she rounded the corner.

Amos, Archer, and a third man were sitting on his flagstone patio, drinking beer and wearing gym clothes. Archer, to Laura's disgust, was shirtless, with far less justification than Amos, who was very well built, and the third guy, who was actually quite a looker. "Hi," she said in a voice that she hoped wouldn't communicate her annoyance at finding Don there.

Amos rose to his feet and gave her a quick kiss on the cheek. "I forgot we had a basketball game this afternoon," he explained. "I'll shower before we go out."

"It's okay," she said. "Hello, Don."

"Laura," he said, with a nod, managing in the two syllables to intimate that he knew exactly what she and Amos were going to get up to later. His eyes grazed her entire body, making her blazer and knee-length skirt feel as revealing as pasties and a thong.

"Have you met Darryl Michaels?" Amos asked, directing her attention to the other man.

"No, I haven't."

Michaels rose to his feet and extended his hand, managing to keep his gaze focused only on her eyes. He was as tall as Don, and blond, too, but the two couldn't have been more different in their manners. "Hello, Laura. I've heard that you're a force to be reckoned with down at the courthouse."

Laura laughed politely. "I don't know about that. I try to do my little bit—you guys catch 'em, I just clean 'em."

"Darryl's not a cop," Archer said.

"Not anymore," Michaels amended. "But I like to think I still wear a white hat."

"Darryl runs a security business," Amos explained. "He and Don are old Secret Service buddies."

"I'm trying to talk this guy into signing on for some part-time work," Michaels said, indicating Amos with a nod of his head. "I could use him."

"No sale," Amos said. "When I get off work, all I want to do is come home. Working another shift has zero appeal to me."

"Jeez, it's not like he wants you to direct traffic, Kowalski," Archer interjected. "Sitting courtside at the Hawks game ain't exactly combat duty, bud. I'd do it in a heartbeat if the mayor would let me," he said wistfully. "He's got a no-moonlighting policy for my squad."

"My clients are mostly celebrities," Michaels explained for Laura's benefit. "I go where they go, which is *sometimes* fun. Sometimes, frankly, I'd rather be at Peachtree and Piedmont, directing traffic."

"Exactly," Amos said. "I wouldn't mind an occasional gig at the stadium, but I'm not interested in trailing around after some guy ten years younger than me and fifty times richer, trying to stop women from tearing his clothes off."

"Sure, easy for you to say, when you can get your own clothes torn off without leaving home," Archer said in an attempt at ribald humor.

"I guess we should be shoving off," Michaels said in the silence that followed Don's leaden joke. "It was a pleasure meeting you, Laura," he said. "And, Kowalski, if you change your mind, here's my card. Always looking for new talent."

As soon as she heard their cars pull away from the house, Laura vented. "That guy—why do you let him hang around with you, Amos? He's such a creep."

"Who, Don? He's got some good points. I don't know why you don't like him."

"He's a goon, and I don't like the way he looks at me."

"He doesn't mean any harm. He thinks you're cute, that's all."

Laura snorted. "How would he know whether I'm cute or not? He's never looked higher than *here.*" She indicated her chest.

"Okay, so he's not the smoothest guy in the world. But I don't think he has a lot of luck with women. You probably make him nervous."

"Sure, he's really nervous around me. I am around him, anyway. I can't even begin to imagine what's going through his head."

"Nothing that doesn't go through mine from time to time," Amos said with a mock leer.

"Cut it out. As a lecher, you're not even in his league. I'd be willing to bet that he has an absolutely encyclopedic porn collection."

Amos laughed. "When you take a dislike to someone, you really take a dislike, don't you?"

"Not without reason, I hope. Anyway, enough about Don Archer. How was your day?"

He shrugged. "It was a day." The tone of his voice was even, but he cut his eyes away as he answered. That was a bad sign; anything might have happened, but Laura knew that it wouldn't do her any good to pursue the matter. He would just clam up more tightly. "Are you too pooped to go out? We can stay in if you'd prefer."

"No, I just need to take a quick shower and change. Grab yourself a beer and I'll be ready in a flash."

Laura did as instructed, and wandered into the living room with her beer. She browsed through Amos's CDs and picked

"The Swingin' Miss D" to install on his freakishly complicated stereo. Dinah Washington was a musical taste—like Joe Williams and Anita O'Day—that Laura had developed since she and Amos had been spending time together. It was an improvement over the shoe-gazing British pop she had favored since college, although she did have to binge on Radiohead from time to time.

She didn't feel like sitting, so she circled the room while she listened. One wall of the room was lined with bookcases that, to Laura's eye, seemed a little barren. Amos wasn't much of a reader; what books he had tended to be biographies and military history—which was fine, Laura told herself. Not everyone has to read. And look at everything else Amos could do—he could build or fix anything, and that was nothing to take for granted. Most men his age, Laura's own brothers included, couldn't drive a straight nail, and as far as fixing the cars they drove—forget it. But Amos could do just about anything, from grouting to wiring. It was a shame that he didn't take the same pleasure that she did in a good book, but it wasn't the end of the world. As Laura's mother had said—she had taken one of her shines to Amos—"Who cares? You can join a book club if you want to talk about literature."

"Ready?" Amos asked. Laura turned and saw that he had entered the room without her noticing, his hair still wet from the shower.

"Sure. What are you in the mood for?"

"Anything, as long as we can walk to it. I'm too tired to fight for a parking space."

"Sure you wouldn't prefer to stay in? We could order pizza."

"I'm not in a pizza mood. Or Chinese, either."

"Okay. Let's just go to Atkins Park and get a burger."

She retrieved her purse from the sofa, but as she heaved it onto her shoulder, a beeper went off. "Uh-oh. One of us is beeping."

"Not me," Amos said.

She was relieved. Pages for Amos were always devastating to evening plans. Hers, on the other hand, could usually be disposed of with a phone call. She checked the tiny screen. "It's Carlton. I forgot to call him. Do you mind?"

"Knock yourself out."

She dialed the familiar number; the detective picked up almost immediately. "Hey, Carlton. Sorry, I forgot to call you."

"That's okay. I tried your office, but they said you never came back after you went to the crime lab."

"Well, I had some plans, and it just didn't make sense to go all the way back into town—"

"Busted! You're at the lieutenant's, aren't you?"

"Maybe. So what's up? Did you interview the witness?"

"*Witnesses,* baby—we got two for the price of one."

"Oh? Who are these concerned citizens?"

"Couple of guys who were hanging out with Roland Jervis the weekend Belew was killed. He offered one of them a ride in a Lexus on Saturday night."

"So they saw him with the car?"

"No, but they described it, the way Jervis described it to them."

Laura's excitement ebbed. "That's interesting, but it doesn't contradict any part of Jervis's story, except the time frame. He says he didn't find the car until Monday."

"But that's not all they said. When they told him they didn't believe him, he started bragging on how he'd jacked the car."

"But they never actually saw it?"

"What do you want? I'm serving up some double-corroborated hearsay and you act like I've stepped in doggie doo. What do I have to do to impress you, lady?"

"I'm plenty impressed. I'm just thinking ahead to what the defense is going to do to them. I'll have to interview them myself."

"No problem. I can get them in here anytime."

"Get them in tomorrow morning, then—say around eleven. I'll have a nice chat with them."

"I'll do it. I already faxed their statements to your office. You, uh, want me to bring you copies tonight?"

"No, I can survive a few more hours without them. I'll see you in the morning." She hung up and looked apologetically at Amos. "Sorry. It's the Belew case. Carlton and Alex Devereaux found some witnesses. I meant to call Carlton earlier, but seeing you must have distracted me."

"You're such a liar."

"Cut me some slack. I do honestly have a lot on my mind. I've got a bad feeling about this whole case. I mean, the mayor and the victim's family offer a reward, and—surprise!—you get witnesses. I can't wait to meet these two."

"I can't wait to meet my dinner. Let's get going; you can tell me all about it on the way." He looked down at her feet and gestured at her sling-back pumps. "Nice shoes. Can you walk in them? I mean, on the sidewalk?"

"Let me change into my flats—oh, shoot, I left my bag in the car."

"I'll get it for you," he said.

"No, that's wasted motion. We can stop there on the way out."

Amos leaned on the car while she changed into more

appropriate footwear. "I didn't even ask you how your day went," he remarked.

"About par for the course," she said. "I went to the crime lab to review the physical evidence in the Belew case. I've got to pull together the testimony for the Grand Jury pretty quickly."

"How's it looking?"

Laura stood up and locked the car door. "I don't know. To be honest, some of the stuff I heard today made me kind of uneasy."

"How so?" he asked, taking her hand. They began to stroll off in the direction of the restaurants of the Virginia-Highland neighborhood.

"You don't want to talk shop, do you?" she asked, hoping that he would encourage her to do just that. She wanted his opinion, because, in addition to his many other skills, Amos was a fine cop. She liked getting his viewpoint on things.

He shrugged. "I don't mind. What did Carlton and Alex Devereaux have to say?"

"Nothing. They were running down those eyewitness, so they didn't go. They'll go tomorrow. Anyway, I went on out there by myself and talked to the lab techs and the pathologist. One of the technicians didn't think that evidence added up." She described Scott's reservations, and the peculiarity of the fingerprints that *weren't* in the car. "And then I talked to the pathologist who did the autopsy. He was a big jerk."

"What does that have to do with the case?"

"Nothing. Just describing the scenery for you a little. Anyway, he was pretty vague about the time of death."

"It's hard to be exact about time of death in anything but the most ideal circumstances. Like when you have a tight time frame to work with."

"Which we certainly don't in this case. I understand that pathology isn't magic, but it's not helpful that he's so wishy-washy on the time of death when the latent evidence is contradictory, too."

"Seems to me you're working pretty hard to undermine your own evidence," he remarked.

"I'm not undermining it; I'm testing it. It has to stand up to some pretty tough scrutiny."

"A Fulton County Grand Jury? That's not exactly a three-point shot," he said dryly.

"I give our good citizens a little more credit than you do, evidently."

"But there's nothing that exonerates Jervis in what you told me. Just get the indictment and worry about the details later. That's what you guys usually do, isn't it?"

"Never mind whether justice is served or not."

"Is that the goal? I thought reelecting Marshall Oliver was the object of the exercise."

"Maybe for Marshall. I want to get to the truth."

"Okay, so what's standing in your way?"

"Just those pesky facts. And the suspect—you haven't met Roland Jervis, but if you had you'd hardly peg him as a criminal mastermind."

Amos laughed. "I don't need to meet him to know that. I mean, cleaning the victim's prints from the car and leaving his own—come on. Sounds to me like he's a candidate for the stupid criminal file."

"Do you really think anyone's that stupid? And whoever cleaned that car was smart enough to wipe the inside of the glove compartment. And the dome light, and every other surface in there."

He shrugged. "The guy killed someone for a car. He's

not firing on all his cylinders. Better look out for an insanity defense.''

''I'm already dealing with an insane defense lawyer. But seriously, Amos, how would he know how to clean a car like that?''

''How should I know? Maybe he used to detail cars or something.''

Laura smacked him on the shoulder in delight. ''That's what I said! I'm getting better at this, aren't I? I'm going to find out, of course, a lot more about Jervis. But what if he *didn't* work the Buckhead car-care circuit, okay? What then?''

''Okay, Laura, how many times have I told you not to get ahead of yourself? Do I have to remind you what's happened when you start developing theories? Once you get an idea in your head, you know what you do—you make all the facts fit that theory.''

''That's not fair. I have to question everything, from every angle. That's what the defense is going to do. Or at least,'' she amended, ''that's what he's supposed to do, the little yutz. Anyway, I have to consider the possibility that Jervis is telling the truth, that he had that car for only a very short time, and that person or persons unknown killed Belew, cleaned the car, and left it where some idiot like Roland Jervis would find it.''

''Ahh, there it is—the conspiracy theory. I've been waiting for it to come out.''

''What the hell is that supposed to mean?''

''Nothing. I just know what you're about to say.'' He lowered his voice and said in a portentous voice, ''Who could have cleaned the prints from that car? Who, but a cop? Don't look at me like that—you know it's what you were thinking. You always think there's a crooked cop behind every unexplainable fact.''

Laura started to say ''inexplicable,'' but thought better of it. ''You are so wrong. That's not what I was thinking at all.''

''So what were you thinking? Spies? A rival clan? Extraterrestrial beings?''

Laura dropped his hand and stopped walking. ''What's eating you? I don't think a damn thing, except if that poor loser had a half-decent lawyer, I might not be able to get an indictment. All I want to say is that there's something wrong with the picture. I thought you might help me hash it out, but just forget it. I'm sorry I brought it up.''

''No, I'm sorry. I had a crappy day, and I shouldn't be taking it out on you.''

He seemed sincerely distressed, or as distressed as Amos was likely to get. Laura took his hand again. ''What happened?''

He shook his head. ''They found a girl's body today, some runaway. Probably forced into prostitution. It was pretty bad.''

''Tortured?''

He nodded. ''But she didn't have any political connections, so it won't make the papers.''

''That's just cynical, and you know it. People do care. I care.'' She put her arms around him, and rubbed the small of his back. ''I wish you had another job. I wish we both did.''

He managed a small laugh. ''Then who would save the world?''

She smiled up at him. ''Captain Justice and his sidekick Tort-Girl to the rescue.''

Equilibrium restored, they were able to enjoy lighter conversation over dinner and the walk home. "You forgot to leave any lights on," Laura remarked as they neared the house.

"There's still plenty of daylight left," Amos replied.

"For the nocturnal lemurs of Madagascar, maybe, but I can't see a thing. Ow," she added for emphasis as she stumbled on the steps.

Amos didn't answer as he unlocked and opened the door. Laura followed him into the darkened living room. "We don't need no stinkin' light," he said. "Not for what I've got in mind."

"I guess we're not going to play Scrabble, huh?" she said.

"Nope," he said, and he pulled her into his arms. "Not unless you insist," he added, gently tugging her blouse from the waistband of her skirt and bending to kiss her.

"I kind of had my heart set on it," she said, when she could come up for air. "But I'll adjust."

Chapter 8

"What in the name of God is this?" Meredith held the blue-jacketed sheaf of paper at a safe distance, dangling it by a corner as if she feared it might carry a legal contagion. Laura recognized the work product of Avery Daniels that she had left on her boss's desk an hour earlier. Avery, having failed to prevail at the probable cause hearing the previous day, had a new angle.

"That? Why, that's the product of one of our finest law schools," Laura answered. "You're not impressed by the finely honed legal arguments contained therein?"

"I haven't made it out of the preamble yet, and he's got everything but *Marbury versus Madison* in there. What's he trying to do?" She plopped into a chair across from Laura's desk and shoved her half-glasses onto the top of her blond head.

"How should I know? You've met Avery Daniels, boy

attorney. Are you saying you're not dazzled by the sheer brilliance of his argument?''

"Does he have an argument in here somewhere?" Meredith asked, rattling the pages impatiently. "I don't have time to find it, if there is—I'll be collecting my pension before I get through all this nonsense."

"Of course there's an argument. If I may direct your attention to Section Four, sub-paragraph two 'b,' you will see that counsel for the defense is moving for dismissal based on—hold your breath—the grounds that the arrest violated the Fourth Amendment of the Constitution."

"Do tell. How did our local jackboots trample the rights of the citizenry this time?"

"You need only read Avery's *extensive* brief—"

"Oh, no, I won't—that's what you're paid to do."

"Then let me summarize for you: racial profiling. It is the argument of the defense that Roland Jervis was stopped and questioned because he was, in short, a black man driving a luxury automobile. Never mind that there was an all-points bulletin issued alerting the police to be on the lookout for that particular car, *and* its owner, who happened to be a black man."

Meredith tossed the motion onto Laura's desk. "How stupid is this kid?"

"He's not stupid at all. Just inexperienced and a little bit of a show-off. His argument turns on the point that the all-points bulletin initially issued on the car gave an incorrect license plate number. So the car Jervis was driving—Belew's car—was not the car described by the APB. Ergo, the *only* reason the police stopped this particular Lexus was that there was a black man behind the wheel."

"Is the judge going to buy it?"

"No. For one thing, the APB was corrected, very quickly,

and Avery fails to prove that the arresting officers had not seen the corrected plate number. For another, I can make a case—if I have to—that the description of the automobile was in itself sufficient to warrant the stop.''

"How do you figure that?''

"I made a quick call to the cops, to ask if any other officers stopped any other tan Lexuses ... Lexii? What would you say?'' Meredith shrugged, and Laura continued. "Anyway, a number of cars matching the description were stopped. Some of them even driven by white guys, and one by a white *woman*. So there goes the argument that there was racial animus on the part of the arresting officers.''

"So why even put this thing forward? He's just wasting the court's time.''

"He would disagree. He clerked for an appeals court, in Virginia, I think, and he saw arguments like this one getting traction with the judges. What he lacks is trial experience, where this kind of argument ... Put it this way: even you or I would throw it at the wall if we didn't have anything more substantial. But it's a moot point, because it is as flimsy as the paper it was printed on, not to mention that there's plenty of substantial stuff Avery could be using.''

"Like what?''

"The physical evidence. It's ... troubling. And the time line is weak. We can only tie Jervis to the car on Monday, and the pathologist at the crime lab seems to think that the death probably occurred much earlier. So where was the car before Monday? And where was Jervis? We don't know.''

"That's not what I hear. I hear that we have two witnesses who can tie Jervis to the car as early as Sunday afternoon, hours before he says he 'found' it.''

"So they say. Have you read their statements?''

"Yes. Do you have a problem with them?" Meredith asked, one brow cocked quizzically.

"No, no—I just need to see them, talk to them, that's all. If Avery comes after them, I have to make sure they're going to stand up to it."

"Well, I don't see any evidence that the defense is concentrating on the weaknesses in our case. He's too busy trying to get appointed to the Supreme Court."

Laura laughed. "He's not an idiot. This is just his first shot across the bow, his bid to impress us with his legal acumen."

"I'm overwhelmed, anyway. That's not quite the same as being impressed, of course. It seems to me that he's conceding the trial and crafting grounds for appeal."

"I think you're right. In the meantime, though, whether he's ready or not, he's got to try the case. And he's got to go though *me* to win it. So don't worry, boss."

"Oh, I'm not worried. Who's hearing the motion?"

Laura rolled her eyes. "Judge Root. He's already had one run-in with Avery. I just hope he doesn't kill him this time."

"No, we certainly don't want to prosecute that one. When's the motion hearing?"

"Tomorrow morning." Laura looked at her watch. "In the meantime, I'm due to meet our two eyewitnesses. Want to come along?"

"I'll pass. I've got a meeting with Marshall. By the way," she said as she rose from her chair, "you do remember about the thingie tonight, don't you?"

"What thingie? Oh, *that,*" she said with a sigh. There was a fund-raiser for Marshall's campaign, and the attendance of all his loyal employees was strongly suggested. "I'll be there."

"Is Amos coming?"

"Are you kidding? He hates things like that. He announced that he has to plane the bottom of the bathroom door, because it's sticking. It's apparently very urgent, and must be done tonight between the hours of six and nine P.M. So, in short, I'm stag."

Meredith laughed. "My beloved husband managed to get called out of town, so I am, too. Who knew that the ultimate result of thirty years of feminist struggle would be that *we* get to do the boring stuff? I'll see you there."

An hour later, Laura realized that, if she didn't get under way, she would be late for her meeting with Carlton, Alex Devereaux, and the two witnesses. She gathered up some papers and threw them in a briefcase, updated her voice mail announcement, and hurried to the downtown command where Carlton and Devereaux had arranged for her to meet the witnesses.

Carlton met her and ushered her toward the interviewing rooms. "We've got them in separate rooms, so you can talk to them one at a time."

"Did they come in together?"

"No, they didn't. They say they don't know each other."

"So they each heard Jervis brag on the car-jacking separately?" Laura said, her voice tinged with doubt.

"Yes. You sound like you don't believe they're for real."

"No, not at all. I'll reserve judgment until I talk to them. One question, though: in the statement that one of them made—I think it was Albert Jackson—he says he ran into Jervis at the pool hall on Saturday. I take it that the pool hall in question was not a legally licensed operation?"

Carlton laughed. "The place he's referring to is technically classified as a 'private club,' so they can skirt the liquor-licensing laws. Every so often somebody gets stabbed or shot in the parking lot, and it gets shut down for a while, but it's pretty much a fixture. When you live in a neighbor-hood like that you've got to have someplace to go to blow off steam."

"I understand, but I'm worried about the character of the witnesses."

"They're both sleazebags, all right, but I wouldn't worry too much about it. It's not like you would expect Jervis to have come across them at church or anything."

Laura shook her head. "Okay, I guess. Let's get it over with."

Carlton led her into the first room, where a slightly built black man, maybe in his late forties or early fifties, was seated at a table. He smiled genially at her, greeting her as if this were a delightful social visit. "Mr. Jackson?" she asked.

"No, miss, I'm Jermaine Clay."

"Okay, Mr. Clay. Tell me what you told the police about Roland Jervis."

"Well, like I tell them, I met him on a Saturday, 'bout lunchtime. We was, uh, at the social club down there on the Bankhead Highway. He comes in, and he's talking to one or two of the fellas. I was just listening, you understand."

"Did you know Jervis?"

"No, ma'am, I didn't. Somebody told me his name, though."

"I see. And what did he say to the fellas?"

"He was bragging on his car. He say he has a Lexus, but the fellas don't believe him. They want to know where is the car, you know."

"Naturally. What did he say to that?"

"He say he don't like to drive it to a place like that where all kind of trash can mess with it. He say he keep it where he stays at, but that soon everybody going to see him driving that car. The boys, they all laugh at that, and that make him real mad. He say we don't want to be messing with him like that, 'cause he's bad to lose his temper and all that." Clay frowned and shook his head. "I didn't talk to him no more after that, 'cause I had to go home then."

"And did you see Jervis with the car at any time?"

"No, ma'am, I never did see that car. He did tell what it look like, though, so when I hear the police was looking for somebody who 'jacked a tan Lexus, I thought I ought to tell them what I heard Roland say 'bout that car."

"Did you know that there was a reward for information about the car, and its driver?"

Clay cut his eyes at Carlton, who remained impassive. "Yes, I knew that. But I would have come to them anyhow."

"Very public-spirited. Thank you, Mr. Clay. Did the detectives tell you that you would be required to tell this story to a Grand Jury?"

"They said I would have to go to court, and that I shouldn't leave town without telling them."

"That's right. We'll be in touch, Mr. Clay."

They left the room, and Carlton instructed a uniformed officer to send Clay home. "What do you think?"

"He seems sincere enough, and it's a straightforward story. I'm still concerned that neither of them saw the car, or Jervis with the car." Alex Devereaux joined them. "Hello, Alex. I was just telling Carlton that our eyewitness testimony would be a whole lot more effective if the eyes had actually witnessed something."

"But you've only talked to Clay. It's Jackson who has more details on the car-jacking itself."

"Bring him on, then."

Devereaux obliged by leading her into a second room, where a far less attractive character than Clay sat at a table.

Albert Jackson was younger than Jermaine Clay, and he sported the thuggish garb of a would-be rapper. He neither spoke nor nodded when they entered the room. "Hello, Mr. Jackson," Laura said. "I'm Laura Chastain, from the district attorney's office. I'd like you to tell me how you met up with Roland Jervis, and when."

Jackson gave a barely perceptible shrug. "It was Saturday, in the afternoon. Maybe about three. I don't remember the date."

"And where did your encounter take place?"

"At the store."

"The store?"

"Yeah, the liquor store. We was hangin' in the parking lot. Just chillin', know what I mean?"

"I guess I do. And Jervis was with you?"

"Naw, not at first. He came along later. But I don't know the man's name, know what I mean? I ain't never seen him before."

"I see. How did he arrive—in a car?"

Jackson shook his head. "He was walkin', but he said he has a car."

"When did he say that?"

Another languid shrug. "I don't know, but somebody says, 'Yo, Roland, where's yo' car at?' so I know the dude got a car, you know what I mean? He says, 'I don' wan to be bringin' my car out all the time, 'cos too many folks be trying to ride in it.' He says he don' wan' folks messin' up the car, 'cos it's a Lexus and all that. I say, 'Yo, man, you bullshittin'. You ain't got no Lexus,' and he say, 'Yes, I do, but I don't hafta show it to yo' sorry self.' He was buggin', you know what I mean? So I say, 'Where you get a car like that, anyway?' and he say, 'I don' hafta tell you where I got my ride.' I say to my peeps—"

"Your whats?"

"My peeps, you know what I mean, my crew. The guys that was hangin' with me. I say, 'This mutha ain't got no car, 'specially not no Lexus.' That make him mad, and he say he gon' beat my ass same as he beat the guy he 'jacked. I say, 'You ain't never 'jacked nobody and you ain't got no car.' Then the man, he goes live on me. He break his forty—"

"I'm sorry—is that a gun?"

"Naw, his forty—his bottle."

"Oh, I get it—a forty-ounce bottle. Go on."

"He break the bottle, and he wave it at me, sayin' he's gon' cut me. Couple of my boys hafta grab him, hold him back, you know what I mean?"

"I guess I do. What happened next?"

Jackson shrugged again. "Nothin'. I laugh at the dude, and he leave. I don' remember 'bout seein' him until I hear some guy's Lexus been 'jacked, and the man dead. Then I call the cops, and say I know a guy say he 'jacked a Lexus. So they come and get me, take me to the police station, and show me a bunch of pictures of some guys. I see the man, and I say that's him, that's the one say he 'jacked a Lexus. That's all. I'm out."

"I guess you are. We certainly do appreciate your helping us out like this, Mr. Jackson. We'll let you know when we need you to appear."

When they were safely out of earshot, Laura turned to the detectives. "He's a really attractive witness."

"We can clean him up," Devereaux said. "The important thing is that he establishes not only that Jervis boasted about the car for a second time, but that he also showed a propensity for violence."

"Waving a broken bottle at some hophead in a parking

lot is a far cry from beating a guy to death with his bare hands," Laura said.

"What's the matter with you, lady?" Devereaux asked, obviously annoyed. "You don't seem to think that either guy is telling the truth."

"I just wish that they hadn't posted that stupid reward money. Neither of them is particularly credible to begin with, and the defense is going to be able to make an issue out of the money."

"There's nothing we can do about that. The important thing is that the two corroborate each other, and they don't have any prior connection, either to each other or to Jervis."

"That we know of, anyway," Laura said, more thinking aloud than anything else. She should have thought silently, because Devereaux took exception to her offhand remark.

"Just what are you thinking? Do you think that we—that I—set this up?"

"That's not it at all. I just think that these guys look like mercenaries, and I've still got problems with the physical evidence, too."

"That fingerprint stuff? You're making too big a deal out of that. He cleaned the car, or had it cleaned. Whose team are you playing for, anyway? You better get with the program, lady. We've turned this into a goddamn chip shot for you, and if you screw it up, I wouldn't want to be in your shoes. Everybody—the mayor, the chief, and even your own boss—wants this taken care of. Maybe there's another assistant district attorney who should be handling this."

"Really? You're not going to find one who doesn't ask the same questions I am. There's no point in being sensitive—if you think I'm asking tough questions, wait until the defense gets hold of your prize witnesses. I'm sorry, Alex; this is just the way I work. Ask Carlton. He knows me."

"That's right. She's got a job to do," Carlton said helpfully. "You just wait until you see her in the courtroom. She'll make those two look like Boy Scouts."

Alex seemed placated. Laura only wished that she shared Carlton's confidence in her own abilities.

Chapter 9

The motion hearing started off badly for Avery Daniels, who was not actually present when it started. Laura, who had arrived safely in advance of the appointed hour, sneaked inconspicuous glances at her watch, hoping, for Avery's sake, that her timepiece was fast and that her hapless opponent was not really late to a hearing in Judge Root's notoriously punctual courtroom. But her watch—and the judge's, and his clerk's—were all scrupulously correct.

The judge entered the courtroom, announced by the bailiff, and took his seat as the matter before the court was announced. He shuffled a few papers on his desk, then peered at the assembly over the tops of his half-glasses. Laura looked straight ahead, although she was tempted to crane her neck toward the courtroom doors to watch for Avery. "Where is the defense counsel?" Judge Root barked. No one—especially not Laura—felt it his duty to reply. "Well? It's his motion. Where is he?"

"Your Honor," Laura ventured, against her strong instinct for self-preservation, "if we could just delay for fifteen minutes I could put in a call to his office and find out what's keeping him."

"You? Why should you do that? You stand to benefit if he doesn't show up, because I will, by God, deny his motion. This court is entirely too busy to be held hostage to the schedule of every half-prepared lawyer in Atlanta."

"I would prefer, Your Honor, that the hearing be rescheduled, if it's all the same to you."

"Well, it's not all the same to me. And why should you care if the motion's rescheduled? Oh, I know what you're thinking, Miss Chastain. You don't want your grand case to be appealed because I was in error in dismissing a pretrial motion on a technicality. Heh—am I right?"

He was precisely correct. Technically, Laura shouldn't have cared a bit if a judge's error resulted in an appeal, or even overturning, of a trial verdict. Her task was to prevail at the Superior Court level, and not to make any errors or omissions that could lead to an appeal. If a judge made an error that opened the door to an appeal, the prosecution wouldn't be held responsible—in theory, anyway. In practice, Laura wished that Judge Root would just lighten up and let her argue against the motion. Then he could feel free to dismiss it in as high-handed a manner as he cared to, because it was, after all, nonsense.

In the meanwhile, the judge was waiting for an answer to his question. "No, Your Honor, I simply believe that the motion warrants argument. Counsel for the defense has, umm, touched upon one or two points that I believe require clarification. . . ."

Judge Root snorted impressively. "Spare me the fertilizer, Miss Chastain. This motion is—"

Happily, Avery chose that moment to burst into the courtroom, a prison-garbed Roland Jervis in tow, before the judge could go on record with a disparaging remark that, Laura sadly feared, would reveal that his mind was already made up.

"Mr. Daniels! Thank you for joining us! I hope we haven't inconvenienced you?" There was, of course, no correct answer to that question, Laura reflected, looking at Avery's flushed face with pity.

"Ahh, no, Your Honor, I mean, of course I wasn't inconvenienced. I was just, umm, I didn't realize what time—"

"May I suggest that in the future you plan to arrive early, as the prosecution managed to do? You've put Miss Chastain here in a very awkward position, young man—she's been trying to argue your motion for you."

Avery glared quickly in Laura's direction, and she stifled a groan. "I'm sorry, Your Honor, but something came up. I was called down to the jail to see a client, and it took longer than I expected." Avery had managed to summon up a little anger of his own, and it went a long way toward restoring his dignity—and toward placating Judge Root, who tended to overuse, in Laura's opinion, the Socratic method. *Good for you, Avery,* she thought.

The judge, his point made, seemed prepared to get down to business at last. "All right, son, I've read your motion, and your brief in support of it. You seem to believe that the arrest of your client was the result of an illegal search and seizure. How do you figure that?"

"There's a large and growing body of case law, Your Honor, that holds racial profiling to be a violation of the Fourth Amendment. In this particular instance, the defendant was arrested when he was driving a tan Lexus sedan. The police were seeking a tan Lexus sedan, but—and this is my first point—the license plate number initially issued was not the license plate number on the tan Lexus that was driven by the defendant.''

"Your Honor, if I may . . .'' Laura said. The judge nodded. ''It is true that the license plate number in the initial bulletin was in error, but the rest of the information, including the description of the automobile itself, as well as the fact that it was owned by a black man, was all correct. I should also add here that the police made numerous other stops in response to the bulletin, including some cars that did not fit the description of the automobile, and at least one that was driven by a white woman. It would be an error on the part of the court to presuppose that the arresting officers stopped Roland Jervis solely because he was a black man driving a certain type of automobile—which is the essence of racial profiling as I understand it—given these other stops that were also made. The defense has also not demonstrated that the arresting officers had not, in fact, received the corrected bulletin.''

''Which leads me, Your Honor, to my second point: that the arresting officers displayed a degree of racial animus in addressing Mr. Jervis, which indicates that race was a factor in their decision to stop him while he was driving the car.''

''What?'' Laura exclaimed. ''Your Honor, this point wasn't raised in the motion!''

''She's right, son. What 'racial animus' are you talking about?''

''One of the arresting officers used the, uh, the 'n' word, Your Honor.''

''According to whom?'' Laura asked, outraged at this

ambush. "Is the defense counsel prepared to introduce testimony to that effect?"

"Are you?" the judge asked Avery.

"I am. My client will testify that one of the officers used that particular racial epithet in addressing him at the time of the arrest."

Laura was incensed. "Your Honor, whether or not this assertion is true, is it relevant to the motion? As I understand the primary argument of the motion, it was the act of stopping the car that constituted the racial profiling. What was—or was not—said to the defendant after the stop was made simply isn't relevant."

"She's right, son. Your argument might hold some water if you could show that the description of the vehicle was sufficiently vague to allow a biased police officer to stop vehicles based on the race of the driver and no other factor. I believe that most of the case law cited in your brief cites vehicles searched in traffic stops, where that type of latitude is given to the police. Here, we had a situation where the police were requested to seek out a particular automobile, and, I believe, its driver, described as a black man in his thirties—a description that also fits the defendant. Regardless of the biases of the arresting officers, which I might add have not been demonstrated or proved, they had full grounds for stopping the vehicle driven by Roland Jervis, and subsequently—since he was, in fact, driving the victim's car—for arresting him in connection with the disappearance of the victim. The motion is therefore dismissed."

Judge Root banged his gavel in an authoritative manner, rose from the bench, and left the courtroom. Laura began gathering up her papers, hoping to avoid speaking to Avery. He didn't have the same idea, evidently, because he started complaining as soon as Laura was in earshot.

"I never had a chance, did I?"

"What do you mean by that, Avery?"

"Oh, nothing. Just a little hometown officiating, I guess. Guess I shouldn't be surprised, given that His Honor is up for reelection this year."

"For pity's sake, Avery, even you can't believe that. Nobody's ever accused Judge Root of anything except maybe being a little crabby every now and then. He's the best judge in the county."

"I'm sure all the prosecutors think so."

Now Laura was irritated. "You can't seriously expect me to believe that you thought that motion would fly. Not even with the little race card you tried to flip in there. Look, Avery, do yourself a favor: try the case first. You can appeal it later."

"You really are an incredibly arrogant woman, aren't you? What makes you so sure I'll *need* to appeal?"

"I'm not sure," Laura said, a little more heated than she liked to be. "Except that if I were defending Roland Jervis, I surely wouldn't be messing around with useless motions."

Avery smiled tautly. "And just what would you be doing, Perry Mason?"

"For one thing, I'd be spending some time at the crime lab, going over the physical evidence."

"I've read the reports," he said with an offhanded wave. "It's pretty cut and dried."

"Have you talked to the technicians who prepared the report?"

"What, they're going to say something that's not in the report?"

"Just do it, Avery. Just defend your client. He deserves a defense. And please excuse me, but I've got to get back to my office." She started to leave, but it was clear that

Avery was still fuming. "I'm sorry," she said in a genuinely contrite tone. "I shouldn't have lost my temper." She laughed. "I don't think they mean it to be quite so literally an 'adversarial system.' Your brief was good, Avery; you did some great research. And the behavior of the arresting officers may not have been relevant to your motion, but if I were you I'd sure as heck make a stab at getting it into the trial transcript. But this isn't theoretical anymore; it's a trial. And a trial is a rock fight. Start flinging some boulders, okay?"

Avery gave her a grudging smile. "Believe me, I plan to. I'm just warming up. Wait until the trial. I'm going to move for a speedy trial, by the way."

"Great. That suits us. See you around, Avery."

Laura returned to her office, ruefully reflecting all the way on her exchange with Avery. *Do men feel this bad after they lose their tempers?* she wondered. No, of course not; it was all part of the give-and-take. Well, if that were true, at least Avery wouldn't have any hard feelings. And besides, he was the one who had called her Perry Mason. She'd have to get back at him for that; the trial couldn't come fast enough to suit her.

But there was another treat awaiting Laura before she got to take on Avery again: that evening's political fund-raiser. Laura and the other assistant district attorneys dutifully packed it in around six-thirty and proceeded to one of the big downtown hotels.

The shindig was taking place in one of the hotel's windowless ballrooms. Atlanta architects had the persistent idea that they could create more appealing vistas inside than nature could provide outside. That was, of course, a self-fulfilling prophecy; downtown Atlanta was liberally supplied with monolithic, narrow-eyed concrete hotels that were indistinguishable from the county jail. The interiors ran the gamut of decorative styles, from Louis-whatever grandeur to fantasy kingdom landscapes. This one had lagoons in its lobby, which served little purpose that Laura could see, other than forcing hapless guests to carry their bags around the "shores" and over "bridges." The ballroom, in the basement, was windowless and nondescript. Laura wearily regarded the floral carpet, dark-papered walls, and white-draped, crudité-burdened tables.

They were a little early; the honorees—Marshall and the mayor, and their entourages—had not yet arrived, but a band was setting up at the far end of the room, and a microphone held ominous promise of stump speeches to come.

Laura milled around with the others, swapping office gossip and sipping an acrid Chablis, until a slight commotion at the far end of the room signaled that the important guests were arriving. The band—a spirited R&B combo—struck up the popular light-rap tune that had become the mayor's campaign theme song. "Boo-yah! Gotta get me some a' that!" the female vocalist declaimed with a spine-dislocating swing of her hips.

Lordy, who would *want* some of that? Laura reflected as His-portly-Honor's shiny bald pate came into view through the applauding crowd. He was followed closely by Marshall, who, although more physically attractive, was every bit as unsexy as the mayor. They both wore the broad, warm smiles that had occupied their faces ever since they had declared for reelection. They were a team, a package, a buy-one, get-one-free political special.

Laura didn't like politicians. She didn't like politics, in fact. It was nothing personal; Marshall was a good enough guy, and the mayor—well, he was about as good as you could expect, given the inherent lose-lose proposition that being a big-city mayor was. Politics seemed like a ludicrous pursuit to Laura, and she couldn't understand why two otherwise bright men would care to seek out the low pay, long hours, and public abuse that came with the jobs they sought so doggedly. Of course, there were suggestions that public service in Atlanta could be quite lucrative if the rules were bent, but the ongoing federal investigation had netted so far only a couple of minor players. The mayor himself was untouched.

The room was full now, giving Laura a faint hope—if she could avoid observation by Meredith and Marshall—of leaving early. She put her half-full glass of wine on a table and began sidling toward the door.

"Hey there," a voice behind her said. "Trying to sneak away, huh?"

Laura fixed a smile on her face and turned to see who had busted her. Of course Don Archer, head of the mayor's security detail, would be here. "Hello, Don," she said. "Just, umm, looking for the ladies' room."

"It's the other way," he said, smiling at her obvious irritation.

"Oh. Well, so long. Good to see you."

"Hey, where's Kowalski?" he asked, apparently not sensitive to a woman's private needs.

"Not here. He had some work to do around the house and he thought this would be the perfect night for it, I guess. Shouldn't you be guarding the mayor?"

Archer turned and looked toward the small knot of people who were gathered around Mayor Broad. "Him? Naw. The most danger he's in tonight is of getting his ass bruised from too much kissing."

Laura had to laugh. "What's he like—really?"

Don shrugged. "Not a bad guy, when he's not running

for office. Of course, a lot of my fellow cops wouldn't agree. They hate him.''

"Why—oh, because of the bonuses.'' A promised bonus had not been paid to Atlanta's police officers the previous year, although the money had been included in the budget. The mayor's explanation was simply that it had been spent on overtime pay, which none of the cops believed, for the very logical reason that none of them had been permitted to work overtime hours. Eventually, the city council had "found" enough money to pay the bonus, but there probably wasn't enough money in ten years of budgets to win back the loyalty of the cops.

"But he's okay. God knows everybody's got a hand out, trying to get something from him. And now he's got the FBI up his . . . well, you know.''

"Is he guilty?'' she asked disingenuously.

"Everybody's guilty of something, aren't they?'' was his answer. She couldn't tell if he meant yes or no, and before she could pursue the subject further, Don saw that the mayor was signaling to him. "Gotta go. I'll see ya later,'' he said as he waded through the throng, a head taller than just about everyone in the room.

Everyone, that is, except the group of professional athletes gathered in an imposing semicircle near the bandstand, surrounded by a picket of flacks and bodyguards. Laura was surprised to see the infamous Shawn Tolliver among them.

Tolliver, as well known for his abuse of fans and reporters as he was for his deadly three-point shot, stood out from the crowd of jocks. For one, he was the tallest guy among them, no small accomplishment given that their average height looked to be about seven feet. He was also one of only two white players in the group. He wasn't as wide as some of the football players, but his fierce scowl made him by far the most menacing. Laura wasn't the only one who noted his displeasure; a petite woman—well, she looked petite next to him, anyway—was talking urgently to him. After a moment, a painful-looking forced smile appeared on his face. He looked at the woman, as if to say "Happy now?" and returned to staring at the middle distance, but with a grin replacing the scowl.

Laura figured that Shawn's attendance at this particular shindig was a part of his ongoing rehabilitation. He had garnered headlines the previous season for using a racial epithet in a dispute with a black referee. It had cost him his seat on the bench for a full month, and his exile had been followed by "sensitivity training" and all sorts of good works, performed publicly under the supervision of a group of public relations specialists and team officials. Backing the mayor's reelection campaign must have been part of the program, too.

As Laura was making these observations, she was surprised to see another familiar face. She hadn't initially noticed Alex Devereaux in the crowd orbiting the jocks, but he was there. He must have been moonlighting as a bodyguard for one of the athletes, Laura figured, because it was highly unlikely that he had paid fifty bucks to rub shoulders with the mayor. Yes, the players were being herded toward the stage, and Alex was going with them. She couldn't tell which body he was guarding—although it was hard to believe that any of these Brobdingnagians would require the protection offered by one medium-sized detective.

"Having fun yet?" Meredith said in her ear, over the racket the band continued to make.

"Sure. Aren't you?"

"Let me see . . . no. I am not having fun."

"When are you leaving?"

"As soon as Marshall makes his speech. He'll go first, so I won't have to hang around for Harrison's sermon—although I am sure it will be very inspiring."

Laura laughed. "Did you ever think about running yourself—I mean, if Marshall quits?"

"Good Lord, no. I have enough trouble as it is. No, if I ever tell you I'm thinking about running for district attorney, do me a favor and hit me with a hammer until I come to my senses."

"You're the boss. Hi, Alex," she said, as the detective approached them.

"Hi, Laura. Meredith."

"Are you protecting the virtue of one of the celebrity guests?" Meredith asked, jerking her head at the stage where they were now gathered.

"Just trying to pick up some coin."

"Which one?" Laura asked.

"Shawn Tolliver." He saw the look of surprise on Laura's face. "Darryl Michaels asked me to do it. Nobody else wanted to handle him, especially not after his latest escapade." Shawn had punched a fan who was seeking an autograph for his six-year-old son. Assault charges had been filed, and just as quickly dropped when defense lawyer Craig Fannin took Shawn's case. "Darryl didn't want to come tonight himself, so he strong-armed me into doing it."

"I hope you're getting combat pay," Laura remarked.

"He's not so bad. He's not a racist, anyway. No more than any redneck who happens to be in a profession dominated by black guys, anyway. I guess he feels alienated from time to time. He sure ain't popular with his teammates. It's gotta be pretty lonely in that locker room."

"That's an awfully sympathetic view for you to take, Alex," Meredith said skeptically.

Alex shook his head. "I tell you, I kind of feel sorry for the kid. Too much money, too soon. Same old story."

"So, Alex," Laura said, seeing an opportunity, "have you had a chance to go over the physical evidence again?"

"Yeah. The guy cleaned the car, Laura. It's the only logical explanation."

"It's an explanation, all right, but hardly a logical one! Just tell me why he would have done it."

"Because he saw someone do it on the TV, that's why."

The crowd was growing noisy, and Devereaux and Laura had to almost shout to be heard. Someone bumped into Laura, sloshing wine on the sleeve of her jacket. She wiped at it irritably with a crumpled cocktail napkin. "You don't think he could have learned it in the service?" she asked.

"Maybe, if he had *been* in the military. And he would have to have been in intelligence, or the military police, to pick up tricks like that. Seems likes a stretch for Jervis."

Laura continued her pursuit of the subject despite a hint of annoyance in the detective's voice. "Well, what about a car-detailing shop—could he have picked up some tricks there?"

"Maybe—who knows? I don't know why you've got your shorts in such a knot over this."

Laura ignored his hostile tone. "Could you please humor me? Just look into Jervis's employment history, and I won't bring it up again."

"If it'll make you shut up, yeah, I'll do it."

Laura started to answer, but Meredith, who had been chatting with a city councilman, hushed them. "Stop talking shop, you two—it's show time!" She pointed at the stage.

The band played a flourish, and Mayor Broad stepped up to the mike. "Thank you!" he said, nodding and flinging his arms out wide. "Thank you all for coming out tonight!

We're kicking off tonight with a party, but let me tell you, this campaign isn't going to be a party—not for my esteemed opponent, at least!'' Laughter from the crowd. ''And not for Ellis Brady, the man who is foolhardy enough to challenge our own district attorney, Marshall Oliver, the big MO! Give it up for Marshall, y'all! Get yah MO-jo going for Marshall Oliver!''

''Good Lord,'' Laura muttered.

''Amen, sister,'' Alex opined. ''Isn't MO a laxative, anyway?''

Laura laughed but Meredith scolded her. ''Be a little supportive of the boss, okay? He's just having some fun with this.''

And he was, indeed. It was a transformed Marshall up there on the stage, far from the dour martinet Laura had come to know and respect. He and the mayor were lapping it up. Arms around each other's shoulders, they waved and smiled.

''Look at him!'' Laura said to Meredith. ''This is the guy who threatened to take away our coffee privileges because we used up all the half-and-half?''

''He's a born campaigner,'' Meredith said. ''And God bless him for it. I sure don't want to wake up next November and find myself working for Ellis Brady.''

''What's wrong with Brady?'' Alex asked.

''Nothing, if you don't mind morons. I'll tell you something: Marshall may not be the nicest guy in the world, but he's a lawyer's lawyer, and he lets me do my job. Ellis is nothing but a politician, and he's got an agenda I don't like. 'Restoring civic values,' my ass. I don't want to spend four years prosecuting jaywalkers. Believe me, this city's got problems that go way beyond litterbugs. So I'm givin' it up for the big MO—whooo-hoo!'' she whooped with genuine enthusiasm that surprised Laura.

Marshall's speech was mercifully short, and, in the applause that followed it, Laura managed to escape. Almost, anyway—Don Archer intercepted her once more. ''Leaving for real now, huh?'' he said.

''Yes, I am. Enjoy the rest of your evening, though,'' she said.

''Lemme walk you to your car,'' he offered. ''It's dark out now.''

''Thanks, but I left it with the valet,'' she lied. She didn't want to venture into a dark parking garage with Don; she would take her chances with whatever unknown menaces might be lurking for her. She felt a twinge of guilt for the lie, though. Amos was probably right; Don was harmless. As she started the car, her thoughts turned from Don to Amos, and she toyed with the idea of dropping by his house instead of heading straight for her own. No, she decided, she could use a good night's sleep. And she wouldn't get it at Amos's house.

Chapter 10

"He's challenging the indictment," Laura said, standing in the doorway of Meredith's office holding another sheaf of Avery-generated paper. Justice had moved swiftly in the week since Avery's first dismissal motion had been denied. The Grand Jury had returned a bill of indictment in less than four hours. But Avery was back at it now.

"Let me guess . . . composition of the Grand Jury?"

"Right on the first guess."

"Racial composition?"

"Partly. And partly a specific challenge to one juror based on—get this—his place of work."

"Which is?"

"A Speedy Tire shop. Because, as everyone knows, Speedy Tire is a hotbed of Republicanism and pro-death-penalty sentiment. And if that doesn't blow the judge's skirt up, we go to exhibit B: a Grand Jury member who happens to belong to the Sons of Confederate Veterans. Which, as I do not need to tell you, is 'an organization composed of individuals dedicated to the preservation of the ideals of the Confederate States of America.' "

"He doesn't really say that!"

"Want to read it?"

Meredith took the paper and glanced through it. "He cites racial discrimination suits against Speedy Tire. So what? Even if the president of the company is an Imperial Wizard of the Ku Klux Klan, it doesn't mean everybody who works for him is. And the SCV stood up for the old Georgia flag with the Confederate battle jack on it. Is this all he has?"

"All that I can see."

"Wasn't there a case like this, some ridiculous challenge to a juror?"

Laura nodded. *"McKibbons versus State.* Avery's cited it, and pointed out that his challenge differs."

"How?"

"Those challenges were 'fanciful.' "

"And these aren't?" Meredith asked, eyebrows at full height.

"He says that the suits against the company are prima facie evidence of endemic racism at Speedy Tire. And everyone knows that the SCV is an auxiliary of the KKK."

"What a load of crap."

Laura sighed and settled heavily into a chair. "You and I might say so, but give Avery this: he really drafts a beautiful motion. Never mind that his logic has a flaw; he has *done the research.*"

"When's the hearing?" Meredith asked.

"This afternoon. And here's the bad news: you know Judge Root is in the hospital, don't you?"

"Yes. Having an angioplasty. I should send the old coot a get-well card. Who's hearing this?"

"Judge Edwards," Laura replied.

There was a moment of silence as Meredith took in the bad news. Judge Marjorie Edwards was relatively new to the Fulton County bench, elected by a narrow margin in a runoff. She brought little criminal experience to her new post; she had been in the city attorney's office for most of her career. And she was notoriously soft on defendants, black ones in particular. Laura couldn't think of a single instance in which she had declined to rise to the race bait when a defense attorney dragged it in.

"You want me there?" Meredith asked.

Laura nodded. "I think it would be best. There's no telling what she's going to say."

"Tell me about it. I just missed spending the night in jail for contempt the first time I was up in front of her. Do you have a plan?"

"I'll do what I can. I have the decision in *McKibbons,* of course, and some more case law to throw at her. But I'm realistic about my chances."

"Fallback plan?"

"Appeal her decision, and reindict Jervis. And hope that Judge Root is a fast healer."

Laura wasn't any more optimistic when she and Meredith presented themselves in Judge Edwards's courtroom. Avery was already there, looking especially pleased with himself. Meredith didn't let that get to her. "Hello, Avery," she called out cheerfully. "Hey, I just bought a new set of tires from Speedy Tire. Whitewalls, of course."

"Ha-ha. Very funny," the defender of the oppressed replied.

"Really? Think I should use it on Judge Edwards?"

"Meredith," Laura said sotto voce. "Please don't tease him."

"What? Afraid I'll awaken his inner Clarence Darrow? You know I relish a challenge."

"Easy for you to say. You're not the one Marshall's going to snap like a twig if we lose the case. Here comes Judge Edwards, anyway. Straighten up and fly right."

"Relax. If we're going to lose, we might as well enjoy it."

Judge Edwards, petite and pretty, seated herself and surveyed the courtroom with a level gaze while the bailiff and the clerk got the proceedings rolling. "Is counsel for the defense here?" she asked.

"I am, Your Honor," Avery replied.

"And who is representing the state?"

"Laura Chastain, Your Honor," Laura said.

"And I see that Mrs. Gaffney is here as well."

"Yes, ma'am."

"Which of you will argue for the prosecution?"

"I will, Your Honor," Laura answered.

"I fail to see, then, why Mrs. Gaffney's presence is required. Is Mrs. Gaffney an attorney of record in this matter?"

"Yes, she is, Your Honor." Laura glanced sidelong at Meredith, and raised an eyebrow enquiringly. *Just what did you do to get this lady's tail in a twist?* she wanted to ask.

Whatever Meredith had or hadn't done, Judge Edwards decided to move on. "I will hear your arguments now, Mr. Daniels," she said.

Avery shuffled his papers and launched into his recital. "Your Honor, I wish to challenge the sufficiency of the indictment on the following grounds: first, that the composition of the Grand Jury that returned the indictment did not reflect the racial makeup of Fulton County. Second—''

"If we may, Mr. Daniels, take your points one at a time. How did the composition of the Grand Jury fail to meet the requirements of the law in this case?"

"The Grand Jury in question, Your Honor, was fully eighty percent composed of whites, whereas the population of the county is fifty-five percent African-American, or, conversely, only forty-five percent white, Hispanic, or other—''

"If I may, Your Honor," Laura interjected. "The law concerning the composition of Grand Juries has never made reference to the general population of the district. The composition of the pool of eligible jurors is the only factor that has been held to be germane—''

"Which was my next point, Your Honor," Avery said in an injured tone. "The pool of potential Grand Jurors from which this Jury was drawn was also overwhelmingly white . . . uh, seventy-five percent white, Your Honor."

Laura went on the attack again. She was enjoying this. "Again, Your Honor, the courts have held that the actual composition of the juror pool is not relevant so long as there is no evidence that the county deliberately attempted to exclude one group or another from it, by, say, requiring property ownership or some other qualification. And, as Your Honor knows, our pool in Fulton County is drawn solely from the rolls of registered voters."

"Which is, Your Honor, skewed toward whites—almost fifty-six percent white, as a matter of fact." Avery waved a sheet of paper indignantly.

Laura was ready. "Your Honor, voter registration rolls are generally held to be the best and the most objective pool for jurors. The standard is 'a fair cross-section' of the population, as in *Lipham versus State,* Your Honor. If counsel wishes to challenge whether Fulton County's voting rolls represent a 'fair cross-section,' he must make a prima facie case that the rolls are tainted because there was an 'opportunity for discrimination' in their selection, and secondly that, being improperly drawn, the source of the jury pool actually produced a 'significant disparity.' *Cochran versus State,* Your Honor. Does counsel wish to argue that Fulton County's voter registration process presents an opportunity for discrimination, Your Honor?''

"Well?" the judge asked Avery. "Are you prepared to make that argument?"

"Uh, no, I . . . well, I believe that the underrepresentation of African-Americans on the voting rolls is prima facie evidence of discrimination, and there's no doubt that it *did* produce a significant disparity in the race of the jurors compared to the racial composition of the county—"

Judge Edwards waved her hand. "Thank you, Mr. Daniels. I think I've heard enough. Please proceed to the second point of your motion."

Avery looked momentarily abashed, but he proceeded gamely to smear the good name of the Speedy Tire Company. "Your Honor, I wish to challenge the qualifications of Mr. Michael Davis to serve on the Grand Jury. Mr. Davis is a manager of the Speedy Tire store located on Piedmont Road in Atlanta. Speedy Tire, as I have stated in my motion, has been party to several racial discrimination suits."

"Has Mr. Davis been named as a defendant in any of these suits?" Laura asked sharply.

"No, not to my knowledge . . . but it has been alleged that there is an overall and pervasive culture of racial discrimination and outright harassment at Speedy Tire stores."

"Any allegations of these occurring at the store Mr. Davis manages?" Laura pursued.

"No, not specifically, but there is ample evidence that senior management of the company holds certain views—"

" 'Ample evidence'?" Laura queried. "Tell me, Mr. Daniels, has any plaintiff in any one of these suits won a judgment against Speedy Tire or any of its employees?"

"Not to date, but there are two suits pending at this time, and the Equal Employment Opportunity Commission has an ongoing investigation into Speedy's hiring and promotion practices—"

"But no judgments have been entered against the company or any of its employees?" Judge Edwards asked, giving Laura hope.

"No, Your Honor," Avery answered dejectedly.

Laura moved in for the kill. "Your Honor, I would like to cite *McKibbons versus State,* in which the Court of Appeals held that a challenge to a juror based on alleged political affiliations encouraged by employers was 'fanciful' and was therefore disallowed."

"Your Honor," Avery said, plucking up a little, *"McKibbons* dealt with the composition of a trial jury, not a Grand Jury."

"Moot point," Laura said.

"It is not," Avery said fiercely. "And besides, the attorney in *McKibbons* introduced no evidence of a pervasive pattern of racial discrimination, as I have done."

"With all due respect, Your Honor, a handful of suits—most of which have been dismissed with no judgments—is hardly demonstrative of a 'pervasive pattern' of *anything.*"

"Miss Chastain, please try not to speak in a sarcastic tone in my courtroom."

"Sorry, Your Honor," Laura said, trying to sound contrite

although she felt a simmering anger. How could anyone *not* speak in a sarcastic tone when confronted with this pile of garbage?

"Thank you. I believe I have heard enough. Mr. Daniels, you have one remaining argument for quashing the indictment, I believe."

"Yes, I do, Your Honor. Specifically, I wish to call into the question the qualification of another Grand Juror, Mr. Henry Porter. Mr. Porter, I have learned, is a member of the Sons of Confederate Veterans."

"Your Honor," Laura said, trying very hard not to let sarcasm creep into her tone, "I have to admit that I don't understand counsel's objection to the SCV."

"It's simple, Your Honor. The goal of the SCV is to honor the memory of men who fought for the Confederacy. As part of that goal, they have—among other things—championed the use of the Confederate battle flag as part of the Georgia state flag."

"I fail to see, Your Honor," Laura said, "how this translates to wholesale racial animus on the part of the SCV's members."

"The battle flag of the Confederacy, Your Honor, is generally acknowledged to be a symbol of racial oppression. I think it's safe to say that most African-Americans find the battle flag highly offensive. It is also a fact that the battle jack was added to the Georgia state flag in 1956 by a group of Georgia lawmakers whose only ambition was to express their resistance to integration in the wake of the *Brown versus Board of Education* decision."

"Your Honor, I don't dispute that the battle flag became a highly charged symbol, and a negative one at that. And I have no doubt that the motives of the men who put it on the state flag were far from pure. But I still don't see the connection between membership in the SCV and racial bias."

Avery darted a triumphal glance at Laura. "Your Honor, Mr. Porter was the Chairman of the SCV's committee to save the flag. He spoke at numerous gatherings in support of the use of the Confederate symbol."

"Did he, at any of these gatherings, explicitly state that his support of the battle flag was rooted in his contempt and hatred of black people?" Laura asked.

"No, but I don't think he needed to say that—"

"I do," Laura said. "Your Honor, my father is a member of the SCV, and to call him a racist would be simply ludicrous."

"I don't know your father, Miss Chastain," the judge replied.

"Well, if you did, you'd know that he wasn't a racist."

"I fail to see the relevance of Miss Chastain's family history," Avery said—sarcastically, which Judge Edwards seemed not to notice.

Laura retorted swiftly. "Precisely. It's *not* relevant, just as Mr. Porter's membership in the SCV is not relevant to his qualifications as a juror."

"I believe that I have heard enough arguments from both sides. I am prepared to rule on the motion," Judge Edwards said abruptly. Laura started to protest, but felt pressure from Meredith on her elbow, and remained silent.

"As to your first argument, Mr. Daniels, that the composition of the Grand Jury was inherently discriminatory, I find that your arguments are insufficient. I agree with Miss Chastain that you have failed to make the prima facie case that an opportunity for discrimination existed. Second, as to Mr. Davis's qualifications, I find that you have not proved to the satisfaction of this court that Mr. Davis's employment by Speedy Tire is necessarily a sign of racial feeling one way or another.''

Avery stood in silence, stunned by the judge's announcements. Laura kept her eyes forward and tried to avoid letting her face pull into an involuntary smile of victory.

"Finally, on the matter of the qualifications of Mr. Porter, I find that counsel for the defense has made a compelling argument. The indictment of Roland Jervis for felony murder is, therefore, quashed." In a single smooth motion, the judge brought down her gavel, rose from her seat, and vanished from the courtroom, leaving Laura standing dumbfounded and gaping in indignation.

"What 'compelling argument' did he make? Did you hear a 'compelling argument'?" she asked Meredith.

"Of course not. But you knew how this was going to go, didn't you? I have to give Avery some credit, too. He served up three screamers, knowing that it would help her look good to be able to reject a couple of them. Then she doesn't look as bad when she rules for him—which she would have done, anyway, of course."

"Don't give Avery any credit. He's got all the strategic ability of . . . of tree bark. I had him cold, on all three of his arguments—"

"Of course you did," Meredith said, interrupting the swelling tirade. "But when did that ever matter? Look, tell me this: did we know before we came into this courtroom that we were probably going to lose?"

"We knew that."

"And did we not come up with a fallback plan?"

"We did do that."

"So quit moaning and come back to the office. Because, my friend and colleague, we have to give this news to Marshall before *he* does." Laura looked in the direction Meredith was gazing, and saw, to her dismay, the crime reporter from the morning paper. "Hi, Bob," Meredith said, smooth as silk, as Bob Harper approached them. "Did you get a load of that?"

"Sure did. Care to comment?"

"The district attorney's office believes that Judge Edwards was in error in making her ruling. We will appeal her decision, and in the meantime, we will reindict Roland Jervis on the charges."

Bob smiled and shook his head. "Why am I not surprised? Where's the big MO today, anyway? I thought he'd be seeing this one through personally."

"He trusts us to take care of the details. You'll see him when the trial starts, I promise."

"Which, of course, will be strategically timed for maximum preelection exposure."

"Bob Harper, you surprise me. What happened to your spirit of Woodward-and-Bernstein idealism? Why, you're turning into as ink-stained a cynic as I've ever seen."

Bob threw back his head and laughed. "If I thought you believed your own bullshit, Meredith, I'd be worried. I'll see you around."

"How can you be so chummy with those guys?" Laura grumbled as they returned to the office.

"If we aren't chummy, they'll skewer us like kebabs. And Marshall's going to be peeved enough as it is without having to read in the morning paper that his assistants blew the big case."

"We didn't blow it!" Laura protested. "She was wrong!"

They had arrived back at the office, where things were winding down for the day.

"Stop being so damn sensitive. Hey, Frances," she said to Marshall's secretary. "Where's the chief?"

His beleaguered assistant rolled her eyes. "Hollering at some poor guy on the phone. I'd wait until tomorrow if I were you."

"No can do. Call me when he's free."

Laura trailed Meredith back to her office to wait for Marshall. She had hardly warmed the seat when he appeared in the doorway. "Well?" he said.

Meredith shook her head. "Quashed. Judge Edwards took exception to a juror's qualifications."

"A Grand Juror? That's ridiculous—she can't do that!"

"Can, and did, I'm afraid. Laura, tell him what happened."

Laura did. Marshall fumed. "That woman's not competent! Any damn attorney can go in there and raise race as an issue. I'm filing a complaint. Damn it, I'm sick of this mess!"

"Relax," Meredith said. "We'll reindict. Of course, if Judge Edwards hears another challenge we'll be out of luck. . . ."

"Well, she won't. I'll call the clerk."

"You can't," Laura pointed out. "The new system assigns judges by computer." *Your* precious new system, she refrained from saying. "We'll have to wait for Judge Root to get back from his sick leave."

"Goddamn it," Marshall said, as he turned on his heel and left.

"That went well," Meredith said.

Laura laughed. Then she was struck by the paradox. Suddenly serious, she asked, "You do appreciate the coincidence, don't you?"

"What coincidence is that?"

"Lawrence Belew designed the new court system. The system that assigned his own case to Judge Edwards."

They were both silent.

Chapter 11

"Okay, here's the deal," Alex Devereaux said. "Roland Jervis worked off and on at Bumper to Bumper Car Wash on Roswell Road in Buckhead for about a year. They haven't seen him there in a while, though." Laura brightened; the detective's phone call was the first evidence she'd had in days that the Atlanta Police Department was still investigating Jervis's story.

"Fantastic!" she said. "How did you find this place—I hope you didn't have to go to every car wash in Atlanta."

"As a matter of fact, I didn't. Someone came forward, a guy who worked with Jervis there. He wanted a slice of the reward pie."

"Back up a minute—we haven't released the details about the interior of the car. How would this guy know he had something we could use?"

"He didn't. He *thought* he did, though. He recognized

Jervis's picture, and he'd been mulling this over for a while. He finally decided to come forward to tell us that Jervis was always talking about how much he liked the Lexus. He said he was going to get one someday. Our man thought that made for a motive."

"That's hardly compelling evidence in a murder case— how many people do you imagine have said they want a Lexus one time or another?"

"About a million. Including me," Devereaux said. "But you're missing the point. This bozo stumbles in with his stupid story—which I'm willing to bet he fabricated, any- way—thinking that we were going to shower him with duc- ats for sharing this breaking news. The guy on the desk who took his statement almost threw him out, but he decided he should at least run it past us. He had no clue we were looking for a car wash where Jervis might have worked. *That's* why I even bothered to talk to the guy."

"Lucky for us," Laura mused. "Clues made to order, on demand."

"What the hell are you bitching about now?" Devereaux exploded. "You asked if Jervis worked at a car wash, and I tell you he worked at a damn car wash. This case couldn't get any sweeter—but you're never happy. I don't get you, lady—or maybe I do understand what bug crawled up your rear. You blew the indictment, so now everybody's got to pay."

Laura was dumbfounded. "Alex, I have no idea what I've said or done to offend you. We're on the same team—why can't we have a little give-and-take? I have to think all the angles through on this case, and I'd like to think I can do it aloud with the detectives without stepping on someone's toes. And, for the record, we didn't blow the indictment— I just came back from the Grand Jury with a brand-new, shiny indictment, thanks to your testimony. *And* the Court of Appeals has agreed to hear our appeal of Judge Edwards's decision, *and* we're going to win that one, too.''

Devereaux failed to be appeased. "So what are you worried about? You're home free, as far as I can see. That kid Daniels couldn't defend Mother Teresa on a jaywalking charge.''

Laura chuckled. "Well, maybe Mother Teresa. You just have to realize, Alex, that—like every NFL coach I've ever heard blather into a microphone—I take all challengers seriously. In fact, I've started to believe that Avery is actually doing all this to lull me into a sense of complacency. Once he gets me in the courtroom, in front of a jury, he'll spring like a coiled snake—and I have to be ready.''

"There's about as much coiled snake in that kid as there is in a Teletubbie. Listen, I'm sorry I barked at you. I've had a lot of late nights lately.''

"Do you have a baby at home?''

"God, no. They're all in high school. But they're still keeping me up late—I'm moonlighting all the time to pay their expenses.''

"Still baby-sitting jocks for Darryl Michaels?''

"Yeah. No more Shawn Tolliver, though. Not unless I get combat pay.''

"What's the problem?''

"Nothing, if you don't mind spending late nights with the biggest asshole in the world.''

Laura laughed. "I thought you felt kind of sorry for him.''

"That was before I got to know him. He really shoulda gone to jail for that crap he pulled last season. There musta been a lotta hoops fans on the jury.''

"He had Craig Fannin defending him, too. When you care enough to pay through the nose for the very best . . .''

"Fannin—I've heard about him but I never met the guy. Is he good?"

"The best. If I ever decide to kill somebody, I'm going to make sure I've got enough money set aside to pay Craig's fee. Which I'll never have, not on an assistant district attorney's salary, anyway."

Devereaux laughed. "I guess I better not strangle Tolliver, then, because I could never pay for my defense on a cop's salary."

"Maybe Fannin would take your case pro bono. Thanks of a grateful nation, and all that."

It was Devereaux's turn to laugh. "Poor Shawn. He ain't *that* bad. Okay, lady, I see Carlton's getting antsy; he wants to go to the Varsity for lunch. I better get going. And I'm sorry I lost my cool with you. I'll send over this ragman's statement, and if you want to meet him I can set that up."

"Thanks. I'll let you know. Maybe we won't need him after all. Is he getting any reward money?"

"Not if he doesn't testify."

Laura sat thoughtfully for a moment after she hung up the phone. She certainly didn't want to seem ungrateful for Devereaux's work, but it was awfully convenient to have all these witnesses popping up left and right with exactly the information the cops and the district attorney were looking for. It could be the reward money; justice and lucre had always had an uncomfortable relationship. She made up her mind that she wouldn't use this testimony unless Avery turned up the spotlight on the fingerprint evidence—which he showed, to Laura's amazement, no sign of doing.

As far as she knew, Avery himself hadn't yet been out to the crime lab. Maybe the public defender's office had sprung for an investigator out of its perennially tight budget. *Damn it,* she thought, *why hasn't he been running an inves-*

tigation? Because, she answered herself, Avery was a supremely overconfident product of our legal education system. Beautiful credentials, but if his client knew anything about the law-school system, he would have felt more comfortable in the hands of a scrappy night-school lawyer who'd never been near a law review.

But you could be wrong, Laura told herself. *Avery might turn out to be a courtroom genius, another F. Lee Bailey or Alan Dershowitz.*

Later that afternoon, Avery proved to Laura's satisfaction that he was neither of those things. Laura, in fact, could hardly keep herself from screaming when she sliced open the envelope that contained Avery's latest blue-jacketed grenade. "Meredith!" she howled as she ran down the hall to the boss's office. "Look what he's done! Look at it!"

"For pity's sake, Laura—get a grip. What could be so bad? Oh, Good Lord. That . . . that *pinhead!*"

"What did I tell you? An *insanity* defense? Even when the client's *actually insane* those don't work!" Laura moaned.

"He's playing for time. He'll have this guy on the couch for a year. You know, now that I think about it, it's not totally dumb. He knows Marshall wants this trial to go forward before the election—he doesn't want this hanging over him when the voters troop into the polls in November. It's clever, really. I bet he's hoping for a plea bargain."

"Will he get one?"

"Of course not. That would be worse for Marshall—and the mayor."

"Then what's so doggone clever about it? It's just another excuse for Avery to pull out his Latin phrasebook, if you ask me. Will you *please* talk to Julia Walton now? This is not going to look good for her office. She should know what her lawyers are up to."

"Okay. I will call her and talk, woman to woman. I wouldn't expect great results, though. I know you don't give him much credit for strategic smarts, but he may have really thought this one through. Or Julia may have thought it through for him. It's the kind of stunt I would have pulled, in a pinch."

"But if it came down to a trial you would have put up a *real* defense, wouldn't you?"

"You're damn straight I would. And trust me when I say that Julia Walton will, too, when it gets down to brass tacks."

Laura gratefully left it up to Meredith to share the latest development with Marshall. His nerves were wearing thin lately, and Laura wanted to minimize her contact with him—especially on this case. And thank goodness Meredith was finally going to talk to the head of the public defender's office about Avery. Maybe Julia would agree to let a pro bono attorney come in and look over Avery's shoulder. There was a consortium of private attorneys available to help out in death penalty cases—good, experienced trial lawyers.

Of course Laura appreciated the limited resources the public defenders had to work with, but in Julia Walton's shoes she would have used what little cash she had available to hire a good investigator. Spending what little budget she had on psychiatrists was a huge waste. If she were in Avery's shoes, she would be mounting an all-out investigation—limited resources or not. She'd whip the press into a froth over the injustice of it all, and let them do the legwork for free. She wouldn't rely on her own limited experience and resources—she'd get some old pros involved. Julia Walton was an okay lawyer, but she was missing the boat on this one.

The whole problem was that Fulton County didn't often

see capital cases. Sure, there had been more in the past year or two—some that Marshall would rather forget—but as a rule, the death penalty hawks nested below the fall line, down in the nether parts of Georgia. There, the system relied on private attorneys who got paid about $500 to defend men who were one step away from the electric chair—with predictable results. If it weren't for a quixotic band of anti-death-penalty activists and the admirable—if under-funded—Georgia Indigent Defense Council and Georgia Resource Center, Georgia's death row would soon grow to gulag proportions. And why Julia hadn't brought some of those resources to bear on this case, Laura couldn't under-stand.

Laura's phone chose this vexed moment to ring. She picked it up and barked a curt "Laura Chastain" into the handset.

"Whoa! Sounds like I just walked into a buzz saw," Amos said.

"In fact, you did. I'm just sitting here brooding on the justice system."

"Guess that means you're not up for going out tonight, huh?"

"No, not necessarily. I don't think that the cause of justice would be advanced by my sitting at home. Why? What did you have in mind?"

"Would bowling have any appeal for you?"

"Bowling? What brings this on?"

"Kenny, actually. He and Cindy have a baby-sitter, and they want to go bowling."

"I'm a terrible bowler," Laura warned.

"That doesn't matter. It's just for fun."

"No, it's not. I've been with you and Ken before. You guys can turn anything into a contest."

"You're exaggerating."

"Am I? Have you forgotten the batting cage episode? You ended up with a sprained wrist, and Ken and Cindy didn't speak to each other for two days."

"That was different."

"How so?"

"The batting cages won't let you bring beer in. We'll have beer tonight."

Laura sighed. "Okay, but I'm warning you: I'm not in the mood for petty bickering."

"What's eating you—this case, the car-jacking?"

"Yes. But I don't think it was a car-jacking."

"Then why are you prosecuting it? I mean, if you think the guy's innocent—"

"I didn't say he was innocent. I'm just saying that it wasn't a car-jacking."

"Okay, what are you going to do about it?"

"I'm trying to decide right now. The defense is just inadequate, and they need help. This kid is fooling around with an insanity defense."

"Will it work?"

"It almost never does. Meredith thinks he's trying to keep the case in limbo past the election, so that Marshall will be willing to make an offer for a plea bargain, just to get it off the radar before the election. Which is not likely; I think a plea bargain would be worse politically than another controversial trial. And, even if there is some idea of putting pressure on Marshall, any leverage they have will evaporate after the election. Assuming Marshall wins. Naturally."

"Did you tell Meredith this?"

"Not in so many words. She's going to call Julia Walton and lay out some of our concerns."

"Do you really expect Julia to do anything?"

"I don't know her that well. But if she's a good lawyer, she will."

"And if she doesn't?" Amos asked.

"I don't know. I'll think of something."

"Just be careful that you don't get on the wrong side of Meredith and Marshall. Like it or not, they are the bosses, and they know what they're doing."

"You don't need to tell me who I work for," Laura said tartly.

"Yikes! Sweetie, maybe you *should* stay at home tonight," Amos said.

"No, no; I'm sorry. I'm just tired. Putting on rented shoes will be just the pick-me-up I need."

"Are you sure? Because I can cancel."

"No. I will bowl, and bowl cheerfully."

Laura hung up feeling bad. She hated sniping at Amos, who was nothing but an innocent bystander. She made up her mind to apologize, profusely. She and Amos did have these little rough patches from time to time, but the making up was always worth it. She resumed her work, halfheartedly, until Meredith reappeared.

"I talked to Julia," she said. "Want to hear what she said?"

Laura nodded. Meredith plopped wearily into a chair. "She hired Avery on the understanding that he would take all the capital cases."

"What? Why?" Laura said, startled.

"He had a lot of experience, on an appeals-court level. In Virginia, where they see a fair number of cases. Julia liked his credentials, so she hired him. She thinks she's lucky to have him."

"If she were running appeals, she might be. But she'd

be better off taking the trial herself. How could she not see how lame Avery is?"

"Maybe she does. The point is, she very politely told me to mind my own business. Which is what I plan to resume doing, right away. And I recommend you do the same." Meredith stood up and looked at her watch. "And now I have to go find Marshall. Have a good weekend if I don't see you before you leave."

"You too," Laura replied.

Stupid Avery Daniels, she thought. Experience with appeals—big deal. He was, as her grandmother would have said, "blinking at gnats while swallowing camels." *I bet he didn't ever go out to the crime lab,* she mused.

As if to prove her point, her phone rang. "Miss Chastain? Hey. This is Tommy Wood from the fiber unit at the crime lab."

"Hi, Tommy. Funny, I was just thinking about you guys. Did you ever hear from Jervis's defense attorney?"

"Nope. Sent him my report and offered to talk to him. So did Scott, and as far as I know he ain't heard pea-turkey-John-Brown, either."

Laura laughed. "Boy, that's an expression I haven't heard since my grandfather died. But, damn it, I wish he had called you. Things are happening that I don't like."

"I may be able to help you, then. Remember that button?"

"The black button? Yes. Did you hear from the FBI?"

"I did."

"What were they able to find out?"

"Well, it's a very nice button. Most buttons are plastic, and most are made in Asia, on the cheap. But this one is made out of natural materials. Horn or bone, probably, dyed black. Antique buttons were made out of bone and shell, or even wood, but most modern buttons are plastic."

"It's an *antique?*"

"No, it's modern. But a button like this costs a lot more than a plastic one. In fact, it's most likely European."

"How can they tell?"

"When I measured it, it came up to an even size in millimeters, but not in inches—I should have known right away that it wasn't American. Anyway, the man they showed it to says the quality of the materials and the size of it made him think the button came from a high-end man's jacket, most likely European—French or Italian, he thinks. Probably a cuff button. It came off of a nice piece of clothing, anyway."

"So it's more likely to be Belew's than Jervis's?"

"Could be. You need to check his entire wardrobe to either show it was his, or to eliminate it."

"Lord, I hope his family hasn't gotten rid of his clothes. But if it's not his?"

"You're looking for a well-dressed guy with a cuff button gone."

Laura laughed ruefully. "That shouldn't be too hard to find."

"Well, I was thinking more along the lines of you finding a guy you thought was good for the murder—then, if he had a cuff button gone off one of his jackets, you'd be able to link him in."

"I see. So all I need to do is find this guy."

"Yep."

"Okay, then, let me ask you the million-dollar question: do you believe there is a guy to find?"

Tommy Wood paused for a long time before he answered. "I'm not a detective," he said at last. "And I don't know anything about your case, except what I've seen in the lab here and read in the newspaper. But based on that, I have to say yes. I think there's at least one other person besides Roland Jervis involved here.''

"You know something?" Laura asked. "I think you'd be a pretty good detective.''

When Laura hung up, she was sure of two things: there had been a second person involved in the murder of Lawrence Belew. And she was going to find him.

Chapter 12

Laura stretched and yawned, purposefully making more noise and stirring around more than strictly necessary in order to wake Amos. It didn't work; he continued to sleep in peaceful oblivion of her design. She tried again, to no avail, and then abandoned subtlety. "Amos!" she said, shaking his shoulder. "It's nine o'clock."

He pulled the sheet over his face and muttered unintelligibly.

"Amos, wake up. I'm hungry."

"Then go eat something," he said.

"But I want to go to the Waffle House," she persisted. "Come on, don't waste a whole Saturday morning. I'll make some coffee—you'll feel chirpier after you've had a cup of coffee."

"I'm not going to feel 'chirpy' no matter how much coffee you give me. Why is it so critical that we get up and go to the Waffle House right this minute? It'll still be there in a couple of hours.''

"I know that. But I want to have my car washed while we eat, and you know what the car wash place is like on a Saturday.''

"As a matter of fact, I don't know, because I don't waste money having my car washed. I do it myself, and I will be happy to wash your car all day—if you'll just let me sleep one more hour."

Laura sighed. "I don't want you to wash my car. I want to take it to the Bumper to Bumper Car Wash on Roswell Road."

He turned and looked at her. "You want to take your car—your 1992 Toyota with eight thousand Diet Coke cans on the floor—to a car wash, and pay forty bucks to have some guy rub the rust spots with a rag?"

"That's right. I do. And it's not forty dollars. You can get a basic wash for twenty."

"That's twenty more than I charge. Laura, what are you up to? It would be a lot simpler if you just came out and told me what your ulterior motive is. I'll find out sooner or later anyway."

"You are so wrong about me," she said, theatrically innocent. "I don't have 'ulterior motives.' As a matter of fact, I'm thinking of taking your advice and selling the car, and I thought it could use a professional cleaning."

"I can do just as good a job. We can take it over to my place, and I'll get out the shop vac. You'll be impressed, I promise."

"I know you can wash a car, Amos. I just don't want us to waste the whole day doing it. If we go to Bumper to Bumper, we can leave it and walk to the Waffle House and have breakfast. Then we'll have the rest of the day to have fun. But not if we don't get moving—by eleven, every jackass in Atlanta will be lined up at the car wash.''

Amos sighed. "The fact that you're willing to be one of those jackasses confirms to me that you are up to something. In fact, I'm curious enough about what that is that I will get up. I'm not going to shave, though.''

"No—don't. Just get dressed and let's go.''

Once having maneuvered Amos to the car wash, however, Laura found it harder to conceal her real mission. "Go on to the Waffle House,'' she said, "and get us a booth. I'll be along in a minute or two.''

"Oh, no,'' he said, "I'll wait for you. It's just going to be a minute, right? I mean, how long does it take to tell them you want your car washed?''

"But you know there will be a line at the Waffle House,'' she said, determined to shake him off.

"Naw, it's not crowded—you can see the parking lot from here. Hardly anybody there. Look—here's the guy to take your car. See? You were right. If you come early enough, you don't have to wait.''

Laura shot him an exasperated glance and rolled down the window to speak to the attendant. "Hi. I'd like to have it washed and have the interior vacuumed.''

The attendant looked at the backseat, which did indeed contain a few beverage cans, and cleared his throat. "You want us to shampoo the mats?''

"Sure, yeah. Umm, are you the manager?'' she asked.

"No, ma'am. That's him over there,'' he said, gesturing with his clipboard to a tall black man.

"Thanks,'' Laura said. "I need to have a word with him.'' She slithered out of the car, handed the keys to the attendant, and trotted briskly toward the manager. Amos followed close on her heels, wearing an amused expression. "What now,

Nancy Drew?'' she heard him say. She didn't rise to the bait. "Hi," she said cheerfully to the manager. "Can I talk to you for a second?"

"What about, lady? We're busy here," he answered, irritably.

"It'll just take a minute. I'm Laura Chastain, with the Fulton County District Attorney's office. I need to know how long Roland Jervis worked here."

"Who?"

"Roland Jervis. He worked here for about a year."

"I don't know nobody named Jarvis," he said sullenly.

"Jervis. And one of your employees told the police that he worked here, on and off, for about a year."

"Well, I don't know nothing about that, and I never heard of the man."

"How long have you been here?" Laura asked.

"Two years," he said. "And I ain't never heard of nobody named Jervis, or Jarvis. So you better let me take care of my business now. I got no time to talk to the cops."

"I'm not a cop," Laura said.

"Yeah, but he is," the manager said, pointing to Amos. "And I don't need no trouble with you or him. You want your car washed, we'll wash it. Otherwise, we got no business."

Laura started to answer him, but Amos stepped in front of her, reaching into his pocket and pulling out his detective's shield. "Please answer the lady's question," he said offhandedly.

"I *did* answer her. And I'll tell you again, slow, so you'll understand: I . . . don't . . . know . . . nobody . . . named *Jervis*. You can flash your shiny badge all you want, but it ain't goin' to change my answer."

"Amos," Laura said, "I can handle this. Look, mister,

this isn't a police thing. I just need a little information. I can get a court order, but I don't think I need one. I don't want to look at any confidential records, or anything like that. I just want to know what kind of employee Jervis was."

"And I'm tellin' you he was *no* kind of employee, 'cause he never worked here. What I gotta do to get you to believe me—and go away?"

"Okay, so you don't remember Jervis. What about . . . Terence Walker?"

"Yeah, I know him. He's supposed to be here right now, but I ain't seen his sorry butt in a week. What's he done?"

"Nothing. He's the one who told us that Roland Jervis worked here."

"Well, he was lying, 'cause no one named Jervis ever worked here that I know of. But Terence did, but he don't no more, 'cause I just this minute fired his ass. Now can I get back to work?"

A small man, who looked Hispanic, had been hovering in the background, listening to this exchange with an appearance of anxiety. " 'Scuse me, boss. I think I know what she is talking about."

"Yeah? Well, you better tell me then, Francisco, before I get frustrated with her."

Francisco nodded. "You weren't here when the big cop came, boss. He talked to Terence about this guy Jervis, too."

"What cop?" Laura said. "A black guy—about his size?" she asked, indicating Amos.

"No, miss. White. And more big."

Laura turned and looked at Amos. "I don't get it. Alex and Carlton are both black. What other cops would have been working this case?" Then Laura remembered what Alex had told her: Terence Walker had come forward voluntarily. No one had come to the car wash looking for him.

"Tell me more about this cop," she said to Francisco. "When did he come?"

"It was Monday, or Tuesday. He came and get his car wash, you see. That's when he talk to Terence. See, we are not so busy in the week, only the Saturdays. And, boss, you havin' your day off."

"That means it was Monday. I'm off on Mondays," the manager said.

"Yes. Monday. And he talk only to Terence. I think that he gives Terence some money."

"What makes you say that?" Laura asked.

" 'Cause Terence tell me he no comin' back to this shitty place," Francisco said. "He said he quittin' and you can kiss his black ass, boss. Sorry," he added. "It's jes' what he say, boss."

"Well, damn it, Francisco, why are you tellin' me this now?" the manager said in exasperation. "I woulda taken on some more crew if I knew Terence had quit on me."

"Excuse me," Laura interjected. "Tell me more about the cop. How did you know he was a cop? Did he have on a uniform? Show a badge?"

"No, miss, he jes' look like a cop. Like this man, your friend, he look like a cop, too."

"So much for my undercover career aspirations," Amos said. "Made twice in one day."

"So he might *not* have been a policeman, then," Laura said.

"Maybe not. You ask Terence, lady. He will tell you. But I know the man give him some money, 'cause he show it to me and he say boss can kiss his black ass."

The boss didn't seem to appreciate hearing Terence's comment reprised. "We know he said that. You don't need to keep on repeatin' it, *mi hombre*. So you found out what you need to know yet, lady? Can we get back to business here, or what?''

"Yes, I guess so. If you don't mind, though, I'd like Terence Walker's home address and phone number.''

"I'll give you what I got. Seems to me he said he was stayin' at his sister's house. I'll go get it.''

A few minutes later, Laura and Amos were walking toward the Waffle House, and Francisco was culling the cans from the backseat of her car. "Want to tell me what that was about?'' Amos said.

"Nothing, really. I just wanted to talk to the guy who said Roland Jervis worked at Bumper to Bumper.''

"Because you didn't believe his statement.''

"I just wanted to check it out. That's what you'd do— check it out, right?''

"Of course. But why not rely on Carlton, or Alex, to do the checking?''

That was a loaded question, and Laura chose to ignore it. "Anyway, I'm glad I did ask. It sounds as if this Terence Walker was lying about Jervis.''

"Why would he do that?''

"For money, of course. Someone paid him.''

"Who? What are you after here, Laura? Did you think Alex Devereaux was lying to you?''

"No. How can you even think that? I just want to be sure of my case.''

Amos held open the door of the Waffle House and allowed her to enter first. "What made you think that Walker might have been lying, anyway? What makes you so suspicious, especially when it comes to cops?''

"This is not about being suspicious of cops. Two, please, nonsmoking,'' she said to the hostess. "Maybe I shouldn't have brought you along. I'm just being a lawyer, Amos.

And yes, maybe I was a little suspicious—not of the police, but of this guy Walker.'' The hostess led them to a booth, and they sat down and ordered coffee. Laura glanced at the menu, unnecessary, since she always got the pecan waffle with bacon and hash browns. "But I was right to be suspicious, don't you think? It sounds as if someone paid him off to put Jervis at the car wash. See, every time I've raised a doubt or a question about this case, miraculous witnesses appear. I ask about Jervis's whereabouts on the weekend of the murder, and I get two eyewitnesses who tie him to the car. I ask how the interior of the car gets so clean we can't even find the victim's prints in it, and I get Jervis's car-wash-career résumé. What does it mean? I don't know. But I know one thing: I think I just got my first glimpse of Mr. Button.''

"Who the hell is 'Mr. Button'?''

"A gentleman of wealth and taste, who sews black horn buttons to his clothes with silk thread.'' Seeing that Amos lacked patience for cryptic answers, she explained the button.

Amos listened without comment. "A button,'' he said, when she finished.

"A button, and some silk thread. I've asked Carlton to check Belew's wardrobe to see if he had any clothing with similar buttons, and to see if one is missing.''

"And if there isn't?''

"I'm going to act on the assumption that there's someone else involved—at least in the disposal of the body. It's never made sense to me that Jervis did this on his own. I'm not saying he wasn't somehow involved, but I never believed that a schnook like Jervis could pull off something like this.''

"So who did?'' Amos asked.

"How should I know? That's for the cops to say.''

"And what are you going to do next?''

"Find Terence Walker. I was hoping you might help me."

"Nope. Not interested. It's not my case, and I don't want to get crossways with the major-cases guys. I need their help on too many cases of my own."

"I understand. I'll follow up by myself."

"Aren't you going to call Carlton, or Devereaux?"

"Not this weekend. There's no harm in my cruising down to this address and talking to Walker, is there? He's one of my witnesses, after all—I need to interview him."

"Let me see the address," Amos said. Laura handed him the slip of paper the car wash manager had given her. "Uh-uh. You can't go here by yourself."

"Sure I can, on a Saturday afternoon. It's not that bad a neighborhood."

He handed the paper back to her. "Okay, you win. I'll go."

"I *win?* What's that supposed to mean?"

"Isn't that what all this was about—manipulating me into doing what you wanted?"

The waitress had arrived with their plates, which gave Laura time to consider her answer carefully. "I don't manipulate, Amos. Yes, I did think it might be handy to have you along at the car wash. I concede that. You're a cop, and you have a certain authority in these situations. But I don't need you to go to Terence Walker's house with me. I'm perfectly capable of asking a few questions on my own."

"Sure you are. But if it's all the same to you, I'll tag along."

"Fine, if you want to. But don't say you were manipulated, because you weren't."

"I wasn't manipulated. I am doing this of my own free will," he said, robotically.

Laura laughed. "Shut up and eat your waffle."

An hour or so later, with a clean car and a wallet lightened by a generous tip to Francisco, Laura drove to the Atlanta neighborhood known as Summer Hill, down by Turner Field. Cosmetic improvements made before the Olympics several years earlier had brought some life back into the area, but there were still side streets that had escaped the brush of urban renewal. Terence Walker's sister lived on one of these streets.

"Not pretty, is it?" Laura remarked as they searched for house numbers.

"No. There's a lot of Section Eight housing down here," Amos said. "I'd like to make some of these landlords live in these places for a few weeks."

"It's the law of unintended consequences. We deplore public housing, and so we come up with a way for the private sector to provide it. And it's worse. Is that the house?"

"I can't tell. I'll ask this kid." He rolled down a window and asked a small boy where number 247 was. The kid looked at him blankly. "Do you know Terence Walker?" Amos asked. The kid nodded. "Well, where does he live?" The kid pointed to a house two doors down. Amos gave the kid a dollar and rolled the window up. "I hope he spends that before some bigger kid takes it from him. Right there."

Laura drew up to the curb in front of a derelict house with a bald patch of front yard and a sagging green-shingled porch. There was no sign of occupancy, and she hesitated before cutting the engine. "Second thoughts?" Amos asked helpfully.

"No. Just planning my approach. Come on—unless you'd rather wait in the car."

"No way."

They walked up the cracked remains of a concrete walk to the porch, and carefully mounted the two bowed wooden steps that led to the front door. The door was open; only a torn screen door served as an ineffective shield against insects and assistant district attorneys. The front room was dark, and there was no sign of a bell, so Laura knocked. "Hello?" she called when no response came. She could hear faint sounds of a television playing somewhere inside. "Hello?" Laura said, louder, knocking vigorously on the door frame. The door itself looked as if it wouldn't stand up to being knocked upon.

The television was turned off, but no one spoke. "Is anyone home?" Laura asked.

Finally, shuffling feet could be heard approaching through the gloomy interior. "Who's there?" a woman's voice said.

"My name is Laura Chastain. I'm looking for Terence Walker."

"He don't stay here no more," came the reply.

"Are you his sister?"

"What you askin' for? Are you the police?"

"No, ma'am. Terence isn't in any trouble. I'm with the district attorney's office, and he's a witness in one of my cases. I need to talk to him."

"Well, he ain't here, and I don't know where he's at. But you can tell him when you find him not to come back here lookin' for no place to stay at. Not 'til he pay me what he owe me."

Laura's eyes had grown accustomed to peering into the dimly lit room, and she could make out the shape of the woman she was speaking to. "He owes you rent?" Laura said sympathetically.

The shape nodded vigorously. "And I know he got the money, 'cause he been braggin' about he been paid a lot of money. I reckon he's off staying with some gal until his money runs out. Then he'll be back around to me, but I won't take him in, no sir. Not 'til I get my rent money."

"I don't blame you. Any idea where I might find him? Does he have friends, or a regular hangout?"

"You can try down to Josie's. She runs the grocery store on the corner, and I reckon he's been in there."

"Thank you, ma'am. I appreciate the information."

"Yeah, but you ain't gonna pay me," the woman said with a knowing chuckle. "That's okay. You just tell Terence not to come back around here. That's all the reward I need."

Laura beat a hasty retreat, with Amos trailing behind. "Sisterly love," he mused. "Nothing quite like it. Are we going to Josie's?"

"I guess so," Laura said. They returned to the car and cruised in the direction indicated. Josie's was a white-painted cinder-block structure, gaudy with beer signs and boasting a milling crowd of brown-bag drinkers in the parking lot. Laura found that her desire to meet Terence Walker was diminishing rapidly.

"May I make a suggestion?" Amos asked.

"No," she said. "Not if you're going to try to talk me out of going in there."

"No, that's not my suggestion. In fact, I was going to say that I think you'd have better luck if you went in without me."

"Why?"

"Because this gang will know right away that I'm a cop. Everyone else does. Might as well make use of it. I'll just stand right here by the car and keep a watch on things. They'll leave you alone." He opened the passenger door and swung his long legs out of the small car. He unfolded his full height, and leaned against the car with his arms folded nonchalantly across his broad chest. Even Laura was impressed.

She walked to the front door of Josie's without so much as a murmur from the congregants. Once inside, she let her eyes adjust to the dim light. The store was small, but neat, dominated by two large glass-doored coolers. An elderly black woman sat behind the counter in the path of an oscillating fan. The counter was cluttered with collection jars marked with various community causes. Most of them were nearly empty. "Hello. Are you Miss Josie?" Laura asked.

"There ain't no Josie. What you want, child?"

"I'm looking for a man named Terence Walker. His sister said he might have been in here recently."

"Oh, yeah—he was in here a couple of days ago, talking big. He want everybody to know that he had some money. I bet he don't have it no more, though," she commented with a chuckle.

"How long ago?"

"Maybe a day or two—no, it was Tuesday, 'cause that's the day I get my delivery. He was here when the truck came."

"And you haven't seen him since?"

"No. What you wantin' him for? He ain't no good."

"I'm beginning to gather that. I'm an assistant district attorney, and he's a witness in a case. I just want to interview him."

"Well, I'll tell him you came by, if I see him."

"Here's one of my cards. I'd appreciate it."

Laura looked around for something she could buy, and decided against taking a forty-ounce to Amos. She settled for a liter of Diet Coke, which the woman rang up without comment. Laura dropped the change from a five into a jar on the counter that bore a picture of a small girl who had leukemia and needed help with medical bills; the coins made a hollow clinking sound. Laura left, unaccountably depressed. She barely noticed the gang outside.

"Success?" Amos asked when she reached the car.

"No. Not really," she said, thrusting the bag containing the Coke into his hands. "She saw him right after he met Mr. Button. He was flashing a wad. But that was Tuesday, and he hasn't been around since."

"It may be that his sister was right—he's holed up with a lady love until the funds run dry. He'll surface in a week or two."

"I guess so," she said, but she couldn't hide her disappointment as she started the car and pulled away from Josie's.

"What's bugging you?" he asked as they drove away.

"I don't know. I just hoped that I could get a handle on this case."

"By which you mean that you want to prove that Roland Jervis is innocent."

"I didn't say that."

"You don't have to. It's what you want, isn't it?"

"It's not a matter of what I want. It's what I believe. Which is, yes, that Roland Jervis is innocent—or at least that he's not the only guilty party in Lawrence Belew's murder."

"You don't trust the police to do their jobs?"

"Again, not what I said. But there has been a certain . . . lassitude in their approach. But I don't blame Alex or Carlton. It's politics. It's the mayor, and the chief, and Marshall who're at fault. All they care about is that one stupid day in November. And the deeper Jervis is buried under the jail by then, the better."

"Can I say just one thing?"

"You're going to anyway, aren't you?"

"Yes. I want you to do me a favor and consider the possibility, just for a minute, that Jervis is guilty. That he did it all, the whole thing, including the clumsy attempt to cover up the evidence, to get that damn car. You're trying to complicate this."

"Not really," Laura said.

"The simplest answer is always the best answer," Amos said. "And what's the simple answer?"

"Cool the Socratic method," she said, irritably.

"Hey, I'm just trying out this Ockham's razor you're always talking about," he said with a disingenuous grin. "The simplest explanation is always the best, right?"

"Okay, the *simplest* explanation is that Jervis killed Belew for his car. But William of Ockham died in the fourteenth century, and Lawrence Belew died last month. And if William of Ockham were here, he'd be a lawyer, and he'd be exploring plurality right and left. Let's drop this, okay? Let's go get our bicycles and forget we ever heard of Lawrence Belew."

Chapter 13

Laura liked to think that Avery Daniels made the decision for her. He indisputably *prompted* her to make it, but she honestly believed that he had left her with no other course to pursue. He chose, in the language of Internet marketers, the negative option: he didn't decide, so Laura had to do it for him.

It wasn't that she didn't try, as she promised Amos she would, to forget that Lawrence Belew and Roland Jervis had ever existed. She did a good job of forgetting their existences, in fact, for the rest of the day Saturday and all of Sunday. It wasn't until Sunday evening, after she returned home from an early dinner with Amos, that they reappeared on her psychic radar screen in the form of a message from Tommy Wood. There was nothing she cared to watch on television, so she ambled back to her small office—actually a hallway with built-in desk and cabinets—to pay a few bills and answer some e-mail. In the course of performing these mundane chores, she took the fatal step of picking up her office voice mail.

Tommy's message had been waiting, apparently, since Friday afternoon. "Hey, Miss Chastain," he said, "I wanted to let you know that I called Avery Daniels, like you suggested. He, uh, didn't seem much interested in hearing about the button. In fact, he said that it seemed irrelevant to him, seeing as how he was going to go with an insanity defense and that the facts of the crime wouldn't be so important. I thought you ought to know. I guess it's good news for you, because it'll save you some time, I mean, if you don't have to follow up on looking through Belew's clothes and all that. But, uh, I thought you might be kind of concerned, too. Anyway, that's the story. You can call me Monday if you want to know more."

Laura hung up the phone in dismay. Avery had really crossed a line now. Not to make even the pretense of defending his client, for whatever reason—stalling tactics, showmanship, she didn't care—was criminal. She reached for the receiver with every intention of calling Meredith at home, but she stopped. What would Meredith say that she hadn't said already? She wasn't going to call Julia Walton again. She had made that clear.

But somebody had to help Avery—no, not Avery; it was Jervis who needed and deserved the help. Laura toyed for an insane moment with resigning from the district attorney's office to defend Jervis herself, but she didn't think that Marshall would allow a move like that to go unchallenged. He couldn't *really* stop her, but he could make noise and make her the focus of the case—which she certainly didn't want.

What Jervis needed was a disinterested lawyer in private

practice to take on the case. There were such animals in
Fulton County, a whole lot of them, in fact. She could
place an anonymous call to the Atlanta Volunteer Lawyers
Foundation. Someone there might take on the case—but
there was no assurance that someone would, or that the
person who volunteered would be right for the job.

In fact, there was only one person Laura considered right
for the job. She flipped through her Filofax and pulled out
a small white card. An office number, a fax number, a cell
phone number, and a pager number were all printed on the
face of the card, but she turned it over. There, written sloppily
in pen, was what she wanted: the home number. She could
punch those ten digits and change everything. Or she thought
she could.

She hesitated, poured herself another glass of Diet Coke,
and wandered around the living room straightening pillows
and magazines. She took the garbage and the recycling bins
to the curb. The little white card lay on her desk undisturbed
when she came back. *Oh, hell,* she thought. She grabbed
the phone from its cradle, without giving herself time to
reconsider, and dialed Craig Fannin's home.

She had no idea what Fannin would say—it could go any
way, from sarcasm, to outright hostility. She knew for sure
that he'd milk the situation for his own amusement. But she
believed there was no other choice. *Any* lawyer she called
might scorn and mock her, and she figured she might as
well be scorned and mocked by the best—no point in letting
some legal hack take shots at her.

A woman with a long-legged, blond voice answered.
Laura couldn't recall if Craig was married at the moment
or if he was between engagements, so to speak. She cleared
her throat. "May I speak to . . ." Laura paused. What should
she call him? She had never addressed him as "Craig." In

fact, she had very seldom addressed him directly at all, usually referring to him to a judge in the third person as "Mr. Fannin" or, when she was really peeved, as "Counsel for the Defense." She decided "Mr. Fannin" would have to do, at the risk of being taken for a telemarketer. "May I speak to Mr. Fannin?"

"Who's calling, please?" the woman asked, in a suspicious tone.

"Laura Chastain. From the district attorney's office," she added, hoping to upgrade her status from annoyance to legitimate business caller.

"Oh. I'll get him."

There was a pause, during which Laura imagined a sotto voce conversation: "Laura Chastain? Why the hell is she calling me at home?" "Probably just stalking you, dear—call the cops." Then Fannin's voice came on the line. "Well, Miss Chastain—what can I do for you?" Fannin sounded genial, at least, although Laura could detect an undercurrent of amused surprise. Or maybe just an undercurrent of Sunday-night Scotch and soda.

"Thanks for taking my call, Mr. Fannin—"

"Craig, please call me Craig. We're old friends, aren't we?"

"Well . . . yes, and please call me Laura. Craig, I have to ask you something. It's . . . well, it's kind of unorthodox. Do you have a few minutes? This could take a while to explain."

"I have all the time in the world."

"All I ask is that you hear me out."

"Of course. For you, I'm one big ear, darlin'. Whatever you say will get my full, undivided, unadulterated attention."

"Okay, here's the situation. You know the Lawrence Belew murder?"

"Doesn't every sentient being in Atlanta know about it?"

"Yes, I suppose so. Can I also assume you know that there's been an indictment?"

"You mean two indictments, I think—one that Judge Edwards very wisely quashed, and the one you managed to shepherd through a more sympathetic courtroom." He was enjoying himself a little at her expense, but Laura didn't care. The important information she gleaned was that he had been following the case, closely. " 'Scuse me just a second—honey, will you top this off for me? I'll be tied up a while," he said to his companion. "Go ahead," he said, returning to Laura.

"Roland Jervis, the defendant, is a guy from the south side with a sheet as long as a Tolstoy novel. But it's all petty stuff—loitering, drunk and disorderly. And what's more, he doesn't seem to be very good at any of it. He's probably spent more time in courtrooms than I have, and he's done a good bit of jail time. He's a loser with a capital L, in other words."

"I get the picture."

"He also has no money."

"Naturally."

"And I would like you to assist in his defense," she said, rushing her words.

"Well, you make it mighty attractive—a loser of a client, and he can't pay either. Why am I being honored with this request? Doesn't he have counsel?" Laura could hear the clink of ice on glass as Fannin took a pull on his drink.

"Of course he does. He has a public defender representing him."

"Doesn't sound like he needs me then. I'm sure his defender is a fully qualified member of the bar."

"Sure he is. And he's got no business being anywhere

near a capital case. For Christ's sake, Craig, a man's life is at stake, and you should see the gooberhead who's defending him! I wouldn't hire this Avery Daniels to defend me from a littering ticket. He tried to plead one of his clients 'guilty' at a first appearance. Judge Root had to give him one of his special little lectures. Now he's filing for an insanity defense. He's hopeless."

"Why does that bother you? I think you'd appreciate having a nice no-brainer drop into your lap."

"Think again. This is a capital case, and Roland Jervis is no more insane than you are. Avery is flailing away at procedural error, but he's not *trying* the case. He's not looking at the evidence, which is . . ." She stopped, not sure how much she should say.

"Ahh, now we're getting somewhere. You don't think the man's guilty."

"It's not that, exactly. I think there is a chance that he did it. But there are . . . questions."

"Such as?"

"Such as there is no physical evidence. Or, more accurately, the physical evidence is inconsistent with the conclusion of the investigators."

"What's that supposed to mean?"

"Okay, take the latent evidence—the only fingerprints inside the car belonged to Jervis."

"So? What's wrong with that?"

"I said the *only* prints were Jervis's. None belonged to Belew, who had owned the car for years. The car was cleaned, Craig. Jervis's story—tell me if you know this— is that he found the car, with the keys in the ignition, late on Monday night, over three days after Belew disappeared. He succumbed to temptation and took it for a ride, but was stopped by the cops less than two hours later. He says he had no idea the body was in the trunk. He only had the valet key, so he couldn't have looked in the trunk if he had wanted to. And that's just the start. The pathology of the physical injuries is very confusing, and there was a button on the body that doesn't seem to belong to either Jervis or Belew. I had the crime lab call Avery to tell him about the button. He said it wasn't important.''

"What's the case against Jervis, other than the prints?" Fannin asked. He was interested now, Laura could tell. The bantering tone was gone.

"Two eyewitness identifications. They both say they heard Jervis brag about 'jacking Belew's car the day after Belew disappeared."

"Solid citizens?"

"One's okay. One's a grade-A creep sniffing for reward money."

"And there was nothing else in the car?"

"Absolutely nothing—no blood, no hair, no fibers. It was as if the car had been cleaned—"

"By a pro," Fannin finished her thought.

"Well, a professional something—I looked into the possibility that Jervis could have worked at a car detailing shop. And lo and behold, up pops another witness who says he worked at Bumper to Bumper on Roswell Road in Buckhead."

"You think this guy's lying?"

"Can't say. I have yet to speak to this one. He seems, however, to have come into a good bit of money lately, because he quit the car wash."

"So what's your theory? Somebody else killed Belew and is framing Roland Jervis for it?"

"You tell me. All I want to know is if Jervis *could* have done it. If he did, fine. If he didn't . . . well, he's good for

auto theft, but that's not a hanging offense last time I looked.
I'll cheerfully convict him for stealing the car—"

"Not if I have anything to say about it. If I take on this
case, you'll be lucky to convict him for anything, sweetheart.
But tell me something, Laura; you're buying yourself a mess
of trouble. Why do this?"

"Because there's something wrong here, and I'm not
about to participate in a judicial murder. Jervis may be a
criminal and a derelict, but he deserves a defense, especially
when his life's on the line. And he's not going to get it from
Avery Daniels, boy attorney."

Fannin laughed. "Okay, but why not beg off? Tell Meredith you're not up for it."

"You know very well why—because the case would
probably go to someone without any scruples about rail-
roading a guy into the death chamber."

"So I'm supposed to show up, decks stripped for action
and ready to give you a real run for your money. What if I
say no? What's your plan then?"

"If you say no, I'll slog it out through the pretrial phase
and then call for an appellate review of the pretrial proceedings. Then I'll hope that somebody on the Appeals Court
notices that the counsel for the defense is an idiot."

"And if that's a no-go?"

"I'll quit the district attorney's office and make as big a
stink as I can in the press."

"But naturally you would prefer not to do something that
drastic," Fannin mused.

"Of course not. I like my job. Not that I couldn't quit if
I had to. Believe me, I thought about this for a long time
before I picked up the phone. I looked at the ethics inside
and out, because I know that this might look like a real
betrayal of Marshall. But my job description says I'm an

officer of the court. My duty is to get the truth, not just a conviction. Convicting the wrong man would be worse than letting the guilty man go; I don't have to tell you that. Calling you, or someone like you, as I see it, is within the bounds of the duties of an officer of the court. I'm obeying the law: I am ensuring that Roland Jervis receives an adequate defense. Going ahead with this farce, knowing that I could have Roland Jervis strapped in the chair without breaking a sweat, that's unethical. That, I couldn't do."

"But naturally you don't want me to tell anyone about this phone call?" Fannin said, raising a verbal eyebrow.

"Well, I guess. Does that mean you're going to do it?"

"I think it would be a ton of fun to have another shot at you in the courtroom, Miss Chastain. And of course my social conscience demands that I do a little pro bono work every so often."

"I should hope so. You can divert a little of the lucre you earned defending Shawn Tolliver. You owe a debt to society for that one," Laura said tartly.

"That poor, misunderstood boy—thank God the underdogs have me to turn to. I tell you what: I'll look into this whole matter. If I think there's a chance Jervis is being railroaded, I'll take his case."

Laura smiled broadly. "Thanks, Craig. Thanks a lot. I really appreciate it, and I hope I didn't ruin your dinner."

"Not a bit, sugar. I wouldn't have missed a chance like this for the world."

"Great. Your client is in the Fulton County Jail, of course. I don't know how you can get in there without going through Avery or Julia Walton. . . ."

"Let me worry about that. I think it's best if we just act like this conversation never happened. You go on and argue your little heart out against every motion I make, just like you normally would. I can take the heat.''

"Of course. I just thought—''

"Never mind. Thanks for the call, Laura. I'll see you in court.''

"Good night, Craig. And thanks again.''

Laura felt an enormous sense of relief, which was immediately superseded by one of pure panic. What the hell had she just done? Craig was right to advise caution; Marshall would be furious if he knew what she had done. Meredith ... well, she wouldn't be happy, but she would understand. Calling in a hot-shot defense attorney, no matter what the ethical framework of the circumstances, was unorthodox behavior for a prosecutor. Laura wondered if this made her unique in the annals of prosecutorial history: the assistant district attorney who sold out the side—in the cause of justice, of course. But she squared her shoulders; she knew that she would be able to defend her decision if she had to. She just hoped that she wouldn't have to.

Chapter 14

Monday dawned, and the world didn't end. Laura sat through Meredith's routine staff meeting without contributing to the discussion, which she hoped Meredith didn't notice. Since the discussion centered on keeping the break room refrigerator cleaned out, her silence was probably not as noticeable as it would have been if the topic had been something that actually mattered. When everyone had finally spoken his or her piece on refrigerator hygiene, the meeting broke up. Laura tried to make an exit that she hoped could not later be characterized as slinking.

"Laura! Hold up a minute," Meredith said. "You're not going to believe who called me this morning." Laura opened her eyes wide and shook her head. Meredith grinned. "Craig Fannin! He's taking Roland Jervis as a client. Doesn't that beat all?"

Laura feigned surprise. "Yes, it does! Did he say why he's doing it?"

"He says he's taking more pro bono work these days, and that he thought this might be one of the few death penalty cases he would see for a while in Fulton County."

"Are you upset?" Laura asked.

"Upset? Why should I be? Craig has every right to take on a client. I can't be upset about that."

"But it'll be tougher for us to make our case with Fannin involved."

"Don't quote me, but this case should have been a lot tougher from the get-go. Avery's too much of a pushover to be running a death penalty defense. I know, I know— you've been saying that all along. So it's a good outcome, really. With Craig defending, there's less chance of errors and appeals."

"So do you think Marshall will be okay with it, too?"

Meredith whooped with laughter. "Marshall? He'll be furious! He'll rupture a vein! I'm off to tell him now. Want to come?"

Laura shook her head. "Pass. But let me know what he says."

"You'll probably hear him yourself."

Laura returned to her desk, a bit weak in the knees. She was glad that Meredith could see the big-picture benefit of having Fannin take the defense. A good prosecutor didn't relish a guilty verdict that was based on error or incompetence of the defense counsel. That didn't mean that Marshall Oliver, fighting for his survival as district attorney, would see it that way. Laura was grateful that Meredith had given her the option of not being there when he heard the news.

Thirty minutes later, Meredith popped her head in. "He's calmer now," she said.

"But he wasn't at first, I guess."

"No. Calm was not the word. In fact, I walked right into a buzz saw: He had just taken a phone call from Fannin. You don't know Marshall as well as I do. I could have predicted how it would go. We begin—always—with righteous anger, and move to self-pity and self-victimization. But we end with rock-jawed determination to prevail."

Laura wrinkled her nose in distaste. "Not really."

"He's a politician, and politicians are part actor. That's good; he needs to be able to draw on a reservoir of indignation to do this job."

"But what's to be indignant about?"

"He believes that Fannin took the case at the suggestion of Ellis Brady's campaign."

"No! That's just paranoid," Laura exclaimed, forgetting for a moment that, if Marshall had known who really gave Fannin the suggestion, he would have had cause for a positively Nixonian level of paranoid anxiety.

"That's what I told him. Craig probably has his own reasons, none of which have anything to do with Marshall, or Ellis Brady. Knowing Craig, in fact, I'd be willing to bet that it's nothing more than a good, old-fashioned love of making trouble and being at the center of the storm. Or maybe he's itching for a rematch against you—he doesn't often lose, you know, and you trounced him pretty well last fall. But I stopped by to tell you that Marshall wants you to talk to Craig. Call his office. Do you need the number?"

"Um, no. I have his card."

After Meredith left, Laura dutifully dialed Craig's office number. "May I speak to Mr. Fannin?" she asked, identifying herself to the pleasant woman who answered.

Craig's voice boomed down the phone line a moment later. "Miss Chastain! Did you hear that I'm representing

Roland Jervis? Looks like we'll be facing off for battle once again—just like the good old days.''

Laura thought he was piling it on a little thick. "The lines aren't bugged, Craig," she said dryly.

"You never know with Marshall. Anyway, I've talked to Julia Walton, and I'm now officially cocounsel for the defense of Roland Jervis. I met my client this morning at the jail, and I've filed an entry of appearance."

"What did you think of Jervis?"

"Pathetic. Not cut out for hard time."

"And Avery?"

"Promising lad. Probably brilliant. I'll get rid of him by the end of the week."

Laura laughed. "You're a piece of work. What's your next move?"

"I've just come back from the crime lab. I met your buddies out there. That guy Scott was delighted to meet someone as paranoid as himself."

"So you're going to follow up on the prints, and the button?"

"Nope. If this thing gets to trial, I can use them to establish reasonable doubt, but, frankly, they all look like dead ends to me—as far as grounds for dismissal, anyway. No, I'm going after the eyewitness testimony."

"How?"

"Hey, don't expect me to open the kimono all the way, sugar. I will say that I've hired a PI to check out their stories. Your pal Kenny Newton, in fact. I was impressed by the work he did for you last year. I'm hoping he turns up something to discredit their stories. If not, I'll try something else."

"Did you talk to the pathologist?"

"That guy. Yeah. Not much help there. I took the photos and his report and sent them to a buddy of mine at Emory medical school, one of the pathology professors. He said he can't be a hundred percent about anything, without actually seeing the body, but he can at least give me an idea of how thorough the autopsy report is."

"You've certainly had a busy day."

"And I'm just getting started, kid—the best is yet to come. In the meantime, you and I should probably keep our contact to a minimum."

"Believe me, I want to. I only called you because Marshall asked me to. By the way, do you know Ellis Brady?"

"Yeah. A complete and total tool. Why?"

"Marshall thinks you're working for him."

Craig snorted with contempt. "That'll be the day. Maybe I should send a check to Marshall's campaign—that'll blow his mind."

"It's already blown enough, thanks. I guess I'll see you around, huh?"

"You bet you will," he said.

Laura managed to make it through the balance of the afternoon without seeing Marshall. She slipped out as soon after five as she decently could, in time to go home and change her clothes before going over to Amos's house. He wasn't home when she got there, so she let herself in with the key he had given her. She pulled a beer out of the refrigerator and settled down to wait for him.

"Sorry I'm running late," he said when he arrived shortly after six-thirty.

"No problem. It's given me an opportunity to thoroughly peruse the latest issue of *Guns and Ammo*. Which reminds me, Emily Bailey wants us to come up to the farm weekend after next." Emily was the sister of Laura's late legal mentor and lover, Tom Bailey. She and Laura had come together in the wake of Tom's death, but the real surprise was the relationship—based on a mutual love of pistol-shooting—that had grown up between Emily and Amos. A weekend at her farm in north Georgia meant horseback riding for Laura, and a blissful two days of shooting at things for Amos. He brightened up at the prospect.

"Great. Did she say if she got that new pistol?"

"Yes, she did, and yes, you can play with it. You two and the guns—honestly."

"And you and the damn horses," Amos replied good-naturedly. "Psychotic animals."

"I still say you were doing fine until the dog got in the way," Laura said. Amos's first and only attempt at riding had not gone well. "Who knew he didn't like dogs?"

"Emily knew it, and she still let me get up on him."

"But she didn't know the dog would run in front of you. And you did a great job of hanging on."

"Until I came off, that is. I know where you're heading with this, and you can forget it. I'm never getting on one of those things again."

"Okay. And I'm not shooting one of those guns."

"I don't know," Amos said. "You're not bad. You've only tried it once, but I was impressed."

"But I don't like it. Guns scare me. How was your day, anyway?"

He shrugged. "Nothing to write home about. You?"

"Same."

"That's not what I heard. What about Craig Fannin taking on the Belew case?"

"Oh, that. Marshall was kind of upset," she said noncommittally.

"Aren't you?" he asked.

"Me? Why should I be upset? Craig can do whatever he likes."

"What he likes to do is makes the cops look bad. And prosecutors."

"He didn't make me look bad last fall. In fact, that's why Meredith thinks he's taking this case."

"What, to get even with you? Some ego you've got going there, kid."

"*I* didn't say it," Laura said indignantly. "Meredith did."

"And why do you think he took on the case?"

Laura struggled to meet his eyes. "He's just Craig Fannin, that's all. He does what he wants to. Now change your clothes and let's go. I'm hungry."

Laura knew that she should have told Amos the truth, but something told her that he wouldn't be happy about it. She deftly steered the conversation away from her case at dinner, and begged off from returning home with him. "I've got a big day tomorrow," she said.

"Yeah, I'm tired, too. I'll talk to you tomorrow." He kissed her good night in the driveway, and waited while she got in her car and started it up. He leaned in the open window. "You need a new car," he said. "This one's going to break down one of these days."

"It's only got a hundred and twenty thousand miles on it," she protested. "Your truck has a lot more than that."

"But I know how to maintain my truck. You've run this heap of junk into the ground. I'm amazed it's still running."

"I do take care of it. I have the oil changed, and I got new tires. And a new belt thingie."

"A timing belt. And a new distributor, but you only did that because I told you to. We'll start looking around for a new car, okay?"

"I'm not ready to spend money on a new car."

"A good used car, then. I'll take care of it."

Laura felt a tiny surge of irritation. She knew that Amos

wasn't patronizing her—he was probably right about the car. But there was something in his tone that she didn't respond well to. "We'll see," she said. "I really should go now." She turned her face up so that he could kiss her once more, and reversed out of the driveway. He stood and watched as she drove down the street, ready, it appeared, to rescue her from all the dangers that might present themselves within two blocks of his driveway. Laura shook her head. Caveman Kowalski, ready to defend his mate. As if she needed it. He of all people should know that she was capable of defending herself, *and* of taking responsibility for her car and herself. Although, she admitted, her reluctance to tell him about her call to Fannin didn't exactly make her the most stand-up girlfriend of all time. Still, she had no trouble falling into a deep and untroubled sleep and waking rested in the morning.

Craig's appearance on the scene created a flutter of renewed interest in the Belew case. Bob Harper had a story on the development in the morning paper, which Laura read at her desk. The reporter seemed to share Marshall's view that Fannin's action was politically motivated, which was fine with Laura—and fine with Craig, she assumed, based on the cryptic quote that Harper attributed to him: "I'm just doing my bit to make sure that the system works for everyone, not just for the folks who can afford to pay a private attorney." Harper had managed to get a huffy comment from Marshall, to the effect that the prosecution's case was overwhelmingly strong and that he hoped that Craig Fannin wouldn't try to distract the public with fanciful theories. Laura put the paper aside with a chuckle and went about her business, hoping—but not expecting—to hear from Craig directly what he was up to.

In fact, she didn't hear from her opposing counsel until Friday morning, and when he did call, he was all business. "I've got to see you," he said abruptly.

"Why? What's happened?"

"I'll tell you in person. We need to meet where we won't be seen together," he said.

Laura knew that Craig's offices were in Buckhead, near her house, but she couldn't think of a place where a locally famous defense attorney could go in that neighborhood without being recognized. "There's a place down on Marietta," she ventured. "Near Northside Drive. It's a hangout for students, and no one from the courthouse ever goes there." She gave him the name and the location, a barren strip of turf west of downtown that had escaped gentrification.

An hour later, Craig joined Laura at a table. "Holy smokes," he said, surveying his surroundings. "What is this place? And what the hell kind of name is 'The Somber Reptile'?"

"I don't know, but the food's okay, if you like Cajun. So what's happened—why did you call me?"

"To tell you that I'm about to blow your damn case out of the water. Frankly, I didn't think it would be this easy." He looked pretty somber himself.

"You don't seem thrilled."

"I'm not. What do you know about Alex Devereaux?"

"Nothing. Except that he's a cop, of course. He's pretty experienced. Seems like a good guy."

"Can you think of any reason he might monkey with a case?"

"No. Are you saying that's what happened?"

"No. But I am saying that there's been monkeying."

"You talked to the eyewitnesses?"

"No. They've disappeared. Kenny's still looking for them. But I checked out the time frame, and they could not have talked to Jervis when they say they did."

"Why not?"

"Because he was at church, believe it or not."

Laura almost choked on a sip of water. "I've got to say 'not,' " she said when she had recovered. "I don't think that Jervis is capable of having killed Belew for his car, but I'm not going to buy into his being a choirboy."

"He's not. He went to church that day, in fact, against his will. One of his aunts died, and her funeral was Saturday. Ever been to a black funeral?"

"Can't say I have."

"It's an all-day affair. Jervis was there from approximately nine o'clock Saturday morning until two that afternoon, allowing for the burial at the cemetery and all. Then he went back to his grandmother's house for dinner. All this took place during the time he was supposed to be hanging in the parking lots of various pool halls and liquor stores, confessing to carjacking Lawrence Belew's Lexus."

"Wait a second. Who saw him in church besides his loving granny?"

"The preacher and about twelve solid, hat-wearing church ladies."

"How come they didn't come forward before now?"

"For one thing, they didn't know that there were eyewitnesses against Jervis. For another, if they had, they all thought that Jervis needed an alibi for Friday night, when Belew disappeared—not for Saturday afternoon."

"But Avery knew—"

"If Avery knew jack-shit, he didn't do anything about it.

I have fired his brilliant young ass, and I'm going to call Julia Walton and tell her to do the same."

Laura felt a warm glow of satisfaction, followed by chagrin for Avery. "He didn't look at the eyewitness statements?"

"You know what I think? I think Avery assumed his client was guilty, notwithstanding anything Jervis might have told him to the contrary, and notwithstanding anything a careful examination of the case against his client would have shown him." Craig was angry, and his voice was rising. Laura placed a warning hand on his arm. "Sorry. The boy genius was so in love with the idea of making new law on appeal that he completely neglected to try the case. Damn it. Oh, and by the way, I never found the guy from the car wash, but Roland says he never worked there a day in his life. I figure *that* will be easy enough to prove, so even if Roland *didn't* have an alibi for Saturday, I've got one lying witness caught cold. I'd still like to find his sorry ass and find out who paid him off."

The waiter approached with menus and water glasses, and Laura hastily ordered beans and rice, with a Diet Coke. Craig tossed the menu down and asked for the same, substituting a Dos Equis for the Coke. "Where were we? Anyway, I don't know where these 'eyewitnesses' are now, but I'm going to find them and I'm going to wring the truth out of them. Someone told them what to say. Someone gave them details."

Laura shook her head. "I'm sorry, but I can't believe it was Alex Devereaux. Or Carlton Hemingway. The guy who talked to Terence Walker at the car wash was white. Both the detectives on the case are black. What does that tell you?"

Craig shrugged and took a gulp of beer. "I don't know.

I never thought it was Hemingway; he's still the junior guy, and he was following Devereaux's lead.''

"But what possible motive could Devereaux have for framing Roland Jervis?''

"I don't see this so much as a frame-up of Jervis in particular. Jervis just happens to be the poor schmuck who wandered into the path of the so-called investigation. In fact, Jervis might actually have been an inconvenience. Whoever did this probably intended that the car be found by the police. That's why there was a tip turned in. And when the cops found not only the car but Jervis, too, somebody had to improvise.''

"You mean Mr. Button?''

"Who? Oh, whoever left that button in the plastic. I'm not so sure about that.''

"Could he be the white cop who talked to Terence Walker?''

"We don't know that he was a cop. A white *guy,* anyway,'' Craig said. "These beans are pretty good. What did your Mexican pal say about him?''

"That he was big, and white, and looked like a cop.''

"That's not much to go on.''

"But he identified my boy . . . my friend Amos Kowalski for a cop right away.''

"You're dating Kowalski? Good man. And he doesn't need to flash his badge to prove *he's* a cop. My granny could make him for a cop. There could be something, though, to this mystery man—Mr. Button, as you call him. If you don't mind, I *won't* call him that. Sounds too much like a name for a kitty-cat. But if we can get one of these two eyewitnesses to admit that someone—cop or not—paid them, or told them they could collect reward money, for telling these tales about Jervis, I might believe there's some sinister force at work. More than likely we're just looking at lazy cops and greedy citizens out for reward money, with the added bonus that it's a politically convenient solution for a high-profile crime."

"But you do believe that there's something else going on—this can't all be down to lazy cops. Not that I think Alex and Carlton are lazy. What about the autopsy report—did you hear anything from your guy at Emory?"

"Not yet. He's been busy. I hope to have something by the end of next week. I don't expect too much to come out of that—at least, not as far as exonerating my client goes. He may see something the cops missed. But it's not my job to figure out who really did kill Belew. I'm only interested in getting Jervis off."

"But don't you care what happened?"

"As a person, yes. As Jervis's defense lawyer, I don't have to. I don't need to play Sherlock in order to get these charges dismissed. Finding the killer? That's *your* problem—yours and the Atlanta Police Department's. I'll be on my merry way after I win my motion for dismissal."

"You really think this is enough for a dismissal?"

"I do. That's why my office is filing the motion right now."

"What do you think I should do—should I fight you tooth and nail, or capitulate?"

"Do what you think is right. I'm sure Marshall would prefer to keep the indictment of Jervis in place—even if you convince him that the case will ultimately fail. It's always better to have a jailbird in the hand in these things."

"Tell me about it. If Jervis gets sprung, the press—and

Ellis Brady—are going to turn up the heat on Marshall. So if you don't mind, I think I'll vigorously oppose your motion.''

"I wouldn't expect anything less from you,'' he said with a smile. "Cheers,'' he added, clinking his beer bottle against the rim of her glass. "See you in court.''

Chapter 15

Going up against Craig, as Laura rediscovered, was like facing down a full-tilt monster truck rally, within the civilized confines of a courtroom, of course. It was hard to remember, in the face of his attack on her case, that she had actually invited him to do this to her, and harder still to believe that only a few days earlier she had been sharing an amicable lunch with this . . . pit bull.

"Your Honor, if I may—" Laura tried to interject to stem the tide of Craig's argument for dismissal.

"Please, let me finish," Craig said impatiently. Laura hoped that he was just overinvolved in role-playing; otherwise, she was going to have a thing or two to say to him. *"None* of the facts of the prosecution's case stand up. There are three witnesses, Your Honor, who have out-and-out lied in order to implicate my client in a terrible crime. And that, Your Honor, is a crime unto itself. A crime for which I intend to seek full justice, Your Honor, once these ludicrous charges against him are dropped. . . .''

"Yes, Mr. Fannin, somehow I knew that you would," Judge Root answered, his attitude apparently not improved by increased arterial blood flow. "But if you don't mind, Miss Chastain does deserve an opportunity to defend her case."

"Thank you, Your Honor," Laura said with an exasperated sidelong glance at Craig. "Mr. Fannin has certainly raised some interesting new evidence. It appears that the reward money that was offered in this case may have attracted a less-than-honest group of witnesses in this matter. The State concedes that the testimony of Messrs. Clay and Jackson should probably be excluded at trial. But the third witness, Mr. Walker, has not been located by Mr. Fannin— at least, not so far as I can tell. And Walker's story— that the defendant worked at a detail shop where cars were routinely and thoroughly cleaned, inside and out—supports the State's case. That is, his testimony shows how Mr. Jervis had the means to cover his tracks."

"If *I* may interject," Craig said with a touch of sarcasm that Laura found most annoying, "Surely Miss Chastain is not trying to argue that my client—though not, I admit, the beneficiary of a fine education—was stupid enough to think that by cleaning the car, eliminating every set of prints but his own, that he could conceal his involvement in a crime. . . .''

"I am not suggesting anything, Your Honor, but that there are inconsistencies in the defense's argument. A couple of greedy people come forward with stories to collect a reward—well, it doesn't reflect very well on the police, or the district attorney's office, that they made it this far, but it certainly doesn't disprove anything else in our case. You'll note that Mr. Fannin makes no effort to deny that his client was driving the victim's car, with the victim's body in the trunk, when he was arrested. His explanation—that he 'found' the car—stretches credibility more than a little. And I *am* arguing that—no matter what Mr. Jervis's educational background may have been—he did have the means to clean signs of a struggle from the interior of the car. That he allowed his own fingerprints to remain is, in that light, meaningless, because he didn't mean to obliterate signs of his own presence—only those of his victim.''

"Come *on,* Miss Chastain—do you expect the court to believe that this criminal mastermind cleaned the interior of the car in an attempt to hide signs of a murder, but *left the body in the trunk?* You know, Miss Chastain, I've always thought you were one of the more logical employees of the district attorney's office. I'm sad to say that I'm being forced to revise my opinion.'' And he did, indeed, look sad. Craig was giving an Academy Award performance, and he was enjoying himself.

"That's enough, Mr. Fannin. We don't need ad hominem observations. If neither of you has any additional facts to introduce, I am prepared to call a recess while I consider the motion.''

"I have nothing further, Your Honor,'' Craig said.

"I have nothing, either,'' Laura said.

"Good. We'll recess until, say, two o'clock. I'll be prepared to rule then.''

Laura didn't look at Craig as she gathered her papers. Meredith, who had been seated throughout the proceedings, watched as Fannin escorted his client—dressed, for this appearance, in what looked to Laura like a new suit, no doubt courtesy of his new lawyer—from the courtroom.

"That went well," Meredith said, her tone implying that she believed anything but.

"Hey, I tried," Laura said. "You could have jumped in any old time, you know."

"Don't bite my head off. You did great. But Craig . . . he's on to something."

"Think so? Think we should expect Judge Root to let us go ahead and let these two dirtbags testify?"

"That's water under the bridge. I'm just hoping he doesn't go all the way to dismissal."

"What's to stop him?"

Meredith stopped and shook her head. "Nothing. It looks bad. I better prepare Marshall for a loss on this one. Let's hope he doesn't fire me." Seeing the dismay on Laura's face, she offered her shoulder a pat. "Don't worry. I'm just kidding. Marshall's not *that* unreasonable. And you haven't done a thing wrong. I could strangle Devereaux, though. This was sloppy police work."

Laura nodded in agreement, hoping that it *was* just sloppy work. The alternative was not very appealing. It occurred to her that Alex Devereaux—and Carlton Hemingway, whom she counted as a friend—could be in a whole lot of trouble if Craig won this motion. She trooped dejectedly back to her office, reflecting that whoever postulated the law of unintended consequences knew what the hell he was talking about. Here was Meredith talking about getting fired, and who-knows-what kind of grief about to rain down on the Atlanta Police Department . . . all of which could have been avoided by Laura's simply keeping her mouth shut. If she had, the only person to suffer any consequences at all would have been Roland Jervis, who was *not* Laura's boss, and *not* a friend. Just a guy who might have been executed for something he didn't do. Knowing that—and knowing that she would have felt worse if she had let it happen—would have to do as shield and buckler for Laura if the going got tough.

Which it very soon did. To no one's surprise, or at least not to Laura's, Meredith's, or Craig Fannin's surprise, after reading statements from one preacher and two staunch aunts, Judge Root granted Fannin's motion to dismiss the charges against Roland Jervis. He did so with a lecture that, although directed at the absent police officers who had investigated the crime, struck Laura as exceptionally harsh.

"To say that I'm disappointed," he rumbled from the bench, "would be an egregious understatement. I am dismayed. Dismayed that the testimony of two such transparent liars as Jermaine Clay and Albert Jackson could be used to indict a man for felony murder. Dismayed that the police spent no more time investigating their false and malicious claims than they would have investigating some petty crime. And especially dismayed that the State—which is charged, as I hope I don't need to remind Mrs. Gaffney and Miss Chastain, with seeing that justice is done—could acquiesce in such a flimsy excuse for pursuing a capital case. I would like to remind all concerned—those present and those not in the courtroom today—of the duties of an officer of this court. The search for justice is of far more lasting importance than any quest for office." Laura cringed especially at that last remark; clearly, the judge thought that all this was a product of Marshall's political ambitions. Which was not, she admitted privately, all that far off the mark. "The charges against you, Mr. Jervis, are dismissed," Judge Root concluded.

"All the charges, Your Honor?" Fannin asked.

"All of them."

"But, Your Honor," Laura interjected, "the felony charge—the theft of the automobile!"

"I consider that a lesser included charge, Miss Chastain. Your case was based on your theory that Mr. Jervis had assaulted the victim with the intent of taking his car. Insofar as I don't believe that you have shown that Mr. Jervis *was* Mr. Belew's assailant, I don't believe that you've shown that he took the car, either."

"But he was driving the car!" Laura declared. This was a little much; she wanted Jervis out from under a death penalty rap, but to try to say that he hadn't taken the car was ludicrous. He was driving the car; it wasn't his car; he didn't have the owner's permission to drive it—q.e.d., he had stolen it.

"Yes, Miss Chastain. And if you had charged him with felony murder *and* auto theft, you might still have an indictment. But you clearly cast the theft of the auto as a carjacking—a felonious assault that resulted in Mr. Belew's death. You can reindict him for theft if you wish, but he is, as of now, a free man. That's all I have to say." With that, Judge Root rose and left the courtroom.

Laura turned slowly to meet Meredith's gaze. In the background, Fannin was congratulating Jervis and the battalion of church ladies who had showed up to support his cause. "Sorry," she said tersely.

"Why? You did what you could. You said all along that the case was shaky. This is what happens to shaky cases."

"But Marshall—"

"Will have a cow. So what? You did your job, Laura. Who could have known that Craig Fannin would take an interest in a case like this? Helluva time for him to develop a conscience, if you ask me," Meredith grumbled.

"It's better, though, don't you think—I mean, not to be

going ahead to trial on such a weak foundation? Sooner or later—even without Fannin—this thing would have collapsed.''

Meredith shrugged. "Who knows? The only important thing now is to decide what we want to do next. And to get out of here without talking to our friends with the green eyeshades—whoops, too late." Laura turned to look where Meredith saw something. It was Bob Harper, the reporter from the morning paper who had been following the case. "Hey, Bob, how are you?" she greeted him as he turned his attention from Fannin and his client to the defeated prosecutors.

"I'm great, Meredith. Better than you, I think. What happened?"

"You were here. What do you think happened?"

"I think you got your ass whupped. But, for public consumption, I'm willing to make it a little prettier."

"What a prince. Well, you can say that the district attorney doesn't believe that the facts Mr. Fannin brought forward change a thing. Roland Jervis still has some 'splaining to do—just what was he doing driving a dead man's car, with, I might add, the dead man as a passenger?"

"Maybe it's just what he's been saying all along—he found the car. And he didn't know Belew was in the trunk."

"You think so? And when was the last time you found a Lexus with a body in the trunk, Bob?"

The reporter laughed. "Okay, it's not the best story. So what's your next move?"

"We're not prepared to say," Meredith answered.

"Will you do what the judge said—reindict him?"

"We're not prepared to say right now. So scoot along and write your story, Bob. I'll call you as soon as I know something." Harper switched off his vest-pocket recorder, gave Meredith a wink, and left. But they hadn't cleared the courtroom before they were approached once again, this time by a well-dressed, handsome black man who looked vaguely familiar to Laura. He also looked angry to her.

"What the hell just happened?" he asked.

Laura remembered who he was. Lawrence Belew's brother-in-law, the husband of Diana Belew. She had seen him at the press conference the day they had announced Jervis's arrest. "You're Julian Arnold, aren't you?" she asked.

"Yes. Diana Belew is my wife. What just happened here?"

Laura shook her head. "Our case wasn't strong, Mr. Arnold. Craig Fannin—the man who argued the motion to dismiss—had us cornered."

"Well, that's just great, isn't it? All along you people have been telling us you had this guy cold. And now, it turns out you don't. I don't know how I'm going to tell my wife about this—let alone my in-laws. Do you *know* what this has done to them?"

"I have an idea," Laura replied.

"What can I tell them? What are you going to do? Can you reinstate the charges?"

"Yes, probably," Laura said thoughtfully. "But our case, without those eyewitnesses, is pretty shaky."

" *'Pretty shaky'*? You catch the guy in Lawrence's car and you say your case is *shaky?*"

Meredith answered him patiently. "You're right that the prima facie case looks bad for Jervis. He had the car, and there's no doubt that the car is somehow connected to the murder. But you heard what the judge said—we tied the theft of the car into the murder. We believed that the car was taken in a car-jacking, and that your brother-in-law was killed in the course of the commission of that crime, and that's how we charged him—as a car-jacker who, in the course of committing a felony, killed Lawrence Belew."

"And that's not what you think happened now?"

Meredith sighed. "I do. But if we recharge Jervis right away, it will have to be with the theft of the car. We don't have the evidence to support the car-jacking at this point."

"Are you saying you can't reindict him for murder?"

Laura nodded. "Not unless we want Craig Fannin to replay this scene again."

"We can hold him, though, on the theft charges," Meredith amended.

Arnold hardly seemed placated by these tepid reassurances. "I'll try to explain it to my mother-in-law, but she's not going to be happy."

"Please tell her that the full resources of the Atlanta Police Department and the Fulton County District Attorney's office are going to be dedicated to gathering the evidence we need to reindict Jervis."

"Or to indict someone else," Laura added, more in the spirit of honesty than of helpfulness. Arnold nodded curtly, and left them without saying good-bye.

"I guess we're off to see the wizard now," Laura said glumly, anticipating another unpleasant encounter, this time with Marshall.

"Yup. Oh, don't look so sad—he won't kill you."

He would if he knew the truth, Laura thought. But Meredith was right. Marshall took the defeat surprisingly well. At first, anyway.

"Bullshit," he said. "Nothing but grandstanding. Fannin drags a bunch of church ladies past Judge Root, and he goes PC. Smug bastard. He threw out the felony murder indictment?"

"He threw out the whole case," Laura said.

"What about the felony auto theft?"

"Lesser included charge, he says, since we positioned it as a car-jacking. He was probably right," Laura added masochistically.

"But we can reindict him for the felony auto theft," Meredith added hastily. "We'll get right on it."

"Well," Laura said. "Let's think about that. What would be the point? We can't reindict him on the murder—not with the evidence that we have—so we'll only look petty and vindictive if we try to hold him on the auto theft charge."

"What do you mean, 'petty'?" Marshall demanded. "How is it petty to keep a car thief behind bars?"

"Everyone would know that's not why we're indicting him. They know we think he killed Lawrence Belew."

"And? I'm afraid I don't see your point. Unless you don't think he killed Belew."

Laura drew a deep breath. "As a matter of fact, I don't. There's too much that doesn't fit. Like, how would he have cleaned the car? Why did all these witnesses step up and start lying their heads off? Don't you think there's something going on that bears looking into?"

"I think the murder of a good citizen of this city deserves looking into, a point of view that you apparently don't share."

"Oh, climb down, Marshall," Meredith intervened. "All Laura is trying to say is that she never felt that this case added up to much. Right, Laura?"

"That's right. It didn't hang together like it should have."

"Why else would Fannin have involved himself? Come on, Marshall, when's the last time you knew him to back a loser?"

"Last fall, when he defended another murderer. Don't

make the mistake of assuming that Craig Fannin was acting out of principle—the man doesn't have any."

"I wouldn't say that," Laura argued. "He's plenty principled, when he wants to be."

"Really? Why do you think he took this case, then?"

"Because he didn't think Jervis was guilty."

"And I say bullshit. He saw a couple of petty inconsistencies in our case and decided to ride in on a white horse. You know what his real motive is, of course." Laura shook her head. "Let me tell you, then. I give it about twenty-four hours before Fannin files a civil suit on Jervis's behalf. It's all about the Benjamins, baby, with that one."

"Aren't you ignoring something?" Laura asked, growing more heated than she liked. "There would have been no *opportunity* for Craig to take Jervis's case, or to file a civil suit on his behalf, if our own case hadn't been a half-baked mess of lying witnesses and dubious conclusions."

"If that's how you saw the case, I'm not surprised that Fannin beat you. You could do me the favor of at least pretending to believe in the cases you prosecute."

"Don't get snide with me, Marshall—you would have lost this one as quickly as I did, because it was bogus from the start and you knew it. If you weren't so focused on your stupid election you might not have pushed to even indict Roland Jervis for auto theft—much less sent him to death row for felony murder."

"All right, children, let's not go there," Meredith said warningly.

"No, I *am* going there," Laura said, truly angry. "For the past six months this office has been run with one goal only: reelect Marshall Oliver. This isn't the first bad decision that's been made with Marshall's political career in mind—"

"I think you should shut up now," Marshall warned. "Because you don't know what you're talking about. I don't need staffers who question my judgment."

"No, you don't. You don't need to have your almighty judgment questioned, and God forbid anyone does. We're all on eggshells around you, all the time—especially since you filed for reelection. That's why nobody in this office can look you in the face and tell you the truth. But I'm going to. Here it is, Marshall: Roland Jervis did not kill Lawrence Belew. He did exactly what he said he did. He found the car, with the keys in it, where someone had left it, cleaned of prints and fibers. Someone who knew what the hell he was doing. Did he mean for some idiot like Jervis to find the car? I don't know. But when he did, and when we jumped on that poor schmuck, whoever did it was only too happy to point us in Jervis's direction. Witnesses were popping up like daisies—need corroboration of something? No problem! One witness, coming up. You want fries with that? I'm ashamed that I went along with it as long as I did. And here's the capper: want to know why Fannin took this case? Huh? Because *I asked him to.* I called him up, and told him I thought the case was being mishandled. And I practically begged him to take it on—because I couldn't live with what was happening."

Even Meredith was astonished. "Laura, why didn't you tell me? Why did you have to go to him, of all people?"

"I *tried* to tell you. I'm sorry, Meredith, I love you to death, but you didn't listen to a word I was saying."

"Why didn't you just resign the case, then?"

"What? And let someone less scrupulous fry an innocent man? I couldn't take the chance."

Marshall had recovered himself enough to speak. "Get out. You're fired."

Meredith tried to intervene once again. "Now, Marshall, think it through. Laura's one of our top performers—"

"No. Get her out of here. I never want to see her again. I don't need some damn Judas on my staff. Leave—go! And you can go, too, Meredith, if you don't like it. That's all."

Both women left Marshall's office. "For God's sake, Laura, did you have to go that far?"

"Yes. I'll get my things and go."

"No, let me try to talk him around."

"Give it up, Meredith. He fired my ass. And I would have, too, in his position. I did what I did knowing there was a chance this would happen."

"You didn't have to tell him it was you who called Craig. Marshall never would have found out."

"No, he wouldn't have. Craig certainly never would have told anyone. But why would I want to keep working for a man like Marshall, who puts his own job ahead of an innocent man's life?"

"And what does that say about me? Do I need to pack my bags and storm out to keep my reputation with you intact?"

"For the love of God, Meredith. That's not what this is about. You know I admire you, and I trust you—"

"Not enough to be honest with me, apparently," Meredith said bitterly.

"Okay, I can see this is going nowhere. I should have told you. I really should have, and I'm sorry I didn't. The last thing I wanted to do was blow up my relationship with you."

Meredith paused, emotions fighting on her face. "You haven't. You're a good lawyer, and you did the right thing.

I wasn't listening to you when you tried to tell me. I didn't *let* you tell me."

"Meredith, I'm so sorry," Laura was crying now, dabbing at her face with the back of a clenched fist to try to hide the tears. "I liked working here. I liked working for *you*."

Meredith put her arms around her now-former assistant. "And you will again, some day. Just give him a chance to cool off."

Laura accepted the embrace, and the assurance, but she knew in her heart that he would not. It was going to be a long, long time before she worked for Marshall Oliver again.

Chapter 16

An hour later, Laura left the courthouse, her career as an assistant district attorney reduced to the contents of a box and a shopping bag. She tossed them into the trunk of her car and got into the driver's seat. She sat there for a few minutes, at loose ends. Relief warred with anger; she didn't respect Marshall, and she didn't want to work for him—but how dare he fire her?

She looked at her watch; it was still early in the afternoon. She had a sense that she shouldn't be out of the office at this time of day; the habit of work was deeply ingrained in her. She could go home, but she thought that seeing her home in the unfamiliar afternoon light would make her feel strange. There would be enough of those quiet afternoons in the coming days and weeks, she knew, but she wanted to spare herself this first one. She decided to go to Amos's house. There, at least, she could sustain the pretense of being on vacation. She backed out of the familiar parking space and headed east.

Amos was surprised to find her waiting at his house when he returned from work two hours later. She was sitting on the porch swing, idly dangling a ball of crumpled paper in front of the delighted cat.

"What are you doing here?" Amos asked, surprised but not displeased.

"Don't we have a date?"

"Yeah, but I didn't expect you until later. Did you get off early today?"

"So to speak," she said. "I'm on vacation."

"What does that mean?"

"It's a permanent vacation."

"You *quit?*" he asked, astonished.

"I didn't get the chance. Marshall fired me before I could fling my resignation at him."

"He fired you?" he said, sitting down next to her. "Just like that? Why?"

"It had to do with the Belew murder, of course. What else? I guess you didn't hear that Craig Fannin won his motion for dismissal."

"I did, but it wasn't your fault. Why would he fire you for that? Did he can Meredith, too?"

"Nope. Just me."

"That's outrageous. Just because you lost a motion?"

"In fairness to Marshall, it wasn't just any motion. He had a lot riding on convicting Roland Jervis. Anyway, it was more the *way* I lost it that he had a beef with. I should have seen it coming; I knew that Marshall was nothing but a self-serving political hack. He'd fry his own granny if he thought it would get him reelected."

"That's not exactly headline news. But his reaction seems

a little extreme. He'll look like a jackass when the press gets hold of this.''

Laura shook her head. ''Maybe so. He was pretty mad, though. I don't think he was thinking about the consequences.''

''What did you do, anyway? He's been mad at you before, but he's never fired you.''

''Well,'' Laura said hesitantly, realizing that this was not going to be easy to tell Amos. ''I guess it is fair to say that losing to Fannin was the proximate cause. Marshall was pretty upset that Craig had gotten involved in the case in the first place.''

''It is annoying that he decided to stick his nose in. But it wasn't your fault.''

''Actually, it was.''

''How could it be?''

''Because I called Craig and asked him to look into the case against Jervis.''

Amos stood up so suddenly that the swing rocked violently. The cat skittered away, alarmed. ''You did *what?*'' he asked.

''I called him. Fannin, I mean. Avery Daniels was missing the forest for the trees, and I thought Roland Jervis was being railroaded to make life easier for Marshall and the mayor. And Avery was making it easy for them.''

''So you decided that you had to take matters into your own hands?''

''Yes. Look, I knew you'd be mad when I told you—''

''So you *were* going to tell me?''

''Eventually. Craig and I thought it was best—''

''Craig thought? That's great. Now you're taking advice from Craig Fannin.''

''Amos, it was a delicate situation. Craig's the best

defense lawyer in Atlanta. I knew if there was something screwy he'd find it."

"And what did he find that was so screwy?"

"The same things I had noticed—the same things I had been trying to get everybody else to pay attention to! The fingerprints, the sleazy eyewitnesses—and no one listened to me. If Avery had been doing a halfway decent job, I would have shrugged it off and said tough luck for Jervis. But Avery was wrapped up in some Supreme Court fantasy. Actually, you're right—I didn't need to call Craig Fannin. I didn't have to get the *best* lawyer in Atlanta involved; pretty much anyone with some courtroom experience and the ability to fog up a mirror would have done as well. But I'm glad I called Craig, and I'm not sorry that he blew my so-called case to hell."

"Your case? Excuse me, but there were some other people involved here. What about Alex Devereaux, and Carlton?"

"I tried, Amos. I really did. But Devereaux was determined to put this one to bed and drive on. And Carlton is still the junior partner—not to mention that, much as I like him, Carlton isn't as open-minded as a detective should be. He went into this thing with some prejudices against Lawrence Belew."

"Really? Then you'll be happy to know that both of them are under investigation by the Office of Professional Standards."

Laura gaped at him, disbelieving. "I never thought—"

"No, of course you didn't. You never thought that you might be taking a chance with the careers of a couple of pretty good cops. Because, let's face it, the cops are the bad guys in your book."

"That's not fair—and it's not true, either!" Laura exclaimed, standing up and once again driving the cat into hiding behind a planter. "Neither Craig nor I seriously thought that Devereaux had cooked up evidence. We thought he was sloppy, sure, but we didn't want him *investigated.*"

"Maybe you didn't, but your pal Fannin sure did. It'll help him when he files Jervis's civil suit. Which, of course, he will be doing."

"He may. Why shouldn't he? The bottom line, Amos, is that Jervis didn't do it. He didn't kill Lawrence Belew."

"What makes you so damn sure?"

"Just what I told you. The evidence points elsewhere."

Amos snorted. "The evidence. Don't you think Alex Devereaux knows more about evidence than you do?"

"Of course he does—and so do the guys at the crime lab. Both of them thought there was something wrong with the setup."

Amos waved a dismissive hand in the air. "What do they know? You don't make a case out of fingerprints and fibers. There's a whole lot more that goes into an investigation. I've been doing this for a while, and I'm glad that those guys are out there, looking through the microscopes and all that, but most crimes I've been involved in get solved by detectives' gut instincts. And luck."

"Okay, then, look at what the detectives had in this case. What about the eyewitnesses, then? They were lying. You can't deny that."

He shrugged. "So a couple of creeps make a grab for some of the reward money. Doesn't mean that Jervis is innocent."

"No, it doesn't. But how come they lied with such specificity? And where are they, then—why couldn't Craig find them?"

"What makes you so sure he didn't?"

"Okay, now you're being ridiculous," Laura said irritably. "What reason would Craig have for tampering with the witnesses? And, for your information, he hired *Kenny* to find them."

Amos shrugged. "There's one thing I know: I don't trust Craig Fannin as far as I can throw him."

"So he's the one who set all this up? You're accusing me of having an anticop mind-set. Well, if that's so, you're antilawyer."

"Why shouldn't I be? I get to see them at work all the time. Go anywhere, say anything for a dollar."

"Just like me, huh? Of course. That explains why I took a fifty percent cut in salary to go to work for the district attorney. I'm so glad we're having this discussion. It's nice to know what you think of me."

"Not of you; of your profession. You, unfortunately, I happen to love."

"Yes, that is unfortunate. And may I say you're doing a fine job of showing it? Amos, you're treating me like I'm the enemy. Don't forget that we're supposed to be on the same team. We're supposed to be working together to catch the bad guys."

"I haven't forgotten, but you did. You called in Fannin, and now Alex Devereaux's entire career is in jeopardy. Carlton will be okay. Like you said, he's the junior guy. I don't imagine you're going to be top of his list, though."

"That would be too bad. I like him, and I consider him a friend. But you—and Alex, and Carlton—have to realize that I didn't go into this to get cops investigated. I wanted the *crime* investigated."

"I'm sure that's what Devereaux thought he was doing," Amos answered.

"Maybe he did. But being a detective isn't like working

on an assembly line; there are no production quotas. If he had taken a little more time—''

"He would have seen it your way," Amos finished the sentence for her. "You haven't learned anything, Laura. You go into situations with your mind made up. You'll discard any fact that doesn't fit your version of events. And if you can't get everyone to see it your way, you'll do an end run."

"Playing a little bump and run with the bad guys is what it's all about. Damn it, if I'd played by the rules this time, whoever killed Lawrence Belew would have gone scot-free."

"How do you know he's not scot-free right now, as a result of your meddling?"

"Meddling? Excuse me, but I don't appreciate that. I could hardly have *meddled* in my own damn case."

"But you did just exactly that. You called in the biggest sleazebag in the Southeast. And—big surprise—he turns up a bunch of witnesses to contradict the witnesses the cops had found."

"Are you saying that Craig got a *preacher* to commit perjury? And a bunch of old ladies?"

"It's worth considering," Amos said.

"Please. Why would they lie?" she said, exasperated.

"Why wouldn't they have come forward earlier? See, when Alex Devereaux brings you a witness, you're immediately suspicious. But when Fannin shows up with one it's the word of God."

"And why would Craig risk his livelihood and his career by suborning perjury?"

"To win a civil settlement from the city, of course. All you did was give him the right ambulance to chase."

"Absurd. Craig doesn't have to go looking for business. He was genuinely disturbed by what I told him."

"Give me a break. Fannin's never been genuinely *anything* in his life. The guy's scum."

"And so am I, I guess. Just a scummy old lawyer. I'm surprised you've put up with me this long."

"I didn't have any choice. I fell in love with you."

"Poor old you. How you must have suffered! I guess I should thank you for overcoming the ancient animosity between our two clans—the lawyers and the cops."

"Stop it, Laura. I don't think we should continue this discussion until we cool down."

"I'm completely cool. And I hear very clearly what you're saying: that I should let Roland Jervis take one for the team, in the higher interest of making the Atlanta Police Department look good."

"Bullshit. That's not what I'm saying."

"That's what it sounds like you're saying," Laura said. The cat twined himself between her ankles, trying to convince her to get back to the serious business of entertaining him.

Amos shook his head. "As usual, you're hearing what you want to. You do that, you know. You filter out everything that contradicts your opinion."

"I do not. I wouldn't be a very good lawyer if I did."

"No, it's actually what makes you such a good lawyer. But I've told you before—so you don't need to get your panties in a bunch when I say it again—you would make a lousy cop."

Laura nodded. "I agree. I would be a crummy police officer—I can't just bag 'em and tag 'em and move on. This may sound silly, but I'm interested in getting to the truth."

"That does sound pretty silly for someone who just partnered up with Craig Fannin. He's about as interested in the truth as I am in German operas."

"What the hell do you know about Fannin? For your information, he thinks you're a pretty good guy. He doesn't see you as *his* enemy."

"I guess I should be flattered. Or maybe not—if Fannin likes me, I must not be doing my job very well."

"That's it. I've had it. I'm going home."

"That's probably a good idea. We should go to our corners and cool off. I'll call you in a day or two."

"Please don't bother," she said. "Good-bye, Mr. Cat." She turned her back so he couldn't see that she was fighting tears, and she didn't look back, even though she knew that he was standing on the porch watching as she went to her car, got in, and drove away.

Chapter 17

Saturday morning rolled around, but for Laura the day was indistinguishable from the previous three—unemployed—days. She got out of bed and ambled aimlessly through her morning routine. She made an attempt at breakfast, but it was a halfhearted one. Laura's reaction to any crisis was to go off her feed; she had survived the days since Marshall and Amos had both fired her subsisting on Diet Coke, pasta with prefabricated sauce, and cinnamon Altoids. It wasn't exactly nutritious, but her jeans fit better than they had in weeks and her breath was minty-fresh.

She was toying with the idea of driving home to Nashville, where she could rest in the bosom of her family. Her brother had just produced an heir, the first grandchild and Laura's first experiment in aunt-hood. Or she could drive up to Rabun County and take Emily Bailey up on her offer of a sympathetic ear. The second idea had a lot of appeal, considering that there was a long-legged, evil-tempered horse there that Laura loved to tangle with. Or she could continue to mope right here at home, wasting another beautiful late-spring day.

Before she could come to a decision, she heard the rumble of a car engine in her drive. Her heart leaped at the thought that it might be Amos come to storm the ramparts in his determination to get her back. A hopeful, surreptitious glance out the kitchen window revealed a sleek silver convertible as far from Amos's old Wagoneer as any vehicle could be. Before she had time to wonder whose it was, the front doorbell chimed.

Laura tiptoed silently to the door—she wanted to maintain the option of pretending to be out—and peered through the peephole. She saw portions of a casually attired Craig Fannin, standing on her front porch holding an envelope under one polo-shirted arm.

She opened the door. "Craig—what brings you here?"

"Figured you could use some company. Mind if I come in?"

"Of course not," she replied, standing aside. *"Mi casa,* et cetera. You've heard the news?"

"That you're a free agent? Of course. I was surprised that you didn't call me. Marshall's an idiot, of course. But he'll take you back."

"Don't bet on it. Things were said that cannot be unsaid."

"He'll be begging you to come back before next month. This is a cute place," he said, digressing, surveying her hallway and living room. "How long have you lived here?"

"A little more than a year. I bought it with the last of my ill-gotten gains from Pendergrast and Crawley, before I became a public servant."

"Prices have gone nuts in this neighborhood. You were lucky to get in when you did."

"I guess so. Have a seat. Can I get you a cup of coffee, or something?"

"No, thanks. I've got someone waiting outside in the car, so I won't linger. I wanted you to see something." He seated himself in an armchair, and Laura positioned herself at the end of the sofa closest to him. He handed her the manila envelope he had brought with him. "I thought you should see this." His normally bantering demeanor departed, leaving him strangely sober.

Laura opened the flap of the envelope and removed the contents, which consisted of a sheaf of papers. On top was a handwritten note that read, *"Craig: As you requested. As I told you, as I was not present at the postmortem examination, I am not able to say anything with absolute certainty. But I found some inconsistencies that I think would be worthwhile following up on. Call me if you want to discuss this."* The signature was illegible, in the hallowed tradition of the medical profession, but Laura knew that the note had been written by Craig's "guy" in the pathology department at Emory University.

Laura put the note aside and examined the papers, which consisted of the autopsy report she had already seen, marked with comments. The photos she had tried to avoid looking at were included as well, marked in numerous places with little sticky yellow arrows, numbered to correspond to the comments.

Craig took note of her frowning attempts to decipher the notes. "It's a lot of technical jargon, but I can sum it up for you. My man at Emory—Eric Hillman—says that the doctor who performed the autopsy is either incompetent or an outright liar."

"What makes him think that?"

"Inconsistencies. Big ones. What did the original report list as the cause of death?"

"Blunt force trauma to the head, I think."

"Right. What do you know about head injury?"

"Not a lot. I know that head trauma can cause bleeding in or around the brain. It's not always fatal, I know. But I didn't delve too deeply, because the facts of the autopsy weren't in dispute—heck, with Avery on the case, *nothing* was in dispute. I had some trouble communicating with Dr. Cooper, anyway."

"Let me give you a short primer on head injury. What kills you isn't the blow itself; it's the bleeding that results from it. That's hematoma. But there's hematoma, and then there's hematoma. Near as I can tell, they have about six kinds. What Lawrence Belew died from was—hand me that report so I can read the big words—a 'subscalpular hematoma, with subarachnoid and subdural hemorrhage.' In the degree he suffered it, that type of injury is almost universally fatal in a short time. According to Dr. Hillman there's no way he could have lived for any significant period of time with that kind of injury. The bleeding was too massive and too traumatic."

"That's consistent with what Cooper said, though."

"Hang on. I ain't done schoolin' you yet, missy. What Hillman saw that disturbed him were the *rest* of Belew's injuries. Bruises, fractures, abrasions . . . all consistent with a brutal beating, right?"

"Right," Laura agreed, cringing mentally at the remembrance of the photos. "He was beaten, literally, to a pulp."

"Twice," Craig said.

"What, *beaten* twice? But Cooper and Hillman both say

that he couldn't have survived for any length of time after he received the injuries.''

''Not after the fatal injury, no. But the first set of injuries, bad though they were, were survivable. And he did survive them—for more than twenty-four hours, near as Hillman can tell from the photos and reports. Maybe as long as forty-eight hours. Hillman believes that Dr. Cooper deliberately obfuscated the time of death.''

''That's absurd—Dr. Cooper wouldn't have *lied*. What advantage does he have in lying? His whole livelihood is at stake.''

''Which is why I allow for the possibility that he was simply incompetent. I'm looking into his credentials. Anyway, let me tell you what Hillman thinks about the sequencing of the injuries. There was a set of traumas inflicted on Lawrence Belew somewhere between forty-eight and twenty-four hours before he died. Then he met with the fatal blow, and died almost immediately. How does he know this? He can look at the photos and tell from the appearance of the bruises that Belew had been injured for some time. How long does it take a bruise to develop on your shin when you bang it?''

''I don't know. Maybe a few hours, or overnight?''

''That's about right. But bruises have sort of a life cycle—it's not possible to say exactly when someone was bruised, but they've made enough of a science of it that they can make a pretty good guess. Recent bruises are bluish black; older ones show yellow and green because of iron in the blood. These are recent bruises, but the important thing is that they're bruises at all. Belew had time, in other words, to bruise before he died. He had, in the jargon, *antemortem* contusions. There were also postmortem ocular changes that are consistent with his being alive much later than Cooper suggests. That means that the fluids in his eyes were still present. If he'd died right away, the fluids wouldn't have been there. And Hillman's guess, based on the degree of bruising, and the condition of the other injuries, the scrapes and cuts, is that Lawrence Belew was beaten to within an inch of his life in the time frame I just gave you.''

''Twenty-four to forty-eight hours before he actually died?''

''Yes.''

''Okay, say your man is right—let's look at the implications. We have approximately eighty hours in the life of Lawrence Belew unaccounted for, if you take the maximum parameters. He left his office Friday evening about seven; his body was discovered about midnight Tuesday morning.''

''That's seventy-seven hours, to be exact,'' Craig added. ''And Hillman says that he believes—although he won't swear to it—that the fatal blunt force trauma was inflicted about thirty-six hours before the body was found and photographed.''

''What does he base that on?'' Laura asked, putting aside the papers and photographs.

''Pathologist savvy, mostly. You know that fixing the time of death is really only possible when you can pin a victim's movements down to a fairly narrow time frame. But a good experienced pathologist can make a guess or two based on the condition of the body. Hillman's is that Belew was beaten—to use the time frame we know about— Friday night. He survived until sometime Sunday morning or afternoon, when a final blow to the head finished him off.''

''Why wouldn't he have gone to a hospital?'' Laura asked. Before Craig could answer, realization dawned. ''Sweet

Jesus, Craig—are you saying he was being held somewhere? That this was a kidnapping?''

"I'm saying it's possible. Belew had also suffered a subdural hematoma, probably in the first assault. That's a bleed between the membrane that covers the brain and the brain itself. It's serious, but survivable—although someone with a subdural hematoma might lose memory, or even be semiconscious."

"So he might have wandered around for part of the time he was missing?"

"It's possible, although it seems that someone would have seen him and helped him. And the condition of the car . . . someone did that deliberately . . . that gives some credence to the idea that he was being held somewhere against his will."

"If he was, if someone beat him, then held him prisoner . . . that's depraved. That's torture, pure and simple." Laura's hands were shaking and her heart was pounding.

"You're damn right it is. But it adds up, at least. We both wondered why the car had been cleaned from stem to stern. It never made sense that Roland Jervis cleaned the car. First, despite what may have been alleged about his employment history, he couldn't have done that thorough a job without training, and by that I mean of a more specialized variety than he would pick up at the car wash. Second, why was Belew missing such a long time, only to be found, right on cue, when the cops got an anonymous tip? The idea that Jervis had been in possession of the car for three days was never plausible, even if I *hadn't* found that he had a solid alibi for the time he was supposedly bragging on his brave deeds of piracy to Jermaine Clay and Albert Jackson."

"So what does it mean to you?"

Craig rose from the chair and wandered to the fireplace,

where he looked nonchalantly at Laura's family photos before answering. "I'm not entirely sure. What do you know about Alex Devereaux and Carlton Hemingway?"

"I know that Carlton would never be party to anything crooked. I know him pretty well. I also saw him the day he caught the case. He was investigating Belew's business—I don't think he would have gone through the motions if he were a party to a cover-up. Or worse." Fannin raised a skeptical eyebrow. "I also know that he's not that good an actor. He wears his heart on his sleeve. Forget it, Craig; Carlton wasn't involved."

"What about Devereaux?"

"I only met him through his involvement in this case. He and Carlton haven't been partnered for long. Carlton's old partner, Randy Travers, retired last year. I think Devereaux was transferred to homicide and assault from the auto theft unit. I had never dealt with him before this case."

"Auto theft, huh?" Craig said, hands in pockets. "Interesting."

"He strikes me as just a regular guy. He's got teenaged children. I know he has to moonlight a little to keep up with the bills," she added thoughtfully. "But if that's evidence of criminal proclivities, better round up the rest of the Atlanta Police Department. Cut to the chase, Craig: what are you thinking?"

"Look, you know that my reasons for getting involved in this case were not purely altruistic."

"You want to sue the city on Jervis's behalf, right?"

"It had crossed my mind."

"That's what Amos said," Laura remarked ruefully.

"Kowalski? I knew he was smart. But it can't come as a shock to you, Laura, that I don't just get on white horses and ride to the defense of the indigent without some self-interest in the mix.''

"No, I'm not surprised. And I have no problem with it. If there's a suit to be filed, I say, file away. This was horrible, sloppy police work, and I don't think it should go unpunished.''

Craig nodded his affirmation. "And it won't. But the larger issue for me now is figuring out if sloppy police work is all we're dealing with.''

"You mean, was there a cover-up?'' Laura asked.

"Correct. And, further, were the police party to it?''

"No—not Carlton, anyway. And I may not know Devereaux well, but I find it hard to believe that he would participate in a murder. Or a cover-up of one. Why would he?''

"Why, indeed?'' Craig mused. "That's the crux of my dilemma. I know there's a case for false arrest. That's a chip shot. I'm wondering, though, if there isn't a larger case lurking behind this one.''

"Such as . . . ?''

"For one thing, a charge of attempted murder. If person or persons unknown deliberately framed Jervis, knowing that he could be sent to death row, I'd call that attempted murder, wouldn't you?''

"Doesn't matter what I'd call it. You'd have to convince a jury.''

"I think I could, with some work,'' Craig said offhandedly.

Laura shook her head. "A *lot* of work. All you've got to go on are the inconsistencies in the police case, plus the opinion of your pathologist. And that's just one expert disagreeing with another—and your expert didn't even see the body. If I were arguing against you, I would crush you on that alone.''

"Exactly, which is why I'm here . . ." Craig began. As he spoke, a horn sounded. Craig was positioned so that he could see out the window. "My friend is getting impatient; I'd better hurry up and get to the point. Look, Laura, I'd like you to come on board with me for this case. You know I fly solo, so I'm not offering you a permanent spot. But I'm very busy these days, and I can't do justice—pun entirely intended—to the Jervis matter on my own. I was wishing that a talented and experienced lawyer was available to help me, and then, like the answer to a prayer, Marshall very foolishly cans you. How about it?"

"I'm not sure what to say," Laura answered, surprised although she perhaps should not have been. "It's been a while since I handled a civil matter. . . ."

"You've handled them as recently as I have."

"How would our arrangement work?"

"I live by a simple rule: you eat what you kill. You take the Jervis case, and I'll give you total access to my offices and staff—paralegals, investigators, paper clips, whatever you need. You get to keep whatever fee you want out of the settlement you win. I get ten percent plus expenses. I'll bankroll a first-class investigation."

"What if I don't win? Will I owe you expenses?"

"I wouldn't be making this proposition if I didn't think you would win. But, to answer your question, no. I'll take one hundred percent of the risk. Are you in?"

Laura hesitated. "I don't know. It's not . . . do you think there's an ethical issue?"

"Do you? The only ethical issue I could imagine would be your revealing something you learned in the district attorney's office and were required to keep in confidence. But the last time I looked at the principles of discovery, anything that the state has is public property. If Marshall and Meredith are still holding on to some pertinent information, I'll go after them for misconduct."

"Of course they aren't. And I guess you're right. Still, it's very sudden. I think I need some time."

"Worried about what Kowalski will say?"

"No!" Laura said, more vehemently than she intended. "I mean, he has no say in what I do."

"Uh-oh. Trouble?"

"He was not happy that I had involved you. He's a police officer, after all," she said carefully, not entirely willing to share her private life with Craig.

"Cops," Craig said. "Gotta love 'em. I married one, you know."

"Really? You?" Laura was now genuinely surprised. She knew that Craig had a reputation for marrying early and often, and there was that old story about one of his wives being a witness in a trial—there had been trouble over that. This must have been the one.

Craig sighed nostalgically. "Yep. Mrs. Fannin number two. She was—is still—a Fulton County Sheriff's Deputy. And did she ever look hot in the uniform. Sorry," he said, catching Laura's glare. "But we came to a parting of the ways. Lawyers and cops are a classic case of opposites attracting, you know. Know why we like them?"

Laura shook her head. She knew why she liked Amos, of course, but she didn't think that Craig was talking about big shoulders, green eyes, skill with mortar and trowel, or any of the other things that made Amos wonderful.

Craig continued his soliloquy. "Police officers have the moral authority that we lack. I'm not saying we're immoral," he added. "It's just that we're prone to question the received wisdom, whereas they accept it whole. How else could they enforce some of these boneheaded laws? They're moral authoritarians. They're kindergarten teachers for adults; they can always tell you what's right or wrong.''

Laura had to admit that he, at least in part, was right. There had been a time when she was grateful to turn over all her decisions to Amos because he was so *sure* about everything. Lately, though, she been finding that same quality more of a problem. Maybe they had been moving toward this point for a long time. Maybe they had used up whatever it was they had had in the beginning that was so good.

But if that was true, why did Laura feel as if she had been cored like a pineapple when she walked away from him the other day?

Craig glanced at his watch. ''I better get going, or Miss Gilmer County of 1989 is going to slash my tires.''

''A beauty queen?'' Laura asked with an arched eyebrow.

''Yeah, I just can't move past the clichés,'' he sighed. ''Maybe that's why she's about to become the fourth Mrs. Fannin.''

''The triumph of hope over experience?'' Laura asked wryly.

''No, just better at drafting prenups than I used to be. Think about my offer. I can't leave it open indefinitely.''

''I know. I'll let you know soon. Monday.''

''Good. And don't worry about Kowalski. He'll come around.''

''I'm not so sure, but thanks for the good thought.''

Laura closed the door behind Craig and stood in thought for a few minutes. Then she walked purposefully to the kitchen and picked up the phone, and dialed. ''Emily? It's Laura,'' she said to the answering machine. ''I'm taking you up on your offer. I'll be there by three. And I'll stop in Clayton and pick up some barbeque. I need your wise counsel, and some spareribs.''

Chapter 18

Emily's farm was cupped in one of the many small valleys in the north Georgia hills. The house was built on a wooded hillside overlooking a pasture, a paddock, a dirt-floored riding ring, and a barn. Emily grew beans, squash, tomatoes, and cantaloupes, but her real love was the exotic hens that she housed in a chicken house at the far end of the pasture. The small house featured two wire-enclosed pens on either side, where the birds could scratch and do whatever it was they did. Emily also housed them in movable pens that she could set down anywhere in the pasture to let the fowl feed on bugs and seeds. It was a good place, for chickens, horses, and people.

When Laura arrived, a leaky paper bag of intoxicatingly scented barbeque on the backseat, Emily and one of her hired hands—a friendly Mexican named Angel who spoke almost no English—were replacing a section of the wiring

on the coop, much to the consternation of the hens. She
called out to them from the front porch of the house. Emily
shouted back, "I would come hug you, but I'm covered in
chicken poop."

"That's okay!" Laura said. "I can wait!"

Laura took her things into the house and joined them.
"Can I help?" she asked, disingenuously. Emily knew that
Laura was not exactly *afraid* of the chickens, but it was fair
to say that, with all their muttering and fluttering and their
unpredictable way of launching themselves three feet into
the air if anything startled them, they made Laura nervous.
Some of them, especially the ones called Buff-laced Polish,
were downright creepy, with weird quiffs of feathers sprouting from their tiny heads. Laura liked the Plymouth Rocks,
though, especially the roosters, whose combination of black
and white feathers with red comb was the image, in her
opinion, of what a chicken should look like.

Emily did a bustling business in these creatures, breeding
them and shipping them all over the country. She occasionally showed some of them, too, although she had admitted
to Laura that, as a sport, chicken-showing didn't really blow
her skirt up. Overall, she preferred shooting at things. Emily
was one of a vanishing breed of southern women who were
equally comfortable in the country and the city, directing
boards and chatting at the club, or hunting quail and driving
tractors. There was nothing she couldn't do, and do well,
but she was relaxed, funny, and an overall good companion.

"We're fine here, but you can muck out some stalls in
the barn," Emily answered Laura's insincere offer. "And
I'd appreciate it if you could give Slim a good workout. I
haven't been able to ride all week."

Laura didn't need asking twice; she had made the drive
in her paddock shoes, so she wouldn't have to waste time

changing. She walked the rest of the way around the paddock, to Emily's three horses—Slim, the chestnut gelding, a gray Arabian mare, and an old black warm-blood gelding that had won many ribbons for Emily in her competing days. Slim was Laura's favorite of the three; at sixteen hands he was just the right size for her tall frame, and he had a demonic streak that made him a challenge to ride.

She stopped for a moment to watch the horses cropping grass, then continued to the barn where three stalls awaited her. Shoveling wet sawdust was the best upper-body workout Laura knew anything about, and it guaranteed that she would sleep soundly and gratefully—something she had been having trouble doing the past few days.

The barn, like the Plymouth Rock rooster, looked exactly as it should: dark red and ship-roofed. The farm—a refuge from the sweltering heat of summer in Atlanta—had been in the Bailey family for a little more than a century. The house dated from the late nineteenth century, but the barn was newer, built in 1920 from a prefabricated kit. Emily had pictures of her grandfather and some local men building it. Eighty years of sweet-smelling straw and leather had mellowed the structure to perfection. In the soft afternoon light, dust motes drifted sparkling in the air. Only three of the twelve stalls were currently used to house horses; others held Emily's workhorse New Holland tractor, dusty lockers of horse tack, and the combined detritus of ten decades of human and animal habitation. A ladder led upstairs to the hayloft, where an occasional fugitive chicken would roost.

She stood for a long minute and drank in the silence that was interrupted only by the occasional flap of bird wings and a scratching that may have been mice in the hayloft. Then she went to work with shovel and wheelbarrow, dumping load after load of muck on the compost heap. Finally, she was able to spread new shavings in the clean stalls and get her saddle and Slim's bridle from the tack room.

She remembered that she needed to add a new hole to her stirrup leathers; they had stretched and were too long for her liking. She opened the small cabinet where Emily kept tools, assuming that there would be a leather punch or an awl that would serve her purpose. What she saw made her take a step backward.

There was a *gun* in the unlocked cabinet, lying among the tools and cans of saddle soap. Laura looked at it for a minute, not sure what to make of it, before she moved in for a closer examination. It wasn't a toy, as she had hoped. And the damn thing looked as if it was loaded. She couldn't fathom why Emily—who was a gun-safety missionary—would leave a weapon in such an exposed place. Granted, the tack room was normally locked, but the key was hidden, not very cleverly, under the seat of a broken-down tractor in one of the empty box stalls.

Laura picked up the gun. It was a little one, as guns went; she recognized it, with some pride, as a Smith and Wesson .38-caliber Chiefs Special, a five-shot revolver, just like one Amos had taught her to shoot, or tried to teach her to shoot. She checked the magazine; it was loaded, with funny-looking cartridges with blue plastic tips that held tiny shot in place of bullets. Laura had never seen anything like them. She guessed that they might be some target-shooting cartridges Emily used; she would have to ask.

Laura swung the magazine back into place, but she didn't return the gun to the cabinet right away. Seeing it stirred up turbulent emotions that she had come here to put to rest, at least temporarily. She didn't like guns; she didn't like the shotguns her father and brothers had used for hunting, and she didn't like the nasty-looking nine-millimeter pistol Amos carried for his job. But the day last fall when she and Amos had been visiting Emily, and Amos had convinced her to try shooting, was a good memory.

The sun had been warm, and Laura had liked having Amos as a teacher, standing behind her with his arms around her, putting hers into the proper position, and praising her when she shot anywhere in the vicinity of the target. She had performed respectably, she thought, even while recognizing that his praise had been a little exaggerated, the same way hers had been when he managed to sit straight in a saddle for a whole hour. There had been so much accommodation between them. Was it all just an effort to avoid acknowledging what Craig Fannin had said this morning—that cops and lawyers would always be attracted to each other, but that they could never bridge the gulf between their outlooks?

Laura looked down at the gun again. No, Craig was a cynic, and he was wrong. She didn't mind that Amos was a cop. She minded what being a cop *meant,* and there was a difference in the two things. She didn't like the danger his job placed him in, and she didn't like the nightmarish things that he saw and knew as part of his job. She had seen him troubled by his worst cases, and she hadn't forgotten how she felt when that idiot with the golf club attacked him. She felt foolish even admitting it to herself, but she felt protective of him—all six feet, two inches of him.

This, she thought, *is going nowhere.* She put the gun back in the cabinet and fished out the leather punch. When she had adjusted her stirrups, she hoisted her saddle onto a rail and slipped the stirrups into place. Then she hung a bridle on a peg, and headed outside with a lead rope.

Slim was on the far side of the paddock, but Laura knew that he was a sucker for a treat. She had brought carrots for all the horses, but Slim, the greediest, was first to reach her. She snapped the rope's shackle onto his halter, and hitched the end of the rope to the fence. Then she doled out the carrots. When they were gone, she untied Slim and led him back into the barn, where she snapped his halter to two restraining lines while she brushed and saddled him and slipped the bridle over his tossing head. She led him outside to the mounting block and climbed onto his broad back.

Two hours later, as the sun was setting, Laura cooled Slim down with a long walk around the perimeter of the pasture and the paddock, then took him inside for a bath and a treat of alfalfa. She rounded up the other two horses as well, and placed them in their clean stalls with plenty of water and food.

By the time she reached the house, it was almost dark and she was happily exhausted. She hadn't thought about Amos, or Marshall Oliver, for hours. Emily was already inside, showering. Laura went to "her" bedroom—she came so often that Emily treated her less like a guest than a family member—and shucked out of her sweaty T-shirt and jodhpurs and headed for the guest bath.

Clean, but fighting drowsiness, she slicked a comb through her wet hair and joined Emily in the kitchen. Emily was heating the barbeque and mixing a healthy gin and tonic. Laura passed on the booze, but accepted a beer. "Hey," she said, "while I remember it, what the heck is a loaded gun doing in the tack room?"

"Oh, that's Angel's idea. We've had some problems with rats, and he's terrified of snakes. So I took one of my old guns and loaded it with shot shells. He can pot away at the varmints without doing too much harm."

"Those blue-tipped things are shot shells?"

"Yes, they're just thirty-eight cartridges loaded with number-nine shot instead of bullets."

"So they're pretty harmless?"

"I didn't say that. A face full of snake shot wouldn't do you any good. But I don't anticipate Angel getting into a shoot-out with anyone. Between you and me, I think he's more afraid of the gun than he is of the snakes. Anyway, we keep it locked up in the tack room."

"Which was wide open today," Laura pointed out.

"But it's not usually. And I'll speak to Angel and tell him that if he wants to keep the gun in the barn he has to be more careful. Ready to eat?"

They had dinner on the screened porch, talking about nothing important. It was only after the dishes were in the dishwasher, and they were back on the porch with ice-cream sandwiches, that Emily brought up the topic of Laura's difficult week.

"So, tell me more about the situation," she said with typical bluntness.

"There's not a lot more to say. I have managed, once again, to dismantle my life with astounding speed and completeness."

"You're exaggerating."

"Let's see: no job, no boyfriend . . . sounds like a train wreck to me."

"I'm not convinced that you don't have a boyfriend. You're just on hiatus until this thing blows over."

Laura threw her hands up in a helpless gesture. "How's it going to blow *anywhere?* Time isn't going to change the fact that I *did* call Craig, which both Amos and Marshall see as a betrayal. I couldn't care less what Marshall thinks, but I care quite a bit about Amos's opinion."

"What if it turns out you were right to call Fannin? What if there is something fishy going on in the police department?"

"I doubt that'll send Amos rushing back to me. There's this thing between us about being a cop and a lawyer. Maybe I should say 'cop *versus* lawyer,' because near as I can tell that's how he sees it."

"I don't think that's what it is."

"It's what Fannin thinks," Laura said. She told Emily about Craig and the sheriff's deputy he had married.

Emily laughed, but she shook her head. "I can't believe you're taking *his* advice on romance. No, what I've always seen about you and Amos is a certain tension that's more related to your backgrounds than it is to any philosophical differences."

"Such as?"

"You're from a privileged, southern family, Laura, and he's not. He's a Polish cop from Chicago. He's an outsider— a wonderful one, but I don't think you can appreciate how these differences matter to a man like Amos."

Slightly irritated, Laura wiped her ice-cream-sticky hands with a paper napkin. "Look who's talking. You say *I'm* privileged? You could buy and sell my whole family, Emily."

"Possibly, but I'm speaking from my own experience here, sugar. I haven't always been the bitter old woman you see before you." Laura laughed. Emily was barely fifty.

Emily continued. "That's right; mock me, but I once had a tender young heart, and I was quite susceptible to men who were . . ." She hesitated, groping for a word.

"Proletarian?" Laura suggested.

"No, you snob. What I liked was men who weren't like the ones I grew up with—because I *knew* I didn't care for those. They were soft around the edges. I liked men who knew how to take care of themselves, because I figured they could take care of me. What I didn't bank on was how sensitive they would be to my family's money. It scared a lot of them off.''

"I don't think Amos comes from such a humble background. He has a college degree, you know.''

"I know. It's just a feeling I've gotten. And when you tell me that he's accused you of being anticop, I have to believe that there's more to it. Because you're not anticop; you just may be opposed to some of the things cops stand for.''

"Not true. But I hate it, Em, that he's in a job where any fool can come after him, and try to hurt him.'' She told her about the golf-club man. "I think that's maybe where all this got started. It got me thinking, I know. It brought out something in me.''

"I can understand that. But is it really because he's a cop? My brother wasn't, and you saw him die, Laura. Is it that you're afraid of—that Amos will die, too?''

"I don't know. I really don't,'' Laura answered quietly.

They lapsed into an uncomfortable silence for a few minutes, which Emily broke with an abrupt question. "Do you love him?''

"Amos? Absolutely.'' It occurred to Laura that Emily might have her own reasons for asking. "I loved your brother, too.''

"You worshipped Tom,'' Emily amended. "We all did. I can't help but think he might still be here if we hadn't.''

"What do you mean by that?''

"He was the golden boy. My parents never thought they'd have another child. He could do no wrong—in their eyes, or mine. But he had to live up to being a miracle every day of his life.'' She sighed, and shook her head. ''If only we'd allowed him some honest failures . . .''

''Don't say that. Tom made his own choices. Some of them just happened to be bad ones. He was a good person. And a great lawyer,'' Laura added. ''I learned a lot from him.''

''And you can learn a lot from Amos. You're lucky, Laura. You're young enough to have a chance at happiness.''

Laura was surprised at the implications of Emily's words. ''But, Emily, you're happy—look at what you have! There are about a million people in Atlanta who'd kill for this setup.''

Emily laughed ruefully. ''Yep. Me and my chickens. We do all right. But you can do better, Laura. You just have to work at it. You and Amos can make it work, I know. Just give him some time; he'll come around. Or you will.''

''Do you think it would upset him if I went to work with Craig on this case?''

''You're not seriously considering doing that, are you?''

''I am. Craig has told me some things that make me want to stay involved.''

Emily shook her head. ''You're playing with fire, Laura. Because, as I see it, there are two things that can come out of this: either you'll be right, or you'll be wrong. If you're right, the cops are the bad guys—and if what you tell me is true, that won't sit well with Amos. If you're wrong, he'll have some justification for saying you're prejudiced against the police.''

Laura disagreed with her friend, and she said so. ''I think you're misjudging Amos. If there's something amiss in the way the detectives investigated this case, and it comes out, Amos will be the first to say they should be punished.''

"You're going to take Fannin up on his offer, aren't you?" Emily said, peering at Laura in the dim light.

"Yes. I am," Laura said.

Emily looked up at the pale blue porch ceiling and sighed. "I'll tell you what you and Kowalski *do* have in common: you're both stubborn, and you both play for keeps."

Chapter 19

"Come on down," Craig Fannin said, obviously delighted to get Laura's phone call Monday morning. "I can put you right to work."

"Where exactly are your offices, Craig? I know they're on Maple Drive, but I can't place the number."

"We're between Peachtree and East Paces Ferry. You can walk it, if you're so inclined."

"I am. I've just come back from the mountains, so I'm in desperate need of a shower and clean clothes, but I can be there by lunchtime."

"Take your time. I'll get an office and a phone set up for you."

Two hours later, Laura was standing outside a modest two-story brick office building. She'd driven this block countless times, but the presence of three nearly identical buildings had somehow escaped her notice. This one had a parking

lot beneath it, which Laura took note of. The half-mile walk
had been pleasant today, but she'd be glad of a parking spot
on a rainy day.

Craig's one-man firm occupied the entire building. Laura
entered the modestly furnished waiting room and registered
surprise. She had expected Fannin's digs to resemble a Bond
villain's lair—leather and chrome, with round sofas and
miniskirted female minions. Instead, a well-dressed middle-
aged black lady greeted her by name. "Miss Chastain? Welcome. I'm Arlene Turner, Craig's office manager. He wants
you to join him in a meeting right away."

Laura shook Arlene's hand and followed her into Craig's
private office. The furnishings were a bit more luxurious than
those in the waiting room, but still reassuringly conservative.
"Laura!" Craig exclaimed, beaming. "You're just in time.
You remember Roland, don't you?" Laura did, of course,
recall Roland Jervis, although without prompting she might
not have recognized this happy, smiling version of him.
"And this is Roland's grandmother, Mrs. Allen, and his
aunt, Mrs. Walker. . . ."

Laura smiled and greeted the family group, a little puzzled
as to why they were gathered here in what appeared to her
to be Sunday garb.

"You're in time for the press conference," Craig said.
"Actually, it's not so much a conference as a little party
for some of our ink-stained friends. They'll be here in a few
minutes."

"Great. Terrific," Laura said, forcing a smile. "Craig,
can I see you for a minute?"

"Sure. Excuse us, folks. I'll show you to your office. I
had to put you upstairs, but it's a corner office. Arlene's
getting the phone hooked up."

They mounted the stairs; Craig threw open a door to a

spacious office decorated in the same British-men's-club idiom as Craig's. "What's on your mind?"

"A press conference, Craig? To announce what?"

"That we're representing Jervis in his civil suit against the city."

"Does there always have to be a press conference?" Laura sighed. "Can't we do a little quiet legwork before we call in the hounds?"

"Come on, Laura. You know half the battle's fought outside the courtroom. You've played the game before—and well, might I add."

"Thanks, I guess," she replied. "I just wish I had a better grasp of what happened."

Craig shrugged off her concerns. "We know enough to file a suit. The Atlanta Police Department failed miserably in its duty to investigate a crime. Roland Jervis was a victim of sloppy police work."

"Is that what you're going to say today?"

"That's all. I'm not ready to start whispering about a conspiracy, if that's what's got you worried."

"It is. Just promise you won't let it get beyond that."

"Of course not. Not until I have a good reason to, anyway."

"So who's coming to this shindig?" Laura asked as they descended the stairs.

"The usual suspects—Bob Harper from the morning paper, and Jan Butsch from the Buckhead weekly. Plus someone I don't know from the evening paper, and that guy from *Terminus* magazine who wrote about the last time you and I faced off in a courtroom, emphasizing the David versus Goliath nature of your victory over me. He wants to interview you."

"I don't know if I'm up for that."

"I made no promises," Craig reassured her. "Just meet him, and if you're comfortable, you can give him the interview. If you're not, he can pound sand. They all can, in fact. Are you ready? Arlene's got them herded into the conference room, eating cheese straws."

"Ready as I'll ever be," Laura sighed.

"I'll get the Jervises," Craig said.

If Craig was right, and this was all part of a great game, Laura wasn't sure who won this round. The ladies and gentlemen of the press, despite the excellence of the cheese straws, seemed to regard Craig with some skepticism, probably based on bitter experience. Bob Harper, the familiar crime writer from the morning paper, seemed downright amused by the proceedings. But they all played their roles, down to Roland and his loving family, and the half-hour conference passed without a major breakdown in either side's facade. Craig remained the concerned citizen, crusading for justice; the press bent over their notebooks with suitably furrowed brows. No one laughed out loud, anyway.

When the throngs had departed, Laura followed Craig back into his office. "Now that we've run down the curtain on that little bit of theater, let's get down to business," she said. "We've got a long way to go."

"I could not agree with you more," he said. "And I'm turning one hundred percent of the work over to you. I've got a new criminal defense that's going to be taking up a lot of my time."

"What's that?"

"One of those federal indictments that's coming out of the FBI investigation of the city's contracting procedures."

"Which crook is yours?"

"My completely innocent client is *alleged* to have bribed certain officials to consider his firm's qualifications for a recycling contract. Which is, of course, nonsense—a citizen is, after all, entitled to make a political contribution, is he not?"

"Of course. I'm sure there's no evidence that any particular consideration was given to him in exchange," Laura said ironically.

"Naturally. The fact that he won the contract is beside the point," Craig said with a straight face. "But it doesn't help that the guy who accepted the check shortly thereafter bought a new BMW. I take that back—it might help *my* client. It would be a shame to have a campaign contribution given in good faith diverted by the campaign treasurer, wouldn't it?"

Laura could see that Craig's mental wheels were turning on this idea, so she hastened to bring his attention back to Jervis. "I see my first priority as supplying the prima facie evidence that the police did inadequate investigation of their case. To do that, I'm going to need to talk to all three of the supposed eyewitnesses. And to do that, I'm going to need to find them. I thought I'd rehire Ken Newton to run them down, if it's okay with you."

Craig waved a hand in the air. "You have carte blanche, as long as you think the expense is productive. I'm relying on you not to break the bank, but I think I can trust you to be prudent."

"Of course." She rose to her feet. "I'll call Ken and get him started. I'll also want to get affidavits from the crime lab technicians. I think that's pretty much the case, don't you? Unless, of course, we turn up some evidence of malfeasance."

"Put it this way," Craig said. "I think we can get a nice quick settlement on the false arrest complaint. If we can show there's a conspiracy, the sky's the limit."

"Speaking as a conflicted city taxpayer, I'd like to think that's an exaggeration," Laura said. "I hate to think I'm taking money from the city coffers that could be used to fill the giant gaping pothole on my street."

"If we left the money in their hands they'd just spend it on golf outings and trips to the Bahamas," Craig said with a laugh. "Don't worry about any of your tax money making it to classrooms and social service agencies."

"It must be nice to be a cynic," Laura said.

"I'm never surprised, anyway," he said with a wink.

Laura returned upstairs to her office, where the phone and the computer were fully functional, leaving her to wonder if Craig had ever been in doubt about her acceptance of his offer. She dialed up Kenny's number right away.

"Hey, boss," he said. "Where are you calling from? I don't recognize the number on the caller ID."

"I'm in my new office," she said. "In Buckhead."

"You move fast. Who hired you?"

"Take a guess," she said.

"Not Fannin! Don't that beat all. What does Amos think?"

"He doesn't know. Not yet, anyway. Have you talked to him?"

"Yesterday."

"He didn't tell you that we've split up?" Laura said, not really surprised.

"No! That idiot. What'd he do?"

"Nothing. It's my fault." She outlined the grounds for the quarrel. "He thinks I'm too inclined to mistrust cops. But that's not the problem. I don't suspect them all of being murderers—I just think there was some sloppy police work done in the Belew case. That's where you come in. I want to hire you again. Are you free?"

"I can be. What's your angle?"

"I want to talk to the eyewitnesses. I can give you names and addresses. They're all lying through their teeth—that much I'm sure of. I want to know why. What could possibly induce someone to lie and say they heard Jervis claim to have murdered Belew?"

"You'd be surprised at how little it would take," Kenny said. "I'm betting that the two of 'em cleared less than five Benjamins on the transaction."

"Make that three of them—I want the creep who claimed Jervis worked at the car wash, too. He's the one I know for sure was approached by someone." She described the mysterious white cop to Kenny. "That's where I do have a little bit of a bad conscience," she admitted. "I know that there's some white guy out there who's involved in this, but Alex Devereaux and Carlton Hemingway are under investigation now. I wouldn't mind clearing them."

"One thing at a time, sugar. If they're not involved, it'll come out. You and Fannin aren't out to solve the murder, are you?"

"No, that's up to the cops. We just need to show that Jervis was wrongly accused based on a faulty investigation. I think Craig has some hope of showing that there might have been a police conspiracy, but I think that would be hard to prove. I think there's more going on than meets the eye, of course, but I can't convince myself that it's the doing of a cabal of corrupt cops."

"It is kind of hard to imagine. But if it's out there, you and I will find out. I'll get started right away," he said. "Give me those names and addresses."

Laura did, and hung up. As she did, she noticed Arlene standing discreetly in the doorway, so quiet that she hadn't noticed her. "Hi, Arlene. What's up?"

"There are two ladies downstairs to see you, Miss Chastain."

"Call me Laura, please. Did they give their names?"

"No. But one of them is Lawrence Belew's mother. I recognized her from the newspapers."

Laura stood up and put her jacket back on. "Helen Belew? What's she doing here—and how did she know I was here?"

"I couldn't say," Arlene answered. "Would you like Craig to come with you?"

"I don't think that will be necessary," Laura said as they descended the stairs. "I think he's busy."

Arlene opened the door to the conference room and stood by silently while Laura went in. Helen Belew was standing on the far side of the conference table, and her daughter, Diana Arnold, was seated in a chair, head slumped. "Hello," Laura said. "What can I do for you?"

"I think you've already done *plenty,*" Mrs. Belew replied. "You've not only set free the man who murdered my son; now you're going to help get him a lot of money so he can actually go out and *buy* a Lexus instead of murdering someone else's son to get one. Thank you. You've done us all a great service." Her tone, heavy with sarcasm, barely hid her rage.

"Mrs. Belew, I don't know where you got your information, or how you knew to find me here, but you're wrong," Laura said flatly. "Roland Jervis didn't kill your son. I don't think sending the wrong man to death row would be justice for your son."

"Don't patronize me, you arrogant bitch. It's just fine with you that my son's murderer will go unpunished. Roland Jervis did you people a favor by getting rid of one uppity black boy who didn't learn his place. You'd rather have a million Jervises than one Lawrence Belew, a proud black man who could buy and sell you. No, you'd rather defend the almighty civil rights of this ni—''

"Mother!" Diana Arnold exclaimed.

Mrs. Belew ignored her daughter. "You'd rather let that thug go, because you know he'll never rise up to challenge you like my son would. To think that I *fought,* that I marched in the streets for people like him—the scum of the earth— so that they could kill my family!"

"Mother, please," Diana said, in tears and shaking. "Please, let's go. It's not her fault."

"It's okay, Mrs. Arnold," Laura said, although she was more than a little shaken herself. "I understand why your family is taking this hard—"

"Taking it hard?" Mrs. Belew shouted. "Do you not understand that this has *destroyed* my family? Look at my daughter—look at her! I never should have let either one of them come to this city. My family left the South sixty years ago, and we should have stayed away. It's no different than it was when my grandfather left Alabama—only now the lynch mobs are more subtle. They use lawyers and juries instead of rope."

The door opened, and Arlene and Craig entered. "Is there a problem?" Craig asked quietly.

"Are you this Craig Fannin?" Helen Belew asked. Craig nodded, and she continued. "I'm glad to see you, Mr. Fannin. I'm glad to confront the man who's murdering my son. Roland Jervis . . ." She spat the name as if it were poison on her tongue. "Roland Jervis only *killed* my son. It's you people who're murdering him—murdering him and burying him under the courthouse!"

"I understand that you're upset, Mrs. Belew," Craig said coolly, "but you're wrong. Roland Jervis didn't kill your son. He stole his car, but he didn't kill him. Laura and I believe that someone very powerful had something to do with your son's death. We can't do anything about that but push the police and the public to find the real killer. That's why we're representing Jervis. The truth won't come out without pressure.''

"You *bastard!*" Mrs. Belew exclaimed. "How dare you stand there and lie to me? You no more care who killed my son . . . you and this mercenary you've hired. All you two care about is your payday. Don't you dare talk to me about some greater good to come from this—the only good that will come from this is that Diana will finally get some sense and leave this city. I told you all along," she said, turning to her trembling daughter, "I told you and Lawrence both not to come here! Your father and I knew how the game was played here—nothing has ever mattered in Atlanta but money. The white folks don't care if they have a black mayor, or black people running the schools—that's not where the real power is. The real power is downtown in those towers where they keep the money, and you better believe no black person's going to get a cut of it. If one comes close, he has to be dealt with. That's why my son is dead, and that's why you two are out to get Roland Jervis his reward money.''

She had a point, Laura had to admit, even if her rhetoric exceeded the rational. Power in Atlanta was strictly measured by bank accounts. That a few black businessmen and politicians had succeeded hadn't changed the basic architecture of the city's economy, which was still dominated by a handful of white-owned corporations. Black progress, at least until very recently, had been more symbolic than real. But she was wrong, too, in saying that *no* power rested in the hands of the minorities. *Look at Marshall,* Laura thought. *He's no Uncle Tom, and he's proved it over and over again.*

"I'm sorry you feel the way you do, Mrs. Belew," Laura said, her courage and confidence restored. "You're wrong, and that's all I can say. I set out with every intention of putting Roland Jervis away for killing your son. From the start, I felt like I owed your son something, and *I still do*. But everywhere I turned I found things that didn't add up. I saw things that made me believe that someone far more clever and powerful than Roland Jervis had something to do with Lawrence's death. You're right about Jervis: he is just a punk, and he doesn't deserve any kind of reward. But neither does he deserve to die. And you're wrong about the money; I don't care about money. If I cared about money I certainly wouldn't have quit a job that was paying me two hundred thousand dollars a year to go work for the district attorney at seventy-five thousand! And I wouldn't be working with Craig on a long-shot lawsuit that may net me a lousy one-time paycheck. I wanted to stay involved in this case, and this is the only way I knew how. If you knew what we knew . . . tell her, Craig, about Dr. Hillman's report."

Craig started to outline the gist of the pathologist's findings, but Mrs. Belew, her fury unabated, interrupted him. "I've heard enough of your lies and self-justifications. Come on, Diana, let's leave. You two will roast in hell for what you've done."

She swept from the room, her shaken daughter trailing behind. As Diana left, she directed a look of contrition at Laura. "I'm sorry," she whispered. "He was her only son." And with that single poignant remark, they were gone.

Craig and Laura stood in silent shock for a moment after the women left. It was Arlene, who had been standing unnoticed in the corner, who spoke first. "She had no right to say those things," she said, her normally even tone disrupted by emotion. "She doesn't know the first thing about Atlanta, or Craig Fannin. I know her type; she and her people have made it, and screw the rest of us."

Laura was taken aback at Arlene's choice of words and at the bitterness of her tone, which grew more pronounced as the diatribe continued. "In fact," Arlene added, "the worse off the rest of us are the better it is for them. Don't look at me that way, Craig. You know exactly what I mean. First the white people had us all down, and when it looked like that wasn't going to keep working, they let a few of us rise up. They didn't much care who, so long as it wasn't too many of us. And it didn't take the Helen Belews long to realize that the pie wasn't going to get much bigger—so they've been trying to keep as much as they can to themselves for thirty years now. And that's okay with you people, and you know it."

"A pox on both our houses, huh?" Craig said wryly.

"You're damn right," Arlene said. "Now if you'll excuse me I've got to get back to work."

Laura watched Arlene's ramrod-straight back leave the room; then she collapsed into a chair. "Wow," she said. "What the hell have you gotten me into, Fannin?"

"Don't worry about Arlene. We have these discussions from time to time. She likes to remind me that I'm the lowest form of life."

"What about Helen Belew and Diana Arnold?"

"I don't know if I'd get too het up about all that, either. You've handled unpopular cases before; you know what the heat feels like."

"Somehow it's never felt quite this hot before. How did they know I was here, anyway?"

Craig smiled at her naïveté. "That's easy. The ladies and gentlemen of the press, of course. How long do you think it took Bob Harper to call the mayor's office for a reaction—

and how long after that do you think it took for him to spread the word? It is unfortunate that Mrs. Belew happened to be in town, but I'm not concerned. You heard Arlene; she won't necessarily get the most sympathetic ear in this town."

Laura waved her hand in the air. "That doesn't matter; let them say what they want to. After all, everyone else has."

"Who? Marshall? And your boyfriend? Come to think of it, with Helen Belew pitching in, you have sort of hit a triple," he said, laughing. "Buck up, kiddo."

"Yeah, right," Laura said, rising to her feet. "I can always look to the silver lining—there are still some people left in town who haven't had a shot at me yet."

Chapter 20

Kenny Newton was normally a fast worker. Laura had sometimes called him in the morning, and gotten his report over lunch. So it was frustrating to wait several days to hear from him, and then to get bad news.

"I found one of your witnesses," he said, settling into a chair in Laura's new office.

"Just one?" she asked, disappointed.

"Actually, not even an entire one," he said cryptically.

"Okay, it's time to stop fooling around with me now," she said. "I've been sitting here for three days doing nothing and I'm ready for a little action. Where is this partial witness, and when can I talk to him?"

"He's down at the Tipton Brothers Funeral Home."

"Let's go, then," she said, starting to stand before she got it. "Damn it, Kenny! He's dead, you mean?"

"Yep. Stone-cold."

Laura sat back down and glared at him. "You and your little games. You couldn't just tell me he was dead. You had to dangle it in front of me."

"You're in a mood," Kenny remarked cheerfully.

"Wouldn't you be? I've got quite a bit of personal capital invested in this case, and I'm about to start thinking I'm going to lose it all. How did he die?"

"At the hand of another," Kenny said melodramatically.

"Really?" Laura said, brightening. "He was murdered?"

"Don't get your hopes up. He was killed in a knife fight in the city jail. I'm afraid it was a random act of violence. Sorry to disappoint. There's nothing I'd like better than to bring you a big ol' conspiracy. But this was just one dumbass punk slicing open another one."

"Too bad. Which one was it, anyway?"

"Albert Jackson."

Laura sighed. "I can't say I'm surprised. He was the seedier of the two—not that it wasn't a close race. What was he in for?"

"There was apparently an old warrant out on him. The cops picked him up some time last week. I don't have any details, but I can get some if you want."

"Would you? I think it would be smart to know as much as I can about Mr. Jackson. Maybe some of his associates can help."

"Maybe. I'm sure they're very helpful people," Kenny said disingenuously.

Laura laughed. "You're a riot. What about eyewitnesses numbers two and three?"

"Number two, Jermaine Clay, is a tough nut to crack. He had no fixed address; he had stayed with various friends and relatives over the past couple of years. None of them have seen him recently, though. Not that they're admitting, anyway. He might just be sleeping on the streets. I'll check the shelters and the parks, and I'll see if they know him at the soup kitchens. Eyewitness number three—"

"Terence Walker," Laura said, referring to her file.

"Right. Former employee of Bumper to Bumper Car Wash. I had about as much luck as you did. He hasn't been seen in the neighborhood. One of his buddies thought he might have gone to Florida."

Laura nodded. "He seems to have come into some money."

"If he did, he'll burn through it quickly enough and come back to his usual stomping grounds. We'll just have to give it some time."

"I don't know how much we have," Laura said. "Craig's not going to bankroll me forever."

"Don't worry; I'll get you something. You got plans for the weekend?"

"No," she replied. "I thought I might go up to Nashville and see my family."

"If you change your mind, come on out to the house and have supper with us. Cindy's always glad to see you and I can make sure that the kids don't bug you."

"Your children don't bug me. Thanks for the invitation. I'll let you know."

Laura really didn't want to go to Kenny's house or to Nashville, but she didn't want to stare at the walls for forty-eight hours, either, so she knew she'd do one or the other unless something else came along. She reflected, ruefully, that she had reached that comfortable stage with Amos where spending the weekends together was a foregone conclusion. This hiatus in their relationship was underscoring something Laura had been only vaguely aware of before: she didn't have many friends in Atlanta.

Laura wouldn't have called herself lonely, or even a loner. She was sociable and had plenty of friends back home in Nashville and scattered over the country. Eight years in Atlanta, however, had not netted her a solid base of acquaintances, especially female ones. The relationships she had formed with the handful of women who had toiled as associates with her at Prendergrast and Crawley had dropped away as one by one they left that august law firm for less-demanding hours, better chances of advancement, or to start families. By the time Laura had left, she was the sole female associate of her rank.

She did have neighbors, and nice ones, but, as the only single and childless woman (as far as she knew) for blocks around, she was sometimes hesitant to take them up on their friendly offers of book club memberships, potluck suppers, and group yard sales. She had bought in the Peachtree Park area because it was familiar and safe. There were days, though, when she wished that she had chosen a more adventurous faubourg, like Cabbagetown, or east Atlanta—or even Amos's Virginia-Highland stomping grounds. But Laura knew that, despite her many sterling qualities, she was not adventurous. And she liked that little house of hers, and she liked the smart, funny women who lived near it. She wished that she knew any one of them well enough to simply call her up and ask her over for a glass of wine and a talk.

She also wished that she had more professional responsibilities. Her deal with Craig strictly limited her to representing Roland Jervis. Experience had taught her that there would come a time when that would be more than enough, but now, at the developmental stage, the case was hardly forcing her to fire on all cylinders. Kenny's news hadn't been very hopeful, either; Laura was resigning herself to more waiting and watching, which meant less lawyering. Craig didn't care how many hours she worked, which was a welcome departure from her past experience with private law practices, where "billable hours" were sacrosanct. But Craig's airy instructions that she take some days off, or go shopping on her lunch hour, fell on fallow ground. Laura didn't feel right unless she was *doing* something. So she sat in her office, day after day, organizing her notes and records, making phone calls that never turned up anything, and researching any obscure legal precedent that might conceivably have some bearing on Jervis's suit.

Two days after Kenny's fruitless visit, she reached for the phone, intending to call him. She had the pretext of calling about the case, but, since she knew Kenny would have called her if he had learned anything, the pretext was tissue-thin. On the other hand, she could at least RSVP to his weekend invitation.

She never got a chance to dial. The phone rang once, then twice while she looked at it in a slightly puzzled manner. She was so unused to hearing its insistent chirping ring that she was slow to pick up. When she did, her expectations were low.

"Miss Chastain?" an unfamiliar, soft female voice inquired.

"Yes. May I help you?"

"I hope so . . . I'm Diana Arnold. You know, Lawrence Belew's sister."

"Of course I remember you."

"Of course, you would—after that scene my mother pitched. I want you to know how sorry I am about all that, Miss Chastain."

"It wasn't your fault. Besides, I didn't disagree with everything she said. Just the way she said some of it."

"You should have thrown her out," Diana said bitterly. "That would have shown her."

"She's grieving," Laura said gently. "We owed it to her to listen."

"Grieving?" Diana said with a laugh. "Grieving like Medea did. You don't know my mother. She doesn't grieve the way another mother would for her child. She didn't lose a child; she lost her *creation*. Now there's no chance that he'll do what she had planned for him."

"Which was . . . ?" Laura asked, feeling a little voyeuristic.

"Senator Lawrence Belew, of course. Then maybe a Cabinet post, then who knows?"

"Did your brother have any interest in politics?"

"Lawrence? You've got to be kidding! He hated politicians. He was doing what he wanted to, running his own business. He made good money for doing what he liked best, which was messing with computers. He was happy."

"I got that feeling," Laura said. "He seems to have been a good guy."

"He was," Diana said.

"I'm glad you called, Mrs. Arnold," Laura said. "I've been feeling bad about you and your mother."

"Call me Diana. I should have called sooner to apologize. I just . . . I just didn't. But now I need to talk to you about something else."

"Sure. What can I help you with?"

"It's about Lawrence. You know, I never really bought the car-jacking story. Lawrence may have been a computer geek, but he was a pretty big guy, and he stayed in shape. The first time I saw Roland Jervis I thought that there was no way he could have beaten Lawrence to death. But no one in my family wanted to hear anything different than the official version of events. I don't know why. Maybe it was just easier for them to believe that it was some random act of violence.''

"But you don't, do you?"

"No, especially not now."

"Why now?" Laura asked.

"I want to talk to you, Miss Chastain—"

"Please call me Laura. You mean you want to meet in person?"

"Yes. I need you to come somewhere with me, and you can't tell anyone—not even your boss—about it."

Laura hesitated. Was this some weird revenge plot? Was the apparently gentle Diana Arnold going to kidnap her and take her to some dank hideaway and hold her . . . for what?

As if she could read Laura's mind, Diana spoke. "It's not like it sounds. There's someone who wants to see *me*, and I'm afraid to go alone."

"Why not call the police?"

"He said no cops. And I can't ask my husband—he'd just call in the police. This guy is scared of something. I think he knows something about who killed Lawrence."

"Who is he?" Laura asked.

"He says he knew Lawrence."

"You can't just take the word of a mysterious stranger, Diana. You've gotten a lot of publicity lately, and you're very lovely. What if this is some guy who saw your picture in the paper and wants to get you alone?"

Diana made an impatient sound. "That's why I'm asking you to come along, too! He can't very well ravish both of us, can he?"

"He can if he has a gun," Laura warned. "Look, I have a suggestion. I'll go with you, but we let my PI follow along.

Don't worry, he's good at it. If there's no trouble, your man will never know he was there.''

"And if there is trouble?"

"We'll set up a time limit. If we're not out by a certain time, Kenny storms the bunker. Which he's also good at," Laura added, although she had never actually seen Kenny storm anything. She hoped that Diana wouldn't notice his pronounced limp.

Diana hesitated for a long moment before agreeing. "Okay, we can do it that way. But it has to be today. And soon—I have to pick my son up at school at three."

"Give me your number. I'll call Kenny right now. Where are you?"

"No, don't come here. Someone might see you. I'll come to your office. Get your private eye there as soon as you can, okay? It'll take me about a half hour to drive there." She hung up.

Laura hoped that she could deliver Kenny in time. If not, she'd have to come up with another plan and quick. She dialed Kenny's office number and got the voice mail. His cell phone number came up "unavailable," so Laura sent an urgent page and hoped for the best. She called Craig's extension.

"So you're calling me now—too good to come downstairs?"

"I can't leave my phone," she said, sketching out the latest development for him. "I've got to get Kenny here in thirty minutes. Do you have a backup plan if I don't?"

"I could try another PI. She might not trust someone you don't know, though. No cops?"

"None at all. I thought about Carlton—wait, here's my phone. I'll call you back. Hello?"

"You paged?" Kenny's voice said.

"Thank goodness. Where are you? Please don't say Duluth, or Alabama or anything."

"I'm on Northside Drive, near West Paces Ferry."

"Hot dog. Come on over here. I need you."

"I'm tailing an unfaithful spouse at the moment."

"He'll continue to be unfaithful. You can catch him again."

"What's the rush?"

"Come to Craig's offices and we'll tell you. Now, get a move on!"

She called Craig back, relieved. "Plan A is operative; he's on his way."

"I don't like the sound of this," Craig said. "You might be walking into a trap of some kind, or just gratifying some nut's cops-and-robbers fantasy."

"I know that. I wouldn't go on my own, although Diana Arnold was ready to. If I don't go, she'll just go alone and who knows what might happen? I don't want that on my conscience."

"You know best," Craig said. "All the same, just be wary of running all over the place drilling dry holes. You've got a case to pursue, and this doesn't sound like it's going to move the lawsuit forward."

"I promise to keep my eye on the prize, Craig," Laura said with an expressive roll of her eyes.

Fifteen minutes later Kenny's anonymous blue pickup pulled into the small lot at the front of the building. Kenny tricked out his truck with ladders and buckets, camouflage that allowed him to park pretty nearly anywhere in Atlanta, which was less a city than it was a large, ongoing construction project. Laura noted with approval that he even had some convincing-looking power tools along this time. She hurried out the door and met him as he walked toward the building.

"Holy smokes, what's got into you?" he asked. "I haven't seen you this agitated since you made me get that possum out of your garbage can."

"This is a lot worse than a possum," she said, escorting him in and leading him to Craig's office. She told Kenny about Diana's call. "So I suggested that you tail us," Laura said.

"I'd rather go with you," he said. "Just following along and waiting for a disaster doesn't sit right with me."

"He said no cops," Laura reminded him.

"I'm not a cop," Kenny rejoined.

"You *look* like one. Look, we'll be okay if you stay close. And we need some way to communicate. Can I wear a wire?"

Kenny and Craig laughed. "Too much TV, Laura," Kenny said. "That would take forever to set up, anyway. Here, I tell you what: I've got a couple of those walkie-talkies in the truck. They look just like cell phones. If you put it in the hands-free mode and put it in your pocketbook, I'll be able to hear what's going on."

"Sure, if I make sure that I keep my purse close to this guy's mouth."

"I don't expect perfect sound transmission, but I can hear you holler if things take a turn. It's not perfect, but it'll have to do."

"So you're coming?"

"I guess so. Under protest."

"Good. Because if this guy is for real, you can help corroborate the meeting. Now, here's Diana." Arlene ushered in the agitated woman and closed the door. "Diana, you know Craig Fannin. And this is Kenny Newton, the private investigator I spoke to you about. He'll tail us in his truck, and I'm going to carry a little radio. If there's any trouble, he's going to pull us out."

"Hello," she said, weakly, as she shook his hand. "I

didn't think this was such a big deal . . . I just thought that Laura and I could go down and see the man. . . .''

"Chances are it isn't anything at all," Kenny said reassuringly. "But always better safe than sorry. Now, where is it that we're going?"

"It's someplace I don't know—somewhere in east Atlanta." She handed Kenny a scrap of paper.

He nodded. "I know it. Best way to get there is to take Memorial to Moreland, then head south on Moreland. Turn off onto Flat Shoals just past I-Twenty."

"I think I know," Diana said. "We should get going, though. I only have a couple of hours before I pick up my son."

"Let's ride, then," Kenny said, smiling. "Come to the truck and get the radio, Laura. I'll give you the fifteen-second course in how to use it."

A few minutes later, Laura was in the front seat of Diana Arnold's Volvo wagon, heading south on Georgia 400. She twiddled with the radio's controls, and tentatively spoke into it. "Ken? Can you hear me?"

"Clear as a bell. Diana, get on the downtown connector and get off at Courtland Street. I'll talk you on down to Flat Shoals from there."

"How do you know him?" Diana whispered.

"You can talk; I've put it on mute. Kenny's an old friend; we've worked on a bunch of cases together. He's very good. And trustworthy."

"I hope so." She was quiet for a minute. "This is kind of exciting, isn't it? I mean, it's creepy, and I wish it weren't happening, because the only reason it *is* happening is that Lawrence is dead . . . but . . ."

"I know what you mean. It feels good to be doing something."

"What made you think that man, Roland Jervis, didn't do it?"

"The physical evidence told me that there was someone else involved, someone smarter than Jervis. I hope you understand what I did, even if your mother can't."

"I think I do. Does Mr. Fannin think there's someone else, too?"

"Yes. He . . . he's seen a lot of cases," Laura said. She had been on the point of telling Diana about the second opinion on the autopsy that Craig had gotten from Dr. Hillman, but she couldn't bring herself to do it. After all, they might be wrong, and why trouble Diana with images of her brother, helpless but still alive, in the hands of his killers?

Kenny's voice came over the radio, directing them to make a turn. They fell silent as they drew closer to the address the mysterious caller had given Diana, a brick building that looked as if it might once have been a store or warehouse, but now, judging from the blinds that hung in some of the windows, was a loft apartment building. "Okay," Laura said. "We're here." She could see Kenny's truck some way behind, and when they pulled over and stopped, he passed them.

"Get on out of the car," he instructed. "Fuss with your purses and whatnot for a minute. I'm going to turn around and get into position." They waited and fiddled while Kenny moved his truck to a vantage point that gave him a good view of the front of the building. "Okay," he said, "I can see you. Now let's see if I can hear you. Laura?"

"I'm here," she replied.

"Laura?" She answered him again, to no avail. "Sugar, I can see your lips moving but I can't hear you. Did you put it on mute so you could discuss me?"

Laura hastily unmuted. "Sorry. We only said nice things."

"What else is there to say? Okay, I can hear you pretty well. Diana, say something."

"Like what?"

"That'll do," he said. "Okay, I'm muting mine, but I can hear you. Stick as close together as you can. And when you get inside talk aloud about what you see. Describe everything, so I'll know the lay of the land if I have to come in."

"Okay," Laura said. "Ready, Diana?"

"I guess so," Diana answered doubtfully.

"Then let's go," Laura said, hoping she sounded more confident than she felt.

Chapter 21

Laura pulled open the industrial-style, aluminum-framed door and held it ajar for Diana. Diana hesitated momentarily before stepping across the threshold. "Look at the lobby, Diana," Laura said, mindful of Kenny's instructions. "Look, there's another set of doors inside, straight ahead."

Diana caught the spirit. "And mailboxes, with buzzers, on our right."

"And the interior doors are locked," Laura said. "I guess that means we have to buzz the apartment."

"Okay," Diana said. "Apartment Two-C. Here it is."

"Is there a name on the box?" Laura asked, although she could see perfectly well there was one.

"Yes. Carl Vuh . . . something."

"Looks like 'Vasovitch,' " Laura commented. "Shall we buzz?"

"I guess so." Diana extended one tentative finger and

pressed the buzzer. There was a long silence. "What if he's not at home?" Diana fretted.

"Why would he have set this meeting up if he wasn't going to be here?" Laura asked.

"I don't know. Maybe he's watching us." Diana peered back through the outer doors as if she expected to see a lurking Vasovitch. She jumped a foot in the air when the intercom popped to life.

"Who is it?" a male voice said.

"It's . . . it's Diana Arnold," she said, her voice gathering conviction. "You called me."

"I'll buzz you in. The elevator's on the left. Come up to the second floor." A loud, harsh buzzer sounded, and Laura tugged open the inner door. This time, Diana didn't hesitate to step through it.

Laura started to let the door close behind them, but Diana caught it. "How would Kenny get in?" she asked.

The radio in Laura purse came to life, "Don't worry about it," Kenny's disembodied voice reassured them. "Piece of cake."

"I thought you weren't going to talk," Laura said.

"I won't anymore. Proceed," he said, and Laura heard a click as he engaged the mute button.

Laura took stock of their new surroundings. "It's a big hall, about twelve feet wide. There are two doors on the right, and one on the left. And that must be the elevator back at the rear."

"Yes," Diana agreed. "On the left. The elevator." The elevator appeared to be an industrial model, and not a new one. There was only a single button; Diana pushed it. The massive doors rumbled open, revealing a utilitarian steel-plated interior. Several colorful flyers, most advertising various oddly named bands, were taped to the walls, and there was a discarded paper coffee cup on the floor. Laura looked at Diana, and nodded. They stepped in, and Laura located the UP button. The doors closed slowly, and the car started upward with a lurch.

"We're going up to the second floor," Laura narrated, unnecessarily, as there appeared to be only two floors. The elevator continued its slow, noisy journey, finally stopping bumpily. The doors peeled back, revealing a hallway identical to the one below. They stepped out, and Laura scanned the numbers on the doors. "Two-A . . . B . . . C is on the left side of the building, on the front. Here we go."

Laura had to admit to a few butterflies as they approached the gray door. She hopped almost as high as Diana had earlier when the door swung open before either of them could gather the courage to knock.

Carl Vasovitch was an extremely tall, thin, pale young man, and he looked more frightened than either of the two women standing in his hallway.

"Mr. Vasovitch?" Laura said, as Diana appeared to have been struck dumb.

"Are *you* Lawrence's sister?" he asked, incredulous.

"No, I'm Laura Chastain. I'm a . . . friend of Diana's. She's Diana Arnold," she added. "Lawrence's sister."

"Right," he said. "Want to come in?" His invitation was breezy, as if he hadn't made an anonymous phone call to arrange this secret meeting. He might have been greeting a couple of Girl Scouts selling cookies.

Diana must have found his tone incongruous as well, or maybe her nerves finally snapped. "Who the hell are you?" she demanded. "What do you mean calling me up and telling me you wanted to talk about my brother?"

Vasovitch cowered in the doorway. "Take it easy, please! I knew your brother. I worked for him."

Laura tried a gentler approach. "Do you think you know something about Lawrence's death, Carl? Is that why you called Diana?"

He nodded. "Yes. I mean . . . why don't you come in?" he asked. "I don't want to talk about this in the hall."

"Okay," Laura said. "You look pretty harmless to me," she said pointedly, in the direction of her pocketbook. "I don't guess you have any evil designs on us."

"Me? God, no," he said. "Can I get you something? A Snapple or something?"

Laura and Diana, now inside his apartment, didn't answer right away. Laura could only speak for herself, but she was too dumbfounded to reply.

The main room of Carl's loft—which Laura guessed was well over a thousand square feet—was, in contrast to the shabby exterior of the building, a high-tech palace. Brightly colored, curvaceous furniture was artfully arranged around the space, but the main attraction was the electronics. A huge flat-panel television clung to one wall; a sleek stereo system inhabited a green-glass cabinet. And there was computer equipment everywhere. It was one vast high-tech playground, the interior decorating dream of a million teenage boys. "Good Lord," Laura said. "This is amazing."

"It's cool, isn't it? I was lucky to find this place. I couldn't have gotten this effect in a regular apartment. Plus this is a cool neighborhood. So you want something to drink?"

"I'll take a Snapple," Diana said. "I could use something. You scared the fool out of me. Why did you have to be so mysterious?"

Carl, fishing in the stainless-steel refrigerator, seemed contrite. "I didn't mean to. I just didn't want to say anything on the phone. I mean, it could be tapped. I think I could tell if it was, but you never know. Anyway, you probably would have thought I was crazier if I had tried to explain things on the phone. You probably would have hung up, or called the cops. Lemonade or raspberry?''

"Lemonade," Diana said.

"You want something?" Carl asked Laura. "Why did you bring her, anyway?" he said accusingly to Diana.

"Why would I come out all by myself to see some kook?"

"I'll have a lemonade, too," Laura said. "And really, you should have identified yourself on the phone. Would it have killed you to say you worked for Lawrence?"

"I dunno. Maybe. Somebody killed *him*, didn't they? Sorry," he said to Diana. "But it's true."

"And you think this somebody might kill you, too?"

"I'm not crazy," he said. "When I heard that Law was dead, it didn't even cross my mind that he was murdered. I just thought maybe he'd wrecked the car or something." He gave Laura her drink and wandered over to one of the jellybean-colored chairs, and collapsed into it. Laura and Diana seated themselves side by side on an aluminum sofa upholstered in a nauseous chartreuse fabric. "I mean, who thinks one of your own friends is going to get murdered? So then there was all this stuff about a car-jacking, and they caught some guy, and I thought, man, that sucks. Law was not a flashy guy. I mean, there have to be about five million absolute *tools* driving Lexuses around this city, but Law, the most decent guy in the world, gets killed for his car." He shook his head. "I tell you what. I traded my Saab for a Saturn the very next day. It ain't worth it."

"But you said you didn't think he was killed for the car," Diana pointed out.

"No, not anymore. I mean, when they let that guy go and said he didn't do it, I thought, whoa! So who *did* kill him?

And I thought that maybe . . . well, it seems kind of weird, I know. . . ."

"What does, Carl?" Laura said.

"Look, I'm not one of these guys who sees a conspiracy in everything. I want you to understand that. But when this kind of shit happens, I think there's got to be something to it. You know what your brother did for a living, don't you?" he asked Diana.

"Of course I do. He was a systems engineer."

"Right. And that's just a way of saying he put together systems for people—for businesses and organizations. He was great at it, too. He really had a head for business, in addition to being a kick-ass programmer. He'd get a contract and hire a bunch of guys like me to work on it. It was a blast. No office; we just worked over a network. There were a lot of different people over the years, but I'm one of the ones who stuck around the longest. I liked the work, and I liked Law. A lot. And the money wasn't bad, either," he said with a broad sweep of his hand. "I live all right, thanks to Law. I mean, without him, I probably would have been some systems puke working for a big corporation. We had a great setup. Which is why I told him not to mess with it."

"Not to mess with what?" Diana asked sharply. "Let's get to it. I have to pick up my son at school in about an hour."

"Okay, okay. I was just giving you the picture. Like I said, Lawrence was the one who went out and got the contracts. We did pretty much anything that came along. Financial systems for banks, a billing system for the cable company. And we did a lot of government work."

"He helped design the case management system for the Fulton County Superior Court, didn't he?" Laura asked.

"Yeah, that was cool, because we were trying to build

an interface so the cops could talk on-line to the district attorneys about their cases. It was going to save the cops a lot of time, so they could stay on the street more. We never got that off the ground, though, because the budget got cut. Anyway, there's this bidding process for government work. And it's supposed to be totally blind, so that the taxpayers don't get screwed because somebody took the guy who makes the decisions to a strip club, or out to play golf.''

"Right," Laura said. "We understand."

"Then you know that it doesn't really work that way, not always. There's some latitude in the contracting process. Things other than price and the reputation and experience of the guy bidding on the contract come into play.''

"Things like race, and sex, you mean," Diana said pointedly.

"Yeah. And I'm cool with that. I mean, how many black people or women would ever get ahead without some kind of leg up? But Law just hated it. I don't know why. I always kind of thought that he *knew* that he was the best at what he did, but he hated it that people thought he was getting all this work because he was black. And—sorry—because his family's pretty big in government and all. He wanted to be taken seriously on his own.''

"I know that," Diana said. "We used to argue about it all the time. He thought that affirmative action and set-asides were keeping black people back, not helping them.''

"Right. I never totally bought into what he said, you know," Carl said earnestly. "But every so often he would get all steamed up on the topic. So, to cut this short so you can get your kid, he cooked up this scam. Well, not really a scam, because he wasn't going to make any money out of it. He set up this one bid where he and I bid separately. He did all my paperwork, and he did this great plan—and he priced my contract real low, too. And I went in and pitched it, you know, all white and all, in a Brooks Brothers suit he bought for me. Then he submitted a kind of half-assed bid in his own name, and made it more expensive.''

"What happened?" Laura asked.

Carl shrugged. "He was right. He won the bid, even though it was screwed up and cost more.''

"And that's why you think he got killed?" Diana said, incredulous.

"That's not all," Carl said, sounding a touch offended. "The whole reason that he cooked up this goofy plan was that some white guy approached him and said that he would pay Law to front for him on bids for systems work with the city, county, and state. All Law would have to do was put his name on the bids. This guy said the rest of it would be 'taken care of.' ''

"What did Lawrence do?" Laura inquired.

"He threw the guy out, of course, and he said he was going to take the whole stinking scam to the FBI. They're investigating the city, I think.''

Laura nodded. "And the county. And then he did this little game, using you, to see if it really was true that he could win a bid just because he was black?''

"Yeah, I guess so. He was pretty bummed about the whole thing.''

"Did he do what he said he would—did he go to the FBI?" Laura asked.

"I don't know. The next thing I know, I hear he's missing, and then he's dead. So you can see how I kind of drew a conclusion. And like I told you, at first I thought it was just some random crime. But when the judge let that guy they arrested off, and the investigation is turned back on, well, then I had to think. And I thought you would be the person to call," he said to Diana. "He talked about you all the time, and your kid. He was real proud of you."

Diana put her face in her hands, unable to speak. Laura patted her on the back and resumed questioning Carl. "Do you have any evidence? Did you keep the bid materials?"

"Sure," Carl said. "That's why I called her. I figured she would know what to do."

"Can we have them?" Laura said.

"Whoa," he said. "I don't know who you are."

"I'm a lawyer," Laura said. "I was in the district attorney's office. I'm the one who got Roland Jervis off."

"The guy they arrested? Why would you do that?"

"I guess it was because I was interested in getting fired and breaking up with my boyfriend," Laura said ironically. "No, the truth is that Jervis didn't do it, and I knew it all along. I guess I was more interested in finding out who really did do it than my boss was, so I kept pushing for answers until he fired me."

"So now you're helping Diana?" he asked.

"Not exactly," Laura allowed. "I'm technically representing Roland Jervis. Diana asked me to come here with her as a friend."

"Did Lawrence tell anyone else?" Diana asked.

"I don't know. No one's come around to ask me anything about it," Carl replied.

Laura nodded. "I don't think he went to the FBI, anyway. Or if he did he kept your name out of it. Otherwise, they'd have been all over you."

Carl looked taken aback, as if he had just realized the gravity of the situation. "You mean the FBI would want to talk to me?"

"Of course. You're a witness in an ongoing investigation."

"What about the Atlanta cops?"

"Them, too," Laura replied, although she could see that Carl was growing more and more uncomfortable. "I'm sorry, but you're involved. You have to come forward and tell what you know."

"Not to mention that you owe it to Lawrence," Diana said. "You don't want them to get away with it. Do you?"

Carl shrugged. "Depends on who 'them' is. If they killed him, what's to stop them from coming after me?"

Diana started to answer angrily, but Laura caught her eye and took a more diplomatic approach. "If you're right, and the people who are involved in the bid-rigging are the same ones who killed Lawrence, they already know about you. And, if that's the case, going to the FBI is the only way I know of that you can protect yourself."

"If I go and talk to them, do you think I need a lawyer?"

"In a word, yes," Laura said.

"Can I hire you?"

Laura shook her head. "I think I have a conflict. I'm representing Roland Jervis, and that means I have a vested interest in cooking up alternative theories on who killed Lawrence Belew. It's not a huge conflict, I admit, but I think you'd be better off with another lawyer. I can put you in touch with someone if you'd like me to."

"Sure. That would be great," Carl said, but he wore a look of serious consternation on his pale face.

"Don't worry," Laura said. "You just tell what you know and the FBI will take care of you."

Diana looked at her watch. "I'm going to be late picking up Martin," she said. "In fact, Laura, if you don't mind getting a ride with Kenny, it would save me some time," she added.

"No problem," Laura said, standing and fishing a card from her purse. The radio dropped to the floor.

"What's that?" Carl said, suspicious. "And who's Kenny?"

"Busted," Laura said. "We've had a private investigator listening in," she confessed. She picked up the radio and spoke into it. "Come on up, Ken. I've blown your cover. And I need a ride."

Diana suddenly laughed. "It seems so silly now that we know who you are," she explained to a hurt-looking Carl. "But you have to admit calling up somebody you've never met and asking to meet is a little offbeat."

Carl managed to smile. "I guess so. But, jeez, I'm totally harmless."

"I hope you're not *totally* harmless," Diana replied. "I'd like to see you do some damage to whoever killed my brother. Laura, I'll call you."

As she left, the buzzer sounded, and Carl admitted Kenny to the building. A few moments later, he opened the door and stood aside to let the big PI in.

"So you're a real private eye?" he asked.

"Yep," Kenny said. "I'm an expert in shadowing, tailing, and general lurking. Man, this is some setup," he added. "What kind of components are those?" he said, moving toward the stereo cabinet like a filing attracted to a magnet.

Carl followed. "Bang and Olufsen, man. These are cool, but you should see the ones that hang on the walls. And the sound—here, let me show you."

"Excuse me," Laura said, "but can we focus on the matter at hand for a minute? Ken, did you hear everything?"

"Enough," Kenny said. "You said you've got all the bid materials, right?"

Carl nodded. "For the bid that I made, sure. I don't have

Lawrence's stuff, and I don't have the letters that he got from the city, you know, offering him the contract.''

"Those are probably at Belew's house or office," Laura said. "I'll ask Diana if we can look for them."

Kenny nodded and continued to interrogate Carl. "And what do you know about this man who approached him—the man who wanted Lawrence to front for him?"

"Nothing, except that he was some white guy. Law never mentioned a name. He said he was a big bohunk, though, and he said he had a connection with the city. He promised Law lots of money if he would just put his name on some bids."

Kenny looked at Laura. "He has to go to the FBI. And the Atlanta Police Department. But he's going to need protection when this comes out. Carl, how would you feel about lying low for a day or two until I can line something up with the Bureau and the cops?"

"I guess so, man. I could go somewhere. I'm due for a trip to Vegas, anyway."

"Why don't you go there for a few days? Just let me know where you'll be and I'll keep in touch."

"Is that smart?" Laura asked.

"No one's looking for him now," Kenny said, "and when he comes back, I'll have a deal for his protection." He looked around. "This building should be pretty easy to secure, actually. Only one entrance, controlled access. Yeah, it'll do."

"You think that the guys who killed Law might come after me, too?" Carl asked.

"I don't know. There's nothing in what you told the ladies that gives us any clue about who these people might be. It just gives a reason to believe that someone had a motive for wanting Lawrence Belew out of the way. And if you're right in thinking that those people actually did kill Lawrence, they might come after you. If they know about you."

Laura frowned. "Ken, don't you think we should just go to the FBI to start? You know the Atlanta Police Department. It's very porous; information doesn't stay secure. What if the bid-riggers find out through the cops that someone's got evidence against them?"

"You've got a point," Kenny said.

"Hey!" Carl said, alarmed. "I'm not so sure I like this."

"Relax," Kenny said. "You're going to *love* the FBI. So, show me this stereo."

Laura sighed and settled back down to finish her lemonade.

Chapter 22

Craig Fannin wasn't as thrilled as Laura expected him to be by the news. "The last thing I need," he sighed, "is to get tangled up with the feds."

"Got something to hide?" Laura asked.

"No. I just can't stand dealing with them. But I don't see any reason that we have to. We don't need to pull Lawrence Belew's killer—or killers—out of a hat to win Roland's suit. In fact, I think we have enough to go on now. We should probably just file the complaint and see where the chips fall."

"I'm not so sure. I don't have much to support the argument. I've got all the affidavits from the grandmother and the aunts and the preacher, and of course there's Carl Vasovitch, for what that's worth at this point. Overall, I think it would be better to wait until Ken turns up one of the other two witnesses."

"Why? You can always get to them later. Anyway, I think affidavits from church ladies are about as good as it gets, lawsuit-wise. It might just terrify them into a settlement."

"It wouldn't scare *me* if I were defending the city. Besides, you said yourself that our case would be better if we had some evidence that the Atlanta Police Department knew that Jervis was innocent when they went after him."

"And I still believe that. However, I also believe that we have plenty to go on now, and we can always add on later. I just want to get the clock started on their response," Craig said, glancing at his desk calendar.

"You're the boss. I'm planning to name the City of Atlanta and the Atlanta Police Department in the complaint, but I'm keeping the individual officers out of it. Is that okay?"

"Worried about what Kowalski will say?"

Laura bristled. "You know better than that," she snapped. "I don't think we have cause to go after Devereaux and Carlton personally, that's all. The real fault in this case lies with the mayor and with Marshall. I'd name them, if I could, but I don't see that it would hold up."

"No, there's no point. We can always add them later if we find out they had an active role in the setup. But you're right: our ability to link in specific individuals is limited right now. Unless we go after your pal Avery."

"Avery? I don't know. There's a malpractice suit out there somewhere with his name on it," Laura said thoughtfully, "but he's just a lowly public defender. Do those guys carry any kind of liability insurance?"

"No. But it's not money we'd be after. It's a stunning moral victory I'd be looking for."

Laura looked at him doubtfully. "It would come at a

pretty high price," she said. "For me, of course; I do want to go back to the district attorney's office eventually, and I'll have to deal with Julia Walton again. But it doesn't seem to me to be the kind of suit you'd want to pursue either."

"You think I worry about what my colleagues in the bar association might say or think?"

Laura laughed. "Based on your history, no. I was thinking of the Goliath-versus-David nature of your—our—suing poor old Avery."

"You're right," he sighed. "My finely honed PR instincts tell me that, however tempting the prospect, I had better not go there."

"Right." Laura stood up. "I'll get you a draft of the complaint before you leave tonight."

"Good. Then we can file tomorrow with all due ceremony."

"By which you mean that you'll make sure all your press buddies know about it, of course," Laura said with a roll of her eyes that said what she thought of them.

"Naturally." He wagged a finger at her. "You were with the district attorney's office too long; you've forgotten how to stir up a good froth of public indignation."

"I *never* liked playing to the press," Laura said. "And I was never that good at it. But I'll do it. And if you can review the draft tonight, we can alert the media first thing in the morning. And, by the way, Kenny has a meeting with one of his FBI pals later tomorrow. He's going to give them Vasovitch's story on a no-name basis and see if they can offer him some kind of protection before he testifies."

"Great. Just try to leave my name out of it, okay?"

"Oh, I see: it's okay to have your name in the papers, but not in the FBI's files."

"You got it," he said. At that moment, Craig's phone

began to ring. He gave her a silent thumbs-up as he took the call and she left the room with her mission clear in her mind.

Laura made short work of drafting the complaint. Years of experience in a civil practice had given her a good grounding in the forms and conventions, and the complaint was really very simple, anyway: Roland Jervis was not guilty of murder, and the police could have easily uncovered his alibi if they had bothered. Laura did feel a twinge of guilt, however, as she put on the finishing touches. It wasn't all the fault of the police; Avery Daniels bore a lot of responsibility, too. Her scruples notwithstanding, Laura hoped that Avery would someday get the public scourging she believed he had coming to him. But she contented herself with naming only the city, in the august person of its mayor, the Honorable Harrison Broad, and the police department.

Craig came into Laura's office, pressed and polished, early the next morning, her draft in his hand. "Perfect. Didn't change a thing," he said. "Print up the final version for filing and take it down to the courthouse."

"Me? Can't we just send it by courier?"

Craig laughed. "You're much more photogenic than any courier I've ever seen."

"Oh, no. You've lined up some photographer."

"Not just a photographer, sweetheart—a television camera."

Laura frowned. "This isn't fair, Craig. You said it was my case."

"I also said I'd help, and that's what I'm doing. I'm lending you the benefit of my experience."

Laura made another bid to duck out. "I'm not really dressed for it today," she said, indicating her trouser suit. "If I had known, I would have worn a skirt."

"You look fine," Craig said. "I think the pants look more professional, anyway. Besides, if you want to change, you're mere blocks away from your closet." He smiled and waved in the general direction of her house.

"You win. But everyone who knows me is going to know that you're behind this, you publicity hound."

"Naturally. But, as I said, you'll make a better segment on the six o'clock news. Did you bring your car today?"

"Yes, I was going to run some errands at lunchtime. But I think I'll take the train and avoid the hassle of parking."

"Suit yourself," he said. "Call me if there are any problems."

Laura set out to walk the few short blocks north to the Buckhead MARTA station. It probably would have been faster to drive at this time of day, but she did have a real issue with parking near the courthouse. It was okay when she had been with the district attorney's office, but as a civilian she would have been at the mercy of the commercial parking lots. So she settled in to enjoy the ride on the MARTA train.

Atlantans were fond of complaining about MARTA, but Laura could find no fault with it. It was fast, clean, and efficient, and some of the stations—Peachtree Center especially—were the best architecture in Atlanta. She chalked up the griping to people who would rather seal themselves into their cars for their commutes, anyway, and who bashed the public transportation system in a more or less prophylactic way, to ensure that they'd never have to use it.

Craig was as good—or as bad—as his word; Laura found a television news crew waiting, along with the ubiquitous Bob Harper, who greeted her with his usual sardonic grin and jerked his head at his fellow media travelers. "Called out the pretty people for this one, huh?"

"Craig's idea, totally," she said. "He told you what's up?"

"Yep. Suing the city on behalf of the downtrodden. Got anything to say to me before you pull out the one-syllable words for the broadcast media?"

Laura laughed. "Sure. Between you and me, I'd think you should watch the skies in the next week or two."

"What will I be looking for?"

"Men in dark suits and sunglasses, with shiny badges."

Harper whistled. "No kidding? Tied in to any particular ongoing investigation that you know of?"

"How would I know?" Laura said with a sly smile. "I'm just a lawyer. Uh-oh, here comes the TV reporter—what's her name?"

"Ariel Saunders," Harper answered. "Ill met by klieg light, proud Ariel!" he said in greeting to the petite blonde.

"Nice line, but wrong play, I think," Laura murmured.

"Close enough for this crowd. Oh, dear, I've upset her. I guess I should be on my merry way."

"Your revels now being ended," Laura said, keeping in theme. He smiled, made a vague salute, and ambled away down the sidewalk.

"Hello, Laura," Ariel said, immediately putting Laura's teeth on edge.

"Hello, Ms. Saunders," she said pointedly.

The point flew wide. "Okay, Laura, let's get this set up. You look at me, not the camera. I'll do a lead-in and then they'll widen out the shot to get you in. I'll ask you a couple of questions, and then they'll focus back on me for the wrap-up. Ready?"

"As I'll ever be," Laura said. Ariel pitched a couple of softball questions, which Laura answered with careful legal diplomacy. It was, all in all, pretty painless, Laura reflected as she went inside the courthouse to make the actual filing. She left a few minutes later, satisfied in the knowledge that the clerk would soon be issuing summonses to Mayor Broad and Chief Sisson. Then it would be their turn to fire a volley in the media war, which she expected them to do right away. They would take longer to answer the complaint in a legal sense, of course, but given that it had gone fairly well, Laura was able to charitably concede that Craig's tactic of opening a second front in the media was a good one.

She was enjoying the walk back to the MARTA station when she heard someone calling after her. "Hey, Laura!"

She turned and shielded her eyes from the early-afternoon sun, unable to see for a moment who had accosted her. Then a large, dark shape loomed up and crystallized into a recognizable acquaintance, if not an especially welcome one. "Hi, Don," Laura said, trying not to show her disappointment at her greeter's turning out to be Don Archer.

"Haven't seen you lately," he said, smiling. "Well, I guess I wouldn't, since the word is that you and Kowalski aren't getting along so good these days."

"Who told you that?" she asked, stung at having details of her personal life bandied about. Surely Amos wouldn't have told tales. If she knew him—and she did—he would be even more tight-lipped than usual about his personal life with his brother officers.

Archer laughed. "Oooh—hit a nerve, huh? Nobody's said anything. It's just that I haven't seen you with the lieutenant lately, and I put two and two together. I used to be a pretty decent detective, you know, before I got put in baby-sitting duty for the mayor. But, hey, I'm real sorry if you guys are having trouble. Say, have you had lunch? I haven't. I was just going to grab a sandwich. Why don't you join me? You can tell me your side of the story,'' he added with a grin that put Laura's nerves on edge.

"No, thanks,'' she said, "I've got to get back uptown.''

"That's right—you work for Fannin now, don't you? You guys are planning to sue everybody and their grandmothers, I guess.''

"No, just your boss,'' Laura said. "In fact, I just filed the complaint, and I better hop along now and get back to work on it.'' Actually, Laura had told Craig that she wouldn't be back for a while; she needed to go to Lenox Square on a panty-hose-buying mission. She planned to take the train to the Lenox stop, do her errand, and grab lunch in the food court before going back to the office.

"Okay. Maybe next time,'' Archer said.

"Sure,'' Laura said. "If you think your boss would approve of your hanging around with me.''

"He don't give a rat,'' Archer said. "Any messages for Kowalski? I'll be seeing him after work—we have a game.''

Laura didn't know what to say; she dug her nails into the palm of her hand and managed a smile. "No, I'll probably be talking to him before you will. See you around.'' She walked away hurriedly, hoping that Archer wasn't watching her rear end as she did, although she knew there was no chance that he wasn't.

Traveling by MARTA had seemed like a good idea in the cool of the morning, but by the time Laura had walked from the courthouse to the MARTA station, run her errands in the marble halls of Lenox Square, and hiked back to the office, the delightful late-spring day didn't seem so refreshing. Footsore and feeling slightly grimy, she had every intention of taking advantage of Craig's liberal office-hours policy. He said that he didn't care if she worked from nine to five, as long as she managed the work flow on the case.

She had noticed that Craig, his two paralegals, and the office staff—other than the dedicated Arlene—seemed to embrace the flexibility. And since she was looking forward to little other than an afternoon at her desk looking for busywork, Laura planned to as well.

But when she entered the office there was a distinct all-hands-on-deck atmosphere prevailing. "What's up?" Laura said to Arlene.

"He just got a call from a client who's been arrested, and he's got a motion hearing in another case tomorrow. He's trying to get the brief on that together before he goes downtown to the jail."

"Do you think he'll let me help on the brief?"

"Honey, he might just kiss you."

Laura grinned and trotted down the hall to Craig's office, where she found the beleaguered attorney hollering into a speakerphone, shuffling papers, and cursing a frozen computer screen. When he saw her he put the phone on mute. An aggrieved woman was continuing to talk about the injustice of her husband's arrest, but Craig turned his attention to Laura. "This damn computer. I tell you, Laura, there are days when I wish I'd stayed with a big firm. I'd have to put up with the partners, but at least I'd have a thousand lackeys eager to do my bidding."

"How about one eager lackey?" Laura said. "I can't get your man out of jail, but I used to write a pretty spiffy brief."

Craig's face brightened momentarily, then fell. "Naw. I can't ask you to do that. I'm not paying you anything."

"Good grief, Craig, I'm not thinking about money. I was so bored I was going to leave early and go home. I *need* to work. Please?"

Craig frowned for a thoughtful moment, but capitulated.

"Okay. Let me give you the file. You'll probably find everything you need in there. It's pretty simple, fairly straightforward. The defendant's accused of fraud, and the state—your pal Marshall—is trying to compel his wife to testify. They say there's no privilege because the marriage is moribund and was at the time the alleged fraud took place."

"Was it?" Laura asked.

"Yeah, but that's irrelevant. She doesn't have to testify. I know there's case law on this. And she also gave a deposition that incriminated him."

"What? It doesn't sound all that simple or straightforward, Craig."

"Okay, maybe it's not. But I need to show that the fact that she gave a deposition is not a waiver of spousal privilege. There's abundant case law in support; I just can't find it with my computer freezing up on me. And I don't have time to do it the old-fashioned way," he added, waving a hand at the shelves of legal books that lined the walls of his office.

"Don't worry; I'll get it done," Laura reassured him. "Why did she change her mind after she gave the deposition?"

He shrugged. "Thought better of it. Who knows? Maybe she doesn't want her kids' father to do time. Maybe she loves him. Anyway, I know it's in good hands. Hearing's tomorrow morning. I gotta run."

And he was off. Laura took the file up to her office and read through it. At first, she felt creepily guilty, knowing that one of her former colleagues in the DA's office had drafted the motion to abolish the privilege. She hoped that it wasn't Meredith, but of course it wouldn't have been, not in a fraud case. Besides, no one would ever know that the brief was her work. She'd make sure Craig was clear on that.

Conscience eased, she plowed into the case law. She read opinion after opinion that supported Craig's argument. At length, she knew she had enough.

She had just begun drafting when Arlene came in. "It's after five. Everyone's gone."

"Is it? Do you need to go, too? If you give me the keys, I'll lock up," Laura offered. "I've got another couple of hours on this."

Arlene looked unsure. "I don't think you should work here alone at night," she said.

"I bet *you* work late all the time," Laura countered. "Anyway, it's a safe neighborhood—at least, I hope it is; I live less than a mile from here. And I expect to finish up before it gets dark."

Arlene reluctantly agreed, and gave Laura a set of keys and instructions for shutting up the office. "Be sure to leave the front light on," she said. "It discourages the night-clubbers from parking here."

"I'll take care of it."

"Okay, then, I'll say good night. See you tomorrow." Arlene left and the building fell into silence.

Laura made short work of the brief. She considered ordering a pizza, but decided that she'd be done in time to go home for dinner. She ran a spell check and sent the document to print. The network printer was downstairs, an inconvenience she didn't notice when the staff was working. She trotted off to pick up the pages, only to find the printer jammed. Clearing the jam took some time, and a few unlady-like epithets. Then Laura realized that she'd have to send the document to print again. Back upstairs, and down again to another jam. After unjamming her brief and running up and down the stairs three more times, she had the bright idea to set it up for manual feed. That worked, but there were errors in the formatting. Back upstairs to correct them she went.

Finally, a crisp brief lay ready for Craig on his desk, with copies for the files. Satisfied, Laura packed up her briefcase and started out. She realized with a start that it was much later than she had expected it to be—in fact, despite her assurances to Arlene, it was already dark. Maple Drive was quiet, but she could hear the rush of traffic on Peachtree, less than a block away, and the boom of bass speakers from the four-wheeled stereos that cruised the bar district nightly.

The noise reminded her of Arlene's instructions about the light over the main door. She flipped it on. It cast a yellow ellipse of light into the pavement of the small empty parking lot in front of the building. Laura looked for her car, and was momentarily startled not to see it. She then remembered that the front lot had been full when she had arrived in the morning, and that she had parked beneath the building. She descended to the unlit lot somewhat reluctantly. Craig's thriftiness with electricity was a running joke in the office. He had installed timers that switched off the outside lights at nine, whether or not anyone was still working in the building.

Despite the fact that she was in her own neighborhood, Laura was on edge as she descended the short flight of stairs to the parking area. It was just the strangeness of the building in the dark, she reassured herself as she walked quickly toward her car. Her heels made hollow noises on the concrete floor that echoed off the low ceiling, giving her the impression that someone was following her. She looked over her shoulder once or twice, and saw nothing but shadows. With relief, she unlocked her car door and hastened to get in and relock it.

She turned the ignition key, and nothing happened. Again, with the same result.

"Damn," she said, checking to see if she'd left the lights on. No, they were in the off position, but the battery was indisputably dead. She had a set of jumper cables in the trunk—a romantic Christmas gift from Amos—but, with no other car handy, they weren't going to do much good.

Laura considered simply leaving the car and walking the mile home, but she knew she'd have to deal with the car sooner or later. Sighing, she pulled her cell phone out of her purse and dialed AAA and reported the dead battery. "Are you in a safe place, miss?" the operator asked.

"I'm in a very good neighborhood." She described her location in detail, taking pains to let them know that her car wouldn't be visible from the street. "Maybe I should meet him up on the street level," Laura said.

"Oh, no, miss," the operator replied. "We never advise anyone to leave a car. Just stay inside it, and keep your doors locked and your windows rolled up, Miss Chastain. That's safest. The truck should be there in about fifteen minutes."

"Thanks," Laura said. She hung up and reached instinctively for the radio before realizing that it, too, would be dead. "Shoot," she said aloud. It was too dark to pull the papers from her briefcase and begin reviewing them. She was beginning to think that the operator's well-intentioned advice was not so good after all—she might be better off standing in the upper lot, or even going back into the building to wait for the truck. That would mean, however, crossing the floor of the garage again, which she was reluctant to do.

Luckily, the truck appeared in fewer than the advertised fifteen minutes. The headlights illuminated the parking lot, and Laura breathed a sigh of relief. She unlocked the door and stepped out of the car to greet the mechanic, a scrawny guy with a ragged ponytail protruding from the rear of his baseball cap. His wiry arms were liberally augmented with various satanic-themed tattoos, but he was a welcome sight. A sewn-on patch on his gray shirt identified him as TREY.

"Hey there," he said. His voice was nasal and his accent thickly southern. "Got you a dead battery, huh?"

"Looks that way," Laura said. "I don't know why. It was fine this morning, and I didn't have the lights on at all today."

"Sometimes they just give out," he said. "Let's take a look." He had pulled a set of jumper cables and a toolbox from his truck, and he popped open the hood with a practiced gesture. He had left his truck running, the lights pointed at the front of Laura's car, so that he could see what he was doing. "Okey-doke. Let's see if she's a goner." Laura watched with interest as he attached some kind of meter to the battery. "No, ma'am, she's alive. Gotta be something else. Let's look around here." He turned on a high-powered flashlight and peered deeper into the cavern under the hood. "Well, I'll be. Your distributor's gone."

"I guess it fell off."

Trey looked at her oddly. "Distributors don't just fall off, ma'am. Somebody's got to take it."

"You mean somebody stole it? Are they that valuable?"

"A distributor for this car'll set you back maybe ten or fifteen dollars," he said flatly. "Don't nobody need one that bad." He looked around the dark parking lot. "What're you doing parked down here at night, anyway? A lady ought not to be in a place like this alone. Can't nobody see you from the street."

"I work in the building, and I had to work late," Laura

explained. "I usually do park in the upper lot, but it was full today."

He peered closely at her. "You havin' problems with anybody, ma'am? You got a boyfriend mad at you?"

Laura laughed lamely. "I sure do, but he didn't do this. He's a cop," she explained. She tried out a mental image of Amos sabotaging her car in order to teach her a lesson, and quickly discarded it. "No, he wouldn't do anything like this. I'm not sure he even knows where I'm working these days."

"Well, somebody done this deliberate. On purpose," the concerned mechanic said. "I think you better call the police." He pronounced it POH-leece, which made Laura smile in spite of the gravity of his tone. "Or that boyfriend of yours, anyway. What do you do for a living, anyway?"

"I'm a lawyer," Laura said, and waited for the inevitable reaction.

"I guess you make plenty of folks mad, then." He looked around the garage. "You didn't see no sign of nobody down here, did you?"

"No," Laura said hesitantly, remembering her jitters when she came down. Had there actually been someone lying in wait for her? "No, and I sat in the car a few minutes waiting for you. Nobody was here." She tried to sound convinced of it. "So, can you fix the car?"

"No, ma'am. I need to get the part. I can get it tonight, but I don't think you ought to stay here. Tell you what. I'll take you home; then I'll come back and fix your car for you. You'll have to find a way to get in to work tomorrow morning, but the car'll be ready."

"Would you? I don't live far away. Just over on East Paces Ferry," she added.

"That's right on my way back to the filling station. Get

your things and hop in the truck. Just shift all that stuff off the front seat,'' he added as he closed the hood of the Toyota and packed up his tools.

Laura did as instructed and they were soon bouncing along in the huge truck. She gave him her address. He insisted on walking her to the door and waiting until she was inside, with the lights on and the door locked, before he left. Back at home, Laura felt much less nervous. She dismissed Trey with sincere thanks and a twenty-dollar tip.

"That's all right," he demurred. "But if I was you, I believe I'd call the poh-leece. Can't hurt none, anyway."

"No, I'm sure it was just a prank. There's a lot of traffic in Buckhead, people just cruising around looking for something to do," Laura added unconvincingly. "Somebody probably saw my car and thought it would be funny to disable it."

Trey shook his head. "It don't seem all that funny to me. You do what you want to, but you lock up, you hear? I'll have your car all ready in the morning."

Laura gave him her spare set of car keys, and thanked him for his help. "Don't worry about it," she reassured him. "I'm sure it was nothing."

He shrugged his thin shoulders and waved a cheerful good-bye. In a minute, she heard the roar of his engine as he started the truck; the headlights flashed briefly through the windows of the living room, and he was gone. She sank into a chair, her knees suddenly weak. She thought for a moment that she really should call Amos, but she shook the thought off. It had probably been just what she said: a prank. She wasn't harmed, and she would be better off not mentioning it to anyone. If she did, she would only make herself look like some kind of paranoid freak.

Feeling better, she rose and went into the kitchen. The clock on the wall said it was after nine o'clock, and she was starving. Food and bed were what she needed, and all this would seem like nothing in the morning.

Chapter 23

"Why was your car in the lot?" Craig asked the next morning. "Did you come in early?"

"No, I left it here overnight. My battery died last night," Laura lied smoothly. "I just went on home."

He frowned. "I don't like the idea of you being here alone. Arlene told me that you stayed late." He shook his head. "No more. You could have gotten into trouble, all alone at night."

"In Buckhead?" she asked lightly. "Come on, Craig. It's not exactly a high-crime zone."

"It didn't used to be," he corrected her. "But all those bars—you get a bad mix of people in Buckhead these days. Suburban jackasses and inner-city kids. I don't mess with it anymore."

"Still, it's hardly Dodge City," she said. "I called AAA

and a perfectly nice man came in about five minutes, anyway. He took me home.''

''What—he didn't just jump-start you?''

''No, I, umm, needed a new battery. My car's pretty old, you know.''

''Oh. Hey, good job on the brief,'' he said appreciatively, holding up the sheaf of paper she had left on his desk.

''Thanks,'' Laura said, relieved to have the subject changed. ''When's your hearing?''

''I'm leaving right now,'' he said. ''I hope I'll be back by lunchtime.''

''Good luck. It should be a slam-dunk. Before you go, I wanted to ask you something. I'm going to talk to Kenny today, to see how his meeting with the FBI went. Do you think there would be any use in having him talk to the pathologist at the crime lab again, to try to clear up some of the inconsistencies in his report?''

''Sure. Just don't let on that we've had another doctor look at his work. That might set him off.''

''Right. Call me if you need me,'' she added insincerely as she left his office. She had no desire to go downtown and appear in a case against one of her erstwhile colleagues, and Craig knew it.

Upstairs in her office, Laura picked up her voice mail. Kenny had left a message yesterday afternoon that she must have missed in her absorption with the brief. ''Hey, Laura,'' he said. ''Reporting in from the field. I talked to my buddy at the Bureau. He was going to get the information to someone involved in the investigation, and I should hear something tomorrow. They'll want to meet Vasovitch right away, I'm sure. He called me from Las Vegas. I think he might be having second thoughts, so I want to hustle the boys along. Call me tomorrow and I should have more for you.''

Laura dialed Kenny's office right away, but the voice mail system picked up. Too impatient to leave a message and wait, Laura hung up and paged him, and ended up waiting.

Finally, he called. Better yet, he announced that he would be in the neighborhood and wondered if she was free for lunch. She accepted quickly. "I want to talk to you about something, too," she said.

"Sounds like a deal," he said. "Meet me out front at noon. We can go to La Fonda and sit outside."

"Perfect," Laura said.

La Fonda Latina was a local chain that served good Cuban food at reasonable prices. Laura was especially fond of the vegetable paella, which came in such generous portions that she could rely on it to provide dinner, too. It was probably past time for an honest-to-God vegetable to get into her digestive system.

Kenny showed up right on time, although Laura, in her eagerness for paella and information, had been waiting in front of the building for a good five minutes.

"Afternoon," Kenny said as he pulled back out onto Maple Drive. "Saw the article in the paper this morning," he commented.

"Ugh. I forgot to buy a copy," she said.

"What, you don't subscribe?"

"Not since the books editor left. How was it?"

"So-so. He only had a paragraph or two about the lawsuit. Most of it was a rehash of Jervis's arrest, and the dismissal."

"I guess there's not a lot else to say at this point. I did hint to the reporter that there might be a tie-in with the FBI investigation. Did that make it in?"

"So that was what he was referring to. Here—I've got

the paper under the seat." He bent down and fished around on the floor.

"Just drive, Ken. I'll get the paper."

"Don't be so nervous, kid. The traffic's barely moving."

"That doesn't mean you can't have an accident," Laura retorted, remembering the mom in the van who had rolled into the Jaguar with such dramatic consequences. Not that anyone sane would come after Kenny with a golf club. She retrieved the paper and pulled out the metro section. To her disappointment, the article—a short one—was concealed deep in the interior. " 'A person familiar with the case indicated that evidence linking the case to other investigations may be introduced at a later date,' " Laura read aloud. "You're right. That's vague. Hey, where are you going? I thought we were going to La Fonda."

"We are. But I don't like the one in Buckhead. We're going to Roswell Road. It's easier to get a parking space."

"That much is true. As long as I get my paella. So tell me about your meeting with the FBI man."

"All in good time. But they're interested."

"When can we meet with them?"

"You're impatient today," he said.

"I hate sitting around doing nothing. By the way, I want you to go out to the crime lab to talk to that pathologist again. Craig thinks it might do some good."

"It might. On the other hand, it might not. There are two possibilities: either he's out-and-out lying, in which case talking to him from now until the end of time will have absolutely zero results. On the other hand, he might have just done a slipshod, half-assed job—in which case he'll be defensive and uncooperative."

"My. You're upbeat today."

"I'm realistic. Every day."

They had battled through the lunchtime traffic in Buckhead and were zipping north on Roswell Road. They passed the Bumper to Bumper Car Wash, which reminded Laura that Kenny hadn't said anything about his search for the remaining two witnesses. "Any progress on finding Terence Walker?" she asked.

"Not a lick. I have a lead on Jermaine Clay, however."

"Really? That's good news," she said, delighted.

"It's just a lead," he said cautiously, "and a pretty darn vague one. I hear tell that he has people in lower Alabama, in Atmore. Looks like I'll have to go there to find out if there's anything to it."

"That should be a pleasant trip," Laura said disingenuously.

"I always enjoy a trip to Alabama," Kenny said in a reproving tone. "I've got a cousin in Mobile; I can run down to Atmore, check out the story, and then go on to Mobile and have myself a good time. Here we are," he said, pulling into the parking lot at La Fonda.

Laura hopped down from the big pickup eagerly, and hiked her skirt, which had slid around her waist, back into alignment. Kenny eyed her. "You don't look like you've been eating right," he commented as they found a table. "Looks like you might have lost a pound or two, even."

"Maybe," she said noncommittally.

"I know what's going on," he said as he picked up a menu. "You don't eat right when Kowalski's not around, do you?"

"It's such a pain to cook for one, and I've been working pretty hard. I didn't get home last night until after nine. I stayed late to work on a brief for Craig."

"Good grief. Fannin's taking advantage of you, kiddo."

"No, he's not," Laura said defensively. She was glad,

though, that the conversation had veered away from the topic of Amos. "I wanted to do it. And I wouldn't have been working late if the printer hadn't kept jamming. Printing the dumb thing took almost as long as researching and writing it."

"Technology. Not all it's cracked up to be." A waiter appeared with chips and napkins. "You ready to order?" Kenny asked her.

"I've been ready. I don't even need to look at the menu. Vegetarian paella, please."

Kenny ordered a quesadilla. "I'm having a beer," he announced. "You might as well, too, so I won't look bad."

"You talked me into it."

When the beer was delivered, Laura resumed her interrogation of Kenny. "So what's the deal? When are we meeting with the FBI?"

Kenny made a play of pulling the label off his beer bottle. "I don't know if you should be there," he said.

"Why the hell not?"

"You don't know the Bureau," he said. "They're going to wonder why you're there, and it might open up a can of worms for you."

"I have no canned worms to worry about," she retorted. "Jervis is my client, and they'll have to share any information they get from Vasovitch that's in any way relevant to the case with me anyway. So what's the big deal?"

"They only want to see Vasovitch and his attorney. They didn't even want me there, but I insisted," he admitted.

"You've already set it up?" she demanded.

"I'm sorry, Laura. You have to do it on their terms. I will tell you everything, I promise, just as soon as the meeting ends."

Laura fought off her disappointment and a bit of annoyance. "Okay," she sighed. "I guess I really don't have standing in the matter. Have you talked to Diana Arnold?"

"No, I thought you'd want to do that," he said.

"Ah. Throwing me a bone," she said with a smile. "You're a prince. I assume that after you get this buttoned up you're off to Alabama?"

"Yep. Unless something else comes up."

"When you get back, I want you to tackle this pathologist at the crime lab. There's got to be some reason that his report is so far off from the one Craig's guy came up with."

"I agree. Do you think he's lying?"

Laura sighed. "It's impossible to say. Why would he? He doesn't have a dog in this hunt—at least, not that you can tell. But he struck me as a strange guy. I had a hard time getting a feel for what makes him tick, but I'm pretty sure telling him that we had another doctor look over his report wouldn't go over real well."

"I'll give him a call and try to wander out that way when I get back from Atmore. And, speaking of Atmore, what's up with you and Kowalski?"

"Very smooth transition," Laura complimented him. "The answer is nothing. I haven't called him, and he hasn't called me. Nothing has changed, and I don't think there's any reason to rehash the discussion."

"You're both being stubborn," Kenny said.

"No, I don't think so. I think we're dealing with a fundamental difference in the way we look at things."

"You're saying it's over?"

"Of course not. Not in my mind, anyway. He may disagree. You and Cindy don't always see eye to eye, do you?"

"Of course not. But we don't turn tail and stop talking to each other for two weeks, either. Because we're not stubborn."

"Leave it alone," Laura said. "Everybody in Atlanta seems to have an opinion on Amos and me. Police departments are nothing but hotbeds of gossip and rumor. I ran into Don Archer when I was downtown filing the suit—you know him, don't you?"

"Big Don? Sure. Nice guy."

"There's where we disagree," Laura said. "He gives me the creeps. I don't know why Amos hangs out with him."

"They don't hang out; they just play a little ball together. And if you ask me, Darryl Michaels is the creepy one. He's a jackass, anyway," Kenny added. "I used to play with them, and he was never my favorite. Archer's okay, though. You're just reading him wrong."

"Maybe so, but he's one of those men who you just *know* thinks about sex every seven seconds."

"I thought we all did."

"Probably so, but some of you do a better job of hiding it. Change of subject: How much do you know about cars?"

"I'd guess I'm about average. I can change a tire and jump a battery."

"Do you know anything about distributors?"

"I know what they do. Why are you asking?"

"I had to get a new one."

He shrugged. "That's normal for a car as old as yours, I suppose."

"I had to get it because mine was gone."

"Gone?"

"Completely. I want to know how hard it is to take one off."

"On a scale of one to ten, about a four. Given the right tools, of course."

"How long would it take?"

He shrugged. "Just a few minutes, if you knew what you

were doing. Where's this going? Are you saying somebody took your distributor?''

"It looks that way. I was parked under the building, and when I went down to go home, I couldn't start the car. I thought it was a dead battery, but the AAA man said the distributor was gone.''

"Who would have taken it?''

"That's what I'd like to know,'' Laura said. "It must have been a prank. The mechanic said they're not expensive enough to making stealing them worthwhile. I think somebody just wanted to get his jollies by inconveniencing me.''

Kenny frowned. "Or worse. Taking the distributor out flat disables a car. Somebody might have wanted you stranded.''

"Please; no paranoid fantasies. It was in the middle of Buckhead, not Beirut. Just forget it. It was nothing. No harm, no foul. Whoever did it had plenty of opportunity to hang around and take advantage of my helplessness. But the only person I saw was a tattooed mechanic.''

"Just the same, I'd be careful,'' Kenny warned.

"I'm always careful. And, Kenny, please don't tell Amos about this. I just wanted a second opinion, that's all.''

"My lips are sealed. You want more chips?'' he asked.

"Absolutely.''

Chapter 24

Laura tried not to be disgruntled at being left out of the meeting with the FBI, but it wasn't easy. She glumly told Craig what was going on. He was, of course, unmoved.

"It's no big deal," he said. "Let the Bureau do the leg-work. If they find out that our client was the victim of a conspiracy, we'll reap the benefits. Otherwise we might be just wasting our time."

"And time is money," Laura commented.

"You say that as if it was a bad thing," Craig said. "Speaking of which, here's a small token of my gratitude for the work you did last night. I didn't hire you to be my associate, and I want you to know that I don't expect you to do work for me without compensation." He handed her a check, which, to Laura's astonishment, was in the munificent amount of twenty-five hundred dollars.

"Craig! This is too much. I just worked a couple of

306 *Lelia Kelly*

hours—my billable rate at Prendergrast and Crawley certainly never got this high!"

"Maybe it should have. Anyway, I feel bad that you stayed here and did this, and then had to deal with your car. I looked at your car this morning, by the way. You really should get rid of it."

"Thanks, but as long as it runs, I think I'll hold out."

"Suit yourself, but it's going to stop some day when it's not going to be convenient—or maybe even safe. Use that as a down payment on something new."

"I'll think about it," she said noncommittally. She didn't need Craig taking up where Amos had left off in the argument over the car.

"And go on and take the rest of the afternoon off," Craig continued, his bounty apparently not exhausted by signing the check. "Go see a movie. You won't make the phone ring by staring at it, you know."

"I know, but I want to stay. I have things to do," she said.

"Suit yourself. Let me know when you hear something. And don't look at me like that. I *am* interested; I'm just not putting a lot of hope into the FBI. In my experience, once they're involved, you can kiss your case good-bye."

Laura returned to her office. She did have things to do—a thing, anyway: call Diana. She tried, but got the answering machine. It occurred to her that Julian Arnold might not know that his wife had been in contact with her. It also crossed her mind that Helen Belew might still be in town, and staying with her daughter. In either case, Laura didn't think it would be wise to leave a message.

That pretty much covered her to-do list. She sat in the slightly battered chair at her desk, and bent a helpless paper clip into new and strange shapes. Laura was not accustomed to inactivity, and she'd had more than enough of it. Maybe Craig had the right idea. Two hours in a brain-cell-killing movie might be just the thing she needed. She pulled out Kenny's newspaper and looked at the entertainment section. There were a couple of appealing films at the art house on Cheshire Bridge she wouldn't mind seeing, and she could still make the cheap early show if she left right away.

Just as she made up her mind to leave, the phone, which had been so silent that she'd actually checked it for a dial tone a couple of times, rang. Laura knew that it wouldn't be Kenny; it was too early, but she hoped that it might be Diana, even if that meant missing the movie. She picked up with alacrity.

"Hey, Laura, it's Carlton."

Laura was puzzled for a minute. Carlton who? She couldn't believe that the detective would be calling her. She hadn't spoken to him since the charges against Jervis had been dropped, and since she had put him at the center of an internal investigation. Carlton might call her, but she doubted that he'd sound this cheerful and friendly if he did. This had to be another Carlton altogether.

But it was Carlton Hemingway, and not only was he speaking to her, he was as cheerful as ever. "How are you?" she asked, trying not to sound surprised.

"Okay. How about you? Things okay with Fannin?"

"Sure," she said, and then she fumbled for something to say next. "So, ahh, what are you up to?"

"Working, as usual. In fact, that's why I'm calling. I need a favor."

"Wait. Back up. You mean you're working again, as a detective?"

"Of course. Oh, that's right—you and Kowalski split up.

I guess you've lost your pipeline for all the Atlanta Police Department news.''

Laura answered him tartly. "We have *not* split up. Honestly, all cops do is gossip. Maybe if you spent a little more time hunting down felons and a little less talking about each other's love lives the crime rate would drop a point or two.''

Carlton laughed. "Hit a nerve, huh?''

"Maybe. Anyway, the last I heard you and Devereaux were the subjects of an internal investigation.''

"Yep. Alex still is. I'm cleared though, and back at the grind.''

"You mean Alex has been implicated in the Jervis case?''

"No, there was nothing to all that. No, he was suspended because he was working unauthorized off-duty.''

"For Darryl Michaels? But everyone knew that! He was at the mayor's campaign rally bodyguarding a jock.''

"But he didn't get it authorized. Which would have been no big deal, except that when the Office of Professional Standards started looking at him for the Jervis mess, they found out that he was moonlighting. So he was grounded for a week, with pay. It's no big deal. He'll be back on the job tomorrow, as a matter of fact.''

"I'm glad. I was worried that you guys were in trouble.''

"No sweat. I mean, it wasn't the greatest thing that ever happened to me, but I wasn't ever really worried. And now, I'm beginning to think that you were right all along. I think we might have missed a thing or two in the investigation.''

Laura tossed the movie pages into the trash can and settled back into her chair. "What makes you say that?''

"It's this new case I'm working, which is related to the Jervis case. You know that one of the eyewitnesses who turned up to testify against Jervis got himself killed?''

"Yes. Albert Jackson.''

"Right. And it just so happens that he was in custody at the time."

"Yes. He got into some kind of fight with another inmate. Which," she editorialized, "came as no big shock. He was quite a little player, wasn't he?"

"But things aren't always what they seem to be. It's beginning to look to me less like a jailhouse beef than a hit."

"You're kidding," Laura said. "Who would want him dead?"

Carlton laughed. *"Hellooo*—that's what I'm trying to figure out. Which brings me back to why I'm calling you. Your man Ken Newton's been nosing around this business. I was hoping I could talk to him."

"Of course. He's tied up this afternoon, but I'll have him call you as soon as he gets free. But tell me more—what makes you think someone was paid to kill him?"

"There are rumors. Besides, the guy who did it had a hunting knife. He had to have some help getting a weapon like that. I mean, the jail's not the tightest-run ship in the world, but they're pretty good at keeping the pointy objects away from the felons. I would be, too, if it was my job to guard them. And then there's a coincidental mix-up in the records when the perp is being transferred to the county jail. Instead of getting locked up to await trial for manslaughter, the guy is released. Needless to say, he ain't been seen around since."

"Wow. It does sound strange."

"That's about all I've got to go on. I was hoping Newton would have had some luck finding the other guy . . . Jermaine Clay."

"As a matter of fact, he does have a lead on where he might be hiding out. It's pretty clear that he *is* lying low somewhere. Although," Laura wondered aloud, "he might be dead, too, for all we know. You think whoever killed Belew is behind all this, of course."

Carlton hedged a little. "Looks like there might be a tie-in. It's still possible that it's all just a bunch of rumors. Jails and cons are notorious for spinning conspiracy theories."

"Just like police forces."

"Yeah. Anyway, you're working for Fannin now. What's that like?"

Laura sighed. "Not exactly a thrill a minute. It's a waiting game." She decided not to tell Carlton about Carl Vasovitch. "You know we filed suit against the city and the Atlanta Police Department, don't you?"

"Yep."

"Nothing personal," Laura hastened to add.

"I'm not taking it personally. Jervis wasn't the right guy; we made a mistake."

"It's nice to hear you say that, Carlton. I think other people *are* taking it personally."

"Well, Kowalski's a hard case. But he'll come around. Want me to talk to him?"

"Absolutely not!"

He chuckled. "I kind of figured you'd say that. I better get going. Have Ken call me when he gets time."

"Sure thing. Good talking to you, Carlton."

"Ditto. Maybe we can grab lunch someday soon."

"Sounds like a plan."

That was a relief, anyway, she reflected. This principled decision of hers had proved pretty expensive in terms of her personal life. Carlton's almost nonchalant attitude gave her hope that maybe Amos might come around eventually, too. Which was all to the good, except that now she had missed the start of the movie, and she still had nothing constructive to do with the rest of the day.

Laura decided that she'd be better off at home than sitting here, scrubbing the bathtub or anything. Kenny knew where to find her. She packed her bag, said her good-byes to Craig and the staff, and started for the parking lot, where she saw Kenny's truck. She practically ran to meet him as he angled into a parking space.

"What happened?" she said, not even allowing him time to get out of the truck.

"Easy," he said. "I'll tell you all about it. Where's Fannin? He might want to hear this, too."

"He's inside. Come on," she said, resisting the impulse to tug at his sleeve.

Craig was happy to see Kenny, although he managed to keep his enthusiasm more muted than Laura did. "Give him a break, Laura," he said. "You want a Coke or something, Ken?"

"That'd be great," Kenny replied. "It's been a day." Craig stepped out to get the Coke. "Don't look at me like that," Kenny said to Laura. "I'm plumb wore out from all of this running around. And now I bet you want me to go to Alabama looking for the mystery witness."

"I do. I've got to tell you about what Carlton said."

"You're on speaking terms with him again?"

"Yes. He didn't get in any real trouble. He called today . . ." Craig came back into the room. "I'll tell you both about it when we've heard your story, Kenny."

"Okay," he said. "Thanks, Fannin." He popped the top on the can, poured the Coke into a glass, and started narrating. "Let me just say first, for those of you who haven't dealt with our colleagues in law enforcement at the Bureau for a while, that things haven't changed a whole lot. In other words, when you have a meeting with the men in black, you can count on doing a lot of talking while they do all the listening. That's pretty much how it went down today. The good news is that they are very interested in what our friend Carl has to say. They were especially interested in this guy who asked Lawrence Belew to act as a front for bids.''

"But Carl never knew who the man was," Laura said.

"No, but I have a feeling that the agent we met with might have known something. He sat right up when Carl got to that part of the tale."

"Did you get a sense that the Bureau thinks Belew's murder might be tied in?" Craig asked.

Kenny shrugged. "Who can say? We'll just have to wait and see what turns up. In the meantime, they've put a guy in Carl's building, and that tells me that they must believe that he might be in some physical danger."

"Poor Carl!" Laura said. "I hope he's not too upset that we dragged him into all this."

"Naw, he's cool with it," Ken said. "I think he really cared about Belew, and he wants to do what he can to make sure Belew's wishes are carried out. But don't hold your breath for any quick breaks. Those guys have an agenda, and they're not going to kite off and start arresting folks just because they get some new lead. They're all set to keep this investigation running as long as it takes for them to get what they want."

"By which I assume you mean getting the cuffs on some more of our elected officials," Craig said dryly.

"You bet your bottom dollar. I think they'd like to land a bigger fish. They've racked up a pretty good head count so far, but most of the guys they've indicted or convicted are pretty small-fry. So don't be disappointed that we didn't set off any fireworks.'' This last remark was clearly directed at Laura.

"I'm not. Besides, I want to tell you about my call from Carlton,'' she said. "You, too, Craig. He's looking into the murder of that witness—Albert Jackson—in the city jail.'' She ran down what Carlton had told her. "And he wants to talk to you about Jermaine Clay, Kenny—when you find him.''

"Okay, okay—I get it. Time to stop sitting around on my duff. I'm off to 'Bama.''

"With a banjo on your knee?'' Craig asked.

"I believe that's Louisiana,'' Laura corrected.

"You're both wrong. It's 'I come from Alabama with a banjo on my knee,' '' Kenny said. "But whatever, I'll call you when I know something. And,'' he added, anticipating Laura's next question, "I called out to the crime lab to see if I could get a meeting with that pathologist. Turns out he's gone.''

"Gone? What do you mean?'' Laura asked.

"He resigned, with no notice. And, no, they don't know how to get in touch with him—or if they do, they're not going to tell some random PI just because he wants to know.''

"I have to say that sounds kind of odd,'' Craig said. "First, the guy does a half-assed job on an autopsy; then he leaves town?''

"Maybe it is fishy,'' Ken said. "Or maybe it's code for 'we fired his ass.' ''

"That's possible,'' Craig said. "On review, Dr. Cooper's superiors may have decided that his work wasn't up to snuff.''

"I'll call one of my buddies out there and see what he knows,'' Laura said, "but it sure does seem like we have a lot of people involved in this investigation who've mysteriously disappeared.''

"Cooper's bugging out is a little strange," Kenny admitted. "But these other witnesses? I'm not a bit surprised. We're not dealing with responsible, productive members of society."

"Understood," Laura said. "Still, it bugs me that Cooper could have—should have—been a witness in the trial of Lawrence Belew's killer, whenever that happens."

"He may be yet," Craig said. "He can always be found. But our case is fine without him. Maybe better, in fact. There won't be anyone to dispute Dr. Hillman's version of events."

"Good for us," Laura said. "But not for everyone. Speaking of which, I should call Diana Arnold and bring her up to date. Kenny, do you have a minute to come up to my office and talk to her? If we can get her on the phone, that is; I haven't been able to so far."

"I'm game, as long as I get to go home and kiss my wife and kids before I go on the next mission."

"We'll keep it short. There's not an awful lot to tell her, anyway, is there?"

There wasn't, and Diana didn't have much time to listen, as it happened. She was trying to get dinner on the table, and her son had a friend from school over. They managed to get through the chaos and communicate what Kenny had learned.

Diana was keenly interested, though, in what they had to tell her, and she listened as intently as anyone could with two six-year-old boys in the background. "Did they seem to think that there was some connection between this man who tried to bribe Lawrence and the murder?" she asked.

"Hard to say," Kenny said.

"Did you get a sense that they might have known who this man was?"

"Maybe," Kenny said. "They're pretty good poker players, but I thought I picked up some interest."

"I guess that's about as good as it's going to get," she sighed.

"For now," Kenny said reassuringly. "We've still got some leads to follow. Laura, tell her about Albert Jackson."

Laura shared Carlton's suspicions. "So *now* the Atlanta Police Department thinks that there might be something to what you've been saying," she commented. "I hope they're usually more on the ball than this."

"In fairness," Laura said, "I think the blame—if there is any—belongs to the higher-ups in the city government. Carlton and Alex were just doing the best they could."

"And now the FBI will do the best they can," Diana added, "and my brother is still dead."

"Diana, I'm sorry."

"Hey, not your fault. I guess I just have to suck it up and get on with my life at some point. No offense, Kenny, but I don't think you're going to have any more luck in Alabama than you did at the FBI this afternoon. Whoever's behind this is one step ahead of us."

Laura hated to hear Diana's tone; she feared that the bereaved sister was slipping into depression. "All we can do is keep trying," Laura said.

"I know. And at least you *are* trying. Which is more than I can say for the police and the city government."

"Don't give up, Diana. That's what they want you to do."

"I'm just taking one thing at a time. Right now, I've got two little boys pestering the cat. I better do something about it. Call me if anything else happens."

"We will," Laura promised.

She hung up and shook her head. "She's depressed, I'm afraid. She doesn't know it now, but even catching the guy who killed Lawrence isn't going to bring her out of it."

Kenny agreed. "But she'll be okay. She's a good strong lady." He glanced at his watch. "I better hit the road. I'll call you from Alabama."

"Thanks. It would be great if you could find Jermaine Clay."

"If I do, I'll tie him to the front grill of the truck and bring him on in like a prize buck. You go on home, too, kid. You're not doing yourself a lot of good worrying about all of this."

"Yeah, I know. Stops me worrying about everything else, though," she said with a smile.

"Cindy says Kowalski is crazy, if that makes you feel any better."

"Your wife is a perceptive and intelligent woman. Be good in Alabama."

"I'm always good in Alabama," he said.

Laura looked at her watch; there was just time to catch Tommy Wood at the crime lab before he left work. She looked up his number and punched it into the keypad.

"You just caught me trying to sneak out," he said. "What can I do for you?"

"What do you know about Jay Cooper leaving the crime lab?"

His reply was cautious. "I know he's gone, but I don't know why. We're kind of a small shop out here, so it gets around pretty quickly when someone leaves. Not always *why*, though."

"Can you say whether or not his departure was voluntary?"

"As far as I can tell, yes. But they're so afraid of lawsuits that they might have wanted it to seem that way."

"So you think he might have been asked to leave?"

"Geez, did I say that? You're worse than that cop."

"What cop?"

"Uh-oh. Now I've done it. Look, a cop from the Atlanta Police Department was asking about Cooper, okay? I gave him the same story I'm giving you."

"What cop was this?"

"I didn't meet him. It was just a phone call."

"But surely he gave you his name."

"It was Alex Devereaux."

"But he's ..." Laura stopped herself. "Never mind. I don't mean to bug you. Sorry I kept you."

"No biggie. Just call if I can ever help."

Now, that's *interesting,* Laura thought after she hung up. *What's Devereaux doing poking around this case when he's suspended?* She spent a minute staring into the middle distance. At length, she realized that she wasn't going to figure it out by sitting in her office all night. It was time to go home.

Chapter 25

Nothing looked wrong as Laura approached her house. It was, in fact, hard to imagine anything that could look more right than this small white-painted brick cottage, unless it was any of the couple of dozen other houses that bordered the quiet street. This part of town had so far escaped most of the depredations of the nouveau riche Visigoths who thought that it was acceptable to tear down a house that had unassumingly provided comfort and shelter to families for seventy years, and to erect in its place a crackerbox mansion. There were one or two hideous new houses in the neighborhood, but none yet on this street. Sometimes Laura wished that the economy would slow down, and that people wouldn't have enough money to build those follies.

She pulled into the little one-car garage at the end of the drive, turned off the motor, and got out of the car. The door creaked every time she opened it; the engine tended to cough and sputter for a minute or two after the ignition was cut. Maybe Amos and Craig were right. Maybe she did need a new car, but she'd rather take Craig's little bonus and use it for a trip to Italy. She and Amos had been talking about going to Europe. Now she'd have to go alone, or get a girlfriend to come along. She felt herself beginning to slide into a little self-pity session. "Shake it off," she warned herself, half under her breath. She walked out of the garage and started toward the house; there was still enough daylight that she didn't flip on the light that illuminated the driveway.

"Hi!" a little voice said, off to her right. It was Evan, her neighbor's three-year-old son, peeking through the gate in the fence that separated Laura's driveway from his back-yard.

"Hello to you, too," Laura said. She liked this little guy, and his mother Lucy, a "retired" lawyer. They had some acquaintances in common, and every so often they would share legal gossip over the back fence.

"I'm having bisghetti for supper," Evan informed her.

"Oh? Me, too, probably. Do you like bisghetti?"

"I guess so." He looked over his shoulder and saw his mother approaching.

"Hi, Laura," she said. "Is he bothering you?"

"Never," Laura replied honestly. "We were just discussing bisghetti."

"You're welcome to join us for some. Mack's going to be working late again, so it's just the two of us." Mack, Lucy's husband, continued to toil toward partnership in one of the big law firms downtown.

Laura started to decline, but changed her mind. "You know, I think I'd like that. If you'll let me bring a bottle of wine," she added.

"You're on. We'll go ahead and feed this guy and you and I can have a little cocktail."

"Great. I'll change and be right over."

Laura was so glad of the prospect of a nice glass of wine and some good company that she almost didn't notice that the back door was ajar. She started to walk through it, but stopped. Had she left it open this morning? It was possible, but she could conjure up a mental image of locking the door behind herself.

Then she looked at the door frame. The splintered wood told her that she *had* locked the door. Someone had opened it by force. She quickly turned away and headed back toward the driveway, to the gate in the fence that separated her house from Lucy's. Lucy and Evan were still in the backyard. "That was quick!" Lucy said.

"No, I didn't go in . . . there's a problem. Have you been home all day?"

"Yes. Except for running out to the grocery store early this afternoon. Why?"

"You didn't see anyone at my house?"

"Oh, my God—did someone break in?"

"Maybe," Laura said, with a meaningful glance at Evan.

Lucy followed her gaze. "Oh. Right. You better go inside and call 911. We'll wait here."

Laura went into Lucy's house and dialed with shaky fingers. She gave the operator all the relevant information. "Okay, Ms. Chastain, we've dispatched a car. Don't go back inside."

"I won't," Laura promised. "I'm at my neighbor's house."

She went back outside, and nodded to Lucy. "On the way," she said tersely.

"Okay, I'll get him in and start supper. And I'll get you a glass of wine. Come on in."

"I'd rather wait here," Laura said. "I'll be okay."

The police car, dispatched from the zone headquarters just down the road, was there in minutes. Two officers, a man and a woman, got out. Laura was thankful that they hadn't used the siren; the less attention this drew, the better.

"You Miss Chastain?" the male officer asked.

"Yes," she said.

"Did you go inside?"

"No, I started to, but I saw that someone had broken in."

"Okay, let us check it out. Whoever did it is probably long gone, but better safe than sorry." His partner was already walking around the back of the house. Laura watched, alarmed, as they both drew their guns before the woman called out "Police officers" and went inside, keeping her back against the door frame. Her partner waited a moment; then he went in as well.

They were inside for only a few minutes; it was a small house. When they emerged, their guns were holstered again. "He's gone, ma'am," the female officer said. "Can you come inside and tell us what's missing?"

"Sure," Laura said hesitantly. The woman went ahead of her. Laura thought, absurdly, that she should have asked her name; she had a nagging feeling that she was being rude. They stopped inside the kitchen. Laura looked around. Nothing was gone, but there wasn't anything to take, except the blender or the toaster, which were in their usual places. The female cop—her name was Debbie, Laura noticed— looked inquiringly at her. "Nothing's missing," Laura said.

They proceeded into the living room; the television, VCR, and stereo were all intact. Nothing was missing in the bedroom, either; Laura's only valuable jewelry was a pearl necklace, and it lay untouched in its case on the chest of drawers. She shook her head. "Nothing seems to be missing."

"Something must have interrupted him," the male cop said. His name was Mike, which was a very good name for a cop, Laura thought irrelevantly. He pointed to the bed. "Strange place to keep a distributor, miss."

Laura looked at the bed, which, luckily, she had bothered to make up before leaving. There was a thing sitting in the middle of it, about the size of a coffee mug, with wires sprouting from it. "Is that a distributor?" she asked quietly.

"Yep. You been having trouble with yours?"

"In a manner of speaking. It was stolen out of my car a few days ago," she said.

That precipitated action. Debbie hustled Laura out of the room. "Can you go wait at your neighbor's?" she asked. "We'll have to call in a crime scene unit, and the detectives. They'll want to ask you some questions."

Laura allowed herself to be led back to Lucy's, and to be deposited on a kitchen chair. Debbie said something quietly to Lucy while Laura watched Evan, in a booster seat, tackle a plate of spaghetti. Debbie left, and Lucy wordlessly put a glass of red wine in front of Laura. Laura picked it up, trying her hardest not to slosh it onto the table.

"Do you want to call your boyfriend?" Lucy asked. "He's a policeman, isn't he?"

Laura nodded. "I'd rather not, though. We're . . . I don't think I ought to call him."

"Okay. You just sit right here. Are you hungry?"

"No, thanks. God, I'm sorry about this. . . ."

"Don't be. You can stay here tonight, as long as you want."

Laura shook her head. "I have to go home. If I don't tonight, I may never."

The detective came, and Lucy led them into Mack's home office, where they could talk behind closed doors. Laura didn't recognize the detective, who introduced himself as Jim somebody. If her name meant anything to him he showed no sign of it. He asked her a series of routine questions— when had she left home that morning, when had she returned, when had she noticed the door had been jimmied? She answered them all by rote; the patrol officers had already been through all of this. Then he got down to cases. "When was the distributor taken, Miss Chastain?"

Laura answered carefully. "Last night. You can ask my boss. I told him this morning that I'd had car trouble."

"Never mind for now, but we will need confirmation eventually. You didn't report that to the police, did you?"

"No. I thought it was a prank, maybe some kids trying to have a good time in Buckhead, you know."

He made a note, then looked up at her again. "Have you had any strange phone calls or messages lately?" She shook her head. "Seen anybody in the neighborhood, or at the office, who doesn't belong?"

"No. No one. Nothing strange."

"Try to think: is there anyone who might want to scare you?"

"Yes. I'm a lawyer, and I'm working on a case that . . . well, I think you know what I'm working on."

"Yes," he said, meeting her eyes evenly. "Would you like me to call Lieutenant Kowalski?" The message was clear: *I know all about you.*

"No. Please don't worry him," Laura said, with an effort to remain calm.

"He'll find out about this anyway, Miss Chastain."

"I know," she said. "But he won't want to be involved."

"Are you having trouble with your relationship with the lieutenant?"

"That's none of your concern," Laura said sharply.

"It might be," he said.

"For God's sake—Amos didn't do this. Are you insane?" The very suggestion galvanized her. "This is some creep who doesn't want me nosing around the Belew murder," she said. "Do you *know* Amos Kowalski at all?"

"By reputation. I have to ask," he said defensively. "The fact that the distributor was placed on the bed . . . well, it's suggestive."

Laura stood up. "And I think the person who did it meant it to be. He probably wanted you to think exactly what you're thinking. Do you have any more questions?"

"Not for now. You can't go back until the crime scene unit is finished."

"I know that. Please let me know when they're done," she said, and she left the room.

Detective Jim followed, and he spoke to Lucy. "Okay if she stays here awhile?"

"Sure. We're just going to put this guy in the bathtub and have our supper. Laura's going to read you a story when you get your pajamas on, Evan."

"I want my bezert first," Evan said. "Who are you?" he asked the detective.

"Just a friend of your mom and dad's," Jim answered. "You'll be okay, Miss Chastain?"

"Yes. Just let me know when I can go back home."

Lucy gave Evan a cookie for his "bezert" and kept up a stream of cheerful talk while he ate it slowly, clearly avoiding the inevitable bath. His mother prevailed, though, and he was soon off to the tub. Laura sat on the john and drank wine while Lucy erased the evidence of bisghetti from his small person. Once he was in his pajamas, Lucy started fixing the grown-ups dinner, and Laura read Evan the promised story. He grew drowsy after the third reprise of *Mike Mulligan,* and Lucy took him to bed. It was all very normal, with the exception of the intrusion of a cop who took a set of Laura's fingerprints. After he left, Laura and Lucy ate dinner without once mentioning the break-in.

Finally, as she and Lucy were clearing up the dishes, Detective Jim returned to tell Laura that her house had been secured. "I called a locksmith to repair the door," he added. "He's there now."

"Thank you," Laura said, wondering if crime victims who didn't date cops got this kind of service.

"You're welcome. Sure you're okay going back alone?"

"I'll be fine." Laura managed a smile. "Don't worry. It takes more than this to shake me up."

Despite the brave words, though, Laura gratefully accepted Lucy's offer of another glass of wine before she left. Mack returned home, and they had to tell him the story. He offered to walk Laura home and see her safely inside, an offer she accepted without hesitation. "Thanks, Mack," Laura said. "And tell Lucy how much I appreciated everything."

"She knows. We're glad to help. We were just saying that we wish we saw more of you, Laura. Maybe not under these circumstances, of course."

"Of course!" Laura agreed with a laugh. "I'll try to keep the crime wave to a minimum. And next time I'll fix dinner."

"It's a deal. Call us if you need anything. Any time, Laura—seriously."

"Thanks."

Once alone in the house, Laura took a minute to assess

the damage done by the crime scene team. Everything had been fingerprinted, and traces of powder remained. A few things had been moved, but nothing had been damaged. The distributor, she noted, was gone. Tagged and bagged, she assumed, evidence in a case she felt sure would never go anywhere. She closed her eyes and pictured the man who had done this. He had a button missing from the cuff of his jacket. "I got your message," she whispered to him, "and you can go to hell," she added defiantly.

Although it was getting late, and she was tired, she set about cleaning up the mess before she got ready for bed. She was working her way through the living room when she heard the sound of tires in the driveway. She involuntarily crouched down in an attempt to make herself invisible. Feeling a little foolish, she crept on hands and knees to a window, and raised her head to peer out.

She saw the familiar silhouette of a Jeep Wagoneer in the drive. Amos. Of course the police department grapevine had lit up with this news. She stood and waited for the knock on the door. It didn't come.

Laura went into the dining room, where she had a better view of the drive. There was just enough light from the street lamps to show that Amos was still sitting inside his truck. She realized that he intended to spend the night there. She sighed and put down the dish towel she had been using to clean, and went out the front door.

He watched her walk across the lawn, but he didn't get out of the truck. Without preamble, she opened the passenger door and got in. "So you heard," she said.

"Yes. Why didn't you call me?" he said, looking at her.

"I don't know. Yes, I do. Because you'd do this."

"Do what?"

"Come over here to protect me."

"Sorry. I didn't realize that was a bad thing to do," he said.

"It's not. But you don't have to do it. I'm fine."

"No, you're not. You're being stalked by some creep. Possibly a dangerous one."

"I don't think so. I think he's just trying to warn me away from the Belew case."

"Think so? He's picked a fairly elaborate way to do it. He could have made a couple of anonymous phone calls, but he chooses to break into your car and your house. He wants you to know that he can get to you whenever he wants to."

"Why hasn't he, then?"

"Because he's playing with you. He'll make a move when he wants to."

Laura shook her head. "I don't think so. He's not going to come after me."

"What makes you so sure this is connected to the Belew case?"

"What else could it be?"

"What else? To me, it has all the hallmarks of a stalker with a sexual motive."

"Amos, please. I appreciate your concern, but that's not what this is about."

"I've seen a few of these guys. I know how they work. He took the distributor out of your car, Laura. He disabled you, literally and figuratively. He made you helpless. Then he puts it back *on your bed.* What do you think this is all about?"

"I don't know, but it's not sexual. He may want it to look that way, but it's just about scaring me, and I'm not going to be scared off that easily."

"Well, I am. I'm officially worried, Laura. And this isn't

about you and me, in case you're wondering. I would be just as concerned about any woman in your position."

"That's very flattering."

"Damn. I'm wrong either way, I guess. I just wanted you to know that this has nothing to do with us. With where we are. In other words, this isn't an attempt to get back with you."

"Thank you for being so honest," Laura said, hoping that she didn't betray the hurt she felt, but not succeeding.

"Shit, that didn't come out right. I didn't say that I *didn't* want to try again, Laura. I just said that this is not an attempt to do that. Can I catch a break here?"

Laura had to laugh. "I'm too tired for any of this. And you're going to be, too, if you stay out here. Go home, Amos. I'll be okay. I'll call you if I hear anybody skulking in the shrubbery."

"If it's all the same to you, I'll stay. You go back in and get some sleep, though."

"Amos, you are not going to sit in this truck all night. You'll be one big cramp tomorrow if you do."

"That's my choice."

"And what about tomorrow night, and the night after that? You can't live in your car, you nincompoop."

"I've spent lots of nights in smaller cars than this," he retorted.

Laura sighed. He was perfectly capable of staying out there in a full upright position all week, and she knew it. She capitulated. "Come inside. You can watch over me better in there, anyway."

"You know I can't do that."

"For the love of God, I meant you could stay in the guest room. I'm not going to take advantage of this situation to try to patch things up, either. And if you don't come in, I'll stay out here with you. And you know I can outlast you." She glared at him meaningfully.

He conceded, not as reluctantly as she expected. "Okay. In the guest room."

"Fine." She opened the door and got out, and he followed. Once inside the house, she took a businesslike approach. "There are sheets on the bed, and I'll put out towels for you. You need anything else?"

"No. Did you throw away my toothbrush and razor?" he asked.

"Of course not. They're still here. I haven't given up on us, even if you have."

"I haven't."

Their eyes met, and for a moment Laura thought that the barrier would fall, but they both looked away. "Okay," she said. "See you in the morning."

They both got ready for bed in silence, behind closed doors. Laura lay awake for a long time, fighting the temptation to creep into the guest room—and wondering if he was awake, too, and thinking along the same lines. She punched her innocent pillow fiercely, and squeezed her eyes shut. It was early morning—after three—when she finally succumbed to sleep, and when her alarm rang at seven, Amos was already gone, the bed neatly made, and no trace that he had been there at all . . . except for the toothbrush next to hers.

Chapter 26

Craig's keen eyes didn't miss much, and they didn't miss the circles under Laura's the next day. "You look exhausted," he commented as she sat down heavily in the chair across from his desk.

"Thanks, Fannin. Just what a lady likes to hear," she said, but she undermined her indignation by stifling a yawn.

"Late night, I guess. I hope it was fun, at least."

"Not really." Laura had already debated whether she should tell Craig and Kenny. She was initially inclined not to, but she knew that Amos would tell Ken if she didn't, and that Ken would tell Craig ... *and they say women gossip,* she thought. It was probably best to make a clean breast of it. "I had a little trouble," she admitted, casting around for a way to place the "trouble" in the best and least alarming light. "Somebody decided to break into my house yesterday."

"Your house? That's weird. I would think that all of the stay-at-home moms on that street would be a more effective deterrent to crime than a pack of roving Dobermans."

"Normally, I think you'd be right. But this guy wasn't after the Chastain family heirlooms, unfortunately." She spilled the story, even though that involved admitting she had lied about the trouble with her car. He listened with a steadily deepening frown on his face.

"Damn it, Laura," he said when she wound it up. "First let me say that I'm fairly hacked off that you didn't feel it necessary to be honest with me in the first place—"

"But . . ." she began.

He held up a warning hand. "And, second, what makes you so sure that this *is* about the lawsuit? You might have a stalker."

"What else could it be, Craig? I'm not enough of an egomaniac to think that I'm high up on anybody's enemies list, or that I have some guy obsessed with me to the point where he steals my auto parts."

"Don't be so sure about that."

"Come on! I don't have any false modesty; I'm okay-looking. But I don't think there's anybody out there who's worshipping me from afar."

"In the first place, although I think you're better than 'okay-looking,' it's not about how you look. A man who would do something like this . . . well, who knows what sets him off? Or maybe I do know. Have you thought that it might be someone you know—well?"

"Oh, no. You don't think it's Amos, too, do you?"

"Who else does?" he asked.

"No one. The detective just asked about my relationship—which he would have known nothing about if it weren't with a cop, by the way. In fact, I doubt he would have asked about my love life if he didn't already have plenty of information on it. You know how much they talk.''

"Point taken; he probably did know about you and Kowalski. However, I don't think that's why he asked about it. Any cop investigating any similar situation is going to ask about the boyfriend first thing off the bat.''

"Maybe just to eliminate a possibility. But no one seriously thinks that Amos is capable of something like this. It's too stupid.''

"He's a guy, Laura. If he was desperate enough to get your attention, I would say he's as capable as any guy of doing something completely idiotic and boneheaded. We all have it within us. Even me.''

"That I can believe. But if this was all Amos's ploy to get back into my good graces, why didn't he try to take advantage last night? He could have . . . well, let's just say he was in a position to capitalize on the turn of events.''

"He came over, didn't he?'' Craig said knowingly.

"Of course he did. He loves me. And of course he heard about the break-in.'' Suddenly tired of discussing her private life, she rose to her feet. "You know what? I'm not going to discuss this with you anymore. You ask Kenny Newton. He'll tell you that Amos would never pull a stunt like this. If Amos wants me back, he knows all he has to do is say so.''

"Are you sure? You can be pretty stubborn, you know.''

"And so can he. And so can you.''

"Don't take it out on me,'' he said.

"Am I? I'm sorry. It's very frustrating for me,'' she said, sitting back down. "Every time I think we're getting somewhere on this case, I get set back. I find a great witness, and the FBI steals him. Or he's dead. Or disappeared. Or he leaves a perfectly good job. It's beginning to look like a pattern.''

"It could all be coincidental," Craig reminded her. "Especially the vanishing witnesses. People of limited means tend to drift from place to place, and they're hard to find. Thugs get stabbed in jailhouse brawls. People—even doctors—get tired of their jobs and move on. As for the FBI, well, don't say I didn't warn you. I don't think Vasovitch's story was ever going to help us, anyway."

"Maybe not with the lawsuit, but I did hope that it might be kind of a break for Diana."

"Who is not, may I interject, our client."

"Yes, Craig, I know. I know what you want me to do: sit quietly and wait until the city answers the complaint. But you know I'm not built for sitting around."

"I know. And I have an idea for you."

"Really?"

"Don't get excited; it's got nothing to do with Lawrence Belew. I was thinking that you might take on an additional case or two. You can handle it and still do justice to Jervis's suit."

"I'm not sure I want to. What kind of cases?" she asked, warily.

"Criminal defense. Things you can wrap up pretty quickly. Efficiently. Same terms: you kill it, you eat it. Or you eat ninety percent of it, to be more accurate."

"It sounds like you might have one or two cases in mind."

"I might," he admitted. "Atlanta is becoming prime territory for criminal defense—the high end, I mean. We're rapidly becoming the jackass capital of the world, and there's one thing you know about jackasses: they have a sense of privilege and entitlement that's always going to get them into trouble. I've got a live one right here that I'll have to turn down, just because I don't have time to take it. It's a woman—her husband is a commercial real estate developer—who assaulted a cop.''

"I don't believe you," Laura said.

"Yep. He tried to ticket her for running a red light. She tried to explain that she was on the phone and didn't notice that the light had changed, and that tickets are for the little people, but that cut no ice with the officer. So she got heated, abused him verbally, and when he tried to arrest her, she maced him.''

"Good grief, Craig—I couldn't defend someone like that. Someone who would attack a police officer for doing his job is indefensible.''

"I just use it as an example. There are a ton of folks moving into this town who think that having a couple of hundred thousand dollars in the bank and a lease on a spiffy car means that they're part of the elect. There's no limit to their arrogance or their self-righteousness. I only bring it up to show you that you don't always have to defend real bad guys; there's plenty of gold in them thar stupid people. The way I see it is, if they're ruining my town, I might as well make a little money off of them while they do it. It's like shooting fish in a barrel, except that I don't have any more room in my creel. But if you don't like the folks who come to me, find some cases on your own—take a couple pro bono for all I care. I hate to see you spinning your wheels. Believe it or not, I'm sincere. I don't want you to regret throwing your lot in with me.''

"I don't. If I did, I would already have left. You've been very supportive. And I'll take your suggestion under advisement. I'm not sure, though—''

"That you want to come back to the dark side,'' he said, finishing her thought.

"I wouldn't have put it that way."

"Of course not. You're too tactful. Okay, this has been fun, but I have work to do. Think about it; that's all I ask."

"I will," she promised. And she would. Craig had been nothing but supportive of her, and it occurred to Laura that this might be his backhanded way of asking her for a little bit of help. The only thing that had stopped her from accepting his offer on the spot was a nagging feeling that if she put her full weight down in Craig's office, she might never leave—and she didn't see herself as a criminal defense lawyer for the long term. Once, maybe, she would have jumped at the chance, but she'd seen too much as an assistant district attorney to make crossing over to, well, the dark side appealing.

There was, however, the nagging problem of her chronic underemployment to deal with. It wasn't money; not yet, at least. Laura was a good saver, and she had a good cushion built up when she left Prendergrast and Crawley. Still, the taxes on her quarter acre of Buckhead real estate would be due soon, and there was the mortgage payment every month . . . she couldn't stay in this state of suspended employment forever. On the other hand, she might not have to. The city might decide to settle Jervis's case rather than fight it. With the summer campaign season almost upon them, the politicians wouldn't welcome a public scrap over police procedures. And that reminded her: she needed to call Jervis. Strange, she reflected as she trudged upstairs, how unimportant he had become in this whole mess. The poor man was never going to be much more than a pawn in someone's game, and Laura didn't exempt herself. Naturally, though, he wanted to know what was going on, and she did owe him the occasional update, not that she had much to report.

Jervis was, unfortunately, a very good argument against

taking up defense again as a career. He was just the kind of pathetic, low-return loser Laura knew she'd end up dealing with. But what she needed to do was get this phone call over with and then try to find something to keep her busy for the rest of the day. She looked up Jervis's number and dialed it. No one answered. Even Jervis, apparently, had a richer and more fulfilling life than his hapless lawyer.

Laura logged on to her computer, checked her e-mail, and then searched the on-line case law for a precedent that she thought might come in handy down the road if the city responded the way she thought it might. Time for research that she *might* need was a real luxury, she told herself. Or a real waste of time. She did love research for its own sake, though, so she was content to burrow into legal arcana for a while. So much so, in fact, that when the phone rang she was actually irritated to have to turn her attention to it.

It was Kenny, calling from Alabama. "Whaassup?" he said.

"Stop it, Ken. You know I hate it when people say that," she admonished him. "Please tell me you're calling with a big fat break in the case. You found Clay, and he told you everything, right?"

"Not exactly, although I did find Clay, in a roadhouse outside of Atmore. He's alive, which is an improvement over the last one. And I did manage to persuade him to come clean. He admitted that he'd been paid to go to the cops with that story about meeting Jervis."

"I love you," Laura said, sincerely.

"Not so fast. The only clue he could give me to the identity of the briber was—get ready—'a big white cop.' "

"You're kidding. Did you get some specifics, at least? How did he know he was a cop?"

"Clay is pretty good at spotting cops. In fact, he tried to

take off out of the juke joint when he saw me coming at him. All he can tell me is big—I figure at least six-two—and blond. Which is a little more than I had, but not a lot. His description pretty well fits any number of guys—me included.''

Laura tried to hide her disappointment, but it was hard. "Did you get the feeling that he could pick the guy out of a lineup?''

"Probably. Assuming we get to that point," Kenny said cautiously.

"I guess I shouldn't have gotten my hopes up."

"Naw, you've got to keep hoping. Something will turn up, sugar. Just gotta be patient a little while longer. This guy—our big white friend—has shown himself to too many people, and not the most tight-lipped folks in the world, either. Any word from Carlton on the jailhouse knife artist?''

"No. Nothing."

"We'll just have to sit tight, then. I'm off to Mobile for the night. I'll be back late tomorrow night, and I'll talk to you day after. Keep your chin up!"

Good advice, Laura thought, *but becoming almost impossible to follow.*

Chapter 27

Laura returned to staring at the computer until the phone rang again. Expecting to hear Roland Jervis on the line, she picked up with a polite, but reserved, greeting.

"Miss Chastain?" an unfamiliar female voice inquired.

"Yes?"

"My name is Natalie Parsons. I'm calling you at the request of Diana Arnold."

"Is everything okay?" Laura asked, immediately concerned.

"Diana is fine, but there is a problem that she thought you could help us with. I should explain who I am. I am— or was—Lawrence Belew's office manager. I've stayed on in the office to close things out. I usually only come in for a few hours every day now; there hasn't been much reason for me to be here lately, frankly, except to deal with the mail. But when I got here today, there were two cars and a van in the parking lot, and four people waiting at the door for me.''

"Yes?" Laura said, wishing that this precise woman would just get on with it.

"I'm sorry," she said, as if she could read Laura's mind, "I just thought I should explain who I was and why I was calling. These men—and there's one woman—say that they're with the FBI."

"Do they have identification?" Laura asked.

"Yes, and I suppose it's authentic, but I can't tell. I called Diana, and she suggested that you might be able to help."

"What do they want?" Laura said.

"They have a search warrant. Or they say they do; I've never seen such a thing, and I'm not sure it's legitimate."

"Ms. Parsons, I appreciate your problem, but I don't think I can be of much help," Laura said, feeling powerfully guilty as she spoke. The last thing she had intended to do was to bring the FBI down on Diana, but now she could see that it had been inevitable. "I'm not representing Diana legally, and I don't think I'm in a position to. And she might not be in a position to challenge the warrant, either, unless she's the executrix of Lawrence's estate."

"She is."

"Didn't Lawrence have attorneys? Personally, or for his firm?"

"Of course. He was always represented by Martin, Shattuck and Forrest. I've called them. His attorney, Dave Stern, is on the way. But frankly, Miss Chastain, I haven't called to consult you as a lawyer. Mr. Stern can handle that. I called you because I think that Diana is going to need you, as a friend."

"Where is she?"

"She's on her way here. She's very upset, Miss Chastain.

I'm afraid that I'm not of much help in these . . . emotional situations. I know Diana, but not intimately. I tried to persuade her not to come; I don't think that it's going to be good for her to see them take away her brother's things."

"No, you're right," Laura said. A bolt of guilt shot through her gut. What had she been thinking? She should never have encouraged Diana to get involved in any of this. The woman was extremely fragile, still deeply mourning her brother. All Laura had wanted to do was to help Diana, but now she had the feeling—inexorable and overwhelming—that she, and Diana, had just moved officially out of their depth. The least she could do was to go down there to Lawrence's offices and help contain the damage she had, with all the best intentions, caused. "Lawrence's offices are on Piedmont, right?"

"Yes. We're in a small converted house near the MARTA tracks." She gave Laura the address.

"I'm just up the road," she said. "I'll be there as soon as I can."

Laura sped downstairs, and looked for Craig. The door of his office was shut. She found Arlene at her desk. "Tell Craig that the FBI is executing a search warrant at Belew's office. I'm going down there now." She rushed past without giving Arlene a chance to say anything.

Belew's offices were a little over a half mile away, and Laura was there in minutes. She saw the vehicles Natalie Parsons had described; their occupants must have gone inside the building. Laura parked and went in through the front door.

The house, a small Cape Cod cottage much like Laura's own, had been gutted and turned into a studiolike space to accommodate Belew's operation. A small reception area opened into one large, open-floored room that housed several workstations, all unoccupied. There were two offices, delimited by frosted-glass and wood walls, at the rear of the room. Four dark-suited agents stood outside the doorway to one of them. In the doorway itself stood a petite brunette woman in her mid-fifties. Natalie Parsons was calmly and coolly standing down the might and power of the federal government. Laura paused for a moment to admire the sight; then she crossed the room quickly. "Hello," she said. "Ms. Parsons? I'm Laura Chastain."

"Yes. Thank you for coming. These are the people who say they're FBI agents."

"I see," Laura said. "May I see your identification, please?"

The three men and one woman wordlessly produced badges and ID cards, which were—as far as Laura could tell—the real thing. "And your warrant?" she continued.

The warrant was undoubtedly the real thing. Laura took as long as she could in reading it, brow furrowed, but she could tell at a glance that it was in order. She glanced at Natalie. "I'd like to speak with Ms. Parsons alone for a moment. Excuse us."

Natalie walked into the office, and Laura followed, shutting the door behind them. "The warrant's good," she said. "Lawrence's attorney can try to stay it, but I doubt he'll be able to."

"What is it that they're after?" Natalie asked.

Laura tried to explain as succinctly as she could. "They want pretty much all his business records. The're going to take the paper files, and the computers—anything located at this address that might be useful in their investigation. They want to find the name of the person who approached Lawrence about shill bidding on contracts. Did you know anything about this scheme of Lawrence's?" she asked.

Natalie shook her head. "No. I'm not surprised, though, that he and Carl would have tried to pull something like that. But are you saying that it got him killed?"

"Maybe. I don't know. I know that it wasn't just a car-jacking, though."

"I knew that all along," Natalie said. "Lawrence wouldn't have resisted a robbery of any kind. He would have given up the car keys and walked away. He wasn't very aggressive—physically, at least—and he didn't care about material possessions. He just liked programming."

Laura nodded. "It felt wrong to me, all along, and I think it did to Diana, too. I think all we can do is damage control. This is all my fault, really. I'm the one who wanted to go to the FBI. I should have taken it to the Atlanta Police Department."

"Don't blame yourself. This might all be for the best."

"I don't know. What I'm afraid of is that the feds will find some connection between the contracting scandals and Lawrence's death. They might make a deal with the killer in order to get his testimony."

"Can't he be tried for murder in Fulton County, too?"

"Yes. At least, I think so. It depends on what federal charges—if any—are filed against him. But to be honest, I've never dealt with any conflicts of state and federal law."

"I think someone has arrived," Natalie said. "We'd better go see who it is."

The newcomer was Lawrence Belew's five-hundred-dollar-an-hour attorney, Dave Stern, a senior partner at Martin, Shattuck and Forrest. As Laura opened the door he was peremptorily demanding to see the warrant. "Hello, Dave," Laura said.

"Laura," he said with a nod. "What are you doing here?"

"Friend of the family."

He turned his attention back to the agent in charge. "Are

you aware that Mr. Belew's business records and personal effects are all evidence in the investigation of his murder?'' he asked.

"Yes, sir," the agent replied.

"And that your seizure of these items might interfere in the investigation being conducted by the Atlanta Police Department?''

"We plan to cooperate fully, as we always do, with local authorities," the agent replied.

"Hah!" Stern said. "That's a good one. Who's working on this in the U.S. Attorney's office?''

"Patrick Dillard swore out the affidavit for the warrant.''

"Maybe I'll just give him a call, then," Stern said, whipping out a silver cell phone, like Doc Holliday slinging a gun at the O.K. Corral.

"If you like," the agent said.

Laura watched all this play out with some amusement, but with little hope that Stern's bluster would result in the suppression of the warrant. While he was engaged in debate with someone at the Federal Courthouse, Diana Arnold arrived.

She stood at the end of the room and looked from person to person. Laura could tell that she was overwrought, ready to collapse from tension and exhaustion. She and Natalie both hurried to her side.

"Mr. Stern's here," Natalie said, reassuringly. "He's trying to stop them.''

"But, Diana," Laura said, as they led the trembling woman past the silent group of agents and into the office, "I don't think he's going to get great results. The warrant's in order.''

"But his things—they can't take his things," Diana said.

"I'm afraid they can. But so could the Atlanta Police

Department. If Lawrence's death was in any way tied to his work, whoever was investigating it would have to have access to everything.''

"And we have the copies," Natalie said soothingly.

"Copies?" Laura said.

"Of course. We always backed up everything to tape. All the tapes are in storage in a fireproof vault.''

"Not at this address?" Laura asked. Natalie shook her head. "Then they're not covered by the warrant. Let's not mention them, okay?"

Stern came into the office and greeted Diana. "Here's the story," he said. "I can try to stay the warrant, and I might succeed—temporarily. They will prevail eventually, however, so all you will have accomplished is running up some substantial legal fees. While that would be to my benefit, I can't recommend that you do it. Natalie, how much work is ongoing?"

"There were no major new projects under way. Lawrence liked to take it easy over the summer, and travel a bit, so he didn't bid for a lot of new business in the spring. But there's the ongoing contractual service that we perform on the systems that are up and running.''

"Can you manage the business without the records?"

"I was just telling Diana and Laura that we have copies of everything.''

"Okay, then. Let them take what they need.'' He placed a hand on Diana's shoulder. "It's all for the best.''

They left the office, and watched as Stern spoke quietly to the agent in charge. Then the FBI began its deliberate and methodical work. Diana seemed calm, or at least resigned, and it was over in a couple of hours. Diana looked at her watch and remarked dully that she should be going. Stern had already returned to his office. As Laura left, she looked over her shoulder to see Natalie standing in the denuded office like Dido in the ruins of Carthage.

Laura returned to the office, but with less than half a heart. Between Kenny's news and the rout at the hands of the feds, she felt as if she'd had pretty much of a day already. Maybe it was time to take Craig up on his standing advice to go see a movie, or at least to have a nice lunch. She parked in front of the buildings, and pulled Craig out of his office. "Let's have a long lunch hour," she said. "I need company."

"Not too long," he said, "but I don't object to getting out on a nice day like this."

They walked down the street to a chic bistro located in a small cottage, one of the last houses left on Maple Street. Seeing it gave Craig the opportunity to wax nostalgic about his childhood in Buckhead. "Believe it or not," he said, "people actually lived here. Walked to shops, walked to work. Hell, my parents only had one car. And I could ride my bike anywhere—down to Wender and Roberts to get a milkshake. They had a real soda fountain. . . ."

Laura was happy to let him reminisce through lunch. He knew an Atlanta that she never had, one far different from the noisy and ill-tempered neighborhood she had accepted as the norm. His idealized Buckhead was not unlike the Nashville neighborhood she had grown up in. Nashville, she reflected, was a nice town. It hadn't been infected by all of the status-seeking and nouveaux riches that had ripped through Atlanta. Maybe she could find a job in Nashville— that is, if Marshall didn't change his mind and take her back.

They returned to the office around one-thirty, but Laura didn't go inside. "If I get any calls, just have Arlene call me at home," she told Craig. "I'm going to work in the yard and do some cleaning."

"Good idea. Blow the cobwebs out. We'll see you tomorrow."

A few hours later, pleasantly tired, Laura fixed a salad for dinner. She made enough for two, thinking that Amos might show up earlier. He was, she assumed, planning to come over, although they hadn't talked. But he didn't show before she finished her supper, so she put away the salad and the dishes. She went into the living room and curled up on the sofa with a book, trying not to check her watch. Eight o'clock, nine o'clock—no Amos. At ten, she decided that he wasn't coming, so she locked the doors and started back to her bedroom.

Then she heard the sound of his car in the driveway. She was relieved, not because she was frightened to be alone, but because she thought he had decided not to come. She waited for him to come through the back door, as he usually did, but she heard a knock on the front door instead. She opened it quickly. "Good grief," she said, "you don't have to knock. You have a key."

"I didn't think it was appropriate to use it," he said. "Can I come in?"

"For pity's sake, Amos, of course you can. Look, if this is going to be silly, I'd just as soon take my chances with the prowler. You can go on home."

"I'll stay," he said tersely.

"Fine. Just don't act like you've never seen me before in your life. Have you had dinner?"

"Yes," he said. "And I'm tired, so I'll just go straight to bed."

He walked past her and a moment later she heard the door to the guest room close. She started to go right back there and knock on the door, but an awful thought crossed her mind. She looked at her watch; it was almost eleven.

Where had he been—on a date? Was he already seeing someone else? She had a fleeting vision of him laughing and talking with some faceless woman, someone who appreciated all his fine qualities and didn't argue with him. With the horrible picture still in mind, she prepared for bed, casting a baleful glance at the shut door of the guest room as she passed it. Altogether, she thought as she pulled the sheets over her head, this had not been a good day.

Chapter 28

When her alarm went off at seven the following morning, Laura raised her head long enough to register that it was raining. She promptly pulled the covers back up around her neck and made a decision to stay in bed. She was discouraged by the events of the previous day—or days. Frustration had been building for a while without release; yesterday's confrontation with the FBI had brought all that frustration to the surface.

Laura had felt something slip from her grasp there in Lawrence Belew's offices. She had lain awake half the night inventorying her position: Jobs: zero; boyfriends: zero; bank account: shrinking. The dismal prospect of defending every mace-toting shrew in Atlanta haunted her, but that's what she would most likely end up doing, gunslinging for Fannin. It would have its good moments, but Laura also intuited that she'd forever have the sense that she was in the wrong place. She belonged in the district attorney's office. She assessed the chance of Marshall's taking her back as another zero.

She finally managed to switch off her brain and get a couple of hours of patchy sleep. It came as a rude shock when the phone rang. A quick glance at the alarm showed that it was after nine—time for gainfully employed people to be at work. It was Arlene, calling from Craig's office. "Laura? Are you ill? Did I wake you?"

"No, no. I was just moving a little slowly this morning," Laura fibbed. "What's up?"

"You got a call that I thought might be important. It's from a Ms. Norton. She says she's a lawyer with the firm that's representing the city in the Jervis matter. She wants to speak to you urgently."

Laura straightened up. "Give me her number; I'll call from here. I'll be in a little later."

Laura returned the call right away, trying to make her voice sound as if it didn't belong to someone who was wearing pajama bottoms and a ragged T-shirt. Amy Norton answered on the second ring, and Laura identified herself.

"Thank you for calling so promptly, Ms. Chastain. I'm with Porter, Samuels and LeBow. We're representing the city in the Roland Jervis matter."

"Yes, I know," Laura said. "Is there something I can do for you?"

"I'll cut straight to the chase: the city wishes to settle the matter without a trial. I'm authorized to make you an offer."

"I see. Are you prepared to name your figure now?"

"How does one hundred and fifty thousand sound?"

Laura chuckled. "Low. It sounds very low. My client was placed on trial for his life, Ms. Norton. I believe he values his life a little more highly than that." Laura made this statement in the full knowledge that, if the city had offered him even fifty thousand, Jervis would have snapped it up without hesitation.

Amy Norton seemed to know that, too. "Really? Perhaps you'd like to present it to him before you decline it."

"Certainly. I'll get in touch with him right away. We'll call you this afternoon."

"I look forward to it."

Laura dressed hurriedly and went to the office. Craig knew about the call, and he greeted her with a grin. "Well?" he said.

Laura named the figure. "Of course I said no," she added.

"What are you thinking?"

"We counter at half a million, and settle at three hundred or three-fifty," she said.

He nodded. "Sounds fair. I knew they'd come back with something. The mayor doesn't want this circus to go on all through the campaign season."

"No, and neither do I," Laura said. "I'd take less, Craig, but I know you'd be more aggressive. It bugs me that this is coming out of the taxpayers' pockets, you know."

"Naturally. But I wouldn't lose sleep over it. Should I remind you that the power to litigate is one of the most important safeguards of our freedom?"

"Please don't," she said, holding up her hand. "I don't have a problem with what you do, Craig. But I've made up my mind on something. I can't be a defense attorney anymore, and I don't want to practice civil law. I want to be a prosecutor."

"What brings this change of heart?"

"Look at what's happened: I've been put into a passive position, Craig. Yesterday brought it all home to me—Kenny's witness is a dead end and the FBI isn't asking me for help. I'm an outsider. And when I settle Jervis's case I'll have no more connection to Lawrence Belew's murder. I'll be just another citizen.''

"So you'll wait for Marshall to take you back?"

She shook her head. "I don't think he will. I was thinking of going back to Nashville and trying to hitch on with the district attorney's office there."

Craig looked surprised. "Really? My, my. You have been doing some thinking."

She stood up. "I've had a hell of a month, Craig, and I thank you for it. But it's all winding down now, and I have to make some plans."

"You'll do pretty well out of the Jervis case. Assuming you get three hundred grand, your take will be ninety thousand—"

"And yours will be thirty, plus expenses. I've done the math, too. And I can sell the house in no time, at a profit."

"You seem pretty determined."

"I am. Don't take any of this the wrong way, Craig. You've been great. I've had fun, and I've learned a lot."

"There will always be a spot for you here. Would it make a difference if I offered you a partnership?"

The offer was unexpected, and flattering to a high degree. Craig was a solo artist; he hadn't had a partner in more than fifteen years. "You don't want a partner, Craig—at least, not one like me. We'd be at each other's throats in no time."

"Because I push you."

"Push my buttons, you mean."

"Will you think about it? Don't do anything drastic."

"I will—think about it, I mean. And I can't do anything drastic until I've settled Jervis's case, anyway. I guess I need to call the client and tell him the good news. He'll have a coronary when I tell him how much they offered."

But she never made that phone call. The phone started ringing as she stepped into her office. She eyed it for a minute, Dorothy Parker's "fresh hell" quip in mind. The telecommunication network certainly hadn't been doing any favors for Laura Chastain lately, and she wasn't eager to get one more piece of bad news. But she overcame her reluctance and picked up.

It was difficult to make out what Diana Arnold was trying to say. Her voice, usually soft and melodious, was torn by sobs, and she seemed to be having difficulty breathing.

"Diana? Slow down," Laura said. "What is it?"

"There's this woman who called me . . . Oh, God, Laura, it's awful. You've got to tell me what to do."

"Who is she? What did she say? Are you at home—I'll come over there."

"No, not here. I'll come to your office . . ." The rest of her words slid into unintelligibility.

"Diana, what did you say? I don't think you should be driving. I'll be right over there."

"You don't understand. She's not here. I have to go to her. She saw it, Laura; she saw everything. . . ."

"What do you mean?"

"She saw them kill Lawrence."

Laura, still standing beside her desk, actually had to grab the edge of it to keep from reeling. "You mean to tell me that someone has turned up, saying she saw the murder? Who? Where is she now?"

"She's in some hotel. She called me. I don't know how she got my name, I guess it was from the papers, but she told me where she's staying. She wants me to come get her. She says she's scared."

"This could be bogus, Diana," Laura said. "There are people out there who'll do things like this for kicks, or out of sheer meanness."

"I think she's for real," Diana said. Her speech had recovered more of its normal tone; she was putting her brain in control now, to Laura's relief. "She's willing to tell us who did it—she says she has names— but she says we have to protect her. She's scared of whoever did this. And I think she's hurt—I think the guy who killed Lawrence hurt her."

"Where is this hotel?"

"Buckhead, near you." Diana gave the address.

"Okay, you come here, and we'll go there together. Did you tell her you'd come?"

"Yes, but I told her that I wouldn't come alone. She said no cops, though. She was adamant; I think there might be a cop involved. I was hoping that Kenny would come with us this time, too."

"Ken's in Alabama. He won't be back until late tonight. I can ask Craig to come. . . ."

"I guess he'd be better than nothing. But we're wasting time here. I'm leaving the house right now. I'll be there in about half an hour."

Laura replaced the receiver, still trying to process everything she had just heard. An eyewitness emerging now— weeks after the crime, and just when every lead had gone stone-cold dead—seemed unbelievable. But Laura remembered something that Amos had told her, more than once. Sometimes the only break you get is the lucky one. Laura mistrusted luck, especially now. She feared a trap of some kind. Whoever this woman was, she had her own agenda, and it would not necessarily be the one shared by Laura and Diana.

Laura pounded back down the stairs and burst into Craig's

office. "Ho!" he said. "You look like you just won the lottery. What's happened?"

Laura paused for a second. Did she really look as if she'd won the lottery? Maybe she was placing too much faith in this unknown woman. She tried to speak calmly as she told Craig about the phone call. "Diana's on her way. We need you to come to the hotel with us."

Craig nodded. "Happy to, but I think we should call the police anyway. I know what she said—no cops. I'm not saying we need to bust in on her with badges and guns. But if something goes wrong, I want the cops on my side."

Laura considered what he had said, and nodded. "I'll call Carlton. I can't give him any specifics, of course, but I'll tell him that we may have something for him later. Will that do?"

"It'll do fine. I'll cancel my lunch meeting. How long will it take Diana to get here?"

Laura looked at her watch. "It's ten-thirty. She'll be here by eleven. Oh, Lord, I never got a chance to call Roland about the offer. That lawyer wants a meeting, too."

"Call Roland and give him the ten-cent summary. Then tell the lawyer that your client needs some time to consider the offer. Schedule a meeting for tomorrow afternoon."

"Aye, aye, sir!" she said with a mock salute.

"What a difference a phone call makes, huh? Hey, when are you calling the real estate agent about listing your house?"

"Stuff it. That was just thinking out loud." She hurried out before he could enjoy himself further at her expense.

It was hard not to be brusque with Roland Jervis, who, God bless his pea-picking heart, was unable to understand why his lawyer would tell him not to accept the largest sum of money that had ever been waved in his direction. "I could use that money, miss," he said plaintively. "I live here in my mama's house and it could sure use a new roof. Summer's coming, too, and I'd like an air conditioner."

"Listen, Roland, I'm going to get you a lot more money. But if you take this, remember our deal—Mr. Fannin and I get sixty thousand dollars, plus our expenses. That leaves you with less than ninety thousand, before taxes. We can do better."

"If you say so," Roland answered warily, with caution born of long experience with broken promises. It hit Laura like a thunderbolt that he didn't completely trust her. She hung up promising herself that she was going to nail the city's attorneys to the wall on this one, just to prove to him that she was on his side.

Amy Norton was more forceful in her objection to the delay. "This isn't an open-ended offer," she huffed. "We can't hold it open indefinitely awaiting your client's pleasure."

"My client's pleasure, Ms. Norton, would be a realistic offer. We'll see you tomorrow."

When Laura met her in front of the building a few minutes later, Diana was visibly shaken. Her normally flawless hairdo and makeup were gone; she'd pulled her hair back into a sloppy ponytail and her face was blotchy with tears. "I can't take much more of this," she said. "It shouldn't be this way. What if you're right, and this is just some kook out for money?"

"She may be," Laura said, "but if she is, we'll file charges against her. Would you rather have the police handle it?"

"She said if any cops showed up, she wasn't going to talk."

"Yes, but she also gave us the hotel she's staying in, and

her room number. We can get her name easily, and I bet if the police arrested her and charged her with attempted extortion she'd spill her story. I've already called Carlton Hemingway—just to alert him that we might need him later on. He'd be more than glad to pick her up. Your call.'' Laura was worried. Diana seemed more fragile, less resilient than the first time they had gone through this whole mystery-witness drill. That expedition had turned into just another dead end, or, at best, a tantalizing hint at the truth that might never be fully understood.

Diana appeared to weigh Laura's words carefully; then she shook her head. ''No. I want to see her myself. I want to look her in the eyes.''

''Okay. Craig is coming. He's waiting inside; I'll get him.''

Chapter 29

A few minutes later, the three of them were in the lobby of the Hyatt, just up the street. "Strange place for a witness to hole up," Craig remarked, surveying the plush lobby. "I'd think it would be easier to hide your identity at an expressway motel where they don't ask questions."

"Maybe she's an employee or something," Laura said.

They took the elevator up to the tenth floor, and found the room number that the woman had given Diana. "Okay, Diana," Laura whispered, "you knock, and answer when she asks who it is. Craig and I will stand off to the side, where she can't see us through the peephole. But tell her that you brought your lawyers. Tell her we're here to help her."

Diana managed a wan smile and a grim joke. "Sure. She'll buy that—lawyers are known for being helpful."

They took up their positions, and Diana knocked sharply

on the door, as if she had gathered up the last shreds of her resolve and channeled it into her knuckles. Laura heard the door open, and saw a triangle of light fall across the hall carpet. Then she heard Diana gasp. "My God," she said, obviously horrified. "Sweet Jesus, who did this to you?"

Laura and Craig hurried to join Diana in the doorway. Standing just inside the door frame, silhouetted against the half-lit room, was a tall, slender blond woman. She may have been young; she may have been beautiful, but it was impossible to discern either. Her face was a swollen mass of bruises. A large laceration on her forehead, rimmed with dried blood, looked as if it could use a few stitches.

"Who are these people?" the woman asked, her Texas-accented voice muffled by her swollen lower lip. "I said no cops!"

"They're not cops. They're lawyers."

"Great. I wanted you to come alone."

"And I told you that I wouldn't. All I promised was no police, and I kept my promise. Now you keep yours," she said, and Laura was proud of her.

"All right. You might as well come in." She stood aside far enough to allow them to enter the dim room. "Here's the deal: I don't tell you nothing until I get certain assurances."

"What assurances can we give you?" Laura asked.

"Like, that you'll get me protection and that you get this person I'm about to tell you about arrested. This person who killed your brother," she said pointedly to Diana.

"I don't understand how we can offer you protection if we're not allowed to involve the police," Laura said. "We don't have those kinds of resources."

"Well, you better get you some resources, then," she said, " 'cause I'm not putting my butt on the line before I know I'm safe."

"Okay," Craig said, "we'll hire a bodyguard for you."

Unexpectedly, the woman shrieked with laughter. "Bodyguards! That's a good one! You don't know shit, do you?"

"No," Laura said in a measured voice, "and we're not going to if you keep playing this game. You don't want police involved, but you don't want private security, either. You have to give us something to work with here."

"Okay, okay. Can't you get me, like, a private eye or something?"

"Yes, that we can do. We have a man we trust," Craig answered, "but he's unavailable until tomorrow. I can find another guy, but it'll take a while."

On hearing this the woman's bravado dissolved. "How long's 'a while'? I ain't got a lotta time. He's gonna be hunting for me by now."

Laura beckoned Craig and Diana aside for a hasty conference. "How long do you think it will take you to find someone?"

Craig shrugged. "It depends. Maybe an hour, maybe a day."

"What if we offer to get her out of town?"

"It might work. Any ideas?"

"I have a friend who lives on a farm up in Rabun County. It's isolated, and I'm sure Emily would stash the girl away overnight, just long enough for Kenny to take over."

Craig nodded. "Offer it to her. But if she turns it down"— he looked at Diana—"we leave. If she's yanking our chains, we'll find out."

Diana agreed, and Laura explained the plan to the woman, who had seated herself on one of the two beds and fired up a cigarette. She demanded explanations of who this Emily was, and where this farm was, but Laura's answers seemed to satisfy her. Finally, she nodded. "Okay. But if I so much as see a cop before you tell me this person's been arrested, I'm just gonna say I was lying to you guys. You got that?"

"Yeah, I got that," Laura said. "Now get this: If you *are* lying, if you're using Mrs. Arnold to settle some private beef of yours, I'm going to make sure you do time. Got *that?*" Laura had been an assistant district attorney long enough to know how and when to call a bluff. She met the girl's eyes—what she could see of them through the puffy black circles that surrounded them—and saw no wavering glance away, no flicker that could betray a lie.

"All right. I hear you. Y'all might as well sit down, 'cause this is gonna take a while, and it ain't a nice story. My name is Michelle, Michelle Blake. At least that's my professional name. I'm a model," she said, and then she laughed sardonically. "I guess I should say *was* a model. Looks like I might have to find a new career. Anyway, when you look like I do, but you aren't all that great at school, you don't get a lot of choices. But it's cool, because I like clothes, and I like to travel and all. I came to Atlanta about this time last year 'cause you can get work here, and it's cheaper to live here than in New York or LA. And it's not like I have delusions about what I can do. I don't have the look they like for the runways and the magazines. But I do a lot of catalog and advertising work, stuff like that. A lot of lingerie, because I have the body for it. That's not being conceited; it's just the truth. Anyway, it's not as glamorous as everybody thinks. I mean, I do okay. I had an okay apartment, and a decent car, but it's not like I was living on Habersham Road and driving a Jag, you know what I mean?

"I'm pretty realistic, too. I know that there are always new girls coming along, and that my time wasn't going to last forever. So I figured my best bet was to find some guy who wanted to say he was dating a model, and who'd take care of me. You know, marry me. A guy who pulled down some serious bucks. I didn't want some chump. So my girlfriends and me started hanging at the clubs in Buckhead. God, you get a lot of losers. You'll leave with a guy who's got, like, a BMW or something, and then he takes you home to some thousand-bucks-a-month apartment. No thanks. I can do better than that on my own, you know?

"So anyway, I'm getting pretty sick of these losers, and I'm ready to move up. And then I met this guy who was, like, no kidding, a player." She laughed. "You don't get the joke, do you? He was a ballplayer, a real pro jock. I didn't recognize him, 'cause I'm not into sports or anything like that, but my girlfriend did. I was, like, omigod, you're kidding. And it was great because he was really into me. We just sorta clicked and all. This was around Christmas, and he gave me this great bracelet. Then for Valentine's Day he took me to a suite at the Ritz-Carlton for the weekend. He said we couldn't leave town because of his playing schedule and all, but I didn't care. It was sweet. I mean, you just don't know—everybody just kissed his ass all the time. No waiting at restaurants, straight into the VIP room at the clubs. Awesome.

"The only bad thing was that he kind of had a bad temper, but he was okay to me. And I could understand how it bugged him when fans tried to talk to him when he was, like, eating and all. I saw him yell at people a few times, and he shoved a guy once. And maybe now and then he yelled at me a little. It bugged him sometimes when I hung on him in public, or when I said something stupid. Shit like that. But he never really lost it with me, you know? Everyone said look out, he's gonna blow up one day, but he never did.

"So we're out one night a few weeks ago. We had dinner

someplace—don't ask me where, 'cause I can't remember. We were really pretty wasted. We wanted to go to one of the clubs in Buckhead, so we get in his Navigator and we're driving there. I don't know exactly where, except he takes some shortcut he knows. I should tell you he's got this bodyguard along. I don't remember the guy's name; he wasn't the regular one. He was a big blond guy. I think he was some kind of cop.

"So we're in the Navigator, and this bodyguard is behind us in his car. We're coming out of this side street—like I said, don't ask me the name of it—but it was real dark and quiet, with a lot of businesses along it that weren't open. Not like most parts of Buckhead, you know? But he hated traffic, so he knew all these little side streets. So we pull out into some intersection, and this guy in a Lexus hits the Navigator.

"Well, my boyfriend goes nuts. I'm, like, calm down; it wasn't even that big of a bump or anything. I mean, we're in a *Navigator.* But my boyfriend—you notice I'm not saying his name, 'cause I have to make sure you're going to make good. I get up to that farm, and *then* you get his name. Anyway, he gets out, and the other guy's already on the street, and he's, like, apologizing and looking at the damage—of which there wasn't hardly none, at least not on the Navigator. I should say that the guy who hit us was your brother. I know because I saw his picture in the paper, lots of times.

"My boyfriend is, like, crazed at this point. He yells, and then he just hauls off and hits your brother. I didn't want to get out of the car. I'm thinking, hellooo? Where is this bodyguard? He's supposed to take care of shit like this. Well, by the time he finally shows, my boyfriend has your brother on the ground and he's just kicking and stomping him. It was awful. Finally, though, the bodyguard gets him under control. But your brother was dead. I could tell; he was just laying there. So, you see, there was nothing I could do.

"I'm thinking, shit, he's not getting out of this one. I mean, this is way beyond shoving some guy in a bar. He's *killed* someone. But this bodyguard just puts my boyfriend back in the truck and tells us to go home. I'm thinking— honest—that he's gonna call the cops and all, and maybe try to work something out so it won't be so bad and my boyfriend doesn't have to go to jail and all that. So we just do like he says and go home.

"When we get there, I see that he's got blood all over his clothes, and that just totally freaks him out. He takes off his clothes and says for me to wash them. I'm, like, I'm not your damn maid, and he goes live on me, and says I'm an idiot, that he can't let the housekeeper see these clothes— he lives in, like, this really big house that you would not *believe*—so I have to wash them. So I take them to the laundry room, and I'm thinking, this could be bad for me. I mean, there's a law against hiding evidence and all, isn't there? So I put the clothes in a garbage bag, and I run the washer with some other stuff in it so he'll think I've done what he said. I thought that was pretty smart.

"Well, he's scared shitless for a while. I never saw that bodyguard again, and I was scared to ask what happened. Then I see on the news that this black guy—your brother— is missing, and I'm like, *shit.* The bodyguard musta gotten rid of the body. And then they blamed some other guy, and my boyfriend's, like, *whew.*"

Diana, who had been listening in quiet shock throughout this recitation, could take no more. "You little whore," she said, her voice shaking with fury. "You watch my brother die, and you say nothing? You're as guilty as your boyfriend and his bodyguard—''

"Hey, I'm here now, and I'm all you got," Michelle said. "I'm no saint, but I can help you, so if I were you I'd lay off calling me a whore and all.''

"She's right, Diana," Laura said. "We have to make the best of a bad situation.'' She met Diana's eyes meaningfully. Promises or not, she was going to serve this girl up to Meredith once they had "my boyfriend" in custody. "Why *are* you here now, Michelle?''

"Look at me! What the hell do you think? He did this to me, and I'm gonna make him pay. And don't say that it's my word against his, or that his slick-ass lawyer's gonna get him off the hook like he always does, 'cause that dog don't hunt.'' With a painful smile, Michelle reached beneath the bed and pulled out a large black plastic garbage bag. "I got him by the short ones. Here's the clothes he wore when he did it. Now, tell me what you're gonna do for me. When am I going to this farm, and who's gonna be my lawyer, so I don't get charged with anything? 'Cause until I know, you don't get his name.''

Craig stood up slowly. "No need to tell us, Michelle. I know who it is.'' He looked at Diana, and on his face there was an expression of heartbreak. "It's Shawn Tolliver. And I'm his slick-ass lawyer.''

Chapter 30

Michelle seemed stymied by Craig's announcement. He had taken away her most valuable chip. Laura would have enjoyed the moment, but Craig was obviously distressed. She felt for him. He wasn't a bad guy, but he was going to take a lot of criticism for representing Tolliver once this story got out. Judging from the expression on his face, Laura knew that he was going to be his own first and harshest critic.

Diana spoke first. "I was right. Knowing is better than not knowing. It's better to know, no matter how horrible." She turned to Laura. "I needed to know who did it, and now I can see that Lawrence gets justice. I know the name, Shawn Tolliver. He's a basketball player, right?"

"Yes, he is," Laura said.

"He has a history of violent behavior," Craig said, "but nothing this extreme. My God, Diana, I wish I had never represented him. He should have been in jail, several times over. Believe me, I never thought he was capable of anything like this.''

''You're not responsible,'' Diana said, although her voice was wavering. ''He is, and he alone. I wish . . . I wish . . . this is hard for me. I don't think you're a bad man, Craig. You're just part of the system, doing a job. It's all wrong, though.''

''It is,'' Craig agreed. ''Even if he'd never done anything this depraved, he still had a history of bad behavior, and the league let him continue playing. Advertisers still hired him. And I kept on defending him.''

''Is he still going to be on the team, after this?''

''No,'' Craig said. ''I, for one, will submit an amicus brief recommending the harshest sentence available. And I'll represent your family in a civil suit against Tolliver at no cost—if you'll let me.''

''I don't think we'll want to sue. We just want this to be over.''

Laura stood by, frowning, during this exchange. Diana was taking it well—better than Laura would have—but she also looked as if she might be in too much shock to fully comprehend the facts. And there were more facts, Laura knew, that she was going to have to take in. ''Diana, can I talk to you for a minute—alone?''

''You can go in the bathroom,'' Michelle said. ''Sorry I couldn't afford a suite so y'all would have someplace nicer to talk.''

They went into the bathroom, and Laura shut the door. ''I have to tell you something. Maybe I should have told you before, but I didn't want to hurt you more. I know what happened to your brother now.''

''So do I,'' Diana said.

"No. You only know part of it. Michelle only knows part of it. Craig and I have suspected the rest of it for a while. You see, Shawn Tolliver didn't kill Lawrence. He hurt him very badly; I'm not denying that. But it was the bodyguard who actually killed him."

"I don't think I understand."

"Craig got a second pathologist to look at the autopsy report. Lawrence's injuries were very bad, but this man— he's a professor at Emory, a very respected doctor—thought that he survived the initial attack. He would have been unconscious, in a coma, more than likely—but alive."

"Where are you going with this?" Diana said, sitting down on the edge of the bathtub and putting her face in her hands.

"I think that bodyguard took Lawrence from the scene. Maybe he thought he was dead. Maybe he thought he was going to dispose of a body and cover up Tolliver's crime. But at some point he realized that Lawrence was alive. Diana, he's the one who killed Lawrence. I suppose it's not ever going to be crystal clear. Maybe Lawrence would have died from the injuries that Tolliver inflicted on him. Maybe not. But at the very least, this man, this bodyguard, would have been guilty of depraved indifference homicide, because he denied medical treatment to an injured person. But we think it went beyond that. We think that he actually struck Lawrence in the head a second time, and that was the blow that killed him.

"I know this is horrible, much more so than you even imagined. And I'm sorry I didn't have the courage to tell you this before. But we weren't sure. What would have been the point in telling you something that was so terrible, without knowing whether it was true or not?"

Diana shook her head. "I can't ever tell Mother this. Who was this man, Laura? How can we find him?"

"Michelle may not know his name, but she can give us some information. Are you okay, Diana?"

"I'm not angry at you, if that's what you mean. I understand your dilemma. But I want to strangle that little skank in there, and Shawn Tolliver, and this other man, whoever he is. They're street trash, and I hate them. I *hate* them!" She rose to her feet, her fists clenched. Laura was almost relieved to see her roused from her earlier, passive state, but she knew that Diana was just now taking the first step on a long and painful trip that was going to last the rest of her life.

"We'll take care of them, starting with Michelle. That one's going to jail."

"But we promised her—"

"We promised? What authority did we have to promise her anything? I'm not an assistant district attorney anymore. I don't have the power to make deals. And you can't waive prosecution in a murder case. No, she's put her foot right in it. But we have to play her a while longer. Can you keep up the pretense?"

"I can."

"Then let's go get as much as we can out of her. I'll call Emily and drive her up to the farm, but only when I have a good idea who this bodyguard might have been."

They left the bathroom. Craig was standing with his back to the room, looking out the window, his head down and his shoulders sagging. More than one journey was starting here in this hotel room.

Michelle was smoking a cigarette, and flipping through the channels on the television with the remote. "What was that all about?" she said.

"Michelle, I'm going to take you to the farm, but we need to know more about the bodyguard. He's implicated in this, too, so you understand that you won't be safe until he's been arrested, too, don't you?"

"But I already told you I don't remember his name! How can I remember something I probably never even knew?"

"Think hard," Laura said, "because if he knows you're talking to us, you're in danger from him." That got through to the little narcissist. She put down the remote and gaped at Laura. "You said he was big. Did you mean tall, or husky, or both?"

Michelle fluttered her hands in the air, sketching a wide profile. "Both, I guess. And he was blond—blondish, anyway. Not as light as my hair."

"How tall? Think about him in relation to Shawn—how much shorter was he?"

"God, I guess Shawn's—what?"

"Six-seven," Craig said.

"This man musta been over six feet, but he was a good bit shorter than Shawn."

"How did you get the idea that he was a cop?" Laura demanded.

"I dunno. The way he acted, I guess. He was all bossy, like he was bodyguarding the damn president or something, and not just some dumb jock. He was, like, 'make way' and 'coming through' all night long. I got kinda sick of it. The regular guy isn't that bad."

"Think hard. Was he introduced to you at some point?"

"I guess."

"Try to remember. Did you shake his hand or anything?"

"No way, it was at the house. Lemme see. He showed up, and I was still getting dressed, so I came downstairs and I was looking for my purse, and Shawn says, 'Michelle, this is so-and-so.' Oh!'' she said suddenly. ''D. His name began with a D. Does that help?''

''Maybe,'' Laura said, her heart pounding faster. ''Was it Don?''

Michelle considered this for a moment. ''Yeah. Don! That was it. He was kind of a creep, too—he stared at my rack a lot. Yeah, that was him.''

Laura needed no further details to recognize Don Archer. It hadn't made complete sense to her that a bodyguard-for-hire would have taken his duty to the extreme length of killing someone to protect a client. Someone who did something like that had to have something more at stake. Don Archer did—or, at least, he did when he realized who the unconscious man lying on the street was. He must have recognized him, and he must have believed that Lawrence could harm him. And the only reason that he would think that, Laura concluded, was that Don was the mysterious white man who had approached Lawrence about acting as a front for a bid-rigging scheme.

Laura looked at Craig. ''Don Archer. He's the head of the mayor's security detail.''

''And you think he was acting as a bagman for the mayor and his cronies?''

''It makes sense, doesn't it? If he recognized Lawrence as a threat, he would have had a motive to get rid of him.''

Craig was unconvinced. ''I still see it going down the way we originally assumed it did. The bodyguard—whoever he was—removes what he *thinks* is a dead body, with the idea of disposing of it. When it turns out that the victim isn't dead, he's got a problem. He can't go to the hospital, can he? He certainly can't go to the cops.''

''Then why didn't they just call you? If it was just another spot of trouble for Shawn Tolliver, why did you never hear anything about it? Someone went to some extraordinary lengths—whether to save Tolliver's ass or for some other reason. Would a disinterested person have gone to this extreme?"

"I don't know," Craig said. "I say it's time to let the cops sort it out. Get Hemingway and Devereaux over here."

"Hey," Michelle said, operating under the mistaken impression that she still had some leverage, "I said no cops."

Laura turned to her in exasperation. "Who's going to lock up Tolliver and Archer? Did you think that we were going to make a citizen's arrest? You have to give them your statement before they run around arresting people. Unfortunately, they won't take my word on it."

Michelle looked sulky, but she remained silent while Laura called Carlton and gave him their location. As a sop to Michelle, and in the hopes of putting her in a more cooperative frame of mind when the detectives arrived, she also called Emily. The answering machine picked up on the land line, so Laura fished out her address book and dialed Emily's cell phone. "Emily? It's Laura. Can you hear me okay?"

"Hang on. Let me put this chicken down. Now I can hear you. What's up?"

Laura explained the situation. "I was hoping we could stash her with you for a few hours—no more than one night—until we make sure that the bad guys are under lock and key."

"No problem. Are you going to stay, too?"

"Probably not. I think I should come home once I've got her settled. I'll have things to do first thing in the morning. But someone will come for her."

"I'm happy to accommodate you. Any friend of yours—"

"I wouldn't go that far. I owe you big, Em."

"One barbeque dinner should even the tab."

When Carlton and Alex arrived, the room seemed impossibly crowded. Michelle was sullen, and demanded room service before she talked. She picked at a salad as she retold her story. When she was finished, Laura added the conclusions she had drawn about the identity of the bodyguard. A look of surprise and concern flashed across Devereaux's face, but he said nothing. Then he and Carlton began probing Michelle for details.

"You say you can't remember where the collision took place," Carlton said, "or where you had dinner."

"Nope. Well, we mighta had dinner at Nava. Yeah, probably. Shawn likes that place."

"Okay, can you remember the route you took when you left the restaurant?"

"No way," she said, picking the last shrimp out of the salad bowl. "Ask Shawn. He should remember."

Carlton and Alex exchanged glances. Laura bit her lip and managed to remain silent.

"Okay, then," Devereaux said, "tell us more about this bodyguard."

"What do you want to know? He was tall, but not as tall as Shawn—but, like, who is?—and he gave me a creepy feeling. He wasn't the usual guy who went out with Shawn. His name was Don. *She* says it's some guy named Don Archer. Can't tell by me, anyway."

Devereaux was puzzled. "But Don Archer doesn't moonlight. It's verboten for the officers on the mayor's security detail."

Laura cleared her throat. "It was verboten for you, too, without permission, but that didn't stop you."

"That was different," he said, a bit huffily. "I'm not as high up as Don, not as visible."

"Maybe he was just doing it as a favor for Darryl Michaels," Laura suggested. "They're pretty good friends, aren't they?"

"Maybe," Devereaux said thoughtfully. "What kind of car was the bodyguard driving? You've got to remember that, at least."

"I dunno," Michelle said. "It was black, or maybe blue. It wasn't a BMW or a Mercedes, I know that. I can recognize them at fifty feet," she added with pride.

Devereaux looked at Carlton. "Doesn't Don still drive that red truck?"

Carlton shrugged. "I guess so. But he could have borrowed a car for the job. Darryl would never let him go out in that stupid truck."

"It wasn't a truck," Michelle said, very helpfully. "And I already said it wasn't red."

Devereaux's face remained thoughtful, but he nodded to Carlton. "Okay. I think we have enough to get an arrest warrant for Tolliver. And we'll pick Don up for questioning."

"Hey!" Michelle exclaimed. "She told me they would be *arrested*."

"They will be," Carlton explained. "Tolliver as soon as we get a warrant and locate him."

"He'll be down at the arena about four o'clock, getting ready for a game," Michelle said eagerly.

"Great. We'll take Don in and ask him some questions, and if we don't get good answers we'll hold him overnight. But you're going to have to come in tomorrow to identify him in a lineup. Right now, your ID is a little on the vague side."

Michelle tossed her hair. "Whatever. As long as you get Shawn. Preferably in front of his teammates—hah!"

"That's it," Laura said. "Can I take her away now?"

"Please," Devereaux said. "And I hope it's not too long a trip."

A trip around the block with the lovely Michelle would have been too much under normal circumstances, but Laura steeled herself for two hours of her company in the name of a higher cause. They took her back to Craig's office, where Diana got back into her own car. "Will you be okay?" Laura said. "Is there someone we can call to come get you?"

"I'll be all right," Diana said. "I'm a little numb now. I may go to Julian's office and ask him to come home early."

"I'll call you tomorrow," Laura promised. She and Craig watched as the Volvo drove away. "Come on," Laura said to Michelle. "My car's right there."

"Eeuuw," Michelle said, surveying the shabby vehicle with distaste. "I thought lawyers made a lot of money."

"We do," Laura said. "Lots and lots. Oh, Lord. Craig!" she called, rolling down the window. "I forgot the settlement conference with Amy Norton."

"What time?" he asked.

"Two o'clock tomorrow. Her offices."

"I'll take it," he said. "Just go on. And don't worry. I'll get a good deal."

"You'll probably get a better one than I would have."

"Sure. You can buy a new car," he said pointedly. "Then Michelle won't be ashamed to ride with you."

Chapter 31

After putting in more hours of driving in one day than she normally would in a week, Laura gratefully took the Buckhead exit from Georgia 400 and headed for home. She was happy to have made it home before dark, and in time to have dinner and watch some brain-numbing television before an early bedtime. She considered a side trip to the grocery store, or even to a convenient drive-through window, but she was simply too tired to deal with it. She had some pasta and sauce at home, and that would have to do. When she arrived at her driveway, however, she realized that her plans were going to change.

Amos's Jeep was parked in front of her house, and he was sitting on the front steps. She checked her watch; it wasn't possible that he had arrived to play watchdog for the night this early. Maybe he had heard about Don's arrest. In her excitement, she hadn't thought about what the arrest might mean to her personally. She didn't want or need vindication, and she had no desire to say "I told you so" to Amos, but her stomach fluttered a little at the thought that he might be seeking a rapprochement.

She parked in the driveway and walked toward him. He rose and approached her, and before they closed the distance between them she could see that this was not a friendly visit. Amos's face was tight with anger.

"Okay, what is it now?" she asked.

"You had Don Archer arrested?" he asked tersely.

"No. The Atlanta Police Department arrested him. I'm just a lawyer in private practice. I don't have people arrested."

"Stop playing word games. You told Carlton and Devereaux that it was Archer who was at the scene when Belew was assaulted, didn't you?"

"Yes, I did, based on information from an eyewitness. Shawn Tolliver should also be in cuffs right about now. You seem to have a problem with that."

"As a matter of fact, I *do* have a problem, and a big one. Don Archer wasn't anywhere near Shawn Tolliver that night."

"Not according to my witness. She says that not only was he on duty protecting Tolliver that night, he intervened in the fight with Belew. I can only assume that it was Archer who cleaned up the scene and removed Belew's body—or I should say removed Belew, because we know now that he was still alive."

"So you think Don's good for the murder, too?"

"It looks that way," Laura said. "What's this to you, anyway? I know Don's a buddy of yours, but this isn't your call, Amos. Alex and Carlton are handling it."

"I know that. Where's your witness? At Emily's?"

"Yes, although I can't see what that has to do with anything."

"Devereaux's gone to pick her up?"

"Yes. Would you care to clue me in about what your interest in this is?"

"You've got the wrong guy. Don's not involved in this. You've put your foot in it now, Laura."

Laura was dumbfounded. "What are you talking about? I haven't put my foot in anything. I gave this girl's story to Carlton and Devereaux, and I got her away from Tolliver and Archer, that's all."

"You say she identified Archer?"

"I didn't have a picture of him in my wallet," Laura said sarcastically, "but, yes, she described him as the bodyguard who was out with Shawn Tolliver the night he got into a beef with Lawrence Belew. She didn't know his name, but she said it began with a D. Big blond cop, name beginning with D. What she didn't know was that Belew was set to turn over evidence to the FBI in a corruption investigation that looked likely to involve Don's boss. It added up. And," she hastened to add, "the arrest wasn't my call. Alex connected those dots."

"He connected them wrong, then. Archer doesn't do security work. The mayor doesn't allow anyone on his bodyguard detail to moonlight. I've heard Don beef about it a thousand times."

"Maybe he was breaking the rules this time. Alex got in trouble for moonlighting as a bodyguard—why couldn't Don? Did you think of that? If Don was breaking the rules, Amos, why should he confide in you about it? Besides, it looks like Don was in on the bid-rigging that the FBI is looking into."

"Don's not capable of keeping something like that to

himself. He's too stupid to be. He's just a big dumb chump
who's over his head. The mayor picked him just for that
reason. Don's a lot of things, but crooked isn't one of them.''

"Okay, if it wasn't Don, who was it?'' In the face of
Amos's certainty, her confidence in her own theory was
beginning to shake.

"Use your head, Laura. Who would go this far to protect
a slimebag like Tolliver?''

"How should I know?'' she asked irritably, and then
realization dawned. "It's Darryl Michaels, isn't it?''

"Right first time. Too bad you didn't take the time to
think it through before you brought the hammer down on
Don.''

"Stop trying to make this about me,'' she protested. "I
asked Michelle if it was Archer, but only after she had
described him to a tee. And she recognized the name right
away.''

"This is why you'd make a lousy cop. Witnesses like
this girl aren't reliable—they're too eager to please. She
had a beef with Tolliver that she wanted to settle; she didn't
give a shit who else she stepped on. She would have told
you it was the pope if that would have helped her get to
Tolliver.''

Laura threw up her hands in frustration. "Excuse me, but
all I see here is a mix-up. I'll call Alex and he'll get Don
released and they'll pick up Michaels. Will *that* make you
happy?''

"That would actually make me real happy, if it could go
down that way. Unfortunately, this thing is way beyond the
point where it can be fixed with a phone call. Michaels
knows about Archer's arrest, and this Michelle's story, by
now. It's all over the department. He also knows that Devereaux's on the way to pick up the witness in Rabun County.

Alex broadcast the location on the radio. It's only a matter of who gets there first—and Michaels is going to be in a much bigger hurry than Alex, you can bet on that.''

"You're just speculating. I'll call Emily and tell her to look out for Michaels, but I think Alex will be there in plenty of time—even if you're right, and Michaels is on his way up there. I should have stayed up there.'' She pulled her cell phone from her purse and began to dial Emily's number. Amos turned away and began to walk toward his truck. "Where are you going?''

"I'm going to Rabun County. Tell Emily to take the girl into Clayton, to the sheriff's office, and to wait for me there.''

"Wait. I'm coming with you.''

"No, you're not,'' he said firmly.

She shrugged. "Suit yourself. I'll go on my own.''

She could see him struggling to contain his anger. "Just for once in your life do what I want you to. Just call Em, tell her to get the hell out of there, and go inside and wait. You've screwed this up enough.''

It was Laura's turn to get angry. "*I've* screwed it up? This thing was screwed way before I put my two cents in. And you can't order me to sit down and shut up. I'm going to Emily's with or without your permission. Which I do not need, by the way.''

He started to say something, and stopped himself. "Get in the damn truck. I'd rather have you where I can keep an eye on you. I'll drop you at the sheriff's office in Clayton. That's as close as you're going to get to this, understand?''

She considered her options. She could just drive herself, but she was bone-tired and the thought of making that drive for the third time in one day was daunting. Plus, Amos could turn on the flashing beacon he was allowed to keep in his truck and make the trip a whole lot faster than she could. And if she went with him she had a chance of talking him out of his anger.

"I'll ride with you," she said tersely, "but I'm not going to take a lot of abuse from you," she warned.

"I'm not *abusing* you," he said. "When I start abusing you, you'll know it."

He was perfectly serious, but Laura couldn't help laughing. For a minute, it seemed that he would, too, and their eyes met with some of the old communication and understanding that they'd always had. But he turned away, quickly, and walked around to the driver's side of the truck and wrenched the door open. She followed and climbed into the passenger's seat.

As he pulled into the driveway to turn around, she dialed Emily on the cell phone. To Laura's great relief, Emily answered after only two rings. "Em? Thank goodness. Listen, I'm on my way back up there, with Amos. Something's gone wrong. This Don Archer isn't the guy Michelle saw. Is she there, in earshot?"

"Yes," Emily said. "Do you want to talk to her?"

"No. Just ask her if the name of the cop was Darryl Michaels."

"Okay. Hold on." Laura could hear the murmur of Emily's question, and Michelle's muffled reply. "Yes," Emily said, returning to their conversation. "She thinks that's it. She's not one hundred percent sure, though. She says she would recognize him if she could see him."

"She may get the chance," Laura said grimly. "He might be on his way up there. Amos thinks you and Michelle should get out of the house now, and go into Clayton. We'll meet you at the sheriff's office."

"That seems a little extreme," Emily protested. "Isn't

the detective on the way here? What will he do if we're not here when he arrives?''

"We'll get in touch with Devereaux," Laura promised. "He'll know where to find you. Better safe than sorry, Em— go on into town."

"Will do. I'll take some protection, though, in case we meet this geek on the way."

"What, a gun? I wish you wouldn't. The guy's ex–Secret Service. I don't think you can take him on, Emily."

Emily snorted. "Secret Service? All he's ever done is shoot at a piece of paper. Don't worry about me; I can take care of myself."

"That's what I'm afraid of," Laura replied.

When she had disconnected, she turned to Amos. "That's taken care of. Is there a way to get in touch with Devereaux? We should tell him to detour to the sheriff's office."

"Yeah. But I don't have a radio. I didn't expect to be on duty tonight," he said in a tone that sounded accusatory to Laura. She let it pass without comment, although the injustice rankled with her. "Call the APD dispatchers," he continued. He reeled off the number. "Tell them to get a message to Devereaux. And give them your cell number so they can contact us."

Laura did as instructed, and sat back. They had progressed down Piedmont Road and were headed toward Interstate 85 North. "I think it might be faster at this time of day to take 400," Laura offered.

"What? And go all the way around Lake Burton? This way's faster once we get outside of the Perimeter."

"Suit yourself," Laura said, although she disagreed. The interior of the truck fell into silence; she thought of the many times she and Amos had made this drive, talking and listening to music. She didn't dare turn on the radio or CD player herself, but she hoped that he eventually would—anything to break this soundless tension.

Amos was keeping his eyes on the road. She stole glimpses of his profile, hoping to catch him looking her way so she could say something to lighten the atmosphere, but he never moved. She noticed that he was wearing a shirt she had given him for his birthday, and her heart gave a happy little leap. At least he hadn't burned all reminders of her. He looked so good in that shirt; it was a pale gray-green, just the same shade as his eyes. This line of thought, she realized, was getting her nowhere—or worse. She could feel tears beginning to form. She turned away and looked fixedly out the window.

The day had held on as long as it could, but the last rays of the sun were being wrung from the air. The Jeep was mingling with the last of the evening's commuter traffic, but even that grew lighter as they passed through Gwinett County. Bridges and overpasses loomed ahead of them, then cast them into deeper gloom as they drove beneath them.

Laura was tired and hungry, and she could have used a pit stop at one of the gas stations they were hurrying past, but she didn't care to ask. She was surprised when Amos did. "You need to stop?" he said as they reached Cornelia, the point where the road headed north toward Rabun County. There were several inviting-looking gas stations on either side of the road.

Pride almost made her say no, but she thought better of it. "If we have time," she answered humbly.

"I don't see why not. Everything seems to be under control. Don't take forever, though," he warned as he pulled into a service station.

Laura hurriedly did what was necessary, and then, on her way out, bought a couple of canned drinks and some snacks.

She climbed back into the truck and held out the paper sack as a propitiatory offering. "Got you a couple of Slim Jims," she said.

"Thanks. I'm not hungry," he answered, and soon they were traveling again in silence. Laura ate some pretzels as quietly as she could. They had gone only a couple of miles when her cell phone rang.

"Hello?" she said.

"This is the APD dispatcher. Is Lieutenant Kowalski there?"

"Yes. He's driving, though. Want me to give him a message?"

"Tell him we can't contact Devereaux. We've called the Rabun County Sheriff, and they're sending a car to the address Detective Devereaux gave us."

"I'll tell him. We told the people at the house to go into town and wait for us at the sheriff's office. They should be there by now."

"They hadn't seen them when we talked to the deputy a few minutes ago. Probably nothing to worry about."

"Yes. Maybe they stopped to pick up some dinner or something," Laura said, only half believing her own explanation.

"Tell the Loo to call in when he gets there and makes contact with Devereaux."

"I will. He will, I mean," she said, and the dispatcher disconnected.

She turned to Amos. "They can't get in touch with Devereaux. And nothing's been heard from Em and Michelle at the sheriff's office."

Amos didn't answer her, but he reached beneath the seat, took out his beacon, and affixed it to the roof of the Jeep. The garish light from the beacon illuminated the gloom

surrounding the truck, and Amos flattened the accelerator
and the truck began slinging around the curves on the moun-
tainous road.

"Amos? Are you worried?" Laura asked quietly.

"Yes," he said. "Michaels is a genuine spook. The
thought of him running around up here makes me very
nervous. He's likely to be heavily armed and pretty god-
damned determined to accomplish his mission."

"Emily's got a gun with her," Laura offered.

"She's a deadeye shot on a target range, but I don't think
she's ever dropped a man. And I've seen Michaels operate
a gun. He's probably as good as she is. And he's probably
made a kill or two."

Laura listened in anguish. "If you knew he was this bad
why did you hang around with him?"

"I don't call playing a few games of ball 'hanging around,'
and, yes, I thought the guy was wrong, just not to the extent
of being a cold-blooded murderer. Unlike you, I'm not quick
to suspect just anybody of being a killer."

"That was unnecessary," Laura said with heat. "I didn't
suspect Don at all, not until this girl described him in detail
and said his name began with a D."

"But then you popped right up and asked if it was Don,
didn't you?" he accused.

"Yes. I did. But I think you would have made the same
connection. I mean, why, for the love of God, would anyone
have removed Lawrence Belew from the scene and then
killed him? I assumed—I believed—that Don recognized
Belew as someone who was lining up to testify against the
mayor. And he *is* the head of Mayor Broad's security detail."

"Which means nothing. I've worked security from time
to time, and there's not a politician I would willingly take

a bullet for—much less pop some innocent bystander to protect."

"But you're not Don Archer."

"Believe me, Archer's not going down for the mayor."

"Maybe not, but Devereaux sure thought it added up."

"News flash: Devereaux ain't the sharpest tool in the shed. In fact, Carlton can run rings around him. Devereaux's in his job strictly because he's senior and well connected in the department. There's a real shortage of detectives in the Atlanta Police Department; they'll take anyone who can fog a mirror. I turned down a request from Devereaux to be placed on my squad."

"Nice of you to tell me all this earlier," she remarked.

"Why should I have? It didn't seem to be relevant."

"No? Not even when you and I were chasing all over town tracking Devereaux's 'eyewitnesses'? Tell me something: did you think at that time that Devereaux might have been dirty? Did you think he'd manufactured the witness testimony?" she asked.

"It crossed my mind, but I thought he was more likely just lazy and was letting stuff drop into his lap without asking the right questions."

"Do *you* think he's dirty? Oh, my God, Amos—do you think Devereaux and Michaels are working together? You know that Alex worked for Michaels, don't you? That's why he was suspended."

"A lot of cops worked for Michaels. So what?"

"Well, then what was Alex doing snooping around the crime lab when he was technically suspended?"

"I would say he was sore about being taken off a case. Look, I know Alex and Michaels well enough to say that they're not in this together. If Michaels wanted a partner, he'd pick someone smarter than Devereaux."

"I suppose you could be right. And Alex did act kind of funny when I told him that Michelle had identified Don. He said he was sure it was someone else."

"Maybe he suspected Michaels. Who knows? Anyway, Devereaux wouldn't have broadcast his destination if he and Michaels were working together. He wouldn't have needed to."

"So Alex is headed straight into a confrontation with Michaels? I don't think Alex is prepared to face down Michaels, not if he's the bad guy you say he is."

"I doubt Michaels would kill a cop," Amos allowed. "He'll sure as hell get him out of the way by other means, though, if he has to."

"You don't think he would hurt Emily, do you?"

"Not unless he has to. That's why I wish she hadn't armed herself. His mission will be to get that girl, with minimal collateral damage. But he'll take on some if he has to."

"You really think he's dumb enough to start killing civilians?"

"Dumb? No. Desperate enough, maybe."

Laura shook her head. "Why did he let himself in for this, anyway? Out of loyalty to Shawn Tolliver? I doubt it. Why didn't he just turn Tolliver in on the night it happened?"

Amos shrugged. "Who knows? He may have planned to get it all sorted out; maybe he didn't know how badly damaged Lawrence Belew was."

"He killed Belew, you know. Shawn Tolliver started the job, but Michaels finished it off."

"What makes you so sure of that?" Amos asked.

"The pathology. Belew suffered one set of injuries that could have killed him, but didn't. Then, some time later— maybe a day and a half later—someone dealt him a blow to the head that wasn't survivable. That's what finally convinced Craig Fannin and me that this thing was way beyond just some lazy police work.''

"I never heard this," Amos said.

"I didn't know until after you and I . . . until we stopped communicating. Craig had a second pathologist check out the report. The guy at the crime lab missed a few things. And then he mysteriously packed up and left town before we could find out why he didn't spot what another pathologist did right away.''

"Maybe he was incompetent," Amos said.

"Or maybe he was lying, and maybe he left his job with no forwarding address because he was scared. You know that it was probably Michaels who had one of the so-called eyewitnesses killed in the city jail, don't you?"

"It makes sense now. When Kenny told me about it, though, I figured he was wrong. I thought it was just a jailhouse beef.''

"I think you didn't want to believe it. You were very determined to be angry at me, I think.''

"That's ridiculous," he argued. They were now headed directly toward Clayton on Route 441, and, although they weren't having any fun, they were talking, which was an improvement over the leaden silence that had prevailed earlier.

Laura disagreed, spiritedly. "No, it's not ridiculous. I think you picked a fight with me over this, and I don't think it was fair.''

"You're wrong, but this is hardly the time to discuss our relationship," he said shortly.

"You're right. We're almost to Clayton, anyway."

Amos speeded up as much as possible for the final few miles, passing cars recklessly and causing Laura's heart to pound. Finally, they rounded a big curve in the road, and they were in Clayton, a pretty little mountain town that was just beginning to suffer from the sprawling consequences of its own charm. Amos headed straight for the square, where the sheriff's office was located. He parked, and they both hurried from the truck into the office, hoping—expecting—to find Emily there.

She wasn't. The deputy on duty looked at them in surprise; he had heard nothing from Emily or Devereaux. Amos took Laura's phone and called the APD dispatchers again. He spoke briefly to them and handed the phone back to her with a frown of concern. "They weren't able to contact Devereaux." He addressed the deputy, and introduced himself as a police officer. "How many men on duty tonight?"

"'Bout seven," came the laconic answer.

"Is the sheriff around?"

"He's at home. I can call him."

"You'd better. Is there a man you can spare right away? We've got to get out to Emily Bailey's farm. You know where that is?"

"Sure. What's wrong?"

"I'm not sure. Miss Bailey has a witness in a murder case with her, and there may be someone trying to get to the witness. There's a detective from the Atlanta Police Department who's supposed to be out there picking her up, but we can't contact him."

The deputy's eyes widened. "I already got a car out that way; I'll radio him that you're coming."

"Tell him *not* to go in. This guy's armed and should be considered very dangerous, understand? Just tell him to look for an Atlanta Police Department car—should be an unmarked navy Crown Vic with Fulton County plates."

"You got it," the deputy answered. He picked up his radio and began making contact with his patrol car.

"Amos?" Laura asked. "What are you planning to do?"

"I'm going out there," he said. He removed his gun from its holster and checked it over.

"I am, too," she said.

"Like hell. You stay here."

"I know that farm," she argued.

"I don't have time to argue with you," he said. "If you come, you stay in the truck."

"That's fine. As long as I'm there."

The deputy interrupted their discussion. "I got a man headed out there. You want to wait for him to report in?"

"No, I'm heading out. Tell him I'm in a black Jeep Wagoneer with Fulton County plates. I'll rendezvous with him out there. And get hold of the sheriff and roll a couple of extra cars for insurance. Ready?" he asked Laura.

"I'm ready," she said, although her spine had turned to ice. "Let's go."

"... Xno got ... Het doctor anyway," He picked up the
radio and began making noises with his patrol car.
"Henry," Jamie asked. "What are you stopped for?"
"The group car three ..." he said. He removed his gun from
its holster and checked to make it open.
"I am on," she said.
"My God. You saw that ..."

I don't care where?" she asked.
"Don't have time to argue with you," he said. "If you
want, you stay in the truck."

"Then let's go. Let's go as long ..."
"Okay." He turned the engine, "I got a man
headed out there. You want to wait or want to come?" he
said. "I'm coming back, but keep it in in a black Jeep
Wagoneer with Union County plates." He reached out and
handed them. And he told of the sheriff and roll a couple
of right on the interstate North," she asked. I am
"I'm scary," she said, although her nerve has begun to
fray. "Let's go."

Chapter 32

Emily's farm was just a few miles on the far side of Clayton, at Rabun Gap. Laura and Amos followed the main road that led north out of town, then headed east on a smaller road until they came to the gate—permanently open—that marked the entry to the farm.

Amos drove past the gate, not even pausing. "You passed it!" Laura exclaimed.

"I know I did. There's a dirt road that leads to the barn, isn't there?"

"Yes. Just past the paddock," she said. "You're going there?"

"That's the plan. I can hide the truck by the barn and then walk back across the field to the house. That way I can scope it out without alerting Michaels that I'm here."

Laura pointed out the track that led to the barn. Before he turned off, Amos switched off his headlights. "No need to advertise that we're here," he said as he drove carefully along the rutted track. There was a sliver of moon to light the way, although it slipped behind the light clouds from time to time. Luckily, the dirt road was straight and reasonably easy to follow in the dark. The big barn loomed up on the right after a couple of hundred yards, and Amos pulled close to it and stopped the truck.

"Okay," he said. "You stay in the truck, and I mean it. You see or hear anything, you call the deputy back in Clayton, and then the Atlanta Police Department. Got it?"

"I understand," she said.

He reached up and switched off the dome light before he opened the door.

"Amos?" she said as he swung his legs onto the ground.

"Yes?"

"Please be careful," she said, trying to control the anxious tremor in her voice.

"I always am. There's probably nothing wrong, anyway. Just an excess of caution, as you lawyers would say." He started to leave, but then, unexpectedly, he turned back to her and quickly kissed her. Then he was gone, before she could speak. She sat in the dark and silent vehicle, still feeling the imprint of his lips on hers.

There was enough light, from time to time, for Laura to see her watch. The minutes dragged slowly by; she felt as if she'd been sitting in the truck for at least an hour, but her watch showed that only five minutes had passed. That was enough time for Amos to have reached the house, at least. If everything was okay, he would soon return.

More minutes ticked by. Finally unable to stand it, Laura quietly opened the door and slid silently to the ground. She had dressed casually for work, so she was still wearing a pair of loafers. They made a slight crunching noise on the loose gravel roadway that sounded to her like fireworks exploding. She stopped and stood stock-still until the silence resettled around her. Then she began carefully picking her way to the end of the barn. She found that she could walk pretty quietly after all, and she managed to reach her goal without alarming herself too badly.

Conscious that she might now be visible from the vantage point of the house, she flattened herself against the front of the barn and slowly moved across it until she reached the far corner, where she could see across the paddock to the house on the hill opposite. She couldn't exactly *see* the house, of course, but she could see that there were lights on in the windows. She peered carefully through the dark, hoping to catch sight of some movement, maybe even to make out Amos's silhouette against the faint light. There was nothing.

Laura started to slip back to the truck, fully intending to return obediently to her post, when she heard the unmistakable report of a gun being fired. She cried out involuntarily and dropped to her knees, waiting for more shots. None came. There were no more sounds at all—no screams or cries, nothing. Fighting off panic, she struggled back to her feet. She tried to stop the monstrous pictures that were forming in her head—Amos, his body torn and bleeding, or Emily, prone on the floor of her own house.

She couldn't leave this to her imagination. She needed to do something. She looked around, seeking some concrete way to act. She was standing directly in front of the heavy barn doors, shut for the night. The familiar smell of horse and leather wafted out, calming her. Almost without thinking, she pushed the door open and went inside. The daytime familiarity of the barn was gone, but she could still see well enough to know where she was going. One of the horses nickered softly at her approach; she whispered soothingly to him as she passed by.

Moving carefully, but with a purpose now, she passed the other occupied stalls and made straight for the box stall on the end where the disused equipment was stored. Without hesitating, she moved directly to the old tractor, and lifted the seat. The key to the tack room was there, just as it should have been.

She took the key and felt her way carefully to the door of the tack room. She fumbled with the key, but managed to get it into the lock after a few tries. The inside of the tack room, luckily, was illuminated by a window, which made it easier for Laura to move unerringly toward the cabinet. She swung open the door, and sighed with relief when she saw that Angel's gun was still there. She checked the cylinder; the gun was loaded, as it had been when she had seen it before, with five shot shells. She looked in the cabinet, hoping to find some more serious cartridges, but she turned up only a box containing more shot shells. It stood to reason that Emily wouldn't leave anything lethal out in this accessible a place. Laura emptied the contents of the box into the pocket of her slacks.

Now that she was armed, Laura felt more confident. She left the barn, sliding the door closed behind her, and slipped over to the paddock. She ducked under the rail and, holding her breath, darted as quickly as she could across the open space.

Once she reached the far side of the paddock, she stopped and assessed her position. There were two ways to reach the house: she could loop back to the main road and go up the driveway, but that would put her in full view from the house. The second way was to take the path that led from the back door down to the valley. She decided on that route; she was sure that was what Amos would have done.

The path was steep, and climbing it with gun in hand was more awkward than Laura expected. She managed to make it, keeping fairly quiet, although every twig that snapped and every pebble that rolled down the path sounded loud as a cannonade to her ears.

Things got easier once she reached the garden behind the house; the damp grass allowed for soundless walking. Laura also had the benefit of knowing the house and its grounds well. She approached the rear of the house with some confidence that she couldn't be seen except from an upstairs window. The only lights, however, were downstairs, so she felt that it was worth risking crossing the open space behind the house.

Once she reached the near side of the house, she slipped inside the hedge that surrounded the house on three sides, then paused and took stock. She hadn't had time to plan what she would do once she got to this point. Reconnaissance, she figured, was the order of the moment. She took a deep breath and crawled to the closest window, then willed her rubbery legs to stand.

She could just see inside the dining room. There was no one in sight, but she could hear voices through the open window. They appeared to be coming from the living room, on the opposite side of the house, across the central hallway. She could hear someone crying, and someone moaning, and a quiet baritone that she hoped belonged to Amos. She wiped her sweaty palms on her slacks, shifting the gun from one hand to the other. She needed to get a look inside the living room, and this meant another trip across the open space of the backyard. She crept to the corner of the house, steeled herself, and broke into a steady jog to clear the distance. Once across, she dove into another protective hedge.

As she crept along the side of the house, the voices she had heard became clearer. Michelle was crying, keening, almost. She could hear Emily cursing someone; every profanity she uttered was deeply reassuring to Laura. But there were disturbing sounds of someone in agony; someone in the room was hurt. She held her breath and listened closely.

Amos was talking, quietly and calmly, so low that she couldn't make out what he was saying. Every so often, a voice—presumably Michaels's—would interrupt him. Michaels spoke louder than Amos, but without heat. He seemed to be in control of the situation. Laura rose slowly, quietly as she could, hoping Emily's ranting would cover any noise she might make. She allowed herself a quick look only; the last thing she wanted was to pop her head above the window frame and look straight into Michaels's eyes.

The living room was long and relatively narrow, and the players were dispersed along its entire length. On a sofa at the end closest to her she could make out Michelle, curled into a ball and wailing piteously. In front of the sofa, Emily was kneeling by the side of a man in a uniform. This must be the Rabun County deputy who had been sent to investigate, and the shot she heard must have wounded him. He was pale, and breathing heavily, but Emily appeared to have arranged some sort of bandage on his lower leg.

Standing at the far end of the room, with his back to her, was Darryl Michaels, and beyond him, sidelong to the window, was Amos. Neither could see her. She ducked back down and listened for a moment.

"I only want the girl, Kowalski," Michaels said. "I'm taking her."

"No, I don't think so," Amos said quietly. "I can't let you do that."

"Don't be an idiot, Kowalski. You see what happened to Barney Fife here when he tried to be a hero. I like you, man, and would hate to shoot you. But I will."

"Go ahead," Amos said, "but you're not getting the girl."

"Like hell. Who's gonna stop me once I get past you— the old lady? The supermodel? Or maybe Barney's just faking it down there. How 'bout it, Barn—you up for another round?"

Emily let loose with a couple more earthy characterizations. "You're going to have to go through me, too, you son of a bitch. You better not plan on leaving me alive, because if you do I won't rest until you're in jail getting gang-raped twice a day."

"Emily," Amos said quietly, "that's not helping."

"Who says I want to help?" she said.

"Darryl," Amos said, "it's over. You can waste everyone in this room, but that's only going to make it worse. The sheriff's on his way with backup, and the Atlanta Police Department and the GBI won't be far behind. You're not getting out of this. The best thing you can do is give up now. You're not looking at too bad a situation—you've got a story to tell on what happened to Lawrence Belew. That's not all down to you. You give up Tolliver and you might be able to swing a deal. But if you start making a lot more people dead, it's not going to be so easy."

"Let me be the one who decides what's good for me, Kowalski. And don't bet on me not making it out of this, my way."

"If you make a move toward that girl, I'm going to jump you," Amos warned. "You'll have to kill me."

"Damn! Who knew you were such a dumb ass? Look, Robocop, I got your gun. I got Barney's gun. What're you planning to do, slap me down?"

"Try me," Amos answered.

Laura had heard enough. She knew what she had to do: she would go in the back door. Emily's house was built like many old farmhouses in the South. A wide hall ran through its center, opening to the front and rear. If she went in the back, she could creep through the hall, position herself just outside the living room. She had the advantage of knowing exactly where Michaels was standing, but she had to hurry before he moved.

She slid back through the hedge and into the rear yard one more time. Her head was clear and her mind was made up. She had realized something: the shot shells, far from being a disadvantage to her, were a good thing. Much as she would like to send a silver bullet spinning through Michaels's cerebellum, neatly coring him and shutting him down once and for all, the chance that she could do it—at least on her first shot—was slim. But the snake shot would scatter, and she knew that she could hit him in the face. It wouldn't matter that the shot might not be fatal. She could blind him. She knew it, and she could visualize it.

She reached the back door; the heavy wooden door was open, so she only had to deal with the lightweight screen door. She closed it silently behind her and walked carefully, trying to be noiseless, through the hall and past the stairs. Two steps, and she was outside the living room, her back to the wall with the gun in both hands. Just like on TV.

She took only a moment to listen; she could tell by the volume of their voices that Michaels was still standing just inside the doorless opening into the room, and that Amos was still just beyond him, blocking him from moving toward

Michelle. She took a deep breath, turned, and stood in the doorway, gun aimed squarely at Michaels.

He was holding a sleek nine-millimeter pistol, aimed vaguely in Amos's direction. "Drop it," she said. He turned and looked at her in disbelief, and then he smiled.

"For the love of God," he said. "Look who's here . . . and with a gun. Listen, sweetheart, your boyfriend already charged in here with a cannon, but he could see it wouldn't do him any good. He had the sense to drop his piece. Now why don't you just give me that little gun?" Laura didn't answer; she couldn't. Her brain was frozen with fear, but she held the gun steady. Michaels smiled. "I bet I know how to get you to drop it. How about I give your boyfriend one in the knee?" He raised his gun, pointing it toward Amos. "Come on, Laura. Don't make me shoot Kowalski. I like him. I don't like to shoot folks I like . . ."

He didn't finish his sentence. Laura felt a searing rush of anger and hatred for Michaels, but all the fear was gone. She pulled the trigger.

The report was deafening, but Laura managed to keep the gun raised and fairly steady. There was a lot of screaming, some of it possibly her own. She took aim again, but her target had disappeared. Michaels was on the floor, crouching with his hands covering his face. He was one of the screamers; Laura lowered the gun and watched in horror as blood seeped between his fingers.

Then Amos was by his side, picking up the gun Michaels had dropped. Laura continued standing in the doorway, frozen, until Emily arrived at her side, gently prying the gun from her hand.

"How about that," Emily said in disbelief. "Got him with varmint shot. Who'd-a thunk this little popgun could do the job?"

Laura leaned back against the door frame, unable to speak. Everything was happening in slow motion, as if the room and everyone in it were underwater. Amos was trying to help Michaels. Blood was everywhere. There were sirens somewhere in the distance. Laura stumbled to the stairs and sat down, covering her still-ringing ears. She felt sick, and faint. She put her head down.

Then she heard Amos; he was sitting next to her and his arm was around her. She couldn't make out the words but the tone was reassuring. She raised her head and looked at him. He had so much blood on him—how did that happen? The left sleeve of his shirt—the lovely green shirt she had given him—was torn, and wet with blood. Rivulets of red ran down his wrist. Realization dawned.

"I shot you," she said. "I *shot you!*"

"Collateral damage," he said. "You didn't hit anything vital."

"But I *shot* you!" she cried.

"Baby, shot scatters. I just got in the way of it. You got most of it where it belonged. That's all that matters. We'll talk later about what you were doing skulking around with a gun in the first place. But we're okay now. We're okay."

Chapter 33

The little hospital on Route 76 hadn't ever seen this much action. Three gunshot cases—two serious—and one hysterical lingerie model seriously taxed the limited resources of the staff. Deputy Andy Partain, the most gravely injured, was treated first, but it was soon decided that he would have to be sent to Atlanta via helicopter. Darryl Michaels, heavily sedated and under guard, seemed likely to lose the sight in his right eye. But, as his condition seemed stable, it was decided that he would be sent to Atlanta by ambulance in the morning.

Amos Kowalski was being treated, but the doctor said that he could be released. He had a peppering of number-nine shot in his left arm, and some in his left chest. He cursed fluently as they picked it out of him. Laura, who could hear what was going on from her seat outside the curtained area where they were working on him, winced with each new outcry. The sheriff was there, attempting to piece together the story by talking to her, but Laura had been dosed with something that left her capable of doing little more than smiling at him.

"This is just about the damnedest thing I ever did see," he said. "I'm getting accustomed to the meth heads shooting at each other up here, but I have to say this is the first time I've had a lawyer turning my county into a free-fire zone. What the hell were you thinking, Miss Chastain? That man in there was dangerous, and heavily armed. He could have killed you and everyone else in that house."

"He tried to shoot Amos," Laura explained, simply.

Emily intervened. "She knew what she was doing, Jim. She took him completely by surprise. Michaels got there just ahead of your deputy. And Andy did the right thing; he offered himself as a hostage, but he didn't surrender his weapon until Michaels shot him. Kowalski surrendered his right away, and tried talking to Michaels, but it was no use. We would have been stuck there until your SWAT team came. Probably still be there, if Laura hadn't taken matters into her own hands. She did everything wrong, of course, but she had an advantage over Michaels. He figured she wasn't much of a shooter, and he also didn't know she had shot shells in the gun. Maybe he thought she didn't have much of a chance of hitting him—which she probably didn't. Not with a bullet, at least. But she was about ten feet from him, and you get a good spread with the shot at that distance. All she had to do was hit his neighborhood. And she did it like a champ. She got him on her first shot. Unfortunately, Kowalski caught some of the load. He's got some shot in his arm and chest. But you aimed too high, sugar—always go for the chest. Not the head."

"I *did* aim for the chest, just like you and Amos told me to. I missed."

"That's okay. I'm right proud of you."

Laura frowned. Somewhere beyond the pink cloud that enveloped her was the sense that she had done something wrong. She concentrated hard. "I shouldn't ever have involved you, Em," she said at last. "I should have put Michelle somewhere in Atlanta."

Emily shook her head. "He would have found her. That was a dangerous man, sugar. Amos told me that he broke into your car and your house."

"I guess he did," Laura said vaguely. "I wonder why."

"He was a bully, sweetheart. He thought he could scare you away."

"Huh," Laura said. "Craig thought Amos did all that. Imagine. Amos taking my distributor. I told Craig he was nuts. Go see if he's okay, Em. Is he mad at me?"

"He better not be. You saved his onions."

Laura nodded. "A guy tried to get him with a golf club."

"Shug, I don't know what you're talking about. As soon as they dig all the shot out of Amos, I'm going to take you both back home and put you to bed. We all need to sleep for about three days. You can have that one," she said to the sheriff, gesturing toward Michelle. "She's a vegetarian. I can take a lot, but there's a limit."

"I reckon the Atlanta Police Department'll pick her up, Emily," the sheriff said.

There was a small commotion at the other end of the room. They all leaned forward and craned to see what was happening. Another deputy was leading in a rumpled and ill-tempered Alex Devereaux. "Found him in the trunk of his car, Sheriff," the deputy announced.

"Alex!" Laura said, beaming as if greeting a new arrival at a party. "Are you hurt?"

"Just my dignity," he answered. "What the hell happened?"

"I could ask you the same," the sheriff said.

"Michaels had a beacon in his car; he pulled me over. I should have known better. He popped me on the melon and stuffed me in the trunk. Where is that son of—"

"He's in there," the sheriff replied, "but he won't be in any shape for you to see him for a while. This gal shot him in the face."

"Laura did?" Alex asked, disbelieving.

Laura nodded. "And I shot Amos," she added tearfully.

"She didn't mean to," Emily amended. She explained the shot shells.

"Good work," Devereaux said.

"You better have somebody take a look at·that bump on your head," the deputy admonished.

Amos emerged from the treatment room, his arm heavily bandaged. The sight of his bloody shirt set Laura off again. "For the love of God," he said. "Who doped her up? She was fine, just a little upset."

"She'll sleep it off," Emily said. "Come on. My car's outside."

"Got any beer at home?" Amos asked.

"You bet your tail I do," she said.

"Then why are we standing here?"

Emily pulled Laura to her feet and led her outside into the warm night air, propelling her gently, with a hand in the small of her back, toward the car. Amos opened the back door, and between them they got Laura in. Amos followed her into the backseat, and put his good arm around her. Laura put her head on his shoulder, and she was asleep before they left the parking lot.

Epilogue

Darryl Michaels's allocution hearing was late getting started. Laura, unused to being a mere spectator in the courtroom, shifted nervously on the bench, occasionally turning to look back at the door. She had been dreading this day for a while now, and she wanted it to be over. Then life could get back to some semblance of normality.

She turned at the sound of the door opening. It was Craig, wearing a dark suit and a deep frown. He slid into the bench behind her. "I thought I was going to be late," he whispered.

"I don't know what the holdup is," she replied. She admired him for coming; she knew that he felt a deep sense of responsibility for what had happened, and it wasn't going to be easy for him to see the Belews. Her professional association with him had ended when the city had cut a fat settlement check to Roland Jervis, but they still talked a couple of times a week. She suspected him of nurturing hopes that she would come and join him, at least for a while, but she hadn't decided what she wanted to do. The money from the settlement was providing some breathing room to work things out, and she was spending a lot of time with her family, visiting friends, shoveling out stalls in Emily's barn. Maybe when September rolled around she would have a better idea of what she wanted to do. For now, though, she was content to smell the roses. Or, in the case of the stables, something else.

There was more noise at the back of the courtroom, and Laura turned in time to witness the arrival of the Belew family. Diana, solemn in black, caught Laura's eye and waved, but neither of her parents appeared to notice her presence. Helen Belew was, as always, perfectly dressed and composed. Laura had some idea, though, of what that pose was costing her today, as she anticipated hearing the man who had killed her son sentenced to a maximum of twenty years in prison.

That was the deal Michaels had struck in exchange for testifying against Shawn Tolliver, who had declined a similar deal and who would soon stand trial on a charge of felony murder. Michaels was going to be Marshall's star witness. It was anybody's call how next month's trial would go, but one thing was sure: Atlanta was going to be the center of the nation's attention as the star athlete and his "dream team" of attorneys played out their case in front of the jury.

The bailiff appeared, and it seemed as though things were finally going to get under way. Laura was looking at her watch when Amos slipped into the bench beside her and took her hand. "Sorry. Got caught up in something."

"So has the judge, apparently," she said, sotto voce. But no sooner had she spoken than the side door opened and Michaels was escorted in. Laura had not seen him—except for the occasional picture in the newspaper—since that night in Rabun County. She gripped Amos's hand a little tighter as Michaels walked to his place, surveying the observers who had gathered in the closed courtroom. The surgeons had been unable to save the eye Laura had injured, and it was covered with a black patch that gave him a fierce piratical look. He fixed his one good eye on Laura for a long moment, and then gave a short laugh before turning away.

Laura's heart pounded. The rage and hatred she had felt that night had dissipated, leaving guilt and remorse in its wake. Laura knew that Amos, although he hadn't said so, was hoping that coming here and listening to Michaels recite the litany of his crimes would exorcise those feelings.

After what seemed like another eternity, Judge Root swept into the courtroom, followed by Marshall Oliver and Meredith. He gaveled the proceedings to order, and his clerk began to read the extensive list of charges, starting, to Laura's dismay, with the breaking and entering of her house. The judge asked for his plea.

"Guilty, Your Honor," Michaels replied in a firm, even tone.

"Please explain why you thought it necessary to break into Miss Chastain's house."

Michaels turned his head and looked at Laura. "She was making a nuisance of herself. It was to intimidate her. I was trying to make it look like she had a stalker, so her boyfriend would get her back in line. I thought if he thought someone was following her around, he might get her to stop working for a while."

"Because she was pursuing a line of inquiry that might have incriminated you?"

"Yes, Your Honor."

"I don't know Miss Chastain's boyfriend, but based on

my experience I don't imagine that he would have had a lot of luck persuading her to stop doing anything.''

There was a mild ripple of laughter in the courtroom. Laura gave Amos a sidelong look. He seemed to be sharing in the amusement.

''Read the next charge,'' the judge instructed. Next up was bribery of witnesses and suborning perjury. ''Let me get this straight, Mr. Michaels. You bribed three witnesses—Albert Jackson, Jermaine Clay, and Terence Walker—in order to build a case against Mr. Roland Jervis, who was arrested and charged with killing Lawrence Belew.''

''That's right.''

''And you bribed a pathologist at the GBI Crime Lab to overlook certain evidence.''

''I asked him to fudge on the time of death a little,'' Michaels admitted. ''None of this would have been necessary, Your Honor, if Jervis hadn't been stupid enough to get in that car. Once he did, though, I kind of had to run with it. I needed it to look like he was the guy who had done it. But what kind of idiot would get in an abandoned car and take it for a ride?''

''That's enough, Mr. Michaels. You're hardly in a position to question anyone's actions at this point. Now, one of these witnesses . . .''

''Albert Jackson, Your Honor,'' his clerk prompted.

''Albert Jackson was killed in the Fulton County Jail. Do you have anything you would care to say about that?''

''No, Your Honor,'' Michaels said. He hadn't been charged with that murder; the killer had disappeared, and there was no evidence of any kind linking Michaels to the crime.

Judge Root sighed. ''I can imagine that you don't. And

this, I believe, brings us to the charges relating to the death of Mr. Belew.''

The clerk read those charges, voluntary manslaughter and the lesser included charges of kidnapping, reckless conduct, and assault and battery.

"How do you plead, sir?'' the judge asked.

There was a long silence before Michaels replied, "Guilty.''

"Please explain the sequence of events that led to your crimes.''

Michaels, who had probably been coached by his attorney, recited the story of the fatal encounter, but with a bare minimum of detail that did not satisfy the judge. "Tell me *why,* when you arrived and found that Mr. Tolliver had assaulted this man, you didn't seek medical aid. And why you didn't call the police. And why, for the love of God, you removed Mr. Belew, still living, from the scene, only to murder him in cold blood later.''

"Objection, Your Honor,'' the defense attorney said. "The characterization of the killing as 'cold-blooded' is prejudicial to my client.''

Judge Root glared, but said nothing. Michaels began speaking again. "I did all of those things at the request of Shawn Tolliver,'' he stated. "Shawn thought that Belew was already dead. I realized that Belew was still alive. Tolliver got in a panic when he realized how bad he'd hurt the guy. He figured it would be all over for him if the guy woke up and identified him. So he promised me money—a lot—if I helped him out. It was Shawn's idea to kill him. I didn't want to, but he raised the ante.''

"To what, Mr. Michaels?''

"One million dollars.''

"And for one million dollars you agreed to end a man's

life, and to cover Mr. Tolliver's tracks, and to interfere with the prosecution of justice. Am I right?''

"Yes, Your Honor."

"For one million dollars. Was it worth it, Mr. Michaels?''

"No. It wasn't.''

"I don't know what disgusts me more, Mr. Michaels— your willingness to do these things, or your seeming lack of remorse for having done them.''

"I am remorseful, Your Honor.''

"Really? You fail to convince me. But I see that I'm making the district attorney nervous. No, Mr. Oliver, I'm not going to upset your applecart. You'll have your trial, and your star witness. Are you ready to hear your sentence, Mr. Michaels?''

"I am.''

"Very well. You are sentenced to serve a period of twenty years in confinement in an appropriate facility. You will not be eligible to be considered for parole before ten of those years have been served. Your friends in the district attorney's office have recommended that your time be served in a minimum-security facility. You are fortunate, Mr. Michaels. I don't imagine that a former law enforcement officer would have an easy time of it in a harsher environment. Do you have anything else to say, Mr. Michaels?''

"No, Your Honor.''

"Then we are adjourned.''

Judge Root left, and the sheriff's deputy who had escorted Michaels into court reattached the manacles and led him from the room. As he went, he turned and looked once more at Laura, and winked with his good eye. She shuddered involuntarily. Amos put his arm around her. "You okay?''

"I don't know. It was pretty tough seeing him again.''

"Hearing what he had to say for himself must have made

it a little easier," Marshall said. He and Meredith had walked back to where Laura and Amos were sitting. It was the first time Laura had seen or spoken to her ex-boss since he had fired her. "So, Laura, what are your plans?"

"I don't have any right now," she said.

"There's a slot open in my office. Think about it," he said; then he turned on his heel and walked away.

Meredith chuckled. "Smooth as ever, huh? But seriously, Laura, I wish you would come back."

"Would I get a shot at prosecuting Tolliver?"

"No," she said, and then, seeing the dismay on Laura's face, "only because there's not going to be a trial."

"He took a plea?" Amos said.

"Yeah. The league found its moral compass and kicked him out of sports for life. The dream team didn't think that was exactly a good omen, so they very discreetly sounded us out about a deal."

"But I thought Marshall wanted a show trial before the election," Laura protested.

"He did, but he's also no dummy. There's no telling what a jury of twelve celebrity-soaked jurors will do. And Michaels's testimony was shaky; Tolliver couldn't be linked to any of the cover-up. I told Marshall to take the offer. It was a gift, really."

"I guess so," Laura said. From the corner of her eye she saw the Belews leaving the courtroom. "Do they know?"

Meredith nodded. "Marshall went to them first. You want to know what Mrs. Belew said?"

"What?"

" 'It's time to bury my son.' "

Laura watched the door close behind the family. "I think he's earned some peace," she said. "We all have."

ABOUT THE AUTHOR

Lelia Kelly lives with her family in Georgia. She is currently working on her next Laura Chastain legal thriller. Lelia loves to hear from readers; you may write to her c/o Pinnacle Books. Please include a self-addressed, stamped envelope if you wish to receive a response.

A World of Eerie Suspense
Awaits in Novels by Noel Hynd

__**Cemetery of Angels**   0-7860-0261-1 $5.99US/$6.99CAN
Starting a new life in Southern California, Bill and Rebecca Moore
believe they've found a modern paradise. The bizarre old tale about
their house doesn't bother them, nor does their proximity to a graveyard
filled with Hollywood legends. Life is idyllic...until their beloved son
and daughter vanish without a trace.

__**Rage of Spirits**   0-7860-0470-3 $5.99US/$7.50CAN
A mind-bending terrorist has the power to change the course of world
history. With the President in a coma, it's fallen to hardboiled White
House press aide William Cochrane to unearth the old secrets that can
prevent catastrophe. After an encounter with a New England psychic,
he finds himself descending deeper into the shadowy world between
this life and the next...

__**A Room for the Dead** 0-7860-0089-9 $5.99US/$6.99CAN
With only a few months to go before his retirement, Detective Sgt. Frank
O'Hara faces the most impossible challenge of his career: tracking
down a killer who can't possibly exist—not in this world, anyway. Could
it be the murderous psychopath he sent to the chair years before? But
how? A hair-raising journey into the darkest recesses of the soul.
